Flotsam is the Stuff that Floats

A first novel by Carmen Squillante, Undiscovered Authors Regional Fiction Winner.

Flotsam is the Stuff that Floats

By
Carmen Squillante

Acknowledgements

Many thanks to Suffolk County Public Libraries, Fire Island Ferries, Sayville Ferries, Harry Anderson and Alistair. Special thanks to my brother Michael.

For Mom and Dad

Chapter 1

The day Bernadette was born was the first time I ever said; 'This is the most exciting day of my life.' Since that time there have been many more exciting days, but I was only five then.

Bernadette was born during Hurricane Grace, back in the days before equal opportunities, when hurricanes were all girls, raging up from the south in alphabetical order.

Her name should have been Grace, after our Aunt Grace, but by the accident of the alphabet, the real Grace of the day, a Cat 4 with 125mph gusts, was such a bitch that our parents couldn't bear to bestow her name on their precious tiny new baby.

It was Aunt Grace's turn to have a baby named after her. In retrospect, I personally think it would have been appropriate to name her Grace, after either the cyclone or our aunt, considering how the baby turned out. Aunt Grace was a bitch too. However she claimed to understand and sympathise, (she didn't) and just as a severely destructive hurricane's name gets forever shelved, so the name Grace was retired from our list of baby names, in spite of the fact that there were three more girls to come.

The day began with an official storm alert on the radio, called, aptly, an Official Hurricane Alert. It was important that it was official, that there were names for the different points in the gestation period of a hurricane, and then, once born, they needed to be graded and placed in categories according to damage potential. Cat 1 meant lawn work, Cat 5, evacuation, windows, and maybe a new roof. It was human nature to want to regulate Mother Nature, and if the storm itself could not be controlled, at least we could gauge how frightened of it we ought to be.

The Official Alert told us that there was a possibility of a hurricane, that it was churning away out there and serious enough to cancel all the other radio broadcasts while the weather drama took over, tracking the storm. That was another good thing about hurricanes, they said. You could predict them, unlike an earthquake or a landslide that just suddenly happened and killed everybody. In truth, everybody knew there was nothing good about hurricanes, but we were sold on the publicity. The radio people kept up a continual banter of scales and statistics, manipulating our feelings, the only thing in their control.

There was a charged atmosphere of importance in our living room. My big brother Gabe quietly brushed up on his Morse code. The excitement mounted when, soon after, an Official Hurricane Watch was announced. Now Grace had direction. She was travelling parallel to the East Coast and had already wrecked parts of Florida and South Carolina. Would she blow off to the Atlantic and fizzle out? Or gather strength and continue to travel north? Oh please God, let her gather strength, we prayed. Let her come to us. We were ready.

We'd bought milk and bread and cans of soup. We had batteries and candles and extra blankets. We'd put masking tape across all of the windows and secured the bins outside and took down the swing set. We brought the dog and the cats inside with us. They too were safe as well as providers of warmth.

Bernadette was premature. Incidents of premature births that day were up 15 per cent due to the low pressure, so it was reported. We were pretty sure the hurricane was coming. We weren't expecting the baby quite yet. But Mother knew.

Oh for God's sake, please, she thought. Let it fizzle out over the Atlantic.

We kids expected to have a little party. All shut in, listening to the wind buffet the shutters, cosy, snug and safe inside, with the fire crackling and the candles glowing. Maybe we'd eat snacks and have a singsong.

The baby bag was packed and placed by the front door. Dad put his coat on and stood there next to it, looking at the three of us sitting cross-legged around the transistor radio.

Frantic now, the announcer told us that Grace's status had changed. This was no longer a Hurricane Watch; it was now a Hurricane Warning. Now Grace was definite, a given, a sure thing. Dad bowed and shook his head.

'Jesus Christ,' he said.

The lamps began to flicker, heralding an impending power shortage. Mother, in a white cardigan, appeared at the top of the stairs, luminous in the dim light like an enormous pregnant angel.

'I'm sorry, but we have to leave now. I have to go to the hospital...' Mother's announcement was less frantic than the radio. She even managed a smile, '...the baby's coming.'

That's when I said, 'This is the most exciting day of my life.'

I was five. Maureen was four and Gabe was nine.

Our cousin Joseph, son of Aunt Grace, was assigned the responsibility of our welfare but he never turned up. Obstacles thrown up by Hurricane Grace prevented his safe journey to our house, he said. He only had to come around the corner, but hurricanes are most dangerous close to home, Aunt Grace said.

We listened closely to the transistor as the wind whipped the house, unafraid, good little children paying attention and following instructions. The radio weatherman said the eye of the hurricane was going to pass directly over Piper Bay, where we lived. The eye was 100 miles wide. Wow. A whole 100 miles.

How wonderful, and although we understood nothing of their talk of surface pressure and surge levels, the radio announcers became our carers and friends.

It was fun. We set up our own hurricane watch, and looked out of the windows as branches and leaves and bits of the earth flew through the air. There was a huge crack and the tree in the front yard lost a major artery of a bough, just missing our front window. We shrieked in awe.

'Let's make some popcorn!' said Gabe. 'Dad bought Jiffy Pop!'

I felt a pang at the mention of Dad's name. We'd kind of planned on having him and Mother there with us.

We couldn't get the stove to work. The lights had stopped flickering and we were left in the growing darkness, with only one small torch between the three of us. We didn't know how to make a fire and were beginning to get cold.

'Gloria,' Gabe looked at me seriously, 'Do you think we should use the matches?' he asked. We thought of trying to light a fire but it was forbidden to touch matches under any circumstances.

'I think we should try. They wouldn't want us to freeze to death,' I said.

'They wouldn't want us to burn to death either,' said Gabe.

'Here.' I handed him the matches. 'You're the oldest. You'll have to do it. I don't know how to light a match.'

Gabe sat and thought about it for a time.

'I don't know how to start it,' he said.

'Here. Newspapers. They crinkle up newspapers.' I gave him a newspaper. Gabe slowly took the newspaper apart and started crumpling pages.

'Here,' he handed some to Maureen and me. 'Help me.'

In a frenzy of crinkling, we stuffed the fire full of newspaper. Gabe lit the first match. It went out before he could light the paper.

'Get closer to it.' Maureen egged him on. The third match got results. The paper caught.

'Put the gate up!' I shouted. It was blazing.

'It needs wood,' shouted Gabe. He threw some wood in, frightened, and hastily drew back and put the fireguard in place. We whooped it up in front of the blazing newspaper, a glorious moment of proud glowing warmth. After a few minutes it had gone out, and the wind had blown most of the smoke back into the house.

'It's not going to work,' said Gabe. We sat back down on our haunches, staring at the smouldering gap.

'I forgot to bring my new bike in,' I said.

'Maybe Dad did it,' said Gabe.

'No. It will have blown away. It will be ruined.'

We huddled under the blankets together and used the torch to renew the batteries in the radio. Maureen started crying. 'I'm scared,' she said.

'There's nothing to be scared of,' said Gabe, bravely.

The winds suddenly died. We sat up. The rain stopped.

'It's over,' I said. Maureen sniffed, wiped away her worried tears to make way for the relief, and stood up to look out the window.

'But stop', said the radio men. 'It's not over. Get yourself some chips and a beer, or cup of coffee if you can boil water, maybe a doughnut. But don't do anything foolish. Whatever you do, don't go outside.' They explained about the eye being in the centre of the hurricane and how the swirling forces created stillness. It was the calm after the storm as well as before the storm, so we knew it was coming back. Our renewed fear took on a darker quality, a fresh dread of this giant Cyclops monster hovering right above us. The people on the radio sounded cheerful, like they were having the kind of time we'd originally planned for ourselves.

We wanted our parents to be there.

However, at that moment, Bernadette was screaming the roof off the hospital, without any help from the hurricane, so they were otherwise engaged. They didn't, apparently, even think about us.

'Do you think it would be safe to look out the window?' I asked.

'I guess if we're careful it will be,' said Gabe.

Outside it was dark and still. I looked up trying to see the hurricane, a giant flying saucer eye passing overhead, revolving steadily, with its roving gaze surveying the damage. Please God, I prayed, let it see that it has done enough. We could hear the crash of the ocean, sounding bigger and coming closer than it should.

'It was my new bike,' I said, trying not to cry.

'Don't worry,' said Maureen. 'Don't cry.'

'I'm not crying.'

Then Grace came whistling back to life, and threw another part of a tree at the house, hitting the window with a loud and threatening bang. The glass cracked in slow motion, the shards held in place by the tape. We all cried then. It got cold, and eerily dark, inside and out. I sat hugging the radio on my lap, my brother and sister on either side of me snuggling under a blanket. We sat in the centre of the room, as if in a house of cards, feeling the rest of the windows straining against the masking tape with each gust of wind for what seemed like many hours but wasn't, I learned later. Hurricanes don't actually take that long, especially directly under the eye, a storm in two parts.

When we woke up it was to a grim, grey daylight. All the lights in the house were on and the batteries in the babysitter had died. It was raining hard and steadily, the front yard a tangle of bits of trees, some floating in muddy puddles.

'That was when Bernadette was born,' Dad told us. 'During the eye.'

'I thought you were going to call it Grace if it was a girl,' I said, accusing them. The baby was still at the 'it' stage. Bernadette had stayed in the hospital with Mother because she was still too small to come home. We'd not yet met her, this new sister.

'Yeah, the name Bernadette's so long,' whined Maureen.

'What would it have been if it was a boy?' Gabe asked wistfully.

'Probably Joseph, after your grandfather.'

'We already have two cousins called Joseph,' said Gabe. 'And an uncle.'

'Well you only have one grandfather.'

'Who is Bernadette named after?' I asked.

He laughed.

'Saint Bernadette,' he said. And then he told us about the girl and her visions of the Blessed Mother, and the spring and the miracles. I was quite taken with the story, being a big fan of Our Lady at the time, and felt a bit jealous of Bernadette the baby. When she grew up she could go and visit this place where her very own saint dug in the mud and found a holy spring that healed people, and knew secrets. She might see a miracle. There were probably books written about her saint. She could even see her saint's body. Damn, now that really was something.

After all, who was Saint Gloria? There wasn't one. She was just my aunt, my mother's sister, a family name, a word in hymns and prayers. No big deal.

To my smug satisfaction, I learned later that it was actually Saint Bernard she was named for. There had been a panic after the baby was born, when Mother turned tail on the name Grace, on account of the severity of the storm. But what? They hadn't thought to be prepared with an alternative, and, being as superstitious as she was religious, she refused to leave the baby unnamed, believing it was bad luck. After some hasty lateral thinking someone at the hospital produced a Catholic magazine with a list of feast days. As luck would have it, there were three

St Bernard's in that very week. Surely this must be a message from heaven. They called her Bernadette, after Saint Bernard, and that seemed perfectly good reasoning to them, if not divine intervention.

So Bernadette was named after a man, really, that is what I thought. Though they tried to disguise this fact, my envy appeased.

I went out to look for my bicycle, a bleak mission undertaken in a black mood. I knew I wasn't going to find anything good out there. It was still raining and I was inappropriately dressed but didn't care. There was an oak tree fallen across our road, blocking any passage. An unfamiliar car was abandoned directly in front of it, like a spooked horse frozen before the jump. The garden was an unrecognisable swampland full of floating crisp packets and decapitated cat tail reeds, vagrants blown in from the beach. Nature had been rearranged - sticks, cans, kid's toys, feathers, chicken bones, pieces of other neighbourhoods, the flotsam and jetsam dumped on our lives by the hurricane who was now on her way to Canada with a fresh load.

I walked around the house, starting at the side. The maple tree was down. Pulled right out of the ground, its roots, strangely alive, scrabbling blindly at the sky, like an upturned spider trying to right itself. My bike was under its branches. I couldn't get to it, the branches and twigs were too dense to crawl through but I could see it was bent.

Well that's that then. I'd never had anything new before.

On my way round to the back door, I found a mouse on the lawn. I got down on my knees and looked very closely at it. It was dead, or sleeping, its fur disturbed and matted. I picked it up by the tail and threw it into a puddle. I thought perhaps a sudden splash might revive it, cartoon like, but nothing happened. No miracles for me today.

Dad appeared at the back door.

'Gloria. What're you doing out there in your pyjamas? Get in here. Now.'

I stood in the kitchen, dripping all over the floor.

'My bike is under that tree.'

'I know honey,' he said, towelling me dry, 'I saw it when I came home. I'll have a look at it when I have time, but not now, okay? I gotta fix that window, too.'

A week later the aunts, uncles and cousins assembled for the great event of Bernadette coming home for the first time.

'Ooh!'

'Ahh, the miracle of life.'

'Such a precious thing, a baby.'

'So soft.'

'So nice of her to arrive early.'

'So perfect.'

'All the more time to cherish.'

'Nothing like the smell of a new baby.'

'So fresh.'

'So new.'

So nauseating, we thought guiltily. Those sorts of comments travelled on a loop around the room. Gabe, Maureen and I were happy to see Mother home again, but were not so sure about the baby. We didn't think she smelled so special. Mother sat perched on the edge of the sofa with Bernadette in her arms. The little face and hands peeped out of mounds of soft white blanket and things trimmed with lace. We examined her closely.

'Her hands are so small.' This was unanimous. We took turns getting her to grip our fingers.

'She's very strong for something so small,' I said. Laughter. Especially from the men, who relished the idea of passing on strength.

'How long before her eyes open?' Maureen said.

'She's sleeping, stupid,' said Gabe.

'Gabe! Be nice to your sister,' said Mother. 'Would you like to hold her?'

Not really, but it seemed expected so we all held her. It wasn't possible to feel her through all the padding she was wrapped up in, like holding a firm pillow but having to be careful with it.

'Can we go out now?' I asked. We'd had enough of Bernadette the baby.

'When're we having cake?' said Maureen.

'We'll call you in for cake,' said Aunt Grace. 'Off you go.'

Outside it was crisp and clear. The leaves were beginning to turn. There was a pile of sticks and branches that we collected off the lawn and put next to the fallen maple tree which would be cleared and cut up for firewood, while the shiny new bike underneath slowly rusted away.

****

Chapter 2

The day of Bernadette's unpleasant baptism wasn't quite as turbulent as the one she was born on, perhaps a stiff breeze rather than a gale force wind - more bee-sting than snakebite. The day came hot on the tail of her birth, so as to wipe away the original sin and put in place the protective coating that would ensure her unblocked entry into heaven. The cool crisp day was book-ended by a glorious dawn and equally spectacular sunset. Nonetheless, it exited with a sense of foreboding and unease.

Misfortune unforeseen, however, we anticipated nothing but pure joy and there would be a party to look forward to afterwards. At this stage in our lives, the chief ingredient required to turn an everyday event into a memorable occasion was cake. Deliberation over what type of cake started early and was an essential part of the anticipation process. Opinions passed endlessly around the kitchen table at mealtimes, which was most of the time, by the endless channel of visiting relatives.

'What about that one we had last November, round at Mo's house? Man, that was delicious. Who made that?'

'Oh, yes that was nice…'

'What are you talking about? We've never had chocolate cake at Aunt Mo's…'

'That's because it was a funeral party, honey. You weren't there.'

'I can't make a funeral cake for a christening.'

'Nonsense, Mary, it wasn't made chocolate 'specially for a funeral. It was a nice occasion. Good cake too.'

'It was such a nice light chocolate. Don't you remember? Joe turned up late.'

'Ah, yes. Poor old Andy, bless him. He would have loved that cake too, we said that, remember, at the time.'

'No. I won't do it. It would be a bad omen, bad for Bernadette.'

'So, what, are you saying we can never eat another chocolate cake?'

'Don't be ridiculous. How about a nice white cake, with that nice fluffy seven-minute icing? All clean and pure. And sweet.'

Should it be round or rectangular, layered, if so how many layers, even layers or graduated tiers, iced or dusted, filled? Fruit and cream, butter or fudge, vanilla caramel and wasn't Tony allergic to strawberries?

They were right about one thing; it would have been a bad omen for Bernadette, who had plenty of dark indications already so it wouldn't have made an iota of difference.

New clothing was another critical build-up component and was to be preceded by numerous shopping excursions involving much fussing, fitting and decision-making as we agonised over the perfect hat or pair of gloves. A whole outfit was unheard of, as usually our only affordable option was to accessorise what we already owned.

This time we shopped for dresses, whole dresses, one each, along with shoes and hats. Maureen and I were matching, deep red with velvet trim. We rubbed our cuffs and collars.

'Real velvet,' we whispered, not wanting to say it too loudly, fearing familiarity would somehow vanish the luxurious pile.

Gabe learned how to tie his necktie and wore a navy blue blazer to match Dad's.

'You look so grown up,' said Mother.

He did.

Maureen learned how to make the sign of the cross. She had perfected this gesture on one of our shopping outings and joyously, obsessively compulsively repeated the action time and again, prompting even our own holy Mother to suggest that perhaps there were more appropriate places for such piety, rather than the Donut Diner and the sock and underpants aisle in Woolworth's. But there was no stopping her. This was the earliest indication of what would be her lifelong religious devotion.

'Oh, look there Jess, at that cute little girl,' a strange woman would say, as I turned around, horrified, to find my sister kneeling on the side of the pavement outside the library.

'Aw, ain't that sweet. She's praying.'

I would kick her, and hiss, 'Quit rattling that rosary. You're making a scene. Get up and come inside,' then hide around the corner of the building when she wouldn't heed.

'Whatcha praying for sweetie?' a strange man wants to know.

'I'm thanking God for libraries.' Angelic look. The people chuckle, like she's adorable.

'You all alone there sweetie?' they say, glancing around, concerned.

I emerge. 'Hurry up, Maureen. Inside. Now.'

I get dirty looks, like I'm the unholy one. Just one of many outings where I, embarrassed by her, would try to be invisible, pretending that this bowed and whispering creature wasn't my sister.

Bernadette's baptism ceremony was to be small, with only the immediate family and her chosen Godparents in attendance. The purpose of Godparents, as explained to us, was to be ultimately responsible for us. If anything 'untoward' were to happen to Mother or Dad, the Godparents stepped in and took over.

This was supposed to be a comforting idea. Instead, it terrified us.

Untoward. In my bed in the sleepless small hours, I couldn't stop the uninvited godparents hammering on my head. I kept my fears a guilty secret, ashamed of conjuring up car accidents when I should have been saying Hail Mary's and Our Fathers, or at the very least, counting sheep.

On the eve of the Bernadette's baptism my worries intensified, expanding outside of the impending grief over losing both of my parents and spilling beyond into our lives after their death.

We learned that Aunt Grace was to be Bernadette's Godmother. I had assumed that if she hadn't been given her name, the whole job was cancelled. I thought someone else would be found, perhaps someone called Bernadette, for in my five year old mind, that's who Godparents were. They were people with your own name.

They were made simple for us to remember as, after the terrible tragedy that killed Mother and Dad, we were to go with the people we were named for. Easy Peasy. We often discussed the practicalities of these allocations, should they ever be realised.

We would be separated, moved into their respective homes, which made Gabe the clear winner, as Uncle Gabriel and his wife Sal had no children of their own. They lived in a pristine new house, owned a dog and a boat. They'd been known to take vacations, the only people I'd ever met who had been on an aeroplane. Gabe, now an only child, would have idyllic weekends out on the bay fishing, digging clams and swimming with the dog, maybe even get up in an aeroplane.

I was assigned to Aunt Gloria who I knew very well as she spent innumerable hours in our kitchen. Being Mother's identical twin, it would be a distressing placement as I was used to two of her, and just one would not be quite right. Her husband, Nick, sat in an armchair with a newspaper and spoke little. Their life was meticulous and orderly, run like a military operation. I would have to be careful there, and skirt round the armchair quietly. I imagined having difficult Cinderella chores, and there were five cousins, loved before me. There were no spare rooms in their house, perhaps I would have to share a room and be resented. Maybe I'd sleep in the kitchen, roll up my sleeping bag every morning and store it away. No brother or sister there to complain to or commiserate with.

Bernadette's fate, though, was almost too much to bear.

Aunt Grace.

Our beloved Uncle Joe, another one of the kitchen crowd, was the elder brother of Dad, his partner at the Fish Shop down at the marina, our livelihood. Dad and Uncle Joe were sparing with their time spent at home. They were always at the shop, down the pier, out fishing, checking boats. The Fish Shop sold bait and tackle, things for boats. They rented mooring spaces, around the shop's dock, and looked after the boats for people. Even during Bernadette's birth, during the eye, Dad left the hospital to meet Joe and check the boats.

They were as much like twins in their togetherness as Mother and Aunt Gloria, without actually being twins. Dark, swarthy, tough-looking men, but Joe was smaller and stockier, a fit and healthy version of our infamously obese grandfather, Papa Joseph. As a child, I saw almost as much of Uncle Joe as I did of Dad. He was always in our kitchen, with a cup of tea, or a beer, until Aunt Grace phoned or turned up and heckled him away. He had kind eyes, a crooked smile, and doted on our father in a big brother, caring style that he would accept from no one else. He made us feel we were his own. He was, though, inexplicably and unimaginably,

24

married to and ruled by Aunt Grace.

We hated Aunt Grace but of course we couldn't say that, being children. I'd once heard a customer describe her as glamorous, but hers was extreme, grotesque glamour, a cartoon villain-ness, a fairy-tale witch. Everything about her was sharp: shoes, voice, nails, nose. Her lipstick was drawn outside the lines of her lips and she was doused in sickly floral scent. She lived in a 'don't touch that' house with custom-made clear plastic covers over the furniture.

She and Joe had three children of their own, our cousins Francine, Joseph and Anthony. We loved them in spite of their mother, but they seemed to love her well enough.

I once enjoyed a jam sandwich while sitting in her lounge.

'Stop that,' she said. 'You'll get sticky fingerprints all over the place.'

She cleaned her sofa around me with window cleaner and then went on to do the rest of the furniture. The sandwich was tainted with ammonia. I chucked it out.

Aunt Grace pretended to like us but when out of sight of others, she treated us like something the cat dragged in. Actually, she was nicer to the stuff her cat brought in; usually small wounded animals that were much dirtier than we were. She loved and nursed them. Once she took a damaged field mouse to the vet.

I'd seen her strike Maureen, twice. I didn't know why, though I figured it was perhaps because Maureen, being the youngest, made more noise and mess than we did. Now Bernadette had arrived to fill that position. Surely, I hoped, she wouldn't hit an infant.

I came out of the bathroom, stood looking down the corridor. I could see her, unaware of me, angry in her kitchen, slamming the coffee mug down. She slapped Maureen's little head sideways, whacking it furiously, on the table. I didn't see what came before.

'Stupid child!' she shouted. Then she saw me, and feigned accident. She stood unsteadily on her high heels as though losing her balance, pretending to topple, and cupping Maureen's head in her hands to my horror. I thought she would perform some atrocity, but she cradled her and said, 'Stupid me! Stupid table! Stupid! I'm so clumsy, you poor thing.'

She continued her charade for some time, repeating the word 'stupid' followed by words other than 'child', a device I expect she thought might wipe my memory, as she knew I had witnessed something. I just looked at her, and she looked back at me but there was no communication in that exchange. She was a lousy actress, so bad that if it hadn't been for Maureen's howling, I might have laughed at her.

Then she did it again, at a beach gathering. Everyone there, Grace's kids, the three of us, more cousins here and there. We piled into her big car, instantly filling it beyond anything that could be considered safe. The elder cousins sat far away in the coveted back space with the cooler, towels and dog while the rest of us crammed into the rear seat and used laps and floors to pack ourselves in so the doors would shut. Mother sat in the front with Aunt Grace, somebody's baby on her lap.

'Keep that dog away from my picnic,' snapped Aunt Grace, by way of a greeting, 'and keep your paws off my car seats.'

It wasn't clear whose paws she was talking about. Her car seats, like her furniture, were also covered in plastic, sticky and uncomfortable, squealing under bare legs in hot weather. Mother turned around and reached into the back and patted my knee. She smiled and did something with her eyes, not quite rolling them, but there was something in them that told me maybe her thoughts for Grace weren't so removed from my own.

This was the beach we had to drive to, which made it seem special, a cut above the ones that were walking distance, crossing the tickle bridge, its corrugated metal surface sending vibrations up through the soles of our bare feet.

On arrival, we met hordes more family and spent a day that multiplied in our memories because it was so well stocked with food (much of it sweet), cousins, sand, sun and swimming

Maureen, a toddler, still wobbled unsteadily as she explored the patch of sand we'd colonised, marked with our umbrella, baskets and blankets. She rooted around the picnic and, after thoroughly examining and handling the contents, decided on her chosen morsel, one of Aunt Grace's avocado and bacon sandwiches, made exclusively. Not for children.

Avocados were the latest trend in food fashion; a rare taste of exotica, and Aunt Grace must have thought she was being very chic bringing them along to the beach. She snatched the gritty remains away from Maureen, slapping her hand.

'You've got sand in everything! You bad girl!'

Maureen whimpered. Apparently, having not completely vented her anger, Aunt Grace then pushed Maureen, who fell back into a sitting position with a thump, opened her avocado mouth wide and started to scream, bringing Mother running to the rescue. Aunt Grace's only witness, she thought, was cousin Joseph, who was an even younger baby and couldn't speak.

Just yards away, Gabe and I, digging holes in the sand, were watching.

'Did you see that?' said Gabe.

'Look at her now,' I said, as Mother appeared on the scene.

'She's giving her cookies,' said Gabe.

'And wiping her face and hands,' I said.

'Now she's all smiles with mother.'

'Look at that. She's kissing Maureen.'

'Bitch,' said Gabe.

This would be poor Bernadette's new Godmother.

On Baptism day, the wail of the vacuum overlaid the sound of the rosy dawn chorus, as Dad began on his quest to banish all dog hair from the ceremony. Several pieces of toast and boiled eggs later, we were ushered, red, navy blue and black velvet, through the sticky end of the cellophane tape carefully out to the driveway and neatly positioned on the back seat of the car. Mother and the guest of honour, resplendent in several metres of white satin, took up most of the front seat, while Dad squeezed in to drive, still blowing imaginary bits of fur off his shoulders.

'Goddamn dog,' was all he said on the ten-minute journey. Mother tutted at him and crooned at the baby, who made no sound.

'The baptismal area is in the west vestibule,' said a dull little nun.

'Yes, we know. We've been before,' joked Dad. He and Mother beamed at us, their brood of previously cleansed children. The little nun didn't laugh.

My limited experience told me that little nuns in big churches were generally quite humourless. Dad viewed it as a challenge, joking with her as we made our way to the west vestibule, a small stony cave at the side of the cavernous church, as cold as the little nun. It was a grey marble pit at the foot of a black, wrought iron spiral staircase and what little room there was left to stand in was occupied by a birdbath. I could hear the echoing drip-drop sound of ancient plumbing, coming from what I thought was a spring in some unseen tunnel, a rest stop on the road leading off to limbo, land of unbaptised dead babies.

Bernadette, wrapped up like a locust, was passed around the room to pass the time until the priest, Father McGlone, theatrically descended from on high. Stepping slowly, he spiralled down the iron staircase, coming to a halt at the birdbath, which I later learned was the baptismal font.

That is when Bernadette started to cry. It started as a snivel and gathered strength during the ritual. She cried and cried. This was no ordinary baby crying, which is bad stuff. This permeated the skin. It was as though she didn't want to live, let alone be baptised. She was sobbing out her whole sad life story before it even began, like she'd rather go to Limbo, and float eternally, unbothered by time, or voices or people. She didn't go to Limbo, though, at least not the one we knew about. She stayed right there and screamed.

'I baptise you in the name of the Father…'

He could hardly hear his own voice over the din.

Aunt Grace wore a hat with a bit of black net that shielded her eyes, and stood with her head bowed, a vision of devotion. Holding hysterical Bernadette in her arms didn't disturb her peaceful demeanour or underlying frostiness. Mother and Dad, experiencing the parental reaction to Bernadette's anguish, were losing colour, the strain showing in their tightened jaws. Maureen and I fidgeted nervously, thinking perhaps Aunt Grace was squeezing Bernadette too hard. Gabe winced each time she gasped for a fresh breath. Maybe she was in pain. By the end of the ceremony she was hiccupping and gasping for breath, and yet still managing to shriek. The Ice Queen serenely handed her to Mother and said, 'There we go. All done. They always cry. I think it's the water.'

She patted Mother's arm. Mother smiled at her in a way that I recognised from the back of the car, on the way to the beach.

Disappointingly, Bernadette didn't stop crying when she was back in her own mother's arms.

'I thought she'd stop when she got given back to Mother,' said Gabe.

'I wish she had.'

'Then it would have been Aunt Grace's fault.'

We begrudgingly had to concede that the crying had nothing to do with Aunt Grace.

Food had been prepared, plates were borrowed and the sacramental white fluffy cake was baked. We went to the party back at the plastic coated house, worrying about touching walls and dropping crumbs.

'Is something wrong with the baby?' asked Maureen.

'No,' said Mother through gritted teeth.

'Why does she keep crying?'

Everyone seemed to know the answer to that one.

'She's just tired.'

'It's a long day for her.'

'That's a hungry cry.'

'Colic.'

'Wind.'

'What is colic?'

'Wind.'

'Here, give her to me.'

'I'll take her.'

'Can we give her some cake?'

'Hand her over here.'

'Babies cry. Don't worry about it. That's what they're supposed to do.' This from Uncle Tony.

She eventually fell asleep.

After that, Bernadette didn't really figure much in our lives for a while, contrary to our high expectations.

'She doesn't do anything,' Maureen complained.

'We can't play with her,' I said. 'She doesn't even look happy to see us.'

'What did you expect?' said Gabe, the voice of experience.

'She's just a baby.'

'She'll get more interesting, don't worry,' promised Dad.

He was certainly right about that.

We discovered about babies needing constant maintenance. Feeding, changing, washing, winding, rocking, cleaning.

Maureen and I followed Mother and the baby around the house. Gabe didn't bother. Old enough to remember, he had already lived through our beginnings and was bored of babies, especially girl ones who held little promise for a young boy.

'Do you remember when I was a baby?' Maureen asked me. I didn't.

'You were always here,' I said.

'I must've been a baby once,' she said.

'You were.' Gabe confirmed. 'I remember you as a baby. You cried a lot, just like this one.'

'But Bernadette doesn't cry anymore,' I said.

'Well. Okay. I guess not that much.'

Bernadette had gone quiet. It was as though she'd taken all her life's misery and dealt with it all at one time, that day, at her baptism.

On the rare occasions that she cried Mother simply had to go through the maintenance tasks to find the correct one. Feeding, changing, rocking. Something always worked. She was an efficient machine. There were never times when she cried and cried and cried and nobody knew what was wrong.

She slept all night long.

She became the legendary family baby, a paragon of baby-good.

'She's wonderful!' all the Aunts shrieked with delight.

'Josephina was nearly two before I got any sleep.'

'Mary, you are so lucky.'

'She's the picture of contentment.'

'And Georgina wasn't far behind her, if I remember rightly.'

'It's a rare thing to get a baby as good as this one.'

Mother just laughed. 'I guess she knows she has to be good. I haven't got time for her to be anything else.' Behind her laugh she hid her unease and her discomfort. This baby was too tranquil. It wasn't normal.

Much later, some would look back and say, 'I knew something wasn't right.' Everybody had an opinion.

She was a quiet baby, that's all. That was mine.

Gabe stayed outside and played with his friends, or Dad took him down to the Fish Shop with him.

Us girls stayed home and tried to be helpful, but to no avail. Life had changed now, with this new person. We'd lost our freedom, our brother, our mother.

Who needs help with such a baby? She lay on the bed, placidly, while she was changed, washed, winded, fed or rocked. Maureen made faces, I made sounds. We clucked and squeaked and sang and jumped up and down and danced around the bed. And what did the baby do? Nothing. She watched us, silently. We didn't use her name, still referred to her as 'the baby.'

We tried harder.

'Will you girls look after Bernadette for a minute while I wash this out?' Mother left, removing the offending article. The smell of it lingered in the room.

Maureen clambered up onto the bed. I followed her.

'Help me move her into the middle,' said Maureen.

We started to bounce. Gently, at first, circumnavigating the baby at the epicentre. She watched us with her big eyes. We bounced higher and higher and Bernadette's tiny baby body began to bounce too. Her little arms extended out on take-off and slammed back into her sides on landing. Her eyes grew wider each time. It was hilarious. Then she did a wonderful thing, she started laughing, a beautiful baby laugh, pure joy. We bounced harder. She was practically flying now.

'One, two, three...'

'She's getting near the edge!'

'Quick, just shove her over next time she lands!'

'I missed!'

'I'll get it!'

'Ok now higher!'

We were nearing the height of our hysteria, and Bernadette the ceiling, when Mother came back. She didn't find it funny.

The three of us turned and looked at her, mid-air, everyone in the room momentarily stunned. Maureen and I landed on our knees and began to edge our way off the bed. Bernadette, having done a half turn in flight, landed on her tummy and started to wail. She wanted more bouncing, but Mother didn't interpret it that way.

'When I grow up I'm not going to have any babies,' said Maureen, later.

We sat together looking out the window, banished to the bedroom.

'You may not be able to stop it, though,' I told her, knowledgeably, 'you can't, when you get married.'

'No, that won't be a problem,' she said. 'I'm going to be a nun. Do you think they've forgotten about us? I'm hungry.'

Then Maureen began to get tearful.

'Stop it Maureen. Don't.'

'Do you think we've damaged the baby?'

We heard Dad's footsteps coming up the stairs. He came into our room with two plates of food.

'Here. Eat this. Then get ready for bed.'

Our supper had grown cold but we ate it anyway and threw the leftovers out of the window for the cats. We didn't know why eating in our room was a necessary element of punishment but we were pleased about it. We didn't let on that it was actually quite a lot of fun.

That was the day that the baby became a person to us, our sister.

'She was fun,' I said.

'Who?' said Maureen.

'The baby. Bernadette.'

'Yeah, she was.'

'We need to figure out a way to do it and keep her quiet.'

'Yeah. She loved it.'

After that, we started calling Bernadette by her name.

****

Chapter 3

Special days came and went, and always came again, some memorable, if only for the cake, and some not so. In the first year of Bernadette's life there were many such celebrations, but the taste from Dad's birthday lingered strongest.

Our family and its extensions all gathered together in one small room created quite a lot of noise, underneath which lay a silence so powerful it could eat up that noise faster than we ate the cake.

We lived in a quagmire of well-known secrets, a sophisticated system of benign deceit, developed over decades and passed from generation to generation. This was no mean feat considering no one talked about it. Nothing of "a certain nature" was ever discussed, unless it was privately, between two people, and those two people might separate and find new partners, and so the thing would spread far and wide and still, though everyone really knew, the secret was still a secret. What "a certain nature" was remained undefined, but it grew in our blood.

As children we mimicked our elders, operating on a simpler primary-school-conspiracy level, stowing away our own little picked over bones in cupboards to await future polishing.

We were aware of unspoken mysteries. The murky, dark world of the adults that frightened and intrigued us, so widely known and yet not understood. We learned never to dare speak of it.

Never ask who, what or why. We hushed younger siblings before they could spit out an offending question, saving them the shame and embarrassment we'd felt as toddlers, stumbling as much over our social faux pas as we did our own feet.

It was Uncle Tony who first taught me the art of the family secret without even realising he was doing so, and it was ironic that in my later years it would be he that revealed the truth behind the mysteries, including his own. Uncle Tony was Mother's big brother.

He was big, inside and out, tall, strong, dark, handsome with a wild head of hair, always windswept, and booming laughter. When he laughed, everyone laughed, because his distinctive laughter was infectious and also because he never laughed unless something was funny. He never laughed to be polite. He was able to anticipate the needs and wants of children without asking, or trying too hard.

We adored him, and everything about him, one of the best being that he owned Gar-barges, a cartage service company that picked the garbage off Beacon Island by boat. Sometimes he let us accompany him across Piper Bay on his weekly collections. He was one of the regulars visiting at our house; because of his flexibility he became the resident babysitter as well as a fixture at all the barbecues, birthdays and celebratory cake eating fests.

It was because of his attendance at one of these particular events that I learned my valuable lesson about family secrets, questions and sudden silences.

It was late in March shortly after Easter and by then the first spring flowers were blooming in our garden. We'd grown accustomed to Bernadette and now she, too, it seemed, had always been there. The last chocolate rabbit's foot had been devoured and any remaining strands of green cellophane grass were vacuumed up on the morning of this party day for Dad.

The days were getting longer and warmer and Maureen and I, full of the joys of spring, went out back to pick sprigs of forsythia to use as table decoration while Mother baked the all-important cake. This particular annual favourite was mocha-flavoured, with maple icing. Not a popular choice among the younger guests, but cake was cake.

Dad and Uncle Joe were at the Fish Shop, down at the marina, they were at home even more sparingly than usual.

Spring was a busy time for people breathing life back into their boats, dreaming of all the blue fish, red snapper, orange blossoms and gin and tonics they'd be reeling in soon, on deck in the hot sun. Dad and Uncle Joe had to be on hand, supposedly just to advise, but they ended up doing most of the work. A selection of the people with the boats didn't often use them, they just liked having them. They came out from the city on hot summer days and took the boat a little way out on the bay, sat in the sun, a little distance away from the next guy. They had to have a nice, freshly painted, good-looking boat. Boats needed a lot of maintenance.

'Just one or two days, they come,' said Dad, 'I don't understand why these people spend their money on a boat. All that work.'

He didn't seem to mind that it was him that did most of the work.

'Who the hell cares,' said Uncle Joe. 'As long as they pay the rent.'

Dad had promised to be home before dark, in time for cold cuts and cake. There was pink champagne chilling in the fridge that all the children would be allowed to take a sip of.

People began to arrive shortly after our bread and butter lunch. Aunt Gloria and Uncle Nick turned up first and Gloria set to with Mother doing their double acting baking thing and as the house filled up with the sweet aromas, Uncle Nick settled down with a beer and to watch the football, staring firmly at the television set while all the action happened around him. We formed a pack of kids, a sort of high tide wave of hunger and high spirits, ready to run wild until it was time to be fed something again.

At the same time, Alice, our elderly neighbour from down the way, turned up at the door to return our dog, Fluke, borrowed the previous night to warn off intruders. Alice's own dog was an in-patient at the vet and she was nervous on her own.

Of all our relatives, Aunt Gloria and Uncle Nick had the biggest family, thus far, so in ascending order, in the mêlée, Mother in her apron conducted introductions, rattling off names, using a sticky wooden spoon as an indicator.

'Oh I'm so sorry - you have visitors...' Alice said.

'Not to worry! Please come in Alice! Please, please, meet my sister Gloria,' Mother pointed to my aunt, the image of herself, while timid old Alice did the familiar double take. They were uncannily alike.

Alice looked from one woman to the other, probably wondering how, as a close neighbour for all these years, she had no knowledge of these twins. Mother just grinned at her, unaware of the confusion people sometimes felt upon meeting her and Gloria together. To Mother, they were just sisters, being identical was a detail she forgot about.

'Hello Fluke!' said Mother to the dog, who was a spinning circle of greeting, beside himself with joy to be back with us, rather than cooped up in the nervous old woman's dining room.

'She ties him to a chair leg,' said Gabe, once, 'so that if he hears something and forgets to bark, he'll move and pull the chair to make a warning noise.' This wasn't true, but Gabe didn't have much time for Alice, who he suspected of confiscating lost balls.

'And her husband Nick, and here boys, don't disappear just yet, come and meet Alice - Josephina, Nick Jr, Georgina, Christina and Joseph.'

Alice declined all the ensuing offers of hospitality, said hello to each child in turn before excusing herself and quickly exiting, obviously desperate to escape, just as Uncle Tony bounded into the house, one arm loaded with daffodils, the other fencing with a branch of pussy willow.

Listening to these introductions, hearing my cousin's names relayed all in a row, combined with Uncle Tony's arrival is what got me thinking about names, in a vague, non-taxing sense. I fell into an idle innocent reverie, a progressive daydream that soon had me climbing up the family tree.

It seemed to me that all of Aunt Gloria's girls had boy's names in disguise, a bit like our Bernadette. Josephina came first and not being born male, got stuck with the grandfather tag anyway. Nick was next, and as they'd already used up Papa Joe's benefaction, they called him after his dad. Then came Georgina, from some Grandfather George on Uncle Nick's side. Christina was born on Christmas Day, which was self-explanatory. Then of course along came another boy, such a nice surprise, so by this time they figured it would be acceptable to use Papa Joe's name again. I personally thought it was a bit ridiculous having a Josephina and a Joseph in the same family, but this, like most other child opinions, carried no weight. I would keep it to myself.

I then went through each of my young relations in my head, ticking off the names and their origins. For each name there was a logical explanation, a good reason, a certain order. It took me some time and I abandoned the running pack of cousins' games for a period of time while I sketched out a primitive family tree diagram in order to keep track.

It was only when I got to my own family that the system failed. Of

36

course the naming of Bernadette was now a legendary family story, even though she was still a baby. I knew Maureen was Maureen because of Aunt Mo, also Maureen. I, eldest girl was Gloria Mary, after Mother and her twin. But why Gabe? Of course there was Uncle Gabe, Dad's brother. But Dad's name was Tony, and Mother's eldest brother was called Tony, and Gabe was the eldest boy. The eldest boy always got his father's name, if he escaped Papa Joe's moniker. It seemed a missed opportunity for my parents not to name their first son Tony. I was curious as to why. I must remember to ask about it, I thought. Big mistake, as I would find out later that day. When I got tired of pondering, I shrugged it off, discarded my sketch and went back to run with the tribe.

Pink champagne preceded the cake, and just like cake, was a requisite for most celebrations. It had to be pink. It certainly wasn't champagne. It was ceremoniously poured for everyone, tiny finger sized portions in order to go round the crowd, with a bit of glass tipping at the end to balance out the levels. It was only the women who liked it, the men preferred beer. It was all bubbles to us, however. Anything in a real glass was special. Then it was time to sing.

'Happy birthday dear Tony -Dad-Uncle-Tony happy birthday to you!'

My cousin Josephina's glass fell and broke on the floor, but no one minded. 'Let Dad make his wish, then I'll get it cleaned up. Careful!' said Mother.

Laughter and clinking of glasses and me, off in a whimsy, thought, this would be a good time, everyone here, remembering about the names again and deciding right then, at the end of the song, to ask:

'Why didn't you call Gabe Tony instead of Gabe?'

And the candles were all blown out leaving us in darkness, stopping the laughter, and no one said anything. Not a word.

There was a silence that was just the right length, like a record on a turntable skipping before the start of a song, that beat or two added on to what might have been ordinary, just long enough to realise that my question was a problem.

During that short but eternally long moment I looked around from face to face. There was no problem with anything else. The birthday song and candle extinguishing was normal, and no one was suffering any sort of health problem such as a heart attack, choking, or shortness of breath. It was definitely my question that caused the silence. It was me, it was my fault. I'd said something dreadful. No one looked at me, or indeed anyone else, fully occupied with the concentration it took to avoid any eye contact in the small, dimly-lit kitchen filled with more than twenty people. No one saw the heat spreading from my neck to my face, my happy smile and curious wide eyes vanishing.

The sound of the fizzing bubbles was amplified. A small room full of twenty odd people, more than half children, and it was the only thing that could be heard.

'Tony, you wanna hit that light?'

Both Tonys started towards the wall, then stopped, then moved again.

It was Mother that got to the light switch first. Click, it went, and with that, the stylus on our life was lifted and readjusted. The lights came on, the party resumed. The cake was cut, doled out and more champagne was popped. Eerily, the festivities continued as effervescent as before and I could almost believe that I'd had a terrible daydream or a hallucination, that I'd only thought my question and not really spoken it. Except for the shame that I felt, a strange unfamiliar sensation, grimy and soiled, not a childlike feeling, but an adult one, that would affect me for the rest of my life. After that, I never asked a question out loud unless I was fairly sure I knew the answer. I stopped trying to find out the reasons for the things I wondered about and simply imagined the explanations, creating the perfect environment for distortion of the truth, mistaken identity, unjust accusations and wild fantasy. With every pink bubble that burst in the fizzy silence that day, another door within me slammed shut and with it went my childhood innocence and absolute trust.

Uncle Joe was kneeling on the floor, concentrating on cleaning up the broken glass. I joined him, in an attempt to recover. His brows were furrowed; he looked deep in tragic thought.

'Don't be so sad, Uncle Joe. It's only a glass.'

He smiled and patted my head.

'It's not the glass,' he said. 'It's what was in it.'

I kept secrets, my own and anyone else's who chose to confide in me. I tried to protect Maureen from the shame, teaching her early how to avoid the forbidden fruit, don't say anything, just listen.

'Don't ask questions Maureen. Just listen, instead, and wait. Children should be seen and not heard.'

'Aunt Grace says that,' said Maureen.

'Yeah, well, she's right there.'

Some of the secrets were darker than others, widely known but not understood and never dared spoken of, such as why we were steered away from playing with Cousin Francine, or why we dare not ask the reason why Aunt Sally and Uncle Gabe had dogs but no children, or why Uncle Tony never married, or whatever happened to the baby that came after our dad and that the hair of the dog and mother's helpers had nothing to do with pets or staff. I thought I remembered a wedding, with a bride in a golden dress, and thought that bride was familiar to me. It may have been a dream but I wasn't sure and couldn't ask.

We became afraid of the answers. We reckoned the adults were privy to such terrible truths that their whole purpose in life was to protect us from this knowledge, lest we be damaged. They whispered among themselves, exchanged knowing looks.

Our own little secret society, unbeknown to us, almost exactly imitated what our parents did. So, for example, I never told anyone that I witnessed Aunt Grace hitting Maureen, except for Gabe, and he swore not to tell. But of course Maureen knew that I'd seen, and all our other cousins hated Aunt Grace too, except her children, of course, so Maureen would tell Georgina. But she would tell Georgina not to tell anyone. But of course Georgina would. The story would spread, two by two, and like the game of Chinese whispers, distort as it travelled so eventually everyone would know, but no one would talk about it, which was the rule. Most of the time, we all had different versions.

On the whole, like most families, we behaved in a perfectly normal dysfunctional manner and would have done the same without all the unnecessary mystery, and would grow up and turn into our parents. Up until Bernadette came along, that is, changing the rules and providing us with the means of avoiding such dull predictability.

****

Chapter 4

Outside, four years after Hurricane Grace, the fallen tree remained *in situ*, save for a few smaller branches which had been removed and burned, leaving a mighty wooden skeleton that served us as ship, train, bridge, house, rocket, hiding place and all purpose general fort and shelter from the lesser storms since then. We owned the tree. A document of our childhood, we'd carved our names into its trunk, hammered planks of wood into it with crooked nails to create stairways, added and removed sails, portholes, wings, steering devices, luxury compartments, radar, curtains, machine artillery, windows and light fittings.

We left to catch the bus for school out the back door, one by one, me first.

'Please don't slam the door!'

The door slammed. It was a sprung door and the spring was broken. It was hard not to slam it.

'Sorry!' I went to the tree to pick up my drawing book, and waited for the others. I hid my book there, in an old biscuit tin, not on account of secrecy though, but the clandestine nature of having something to hide added some glamour to my life.

Maureen was next. The door slammed.

'Sorry!'

I was ten and Measles was about to spread through our family like the rash that was its hallmark, attacking us in the order of our ages, spreading downwards, starting from the eldest. The first sign of it came from Gabe. He took too long to leave the house. He didn't let the door slam.

En route to school, he leaned against the window, eyes staring into nowhere, his lids gradually closing until we rolled over a bump in the road or stopped to collect someone. Then he would lift his heavy head, rejoining the rest of the world for a moment or two, looking around as though faintly surprised to find himself on the school bus, before sliding back into his fever. He didn't talk to me. His face sagged and looked deformed, flat against the glass, his upper lip sneering at the traffic.

On the way home he was missing from the bus.

'Your brother got sent home sick,' someone said.

'Did he throw up?' Maureen asked.

'No, I think he fainted.'

Maureen and I sat together. 'I wish it was me,' I said.

'Me too,' said Maureen. 'Maybe we'll catch it. Then we could stay home with Mother and Bernadette.' Our wish was to come true. Staying home with Mother and Bernadette was immeasurably preferable to being with strict nuns who concealed weapons under their habits - rulers, chalk missiles and pointing sticks. And who took us on seemingly endless visits to church, walking silent and straight, up and down hard pews, kneeling, sitting and standing.

'I said straight,' they said. 'We'll stand here until we think this line is straight.'

A piece of chalk would whistle through the air; scald an ear. The nuns themselves seemed to be able to withstand any extreme weather condition imaginable. Even in the bright warmth of early summer, the days were long and cold, marble and stone.

At home with Mother and Bernadette, on the other hand, was the soft fluffy world. Our revered Mother, whose saint-like ability to care for the sick could only be outstripped by her namesake, wasn't called Mary by accident, for sure. Bouncing Bernadette, with her delightfully long curly angel hair and her infectious giggle, was just the right age to be fun and full of adulation for her older big-girl sisters - and quite a willing slave as well.

Staying at home with Mother and Bernadette meant cuddling up on the sofa watching television. It meant playing with colourful fishing flies, cutting out paper dolls and a steady stream of small gifts from Dad, and Aunt Mo. Uncle Joe sneaked in sweets. The morning dancing, dusty rays of the sun would shine in and warm the carpet, the cats Skip and Jack would make picky-paw nests on the woollen blanket before settling down on top to be our living, breathing hot water bottles. Dad would come in from the Fish Shop, smelling of the sea and hugging us through the blanket, Uncle Joe with him, another big hug. Then they'd go into the kitchen and discuss the patient in hushed tones, just loud enough for us to hear that we were the objects of their chief concerns, the most important thing in their world at the end of the day.

It wasn't like that for Gabe just yet, however. Rushing into the house, Maureen with a news flash, shouting, 'Gabe threw up and fainted at school!'

'Shhh! Quiet! Don't shout, and especially not such nonsense,' Mother said. 'He did not throw up and faint. He's come home with a fever. He's in bed sleeping and I want him to stay that way. You'll have to go outside and play.'

'But -'

'No buts. Get changed and go out. And be quiet about it. Bernadette's already out there,' she said.

The vision of our saintly mother serving up hot chocolate and buttered toast vanished into the air like steam.

'Goodness, she's grouchy,' whispered Maureen, as we discarded our school uniforms on to the floor.

'Maybe she doesn't feel well,' I said, attempting to make sense of her behaviour. 'Maybe she's catching what Gabe has.' It wasn't usual for Mother to be irritable, to throw us outside. Outside though, was our territory, it belonged to us, not to them. They knew the trees and the boundary hedges and fences but not the way we did, and once outside, we didn't mind. We could not feel banished to our own kingdom.

We found Bernadette, sitting silently and patiently behind the up-ended root holding a string leading to a stick propping up a cardboard box under which she had placed a slice of bread.

She brightened when she saw us. 'Shh!' she put her hand dramatically to her lips. 'Gabe's sick. I'm trying to catch a bird.' Maureen looked doubtfully at Bernadette's bird trap.

'The string isn't even tied to the stick, Bernadette,' she said, 'do you want me to tie a knot for you?'

'Shhh.' Bernadette whispered. 'It's wound around. It works okay. There were lots of birds before you got here.'

'Maybe we should go play somewhere else,' I whispered to Maureen.

Bernadette looked stricken. 'No! Don't go away!' she pleaded, still whispering.

'Bernadette,' said Maureen patiently, 'I don't think that box will catch any birds. And it's no fun for us to stay here, having to be quiet .'

'Okay, we're going somewhere else to play', I declared decisively, 'and you can stay here on your own or come and play with us.'

Bernadette didn't move, but sat tight, her hunched back giving no indication of whether she was sad, angry, sullen or stubborn. We waited in the silence, not quite sure what to do next.

There was a soft thud, the sound of cardboard hitting grass.

'I GOT ONE!' Bernadette shrieked. She turned around to us excitedly, accusing. 'See? See? I told you it would work! And you thought it wouldn't be fun!'

I was doubtful. 'Bernadette, you didn't catch any bird. That box isn't heavy enough. It was probably the wind.'

'I saw it! It's under there, a blue jay,' she cried. 'Go on, go away if you don't believe me. Go play somewhere else and I'll have it all to myself.'

The three of us regarded the overturned cardboard box. I felt sorry for Bernadette. She was so hopeful, and trusting. I knew better.

'Well, nothing's moving at all,' I said, after a few moments. 'You might have some better luck with a smaller bird, maybe if you wait a little longer. Or we could try and make a better trap for another day.'

'That's it!' said Maureen, seeing the perfect solution, 'We'll go and find stuff to make a better trap!'

But Bernadette wasn't listening, having moved to the other end of the string, she was peering into a hole in the top of the box, cooing softly. The box, motionless, sat on the ground looking exactly like what it was, a discarded piece of junk. Then, as we approached her, expecting to offer a bit of comfort and support when she realised it was empty, it moved. Just a bit, a tiny breath; a shift in position accompanied by the unmistakable sound of feathers beating against cardboard. Maureen and I stood, humbled and full of wonder.

Bernadette, without taking her eyes off the box, said, 'Be quiet... you're scaring him.'

Maureen, her brief moment of humility over, affronted, said, 'You're the one who trapped it.'

'Shut up Maureen,' I said. This was exciting. 'What should we do with it?'

'I want to feed it,' said Bernadette, and Maureen ran in to get some provisions. She returned with a crust of bread which, fed crumb by crumb through the hole in the box, was largely ignored by the stricken blue jay, still imprisoned in the dark with an entire slice of the stuff, hunger probably not its chief concern.

My sympathies shifted from Bernadette to the bird.

'It's not hungry, Bernadette. It's too scared.'

'It will eat,' said Bernadette. 'It just needs to get to know me.'

'I don't think so. I think it would be happier going off finding bugs or something.' She ignored me and kept at the bird. Boredom soon set in and Maureen and I gradually wandered away, whiling away the remainder of the afternoon in surrounding fields and up trees.

When we returned much later, Bernadette had cut a door flap in the box and had the bird eating bits of fruit from her fingers. She proudly demonstrated this, the end result of her steadfast patience, and then said, 'I think it's time to let him go.'

Maureen and I sat down on the fallen tree and were silent, trying to give the event the reverence it deserved, while Bernadette, sitting on the ground, lifted the cardboard box and like a magician, revealed the blue jay to us for the first time. It stood for a moment, dazed by the light, cocked its head, squawked, hopped a few steps and then flew away. Bernadette, still holding the cardboard box, smiled on, watched its flight like a proud mother.

'See. I told you I could do it,' said Bernadette.

'Yeah, you did,' I said.

'I could do it again tomorrow, too, if I wanted,' said Bernadette.

'You have a special gift with animals, Bernadette,' said Maureen, 'like Saint Francis.'

'Oh, don't go getting all holy now Maureen,' I said, annoyed.

'You didn't believe her either.'

By the time darkness fell and supper was prepared and we were allowed back indoors, it was becoming evident that Gabe was suffering from something more serious than a bad cold. Aunt Mo came over to consult, and Dad arrived home from the Fish Shop with Uncle Joe who also had a look. Folded arms and nodding heads ignored the rest of us, decided that the doctor needed to be called, tonight, not tomorrow. Afterwards, Aunt Grace appeared to collect Uncle Joe, all red fingernails and black eyeliner, coral lipstick overstepping the outline of her mouth, and offered her unsolicited opinion. A mother of three older children, as she often reminded anyone listening, she considered herself a bit of an expert. Marching into Gabe's bedroom and punctuating her lengthy diagnosis with tut tutting and short sharp intakes of breath through her teeth, she ran through a gamut of childhood diseases, from scarlet fever to polio and even plague, all the while prodding and pinching my poor defenceless brother.

When Aunt Grace left, planting greasy coral lip prints on us - she aimed for our mouths and you could tell by the position of the marks left on our faces who was the quickest to avoid her - Mother said, 'Honestly. Plague. What a nerve, implying that we live in a house full of rats.'

Finding ourselves overlooked again, we grabbed a few empty jars and a screwdriver; and went back outside in the dark to pass the evening catching lightening bugs. I punctured the lids, hammering the screwdriver with a rock before we started hunting.

'Over here's good. They like these bushes,' said Maureen from the hydrangeas.

The yard was different by night. The fallen tree became a more sinister silhouette casting shadows that could be mistaken for holes in the earth, or snakes, depending on your mood. Maureen stood by a wall of dark brush topped with clumps of snow. On closer approach, intermittent flashes from the insects changed the snow to blossoms and back again. It was an eerily luminous night with long shadows cast by a full moon.

'I got one!' Bernadette's voice, from behind the shrub, shouted triumphantly for the second time that day.

'Got what?' said a man's grinning voice. We froze, gripping our jars, frightened.

'Hello children,' the man said again, and we saw the long teeth of the dreaded Dr Shapiro, his face grotesque in the phantasmal glow.

Inside, he made his diagnosis.

'He's got the measles,' Maureen reported to the bedroom later.

'That'll be two weeks off school,' I said. 'At least.'

'Do you think we'll get it?' asked Bernadette.

'I heard them,' said Maureen. 'It's a sure thing. We'll all get it.'

'Will we have rats?' asked Bernadette.

'What are you talking about?' Maureen said.

'Mother said we had rats,' said Bernadette, anxiously. I'd heard the comment about rats, and didn't understand it either, therefore ignoring it but as the eldest present felt it was my duty to offer an explanation that would calm her fears.

'No, that's not what she said, that's a different sickness.' I explained, adding, 'Rats won't live in a house with measles.'

Gabe developed a rash over the next few days, and lay in bed quietly. After school on the third day he was sitting up in bed, still a bit listless but able to talk and read the magazines and appreciate the gifts everyone was bringing to him. Maureen and I sat on the end of his bed.

'How bad is it?' Maureen asked.

'It's not too bad as long as you can stay in bed. It was the worst in school, though, and on the bus,' he said.

'I'm worried about getting it,' said Maureen, looking at his rash.

'It doesn't itch, or hurt at all,' said Gabe. 'And it's okay if you're in bed. You need to sleep a lot. But they give you lots of stuff to read, and there's no horrible medicine.'

'Not like that stuff we had to take when we got worms,' said Maureen.

'Eww. That was disgusting,' I said, feeling the taste of nausea creeping up the back of my throat at the bitter amber memory.

Bernadette, silent up until now, perked up.

'Worms?' she asked, a look of horror on her face.

'No, no, not real worms,' I said, quickly, 'that's just what it's called, it's just a stomach upset and you didn't get it, you weren't here.'

Bernadette was relieved, and went to bed. I stayed with Gabe for a while longer.

'Is it really not too bad?' I asked.

'Well, maybe it's a little worse than I just said to them, because they're worrying about it,' he said.

'Maureen's only worrying about being sick. Bernadette worries about everything,' I said.

'She's so weird sometimes,' said Gabe.

'Who? Bernadette?' I said. 'No she isn't. What do you mean?'

'She's just – I don't know, different.' Gabe was whispering.

'No. You're just sick. She's fine. She caught a bird today.'

'I'm going to sleep.'

Bernadette had liberated four lightning bugs to twinkle our fancies in the dark bedroom. The crime of imprisoning wildlife, as applied to the blue jay, didn't operate in this instance.

Watching them, I heard an imaginary musical ting in my ears every time they lit up. It was soothing. Bernadette gave them names, Goldfish, Mermaid, Seahorse and Starfish using the customary family pet naming system. Everything we owned was named after a fish, even the fish.

The game involved trying to follow the bugs, guessing each new position between flashes, until our own lights were extinguished and we fell asleep. In the morning Bernadette re-captured the insects.

'I know what they look like in the daytime' she said wisely, and set them free.

Not long after, I developed a headache. The doctor came again. This time Aunt Grace didn't have the satisfaction of casting her doomed predictions onto us, as it was pretty much a given that I had the same illness Gabe did. She compensated by talking about the complications that were possible with measles, and of course with four children - and one in every two hundred, was it? - developing these complications, some of them indeed fatal, then the chances were quite high weren't they, for our family?

They weren't very high, actually, but nonetheless, when ten days later Gabe and Maureen relapsed with an ear infection, and I began to vomit, and Bernadette, the last to fall, collapsed into bed with a headache, Mother was worried enough to call the doctor out again.

We didn't like the doctor. I personally, would have rather stayed sick for an extra ten weeks than have to be examined by Doctor Shapiro. He was dry, papery skinned with long hard fingers, always poking too hard in what I considered to be an inappropriate and unnecessary manner.

He sniffed the atmosphere and criticised the air quality in our house.

'It's far too damp in this house,' he said. 'No wonder they're all sick' – his tone implied. His icy stethoscope probed beneath the blankets and he stuck sticks down our throats, heavy breathing his antiseptic tainted breath in the silence of the bedroom, his nose hairs nearly long enough to touch our faces, my parents standing away back in the doorway as though he were some sort of mystic, anxiously awaiting his verdict. We had to see Doctor Shapiro, because he had always been the family doctor, just as we had to be baptised by ancient Father McGlone, because he performed all the baptisms. Doctor Shapiro had delivered my mother and her sisters; it would be unthinkable to go to any other doctor.

His office was in a room in his house, an old, ill-maintained house surrounded by gnarled apple trees. The overgrown garden prevented any sunlight getting through. I remembered being vaccinated for something; looking out of the window into his horror-movie garden, the trees with human-like limbs and faces.

'Stand up here on this chair for me, young lady,' he said. 'That way I don't have to stoop to reach your bottom.'

'Will it hurt?' Pants down around my ankles, scared and humiliated.

'I'm right here, honey,' Mother stood by my side, holding my shoulders.

'Not at all. You'll not feel anything,' he said, through his heavy breath.

It was sore for days.

I never believed anything he said after that, and credited recovery from any illness on which he'd been consulted more to God and my own prayers than to his medicine.

We'd look out the window on the way to his practice and see single storey, clean, modern yellow brick buildings being built that became

'Medical Centres' where there were smart young doctors in suits. We secretly longed to go to one of these places instead. In the meantime, we hid our illnesses, avoiding the doctor except in cases of near collapse.

Dr Shapiro diagnosed Gabe and Maureen with an ear infection each, a side effect - or complication as Aunt Grace would have it - of the measles that Bernadette was just coming down with. I was vomiting simply out of bad luck because I had caught a stomach virus that would no doubt also spread throughout the family and there wasn't much we could do about it except stay in bed and drink water.

He then produced a large bottle of a foul tasting substance for Gabe and Maureen and went on his way. I had to turn away, unable to keep my stomach at the sight of the medicine.

'Why does he carry it with him?' I said to Gabe. 'Other people's doctors prescribe medicine, on pieces of paper and you have to go and get a pharmacist to make it. Do you think he makes it himself in his basement?'

'Go back to bed Gloria,' said Dad, dispensing the brown liquid into Gabe, 'you're not helping.'

'What does it taste like?' I said to Gabe.

'Bed!' said Dad.

I returned to my room, my bed, and my just-in-case-you-don't-make-it-to-the-bathroom basin. I warned Maureen of medication being imminent. She groaned.

'Don't worry,' I said, 'It could never be as bad as the worm stuff.'

Bernadette slept soundly in her little bed, hot and rosy cheeked with oncoming illness… innocent.

****

Chapter 5

Uncle Joe referred to our home as the Sickhouse throughout the grim period of measles and stomach upsets. He and Dad spent even more time at the Fish Shop pretending it was busier than usual while we at home grew thinner, paler and more helpless.

Uncle Joe dropped Dad off without getting out of the car, withholding his usual short evening visit, leaving us with nothing to look forward to except getting well again. Bernadette suffered the most; sick enough to be taken again to the dreaded Dr Shapiro, who looked her over, prodded her with cold instruments and declared she had an extra severe dose of The Stomach Virus.

Finally even our stoic mother Mary succumbed. Weakly, and somewhat timidly, she mentioned her plight to Dad, who was normally very sympathetic and protective over her in times of illness. This time she had to ask. This time he couldn't meet her eyes.

'I'm sorry, Mary,' he said, 'I just can't do it, I can't be around to help, it's too busy at the shop. It's – the sick. And the smell of that disinfectant makes me want to puke up myself.'

I was lying on the sofa, the start of my recovery phase. I opened my eyes to see Mother's expression, which I read as a cross between disgust and pity. She, however, was too ill to feel anything but nausea and simply sighed and closed her eyes. I realised my interpretation of her reaction was really my own. The discovery of Dad's fear of vomit depressed me. At ten years of age, he was the only man of my dreams. The idea that he had failings hadn't yet occurred to me.

'It's just a bit of throw up,' I mumbled under my breath. He looked at me and left the house again.

'Don't worry about it,' said Mother. 'Aunt Mo will help out if we need it. It'll be all right. It only lasts a day or so.'

In her case it lasted a lot longer than that. She shuffled from bedroom to bathroom, soon without even the strength to fasten her thin cotton dressing gown. She took Bernadette into bed with her.

Gabe, Maureen and I were well enough to fend for ourselves.

'What do you want to eat?' I said.

'What is there?' said Maureen.

'Cereal,' I said.

'I could make toast, too,' said Gabe.

'Okay let's have that.'

We visited the sick room for weak smiles. Gabe made tea for Mother, juice for Bernadette, poured cereal for us.

'You look good, Gloria. How's your mother?' said Dad, arriving home, late.

'Sleeping. Her and Bernadette are sleeping,' I said. 'They sleep all the time.'

'That's what they need. Did they eat anything?'

'A little tea,' I said. 'But that's it.'

He looked in on them, went into the bedroom and closed the door. A while later he came out.

'I'll sleep on the couch,' he said. 'Let Bernadette stay there.'

A fair amount of cereal after that, came the day they wouldn't wake up.

I ran down to the Fish Shop, tucked in among the nest of cabin cruisers at the far end of the long marina. It had no proper sign, always known to us as the Fish Shop. On a blackboard outside the words Bait and Tackle were chalked, requiring retouching after rain. The Fish Shop was a big part of our world. It was my favourite part. Still is.

The shop had modest small town beginnings. Following their mother's death, Uncle Joe, Dad, and Uncle Gabe moved out of their Italian neighbourhood in the city, out here to the island. Joe was just ten. Papa Joseph bought the shack at the end of the marina, at the time just a dirt road on a sandy finger pointing into the bay. He started selling bait to local fishermen, supplying them with slithery shiners, killies and chopped up squid, passed in buckets through a hatch in the side of the hut.

Dad and Uncle Joe took over Papa Joe's shack when he decided to retire, and they raised its profile somewhat, adding a few shelves and some stock, building it into a small bait and tackle business. They were successful enough for them both to make a modest living.

It was a busy little shop which spouted three more handmade, hastily tacked on rooms as needs arose, sturdy and watertight in spite of its ramshackle appearance. The Fish Shop couldn't survive without fish, although apart from the live bait, it didn't actually sell any. It supplied all manner of accessories to the fishing, boating and beaching realm as well as various bits of hardware, pharmaceuticals, newspapers, snacks and sundries. With the added rooms came paving for the dirt road, car parking spaces, the boat moorings and more customers. It was a predominantly male environment, men in undershirts gossiping about swells, storms and sharks, drinking coffee out of unwashed enameled tin cups and beer out of the can.

Nobody knew what the original draw was for a city boy like Papa Joe, why he turned and headed away from the land of opportunities to this backwater. Back then the island was marshy and quiet. No place to get rich. Every regular had a theory.

'I heard him talk about his own father from Sicily. He's got fish in his blood.'

'That's right. Spent most of his boyhood out squiddin' all night.'

'Nah. He told me he was in trouble with the cops. Came out here to hide, protect his family.'

'It was trouble, all right, but not cops. Gangs. I think he was into it deep.'

'I heard his wife was murdered.' (This in a whisper)

'Her last wish, get the boys outta here.'

Uncle Joe and Dad had little to say on the subject.

'He didn't talk much,' said Dad.

Aunt Grace proposed opening a coffee and cake bar adjacent to the Fish Shop, but was ridiculed for having such silly ideas, who did she think she was, with these female delusions of grandeur? When Aunt Grace, being Aunt Grace, persisted, or kept nagging, as Dad would have it, she was strictly forbidden on the grounds that it was not only an unrealistic business venture but might even damage the existing bait trade. A year later Uncle Vinny, Mo's husband, stole her idea, substituting clam chowder for cake - with Dad and Joe's blessing and some investment. The business, as predicted by Aunt Grace, was booming within weeks. She was seething.

Maureen and I, however, always felt welcome in spite of our inferior gender. 'Welcome', perhaps too strong a word for what was really going unnoticed. We came and went and didn't get thrown out, sat on the floor until we became invisible, eavesdropping. I gained most of my misinformation that way.

On this particular night, it was late, after supper, when I got there, lungs fit to burst, and the place was dead, Uncle Joe slouched into a newspaper and Dad sitting on the floor surrounded by odds and ends, so absorbed in untangling some knotted fishing line that he didn't see or hear me enter.

'What are you doing?' I asked. He jumped upright, startled, and kicked away the debris at his feet.

'Hey Gloria! You're late tonight. What's up?'

'Nothing. Just visiting.' I said. 'It's late for you to be working, isn't it?'

'Yeah, well, we'll be closing up soon.' He said.

'Can I wait for you?' I asked, not quite sure how to introduce my purpose.

'Sure. I'll just tidy up a few of these fiddly things and then we'll go.'

'Can I watch the fish?' I asked.

'Sure. Grab a chair,' he said. 'Want some cream soda?' He poured us both a glass and sat down with me to look at the fish.

Dad and Uncle Joe loved fish. They loved eating them, catching them, selling them, gutting them and chopping them up. They loved anything and everything to do with any kind of fish, so it seemed natural that there was a tank of tropical fish in the shop, behind the counter. These pets kept their own names, Angel, Guppy, Snail and Neon. I was usually fond of sitting and watching them but tonight my heart was pounding, breaking through my chest. I was afraid.

'Glad to see you've escaped the Sickhouse.' said Uncle Joe, from behind his newspaper. 'How's the rest of them?'

This gave me the opening I needed to broach the subject. The rest of them weren't very well, and this was troubling me, as being only ten, I wasn't sure what to do about it. I was not in control of the situation. I did not welcome this responsibility.

Gabe had gone off to a friend's after school, one of many surrogate families that he'd been scrounging meals off of since he'd recovered. Maureen was technically well but still not going to school, just to be sure.

We couldn't rouse our ailing Mother to help when an even sicker Bernadette couldn't answer a simple question, couldn't even keep her eyes open, when she looked at me and opened her mouth as if to speak and closed her eyes again. I didn't know then that it would be the last time I saw Bernadette, my Bernadette, our Bernadette, the Bernadette we loved. Maureen decided I'd better take charge.

'You have to go down to the dock and get Dad,' she said.

Nervous about his aversion to the illness, I was uneasy about calling on Dad's services. I didn't think he wanted to be disturbed.

'I think Bernadette is getting sicker. She's a lot worse,' I said.

'Ah, well, your mother will know all the right things to do,' said Uncle Joe.

'She's asleep, though,' I said, uncertainly. 'We keep trying to wake her up but she keeps telling us she'll be there in a minute, but then she just flops over, back to sleep. We can't wake Bernadette up either.'

Before my words were out Dad was switching off lights and putting on his jacket and Uncle Joe was shepherding me to the door with the keys to the car in his hands.

Then we were racing along the marina in the dark, past the steamy parked cars facing out to sea that, came to watch the submarine races at night, as Uncle Joe would usually point out. No jokes tonight. The ride home was silent; I sat forgotten in the back seat.

The doctor came and went, and the ambulance came and went, and then Dad went, and Gabe came home and once again he, Maureen and I were home alone while momentous things happened to Mother and Bernadette in the hospital as Dad looked on anxiously.

This time there was no hurricane to help pass the hours or shift the focus of our worries. We were older, wiser and self-sufficient and could have managed to make a fire, should we have needed one, or to cook popcorn if we'd felt hungry. We sat silently in the living room, feeling like abandoned orphans in a desolate ghost town, and would have expected an arid breeze to blow tumbleweeds through the halls had we not lived on the damp north east coast. Instead of huddling together for comfort, we sat apart, careful not to touch or make eye contact in the small room.

'Should I turn on the television?' asked Maureen.

'I guess so,' Gabe said. 'There isn't much else to do.'

Maureen got up and switched it on, and sat down again on her chair, and we stared at it for a while.

'Change the channel Maureen,' I said. I couldn't see what was on. My eyes were misting up. Maureen duly got up and flicked over the switch a couple of times.

'What do you want?' she said.

'I don't know. You pick,' I said. She settled on a sitcom for a moment.

'Yeah, right, Maureen,' sniped Gabe. 'Like this is appropriate.'

'Then you do it Gabe,' I said. 'If you think you're so smart.'

He drew a sharp breath.

'I'm sorry I wasn't home,' he said.

'It's all right. It doesn't matter,' I said.

'It wouldn't have made any difference.'

'I might have gone to get him sooner, though, if I'd been here,' he said.

'Well at least I went; at least I was here to go,' I said, and let go of my emotions and once I started I couldn't stop. I lay on the sofa and sobbed and sobbed.

'Stop crying!' said Gabe, becoming upset himself. 'It isn't helping!'

This made me feel even worse.

'Nothing I do is helpful,' I moaned, in between shrieks. Maureen, up off her chair, knelt next to me with the intention of offering comfort. I kicked her away, hard. 'Get out of here! Get away from me!'

'You kicked me!' she shouted. 'All I was trying to do was help you!'

She then robbed me of my escape by running to the bedroom in tears, slamming the door behind her, leaving me shipwrecked on the living room sofa.

'Gloria' - Gabe said shakily, also beginning to crack.

'Oh go away too you Mr I-could-have-done-it-better!' I screamed. I wanted to be alone and as Maureen had taken to the bedroom I had no option other than to drive my brother away.

'You're right! If you had been here it would be fine, you'd have gone sooner and done the right thing and they wouldn't die!' I stopped shouting. 'They're going to die and it's my fault. Our mother is going to die. They might already even be dead.'

Gabe left the room, up the stairs, followed by another slam.

I woke up there on the sofa early the following morning, covered in pets, saliva seeping out of the corner of my mouth, my eyes crusty with dried tears, to the sound of the key turning in the door. Dad came in. A look of exhausted surprise crossed his unshaven features when he saw me sit up, emerging from a pile of cushions on the sofa, sending cats flying in all directions. Fluke dragged his back legs past him out the door. I rubbed my eyes and waited for Dad to speak.

Maureen appeared at the top of the stairs and, always one to get right to the point, said 'Are they dead?'

Dad rubbed his face. He looked as though he were in physical pain.

'Oh, no, no, honey, they're not dead. Your mother will be home later today, but Bernadette will have to stay there longer. They're gonna take good care of her. She's very sick.'

'Will she get better?' said Maureen.

'What's wrong with her?'

'I'm sorry I left you here alone. I didn't think we'd be there all night.'

He looked around at the two of us.

'I feel awful about that. Were you all right?'

'Will she get better?' Maureen repeated. He was silent and looked at each one of us in turn, considering his reply. By this time Gabe had emerged from his room.

'Yeah. She will get better.'

I wasn't convinced he was telling the truth but let it go.

'What was wrong with Mother?' I said. He smiled at this, and sat down.

'There's nothing wrong with your mother,' he said.

'She's going to have a baby.'

This silenced us, something we'd never considered. We felt complete enough as things were. This wasn't the news I expected, or wanted.

'A baby?' I said.

He smiled again.

'Yeah, a baby. Whatdya think of that?'

'I don't know.' It was the truth. It made him laugh, and shake his head.

'Well, let's be happy about it then,' he said.

We spent the rest of the day tidying the house preparing for Mother's homecoming. Dad shouted out orders and hoped we knew how to carry them out, having little or no idea about the business of domesticity himself. We again survived on breakfast cereal and a box of doughnuts from the bakery that Uncle Joe brought. Gradually, the aunts appeared, starting with Aunt Mo and Aunt Gloria, bearing gratefully received food supplies. Uncle Tony bustled in a while later, armed with a large bunch of flowers from his garden and a bottle of Chianti. It was almost approaching a cake-crowd, although not quite reaching the pink champagne level. Uncle Gabe arrived, but Aunt Grace never turned up, by happy accident or deliberate design I didn't know and didn't care, and enjoyed the atmosphere created by her absence. They were all, apart from Uncle Tony, more relaxed, funnier, louder, easier without her there, nit picking. The laughter wasn't regularly pierced with sharp comments. Uncle Tony, he was always relaxed, regardless.

There were the usual secretive undertones that I was vaguely aware of, but I was preoccupied by skirting around Maureen and Gabe self-consciously until I could decide who deserved an apology, for the previous night's upset, them or me. Tired of the dance, I finally relented.

'I'm sorry I shouted last night,' I said, not looking directly at either one of them. Gabe shrugged, glad to be free of it, Maureen on the other hand, departing from her usual Christ-like ways, demanded a bit more.

'I have a bruise where you kicked me,' she said. 'You were horrible to me when I was trying to help you.'

'I said I was sorry,' I said, trying not to become angry all over again. 'I am sorry.'

She glowered at me briefly and said, 'Okay, Let's go get some food.'

The idea of something to eat other than cereal cured any ill feelings. The sandwiches and salads supplied by Aunt Mo and Aunt Gloria were attractively laid out on the kitchen table and rapidly disappearing. The conversation stopped as we entered the kitchen, the silence a sure sign that I had been correct not to believe Dad when he'd said Bernadette would get better. This could mean that she was going to die, or that whatever was wrong with her was going to become another family secret. Which of course, could not be talked about above a whisper or mentioned in the presence of more than two people, and any knowledge I would gain about it would need to be through snooping.

Mother came home and we stuck close, asking hospital questions.

'Was the food nice?' said Gabe.

'Is there a chapel there?' said Maureen.

'Did you get to see Bernadette?' I said.

She looked tired, pale, thinner in spite of pregnancy. We touched her, making doubly sure she was still there and alive, aunts and uncles fussed, all the while throwing knowing looks between themselves to remind us that we weren't allowed to know what was wrong with our little sister.

'Well, you're going to have yet another little brother or sister,' she said. 'Isn't that exciting?'

It wasn't, actually. We'd already had one of those, but we nodded and agreed for the required period of time, and then asked, 'When will Bernadette come home?' She was our little sister; this future baby wasn't reality, not yet loved by us, was already sapping too much parent attention, bedroom space, and above all, lacked silky blonde curls, big brown eyes and a way with wild birds.

'Hey, look, you're not the only pregnant lady in this house,' said Uncle Tony, cradling a billowing cat in his arms. Skip and Jack, who were the late Tuna's offspring, were now both expectant mothers. Jack, mistakenly sexed at birth, circled the floor beneath our feet. Mother reached out and exchanged her glass of Chianti for Skip. Uncle Tony hoisted Jack in his free arm.

'Oh, poor Skip, we've all been so busy, we didn't even notice!' she cooed, adding, 'Good Lord, both of them.'

I took Jack from Uncle Tony; her kittens were a much more tangible and exciting prospect than another sibling. 'What on earth will we name them?' I said. 'We must have run out of fish by now.'

'We will never run out of fish,' Uncle Joe declared sagaciously.

And so the evening continued in a repeated pattern of laughter, choked back tears, cryptic comments and forced silences until the aunts and uncles trickled away again and we all went to bed, me not forgetting that Mother still hadn't answered my question about when Bernadette would come home.

****

Chapter 6

An Angel Food cake was prepared for Bernadette's homecoming. The finished sugar-dusted mound had an appropriately soft, pure look about it. Multi-sensual, it was delicious to the eye, the fingers and the taste buds. Velvety smooth, light and delicately sweetened, it was like eating a cloud. It disappeared on the tongue like candyfloss leaving you hungering for more; a cake no one could refuse. It was a bit like Bernadette herself. Aunt Grace manoeuvred a wedge of it into her mouth with her pincer-like nails, 'Mmm, angel cake,' she said, chasing crumbs round her lipstick, 'Did you know it was fat free? It's a nice one Mary; Betty Crocker or Duncan Hines?' I watched Mother's back stiffen almost imperceptibly before she replied.

'Neither, Grace, I made it from scratch. I never use cake mixes.'

Did I detect smugness?

'Oh my,' said Aunt Grace, not to be outdone, casting her eyes disparagingly over the kitchen, 'I'm surprised you find any extra time at all with everything else that needs doing around here. And in your condition as well.'

'It's made with all egg whites, isn't it?' said Uncle Tony.

'That's right,' said Mother, 'one and a half cups.'

'Such a waste of all those yolks.' Aunt Grace sighed, somewhat dramatically.

'Oh no, I wouldn't let them go to waste,' Mother said, 'we'll make pancakes out of them tomorrow.'

'Must be awfully rich pancakes,' said Aunt Grace, relentless in her pursuit of the last word.

Behind her, sitting quietly at the corner of the kitchen table, Bernadette spat her angelic mouthful onto the table in front of her.

'I don't like any kind of eggs,' she said, 'especially in cake.' Aunt Grace looked on almost triumphantly at Bernadette's scowling little face. Under the table, the dog drooled.

'Bernadette, honey,' Dad said, mopping up, 'don't spit, honey, if you don't like it, there's a napkin right here, let me get that.'

'She's tired.'

'They just don't know how to treat children in hospital.'

'She doesn't feel well'

'She's had a terrible time.'

'She needs to rest.'

'She's still recovering from the shock.'

'She doesn't mean it.'

'It's not just the sickness. It's the whole scary experience.'

'Lots and lots of sleep.'

Apart from Bernadette's spitting, the day was as jovial as ever. Even Aunt Grace's caustic remarks had by now become part of the recipe for cake days and we paid her little notice except to take bets on who she would pick on before she arrived, and goad her skillfully in the direction of our choice.

Bernadette, although a quiet child in general - the germination of the baby that never cried - was unusually subdued on this, her homecoming. She seemed fundamentally unhappy.

Gabe, Maureen and I had assembled an explanation for Bernadette's hospital stay from our pooled collection of eavesdropped conversations.

We held secret councils late at night while the adults whispered through the floor below.

'She has a measles complication. You remember. Aunt Grace talked about them. Complications.'

'What's that? I don't remember. I heard them say something about monitors.'

'That's someone to watch you all the time, a monitor. Like in school, only in the hospital.'

'A complication is when measles turns into something worse.'

'No it's not, it's an extra thing, added to the measles.'

'Mother said she sang to her.'

'But Bernadette couldn't hear.'

'But she thought she was getting through.'

'She sang hymns, I bet.'

'She thought singing would wake her up.'

We concluded the case had evolved into one of Aunt Grace's predicted 'complications' and Bernadette had become very ill, losing consciousness for some of the time. We assumed we were correct, even though we were told nothing about Bernadette's condition during her absence or on her return. The inaudible whispering frightened us. If we expressed concern they told us to pray; that would make us feel better. As if.

Then came joy, floods of relief. She was coming home. We had been so excited. Bouncing, beautiful blond baby Bernadette, not a baby anymore at all, but she would always be the baby, our baby. We'd all helped, even Gabe, to make the angel cake, sifting, whipping and folding all morning because it was her favourite. We were hurt by her actions.

'Why is she spitting it out?' Maureen turned to me and asked. She was afraid to ask Bernadette. 'I thought it was her favourite.' Now we were the ones whispering.

'Maybe her tastes have changed,' I ventured. 'Sometimes medicine does that.'

'I thought she'd be happier to see us,' said Maureen. 'She hasn't even given me a hug.'

'No, me neither.'

'Maybe she's tired.'

'Maybe she doesn't feel well.'

'She's had a terrible time.'

'She needs to rest.'

'She doesn't mean it.'

Of course she meant it. I gave up making excuses for her. The way I saw it, Bernadette went to the hospital with one illness and came back with another one. She looked the same, but that was all. This was the first time I could remember feeling anything at all negative about Bernadette. It was a sense of doom, and I was right to feel it.

But on this day, the day Bernadette came home, all she did was spit cake out and become irritable. There should be no reason to feel so threatened. She was put to bed, poor dear, tucked in, and kissed night

night.

'She'll be fine after a good night's sleep.'

Maureen and I continued to speak in whispers that night while Bernadette lay in the bed beside ours getting her good night's sleep.

'Do you think Bernadette is different?' I asked her, troubled by it.

'Yes,' said Maureen. 'She didn't get better.'

'Everyone seems to think it's because she's tired.'

'I don't think the grown-ups can see it,' said Maureen.

I asked Gabe, as soon as I had the opportunity.

'No,' he said. 'I told you, she was always that way, she's just more like that now.'

'Maureen thinks that grown-ups can't see it.' I said.

'They see it, Gloria,' he said. 'They're just pretending not to.'

He was right about that.

Between us we'd missed quite a lot of school during the illness. Now it was already early summer and it was nearly finished. There was only a week left, most of it occupied not by learning lessons, but by going to mass, constructing a summer catholic calendar and an end of term school trip to the local beach, followed by the public library. The calendar was to be taken home for daily consultation to ensure we prayed to the correct saints and attended mass on holy days of obligation, for it was naturally assumed that we would overlook the Assumption of Our Lady in favour of a picnic or other summer excursion.

We paraded en masse along Bayberry Avenue under the hot June sun in our woollen school blazers and berets – for we had to appear in full uniform if we were to be allowed to go. We each carried our packed lunch and a library book. The local beach was at the end of Bayberry Avenue, on the opposite side of the marina near Uncle Joe and Dad's Fish Shop, a fact that made me feel simultaneously privileged and embarrassed when they came outside and greeted us with our teachers, the nuns.

Uncle Tony's boat yard was across the dock, at the dead end of Pine Street and he walked out onto one of his barges laughing and waving and shouting hello, which for some reason troubled me less, perhaps because of the distance. He had Bernadette with him, no doubt for the purpose of giving Mother some time to nap in a futile attempt at the end of pregnancy to try and store up sleep. Bernadette waved to us as well, which I found encouraging, and I smiled.

I thought how exciting it must feel, to be four, and to stand on a barge, bobbing gently, waving to your brother and sisters across the water.

We arrived at the beach and sat on the sand in our uniforms, for once not in rows, and delved into our brown paper picnics while the nuns remained upright, pacing up and down, in opposite directions. They surrounded us, two on the tide line, two on the boardwalk, two on each sandy side. They walked, not in pairs, but singly in rigidly straight lines towards each other, nodding as they passed, until they turned on an invisible mark, retracing their steps in the sandy channel they trod. They always turned at the same time. The nuns in school loved straight lines and symmetry, and I sat eating my gritty sandwich, mesmerised, watching this choreographed barrier march around and around us like a giant clockwork toy. The sea breeze wafted their voluminous black habits in all directions, making whip cracking sounds with the fabric of their skirts and lifting their wimples and veils, giving us a brief glimpse of neck or hair if we were lucky.

When we had finished our sandwiches we were permitted to buy an ice cream from the ice cream van where we had to stand and eat them quickly before they melted and dripped onto our dry-clean only blazers. Then we gathered up our library books and headed back down Bayberry Avenue to the public library to return our books and enjoy a few minutes out of the sun in the cool stone building. Those were our treats and that was the end of our last full day of school.

'I saw you today from the beach, Bernadette,' I said when I got home. 'On the barge with Uncle Tony.'

Bernadette was concentrating. She was on the floor sprinkling a shaker of salt onto Skip. 'I want an all-white cat,' she said. Skip was a black and white cat. Uncle Tony was there, watching as Bernadette seasoned the cat. He'd brought her home and would stay the night.

'I said I saw you today, Bernadette,' I repeated. 'Was it fun to be on the barge?'

'No,' said Bernadette, without looking up.

Mother came through from the kitchen and laughed when she saw Bernadette. 'Bernadette, that isn't going to change her colour. Give me the salt please. Maybe Skip will have a white kitten.' She bent down to retrieve the salt shaker, and as she did so, Bernadette hurled it at her, missing, and sending it crashing against the windows at the other side of the room. I watched, aghast, as Mother committed herself to totally ignoring this action. I looked at Uncle Tony, whose expression was troubled but he made no comment. I thought I might talk to him about it when an opportune moment arose. I didn't know what he'd do, maybe shed some light, share my feelings. But I could tell by his body language that he was thinking things were different, too.

That evening Dad was taking Mother out to dinner, their end of school year outing, a traditional gift to themselves. They would go to the end of another marina, a few miles along the bay, and look out at the sea and eat seafood caught no doubt by the fishermen Dad sold bait to. Uncle Tony would baby-sit for us, and take us out for soft ice cream and a drive-in movie and let us stay up late when we got home.

It was most memorable for being the only day of the year we got to eat ice cream twice.

'Chocolate or vanilla?' asked the ice cream man. He wore a striped jacket and matching chef's hat. He smiled at us and asked his question in the space between his shop's and our car's windows. We lived in a drive-in world.

'Three chocolates, two vanilla, all dipped.' Uncle Tony ordered for us all. We watched as the ice cream man deftly manoeuvred each swirly cone, filling it with gloopy white ice cream and then magically turning them upside down to be dipped into the chocolate syrup that hardened on contact with the cold ice cream. We ate them silently as Uncle Tony drove, one handed, to the drive in movie theatre. After paying at the entrance we drove around to find a parking space we all agreed on. It was a huge lot with space for several hundred cars. Uncle Tony positioned the car centrally, in a row as close as possible to the screen. We wanted to be in the front row but the lot was filling steadily. Beside each car was a pole with a speaker on top of it, attached to a wire that disappeared down the pole and into the ground to some central broadcast headquarters which could have been located underwater, judging by the sound quality. The speaker went inside the car and was held in place by winding the window up.

Once we had parked the car, we went to visit the small amusement park and snack bar at the back of the lot where we played on the monkey bars and Uncle Tony gave us nickels for the candy machines while we waited for it to get dark enough for the film to start. We, like all the other children in the park, were in our pyjamas. It was de rigueur to be wearing pyjamas.

Bernadette wanted to go on the merry-go-round, a rotating disc with handles that you ran around with until it was spinning very fast, at which point you jumped on. There was little to be merry about. It was a lethal piece of playground equipment and one I was frightened of, ever since I witnessed an accident. My mother had said, 'Look at that poor child covered in blood,' not realizing for the first few minutes that underneath the blood was my cousin Georgina. Uncle Tony wouldn't allow Bernadette to go on the merry-go-round.

'Not tonight, Bernadette,' he said. 'It's too busy with bigger kids, too dangerous.' Bernadette, who didn't show much interest in playing with the rest of us anymore, reacted badly to his decision and became surly and difficult, doing her best to ruin the rest of the evening.

The film was an adventure story, *A High Wind in Jamaica*. There was a moment in it when a young girl about my age fell from a great height onto the floor of a ship, followed by a large rusty stake, which punctured her thigh and pinned her to the deck. The camera looked down on her from great height. I was horrified by the image, which stayed with me for years. It was the only scene I remembered, the leg, the only body part. I didn't remember what the girl looked like, or what happened next. Whenever I recalled it I felt weak in the legs, as though I was immobilised, and needed blood.

Because of the poor quality of drive-in speakers, which broadcast more static than anything else, and because the audience was made up mainly of restless children crammed into cars, teenage lovers, or dubious men on their own, there were many distractions. The rising stars of the screen competed with the shooting ones in the sky above it, as well as airplanes and seagulls and the sound of nearby trains. The show at the drive in movie was never the film.

'I want to go home,' said Bernadette, hoping to be awkward but unintentionally voicing what we all felt. We took a vote, and left for home. As the evening had not yet reached enough of a zenith for us to consider it special, we were permitted to go outside and play some more. Uncle Tony sat on the front steps watching while my pyjama clad brother and sister disappeared up a tree. Bernadette took a jar from the kitchen and headed around the back of the house.

'Be careful up that tree in the dark,' Uncle Tony cautioned. 'Don't fall out.'

'We're okay,' Gabe's voice came out of the leafy dark shadow.

'We're just sitting in our house.'

We had constructed a primitive sitting area in the tree, by using discarded planks of wood laid across branches on several levels. It was our tree house. I stayed on the porch with Uncle Tony.

'I think they want to be away from Bernadette,' I whispered. He looked sideways at me and smiled. He lit a cigarette. I savoured the aroma of the extinguished match.

'It's a good year for June bugs,' he said, not taking the bait.

I tried again, boldly. 'Do you think Bernadette enjoyed any of tonight?' I asked him. 'She seems a bit off-colour, don't you think?' What I really wanted to know was if he thought Bernadette had changed since her measles, like I thought she had.

'I think she liked the ice cream.' He laughed his big laugh, making me laugh too. 'You ought to see these bugs over at the beach, Gloria. It's like a starry night all around, from ground to sky. They light up everything, the dunes, the water. It's amazing to see. I'll take you over there if you like now that school is out.'

He wasn't going to talk about Bernadette and so chose a subject to easily distract me.

He lived on the other side of Piper Bay, on Beacon Island, not much more than a spit of sand left behind by the tide, accessible only by boat.

'Can we go tomorrow?' I said. I loved Beacon Island. Uncle Tony laughed again. His divertive tactic had been successful.

'Not tomorrow, I have guests staying. But next week.'

'Will the bugs still be there?' I asked.

'Will it still be June?' he said. I calculated quickly in my head.

'Yes, there will be a week left.'

'Then they'll be there. That's why they're called June bugs.'

I called them lightening bugs. They were also called fireflies and glow-worms, but they were actually luminous beetles and not flies or worms at all. They used their lights sometimes to attract mates and as a warning to predators. 'Look at me, I'm full of chemicals, I taste bitter.' Extremely energy efficient, their light was one hundred percent illumination, they expended no heat with it at all, and they were very bright. I once let one crawl on the page of my book and was able to read by it's glow, although gave up as it was an altogether unreliable torch and didn't really contribute much to my enjoyment of the literature. There was no way to know how their on-off switch was triggered.

Our unspoken thoughts about Bernadette drifted away with the cigarette smoke, in favour of the subject of the Beacon Island house, situated in the tiny community of Deer Path Cove. Uncle Tony's beach house was a simple square wooden box that stood alone, on stilts looking out over the bay to the mainland. There was a tottery wooden dock leading from his deck into the bay where he could moor his barges; flat boats that were retired ex-Hudson Bay vessels no longer big enough to suit the needs of a growing city.

His main boat yard was here on the mainland, where he also had an apartment. I now had something to look forward to, heading over to the island on one of the barges, leaving behind the long dull summer days at home.

Bernadette returned with her jar of bugs and sat on the ground, away from us, strangely and silently.

Uncle Tony extinguished his cigarette, looked up into the tree.

'Okay,' he said. 'Come down from there now. Inside everybody. And be quiet. Your parents are sleeping.' It felt very late.

Unbeknownst to us, Mother and Dad had come home before us and were soundly sleeping in their own room while we played outside.

Already dressed for bed, he checked us for ticks and sent us to our rooms.

Bernadette didn't speak to anyone, before or after we got to bed. She curled up under her blankets and put a jar of lightening bugs beside her bed. This buoyed me. Perhaps she wasn't so different after all, and I quietly hoped for her to release them and let them tell their stories as they flew around the room. Waiting for her to speak, I fell asleep and in the morning they were still there, dead in their sealed coffin. Bernadette's bed lay empty.

'She never put holes in the lid.'

'She must've forgot.'

'That's not like Bernadette,' said Maureen.

'No, I guess not,' although I wasn't sure what was like Bernadette anymore.

****

Chapter 7

During that long hot summer the baby inside Mother ripened and she swelled. I didn't think it was possible for a woman to grow as large as she did during pregnancy and found it an uncomfortable yet miraculous process to witness. More uncomfortable for her, however, as none of her clothing fitted her, she wore the same pair of stretch maternity trousers everyday, the elastic window across the tummy growing thinner and more knotted. She washed them out each evening, along with a couple of old shirts of Dad's. She had difficulty getting out of chairs.

'Could you tie my shoes?' I asked.

'It's about time you learned to tie your own shoes, Gloria,' she said.

'I know. I've been practising. I can't get them tight.' I was embarrassed.

'Gloria, I can't even tie my own shoelaces. You'll have to manage.'

I was resigned to wearing school loafers, or loose trainers. Her normally energetic and brisk pace slowed considerably and her standards of housekeeping suffered. The house was kept busy with people dropping in trying to help out. Aunt Gloria came, but with so many of her own children in tow, seemed to succeed only in accelerating the confusion and clutter created by a young family over a day. Aunt Mo called in twice a week to prepare a meal and wash dishes. Aunt Grace came to do her hair, never failing to take a quick tour of the house first so that she could comment on the state of it.

'I can tell by that stack of laundry how tired you are Mary,' she said, cackling. 'It's like a thermometer, going up all the time.' Mother gritted her teeth. She wanted a decent hairdo.

Gabe became more and more independent and roamed the neighbourhood and the surrounding woods and beaches with his friends. Some girls were included in his group of friends now. Not us. Maureen and I didn't play together much, our closeness in age divided rather than united us. She did, however, still spend time with Bernadette and most other times would be in her room worshipping the Holy Mother, Father or

71

Saint of the day. Maureen was becoming very religious and had decided she wanted to become a nun when old enough. In the meantime, she constructed a makeshift altar in her room from found objects not needed around the house, its base being a small table covered in some blue fabric. On the table was a comprehensive collection of statues of Our Lady, in a variety of poses, for the altar was almost exclusively a monument to the blessed virgin apart from two appearances from Jesus, one on a crucifix presiding over the whole scene. She sourced the statues from a selection of suppliers, most on loan from relatives, although she did have her own small replica of the Pieta, which held the other Jesus, given to her by Aunt Gloria who'd bought it at the World's Fair some years before. She also had a classic version of Mary, fair-haired, blue eyed and cloaked, head bowed, hands clasped in prayer. That was a gift from Mother, who was delighted by Maureen's show of devotion and keen to encourage her.

'Imagine having a nun in the family,' she said.

I couldn't imagine a nun in the family and nor did I like being at home with the novice. It was a boring summer, the heat was oppressive and instead of staying home to help where I was needed, I would slope off guiltily down to the marina where there was a breeze and daydream. I could be free to roam up and down the dock, watching the surf casters and the ferries and transactions happening between restaurateurs and fishermen. Or I could walk around the docks and read the names on the boats: *Miss Conduct, Fantasea, Irish Ayes, Its-o-fish-Al, Reel Obsession, Just Jennifer.* Inside the shop I could sit and stare at the tropical fish, so far away from home, or just listen to the conversations between the customers and my Dad and Uncle Joe and the clanking of the surrounding docked boats.

'You got the Kittie Bits?' said Dad.

'Yeah,' said Uncle Joe.

'How much?' said Dad.

'Plenty. A couple of bags, full of cans. Must be fifty or so. I also bought oil,' said Uncle Joe, carrying one of several heavy crates into the back of the Fish Shop.

'Whatcha doing Uncle Joe?' I said.

'You'll find out soon enough honeybunch.'

'Hey Tony, Joe. What's up.' Another customer.

'Just getting ready for the big day, Larry.'

'What's all that stuff for, Dad? It stinks. And what do you need those big bags of cat stuff for?'

'Shhh!' Gloria. 'Quiet. You know it's a secret.'

I would wave to Uncle Tony across the water. My boredom was spectacularly broken on two occasions when I was invited to accompany him on one of the barges over to his house on Beacon Island, the barge slower than other boats, rising and falling gently on the tide, and Uncle Tony standing proudly surveying his domain; the barge, the bay and the barrier island. We sat on his dock late into the evening, bitten by mosquitoes and not caring. Sometimes Uncle Tony had friends to visit, educated, erudite and interesting people who weren't like anyone else I met in my world of aunts and cousins. Not the company one might expect a seafaring garbage man to keep. They came by water taxis and stayed late into the night drinking wine with Uncle Tony by the glow of hurricane lamps and I would fall asleep with the sound of the ocean close by. As more stilted houses were built on Beacon Island Uncle Tony added building materials to his cargo and procured two more barges and barge boys, as they came to be called, to captain the barges, helping to operate the increased service demanded. This summer was his busiest yet and his invitations to me were scarce.

When it rained or thundered I would sit in the cupboard at the back of the Fish Shop and read. Known as the cupboard, it was actually a small storage room tacked on to the back of the shop with an opening looking out over the bay, a window with no glass, a gash in the wall. We called it a hatch. The cupboard wasn't secure and therefore was not used for storage. It contained nothing other than an old armchair, slightly dampened from the sea breeze, perfect for a girl and her book.

This was the cupboard that interested Aunt Grace, who was a frequent visitor to the Fish Shop that summer, trampling on my privacy at regular intervals. I could sense that Dad and even her husband Uncle Joe didn't relish her presence any more than I did. She had tried to convince them that her entrepreneurial flair could turn the cupboard, ideally placed for such things, into a successful coffee, tea and cake bar. They laughed her out of the shop that time.

Aunt Grace had 'emigrated', as Dad said disparagingly, from 'somewhere in the Midwest' and as far as he was concerned had no coastal credibility whatsoever. She was actually from New Jersey but that was far enough inland for him to dismiss her. Coffee and especially tea and cake had no place in this man's world of bait and tackle. They were items that were either imported from the Italian bakery adjacent to the train station or brought from home, and home made. They drank cream soda, seltzer or Budweiser bought in cases from the local distributor. Nothing fancy.

Aunt Grace had moved to the shore to open a hairdressing salon, hoping to capitalise on the growing population due to developing housing and tourism. She secured a small apartment on the upper floor of one of the new split ranch houses, which, in defiance of its name, was not a house cut in half but rather more like one on top of the other and bearing no evidence of ranching. Here she opened her salon and later when she married Uncle Joe they bought the lower floor and occupied the entire house.

It was that summer Aunt Grace came into the cupboard with her new idea, a development of the tea and cake place. I was sitting on the dock outside, underneath the window, dangling my legs over the side. A searing hot sunny day and I'd been burning up my available energy watching a pair of cavorting jellyfish in the still water, their drift occasionally broken by the wake of a passing ferry. I heard the click of high heels as she entered the shop and then her ascending voice as she approached the cupboard behind me. I could smell her garlicky scent masked with what she called 'toilet water', which the receptors in my brain could not translate into a pleasant fragrance.

'Look here, Joe, it would be perfect. Just a fridge and a stove,' Aunt Grace was excited. 'Beer and chowder. That masculine enough for ya? Maybe some soft drinks.'

She outlined her plan while circling round and round the small room, then leaned out the window above me. 'We'd need to put a door on this hatch so we could lock up, but we could serve right out of here in foam cups. The guys could take it with them, something nice and warm for them on their boats. Maybe get a few bar stools for them that want to sit here.'

She looked down at me, not really seeing. 'Phew, Joe, it stinks in here,' she added, significantly, I thought, considering she'd just looked at me.

'Don't be ridiculous Grace,' I heard Uncle Joe say. Aunt Grace removed herself from the hatch and I heard them walk back indoors, Dad and Uncle Joe's dismissive tones and Grace's enthusing, beseeching. Around the corner, outside of the shop, I heard Uncle Joe's finality.

'No Grace. Now go home and do some haircuts, will ya?'

Aunt Grace walked around the back of the shop to where I sat and took another look at the hatch, this time from outside. She finally registered my presence.

'What do you do, sitting there all day?' she said, frowning. Before I could answer she said, 'you and your sisters are strange children, you know that? Especially that Bernadette,' and walked off, angrily.

I was glad of the differentiation she offered, on the one hand, about Bernadette. At least she acknowledged it, said it out loud, unlike the others. On the other hand I didn't think holy rolling Maureen was a typical example of childhood and resented being included in that group as just another strange sister.

It stank in the Fish Shop because Dad and Uncle Joe were cooking up their annual mythical chum recipe. It was their secret. Competitive shark fishing was becoming popular. Previously people fished for marlin or tuna, which were harder to catch but better to eat. There were lots of sharks but no one wanted them until one day a local man harpooned a giant one, in a manner that would be more accurately described as performance art than shark fishing. He became known for his flamboyancy and continued to repeatedly and dramatically catch record-breaking beasts. People travelled to see him. The idea that sharks could be exciting dawned on the fishing communities and thus the annual shark tournament was born, the big game hunting of the sea.

I had never been to the shark tournament before but boredom brought us all down to the marina that day, even Gabe. At first nothing much happened, and we waited expectantly at the deserted marina, listening to the sound of a few boats sloshing in their spaces and the flapping of the flag bunting strung up for the occasion. Most boats were out, those involved in the contest and spectators had set off early in the morning and not much would happen until after lunch when the catches began to come in. It was quiet in the Fish Shop, with a bit of talk of technique, past conquests. The fish had to be line caught.

'I decided to try and get his attention, grabbed my hand gaff and splashed it, tapped it on the outboard now and again...'

'It worked...'

'Headed right at us...'

'Perfect cast...'

'After the hook hit home we ran him for at least an hour...'

'Quite a show.'

'He became very cooperative after that...'

The tournament was a highlight in Dad and Uncle Joe's calendar, and tension mounted, because of their homemade chum. They supplied it at a good price and included a bucket full of drilled holes. Chum was the very unfriendly substance that the fisherman used to attract sharks, in most cases in tins or buckets tied to the boat forming a greasy, odorous slick on the surface while it drifted along. Its ingredients were mysterious because the recipe was a secret. It was believed that chum was instrumental in the size of fish that could be lured, and if one of Dad and Uncle Joe's customers won the tournament they would be written about in the local paper, raising the Fish Shop's profile. Dad and Uncle Joe were particularly proud of their chum this year, having added a new ingredient and were anticipating good results.

In addition to the with flag bunting, there was an enormous scale next to a raised platform and an apparatus equipped with a butcher's hook from which to hang a large fish. There wasn't much to do at the Fish Shop except wait. We did what unemployed children do. Gabe left and went to Uncle Tony's boatyard to see if he could help on the barges until the sharks started coming in. Uncle Tony didn't like the shark tournament, he said.

Maureen and I strolled up and down the marina, her with her rosary, a foot in both camps praying for the sharks, and the fishermen, me with no particular purpose. Uncle Joe made a primitive fishing rod out of a stick for Bernadette who sat pensively on the edge of the dock hoping to catch something.

'I will catch the best fish,' she said.

'Uncle Joe has given me some of the secret chum and I know what's in it.'

'Does she have a hook on there?' Dad asked.

'Just the smallest,' said Uncle Joe.

'You be careful, Bernadette, and call one of us if you get a bite,' said Dad.

Dad was making a kite for me and called me into the shop. I gratefully left Maureen with her prayers and joined him. The kite was meant to be a secret as a surprise for my birthday, which had long since passed. Unlike the painful secrets they could all keep so successfully, the nice birthday ones got leaked. I was so often in the shop he gave up hiding it and enlisted my help instead. We used paper and very thin sticks of bamboo and cellophane tape and some torn up rags for the tail.

At lunchtime, Dad and Joe ate their sandwiches standing in my reading cupboard while I put the finishing touches to my birthday kite. I listened to them enthusing about Aunt Grace's idea of a chowder bar.

'There's plenty of room in here for a little stove, maybe a fridge.'

'We wouldn't need much else.'

'A coffeemaker.'

'Not a lot of outlay, and good profits. We could dig the clams ourselves.'

'Vinny could do it. He makes great chowder.'

'Kill two birds. It could double as his office.'

'Everybody wins.'

This confused me because of the reaction I'd witnessed when Aunt Grace had suggested the same thing. I put down my tools and remained still and silent, having learned that I could learn much more that way.

They had become so accustomed to my presence in the shop that they often forgot about me and I was party to many private conversations. It was Uncle Vinny they wanted, who sold insurance from his living room, to run the chowder bar for them. He could still sell insurance and run the chowder bar.

Tourists started to gather along the marina and the atmosphere began to shift into a higher gear. Boats became visible along the horizon, coming in from the ocean beyond the barrier island.

The afternoon was a gruesome festival of carnage. Carcasses with gaping shark smiles were on display, lashed to the sides of boats and applauded as they motored by. Bleeding great hulks hung from the butcher's hook next to their beer-fisted captors, most of them sun raw and bare chested, fat bellies hanging below belts, being photographed to record their conquest. Blood and entrails spilled out of the countless carcasses, many slit wide open the length of their undersides, covering the surface of the marina and discolouring the inlet, filling the bay with a red cloud. It was a spectacle that both fascinated and appalled me.

I was scared by sharks when they were alive, and discovered that this fear wasn't abated by the fact that they'd been slaughtered, in fact it was heightened and I retreated into the Fish Shop to peek safely from behind the door. The winning fishmonger received a shiny trophy and was photographed for the press. His shark was too big for the scales and would have to be transported elsewhere to record its weight. As hoped for, Uncle Joe and Dad were photographed outside the Fish Shop because they supplied the chum.

'Smile and say "recipe,"' shouted the photographer.

'Biggest catch yet,' said Dad, raising his beer bottle.

'Just wait till next year!' said Uncle Joe.

The crowd revelled around them, kings for a day.

Fearless Bernadette, asked to be lifted up so she could touch the prize carcass's teeth, making me shudder, for the beasts looked as dangerous dead as they did alive, retaining their terrible might without any of their beauty or grace.

'It's the kittens that they put in the chum,' she said to me afterwards.

'I know.'

'What are you talking about Bernadette?' I said, horrified by her.

'It's Skip's dead kittens. They put them in the chum.' She was smiling. It was true that Skip had by now had several litters of kittens, the first two disposed of by way of a more traditional method. I knew this to be fact because of things I overheard at the Fish Shop but was also certain that my Dad, practical as he was, may possibly include cat food as an ingredient but would absolutely draw the line at chopping up kittens to use as shark bait. The most recent of Skip's litter's had been allowed to survive only because we, the children, had hidden them. I felt the need to go and see them, check they were all right. I was disgusted by the shark tournament and by Bernadette's comment.

'Bernadette, don't say things like that.'

The late afternoon pink sun was reflected in the wet face of the dock outside the Fish Shop as Dad hosed the blood off the surface at the end of the day. The carcasses were removed, the scales dismantled, the bunting taken down to be stored and the tourists dispersed.

We would go home and have to have shark for dinner, no objections permitted.

'Eat it. It would eat you if it could.' Dad would say.

We couldn't argue with that logic.

At the end of the day, I flew my kite as the sun set, and watched the dismantling of the event. I could see several barges out on the water piled high with dripping shark shells that Uncle Tony would have to dispose of, as well as one transporting the winning fish to a bigger weigh station. It was not surprising that he didn't like the shark tournament.

Later at home, motivated by Bernadette's bloodthirsty comment, I went in the fading light to see the hidden kittens in the woods, hoping that Skip hadn't moved them on. I found Bernadette there. I froze for a moment, mouth open unable to bring forth any sound for she had tied her fishing line around the tails of two of them and was gleefully swinging the creatures back and forth, squealing pendulums. Finally I managed to scream.

'Bernadette, stop, that hurts them. Stop.' I rescued the kittens, distressed but unharmed, and tried to comfort them. Bernadette, eerily, said nothing.

'Where is the fish hook?' I said. 'Do you have a fish hook?'

She handed me the fish hook.

'I'll take this, it's dangerous. Bernadette, that was cruel. You could have killed them.'

She still said nothing, her soft blond hair standing out as her features darkened in the twilight. I searched her face, looking for something, and could see that she was frightened, but not of me.

I wrapped the hook in a piece of paper, and took her hand, to walk back to the house.

'Bernadette, why were you doing that to the kittens?'

She looked at the ground, didn't answer.

When we got back to the house there was no shark to eat. Mother and Dad had gone to the hospital; the baby was coming. Soon after we discovered that the baby was a pair, twin girls. Maureen was praying nineteen to the dozen. Even I blessed myself. Holy shit. Another two sisters. I forgot about Bernadette and the kittens.

****

Chapter 8

By the time the twins, Theresa and Mary, were three months old Mother was expecting yet again although we were left to discover this fact ourselves when the forthcoming sibling became a conspicuous protrusion on her front end. And then we weren't informed voluntarily but had to ask, disbelievingly, after some initial debate among ourselves.

'Gabe, what do you think of the way Mother looks these days?' I cornered him in the front yard.

'What do you mean?' he said.

'Do you think she looks pregnant?'

He shrugged, 'I don't know Gloria. I gotta go.' He was in a hurry, back to his cigarettes and girls. He took little part in our discussion, and wasn't really missed, having reached that boy age where his conversations were sparse and monosyllabic, composed of grunts rather than words. He had no interest in this future birth; already oversubscribed with sisters and too old to hope for a baby boy, which for him would only mean having to share his much-coveted own bedroom with a noisy, snotty baby and interrupted nights.

Bernadette was quizzed but also declined to join in the speculation, and having not reacted very well to the appearance of Theresa and Mary; the sudden alterations they brought to our life, we didn't press her. Bernadette's bad ways got worse. She was dismissed as the perfectly naturally, normal jealous youngest child, her insular behaviour was overlooked. As instructed by the book, her parents should give her barge loads of extra attention as compensation for these two little intruders. They did, at first, when they remembered.

So it was Maureen, the little nun, and I, who were left to deliberate whether indeed there was a new life blooming and what this might mean for the rest of us.

'She could just be getting fat.'

'But it's all in one place.'

'How could that be possible though? So soon? Gosh, I didn't think it could happen that fast.'

'Gloria, don't be silly, it's God's will.'

'Oh, yeah. Right. I forgot about Him. You'd think he'd give us a break in between.'

'What if it's a girl, where will it sleep?'

'What if it's more twins?'

'She got sick the other day, did you hear that?'

'Yeah, I did, she threw up twice.'

'Do you think she is?'

'I think she is. Do you?'

'Should we ask her?'

'Let's ask her.'

We did, and she was. Incredulous, we approached Dad for a second opinion.

'Did you know Mother was having a baby again?' we asked him.

'Yes, Gloria. Of course I know.'

'But it's so soon! Theresa and Mary only just got here.'

'Yes, Gloria. I know that too.'

I detected in his tone that he didn't think it could happen so fast either. So it was confirmed. We calculated that when Theresa and Mary were still savouring their first birthdays, while we still scoffed down the cakes and guzzled the pink fizz, we'd have yet another brother or sister.

Maureen was delighted, seeing Mother as God's perfectly oiled baby machine, churning out more Catholics quicker than she could say Hail Mary's. I, more selfishly, was concerned about my place in the world and, in particular, my space in the home.

That would make nine of us. Our house didn't have the capacity to hold such a big family. Our bedroom, the girls, had previously been an attic. Located under the pitched roof, it had sloping ceilings on two sides. It was, however, the biggest room in the house as far as floor area. We were crowded before the last arrival with just three of us, and now, with Theresa and Mary in their cribs and a set of bunk beds whose height dictated that they be placed in the centre of the room in order to fit in with the sloped ceiling, it had the feeling of a dormitory about it. Or hospital ward. Or junk shop. Going to bed at night was like navigating a maze. Another girl child would severely increase the congestion in the bedroom, not to mention the dressers and wardrobes, already overloaded and cramped. And that was supposing it were just one, as since the arrival of the twins we recognised that babies didn't always come singly.

Theresa and Mary were identical twins. Mother had an instant special affinity with the babies, being a twin herself. Aunt Gloria became a fixture in our home and the two sets of twins became a living diorama, seen through the kitchen door repeatedly performing the routine tasks of mother and babyhood. The four of them, dark eyed, dark haired beauties, quite often indistinguishable from one another except on close examination, like carved Russian dolls. Aunt Gloria and Mother had been dressed alike as children and would sometimes do the same as adults. If Mother, whilst out shopping, found a pair of shoes or item of clothing she liked she would buy an extra one for Aunt Gloria, and vice versa. They often would wear the same clothes on the same days without prior consultation. Theresa and Mary were dressed alike and passed between the mother and the aunt, back and forth, until like the magician's cups, one's vision became unreliable and the eye confused which was which. Mother and Aunt Gloria spoke the secret language of twins, finished each other's sentences, anticipated needs and understood the new babies telepathically.

'What's wrong with Theresa?' asked Maureen. 'Why is she crying?'

'Nothing's wrong with Theresa,' said Mother. 'You have them…'

'Mixed up. You can't tell them apart,' said Aunt Gloria.

'How can you? They're exactly the same.'

The two big twins exchanged a look.

'Nonsense,' they said.

'It's Mary that's crying,' said Mother.

'She wants…' Aunt Gloria swapped babies with Mother.

'Feeding,' said Mother.

The babies responded.

Babies were special, precious, and two of them doubly so. They were lavished with adulation, as babies should be but there was something magical about their duplicity, as well as a fear of negligence, for surely if there were two of them one must be ultra careful to divide the attention equally, lest one them feel less valued.

As a result, the two new babies thrived and everyone else was neglected.

The appearance of Theresa and Mary was the dawn of a new era in our home. Their first year was a turbulent one for the rest of the family, the babies cried, Dad worked harder than ever and thus was missing from the house on many evenings and weekends, meals were rushed and the menus dull and repetitive, newspapers and junk mail piled up, dust accumulated, socks were not mended, shoes not polished, buttons not replaced. It was the beginning of self-sufficiency for us, the older children - or not - as the case may be.

If we were to vomit somewhere outside of the toilet, we had to clean it up ourselves. We were responsible for our own hair and nails. This was a disaster for Gabe who was appointed to delegate these responsibilities.

He didn't, and left to our own devices, we became those scruffy, slightly grimy children at school that the other children avoided and told tales about.

'They haven't got any running water in their house.'

'They all live in one room.'

'Their father gives them fish bait to eat.'

'They only get washed once a week in the bay.'

'They have worms.'

'They've got lice.'

Repeated enough, it felt like truth. I was guilty. This sort of thing least affected Gabe, being slightly older and male. He still moved in the same circle of friends and was no grubbier than usual. Maureen dealt with her pain through God and prayer. I had a few friends, but being at the age when girls are most cruel, they talked behind my back. I backed off, hurt, isolated myself, and became a loner, spawning more rumours. Bernadette wasn't at school yet so her misery was contained at home, carving deep wounds in her already faulty psyche.

The winter was memorable because of two coinciding events, one being that the bay froze and the other being the acquisition of a colour television, an idea introduced on Thanksgiving Day.

Although there was no shortage of babies, the babysitter wasn't required, as our parents were too exhausted or busy to consider going out. This meant the much-reduced attendances of Uncle Tony, another cross to bear. With my increased feeling of isolation I longed for an occasional escape or at very least, a conversation with someone who didn't live with me, or think I had lice. He did come to Thanksgiving Dinner, though, a welcome interlude even if our home was the inappropriate chosen venue. It was our turn. Thanksgiving Dinners were taken in turn and that was that. I gathered from her reaction to the numerous takeover offers that Mother would rather die than forfeit her duty, and when Aunt Grace suggested standing in I could understand why, as her turkey would be generously peppered with comments designed to remind us of her generosity in taking on the task. So, with two new babies and growing heavy with the next one, as well as having four disgruntled, dirty older children and a chaotic house to tidy up, Mother tackled her task with what can only be described as cranberry relish. Aunt Gloria was there to assist with the twins and as pastry chef, and Uncle Tony was called in to provide the rest of us with distraction and amusement and would stay the night, agreeing to sleep on the sofa.

Over his two days with us Uncle Tony would have ample time to observe and assess our situation. He arrived at the school on Wednesday afternoon to collect us. Spilling into the schoolyard, with the other children at the close of the day, overjoyed, I started to run to him only to be brought to an abrupt halt by my teacher, a grim faced nun.

'Where do you think you're running to?'

'I'm going home sister, my uncle's here to pick me up.'

'You know that man?' She said '*that man*' like she knew him.

'He's my uncle.' I said this with pride.

'Isn't that the *garbage man*?'

'It's my uncle Tony.' I wanted to run away from her but was too frightened and now she made me feel ashamed. She gripped my arm tightly.

'Doesn't he live on that island?' she said '*that island*' in the same disparaging tone she used for '*garbage man*'. I could see Gabe and Maureen already at Uncle Tony's side. 'May I please go now Sister?'

She loosened her grip and I walked over to them slowly, the desire to run demolished, having lost the chance to be the first to reach his side.

When I joined them Uncle Tony took my schoolbag, ruffled my hair and looked long and hard at the nun who'd detained me.

'What did she say to you, Gloria?' he said.

'Nothing. She wanted to know who you were.' We turned to walk home.

'They don't trust anyone, these nuns. Especially guys like me.'

'What, garbage men?'

'Is that what she called me?' Uncle Tony roared with laughter, and spasmodically erupted into giggles the entire walk home.

Even as a child Thanksgiving was stressful, although we didn't call it that. Stress wasn't an overused word then. We might have described it instead as busy, or hectic, or if pushed, a day intended to be enjoyable that was ruined by other people. Which is what Mother might have thought when she got up that morning at dawn, with babies sapping her energy from both inside and out, a twenty-odd pound turkey to dress and roast, pecan, apple and pumpkin pies to be made and potatoes and onions to be peeled, gravy to worry about. And all that before catering and cleaning up breakfast for nine.

Aunt Grace, heavily disguised as kitchen help, arrived first, really more interested in collecting and spreading gossip and scandal. Uncle Joe came with her, as it was one of the few days in the calendar that the Fish Shop was closed. Of their three children, only Francine came with them, a surly fifteen year-old who was as nasty to us as her mother was, although this was one of the characteristic blind spots typical of our family elders, another elephant to skirt around in the living room.

Only Bernadette welcomed Francine, in who she must have recognised a kindred spirit, for although we caught fleeting glimpses of her former charm, Bernadette had become a miserable, misbehaved soul. Since, according to me, her stay in hospital, but according to Maureen, it was since the twins were born (and this was only a temporary phase she would get through with the help of the Lord), whilst according to Gabe, she was just born that way. Mother and Dad ignored her behaviour; in a way that they would never ignore the same conduct in the rest of their children, and it was clear to us that we were to ignore Mother and Dad's ignorant behaviour.

Bernadette sat next to Francine and was entertained by Francine's snide comments, sotto voce, about the arriving guests. Our small living room filled to capacity and spilled into the kitchen and the hall.

The sofa where Bernadette and Francine sat was traditionally reserved for Papa Joseph, our patriarchal grandfather, on Thanksgiving, one of the four days of the year he came to see us. It was tradition born out of necessity, as Papa Joseph was so fat that we had no other furniture suitable to accommodate him. Dad would go to his apartment downtown to collect him shortly before dinner was served and he would stay until dessert, eating from a plate on his lap. He would then be helped up and after giving each of his grandchildren a pat on the head and a shiny silver dollar, he would be taken home again.

'I'll never forget that day,' Uncle Tony shook his head as he and I talked about this much later, 'and how your grandfather showed up and those two still on the sofa, in his spot, and it was one of those moments that we always had with Bernadette...'

But this was long before I knew that Uncle Tony could see the blindness of the others, and that he felt as baffled and helpless as I did.

'It cost me a fortune,' Uncle Tony laughed. He could laugh about it years later but it wasn't funny at the time.

On that Thanksgiving it rained and when Papa Joseph arrived, every chair and floor space was taken up with a body and the kitchen was reaching the hot and sweaty heights of serving time. Papa Joseph came in, rain dripping off his huge body, and nodded as he lumbered around a table to reach his place on the sofa, stopping short at the sight of its occupants. Even Francine cowered under the great man's gaze, and she got up and moved. Bernadette did not. She sat there defiantly, looking not at Papa Joseph but into her lap, motionless. The room entered one of the suspended moments in time we were becoming accustomed to, a moment needing to be addressed urgently but left unacknowledged; creating a silence so awkward it damaged the ears. Mine rang, straining for relief.

Uncle Tony, hiding behind a newspaper, appearing unnaturally small for such a big man, looked up casually.

'What this house needs is a colour television,' he said.

'Come and look at this one, kids, and see what you think.' Like bees to honey, every child surrounded him in an instant, including Bernadette. Over his shoulder, inside the newspaper, he pointed to a Sears' advertisement. While we gawped at it, Papa Joseph, patriarch, founder of the Fish Shop, in a house teeming with his namesakes (for in this family if your first name wasn't Joseph your middle name was likely to be), sat down with a raspy wheeze and demanded a glass of his usual tipple, red wine and cream soda.

Prior to this we possessed only a small black and white portable TV, which was so often in disrepair we abandoned it, and unnoticed by us, it had found its way to Mother and Dad's bedroom, where it could light up the broken nights. Now that the days were shortened by the winter we found ourselves indoors and together with too much time, too little space and of course Bernadette who, with no kittens to torture, would turn on her brother and sisters instead, disrupting any attempt to read, or do homework or some other occupation.

Skip's kittens had sensibly adopted a more feral lifestyle and were rarely sighted, and their mother finally had been 'seen to' and now lived an armchair life, like her sister Jack and they would simply leave the room or crawl into an unreachable napping area at the first sign of Bernadette's approach. Maureen had an uncanny ability to avoid Bernadette's worst attentions, perhaps purely by her faith in God. Gabe, embarrassed to bring his friends home, spent his time at their houses. This left me, as Bernadette's prime target, failing to divert her interruptions by a variety of methods, that is, until the twins grew big enough to torment. Bothering me was one thing, she could knock a glass, scribble on a book. But when the twins grew older and the new baby came along, Bernadette would find a way to really make her mark. Right now she was a pesky irritation. She hadn't yet become a monster.

Uncle Tony was right; the house was sorely in need of something, not just at this well-chosen Thanksgiving moment, but overall. A colour television was a poor substitute for the kind of support that would have been really useful, but it was all that was on offer and would suffice for now.

As promised, he duly went to Sears on his next available shopping day. He took Gabe with him, as colour TV purchase was deemed to be an all male activity, and also because much to my jealous irritation, Uncle Tony treated us all equally. He bought the very same set that he'd pointed out in the newspaper and arranged to for its delivery to his house on Beacon Island, via one of his own barges, shortly before Christmas. As he quite rightly said, 'You've lived without it for this long, you can wait a couple of more weeks,' adding, 'and I'll be damned if I buy you a Christmas present on top of this.'

Not included in his scheme was the early and severe spell of cold weather, and both he and our television set spent Christmas separated from us by sheets of ice, unable to be navigated by boat or barge. Piper Bay was the largest of a number of inland bodies of water sheltered from the Atlantic Ocean by barrier islands like the one Uncle Tony's house was built on. Because of the size and depth of the bay, it rarely froze and the temperatures had to hold well below zero degrees Fahrenheit for a sustained period of time before that could happen. It didn't freeze entirely, only the most important section - which was the area blocking the route that our television would take across to us. We spoke to him on the crackling phone line, begging.

'Can't you slide it across somehow?'

'How about we skate or walk across to your house and watch it there?'

'It's not safe. No. No. No.'

'But those eel guys go out there.'

'Yeah. They don't fall through.'

The eel fishermen carved holes in the surface of the ice, like misplaced Eskimos, jabbing and stabbing into the icy dark water with long pronged sticks.

'No. Those guys aren't safe either. I bet sometimes they do fall through. They're crazy. They'd have to be. Who else eats eels?'

There was no safe option. We had to content ourselves with visits to the marina, to look out on to the seven miles of solid ice that was Piper Bay. We were not there to marvel at the spectacle of nature, solid white waves, visible crystal tides, echoes of an ice age long dead brought back to still life.

We had no interest in waxing lyrical about the beauty of the frozen world. We were only there to check on the progress of the thaw. The sooner the ice melted, the sooner Uncle Tony could get a barge in the water and we could start basking in the supposedly radioactive, warm rays of living colour.

Selfishly, a rare thought was spared for Uncle Tony, who told us later of his hardship. He spent the ten days in his freezing house built chiefly for summer use, warming his hands on the small fire while the heat escaped into the non-insulated night and having to fish through the ice for food, avoiding eels. We sympathised little, though, as he was the one with the television and any one of us would have gladly traded places.

However, all was forgotten when the gift was delivered, and long after the holiday, Uncle Tony stood with his frostbitten hands on his hips, and said smiling, 'Merry Christmas.' And for a few cherished dark winter weeks, peace reigned.

****

Chapter 9

We blinked and another sister was born, christened Angela, which was bad luck for her from the start. Although she arrived hot on the heels of the twins, she was well received by everyone with the exception of Bernadette. She received her first Brownie points simply by coming alone; a welcome relief to all for another pair of twins would have been crippling at this stage and, as we knew was possible, Mother could already be incubating yet more siblings.

Angela, however, although I didn't know it at the time, was to be the last child born into our family. Not for want of trying, as I discovered later there were two more failed attempts, but Mother's ageing egg factory was finally shutting down production.

Angela was a beautiful baby, with fine blonde curls not seen since the birth of Bernadette who had been unique in her fairness of hair and eyes. The rest of us were dark and swarthy, like our parents. Bernadette had always stood out among us as a group, not just because she was so strange, but she was light and angelic, different, and when we entered our grimy era, her golden aura lent her a glow. When our hair looked greasy, hers shone. A dove among cattle, she had a cleaner and more groomed appearance than the rest of us.

The Bernadette-Before, when I brushed her hair, would giggle and say, 'I have angel hair, I am Mother's little angel.' Indeed, in the recesses of my memory I can recall Mother's acknowledgment of Bernadette's statement.

'Yes, you are my little angel, Bernadette.' Unfortunately the angel memory was lodged much further forward in Bernadette's mind than anyone else's.

It was the last straw for the Bernadette-After when number six baby had the audacity to tumble out of the womb with blonde hair and blue eyes, and be so utterly beautiful that Mother and Dad were so much reminded of an angel that they were moved to call her Angela, an outsider in the family of traditional names. There were no aunts with that name.

We'd run out of aunts.

'Look at her.'

'She's so beautiful.'

'So fair.'

'She looks so fresh and new.'

'Like she could float away on a cloud.'

'Just like an angel.'

Well, that settles it, I thought. Blondes do have more fun. Thanks a lot. I shrugged off the unintentional insults. It was different for Bernadette, though. I could sense by the look in her eyes and the inward lean of her posture that Bernadette felt robbed of her identity by this new baby, feeding the bad seeds in Bernadette, the original blonde cherub. I struggled to remember the quiet baby, the one that we had to bounce to hear her laughter; the caring, loving child who showed such tender kindness to animals and insects. That one was becoming a fast fading memory. That was the Bernadette-Before. Before she changed.

Life was divided into two parts, marked by the Bernadette-Before and the Bernadette-After, simultaneously recognised and denied. At first Maureen and Gabe and I discussed her transformation like idle gossips, speculating on when it began and what could be its causes. We waited, fully expecting the return of the Bernadette-Before. We never thought it would be permanent.

'It'll just be a phase she's going through.'

'She'll get over it. She'll get better, like she was before the hospital.' We spoke of her as if she were a temporary weather system, viral infection, or power failure, something that would come to an end and return to normal.

But time passed and we forgot about the hospital, and the exact point of her change was blurred and disputed, an unreliable memory. I observed my parents with Bernadette, allowing her worst behaviour to slip by with no comment. It was obvious to me they could see the difference in her. They didn't talk about it, but they exchanged looks. Meaningful looks, loaded with more garbage than you could fit on one of Uncle Tony's barges. They exchanged those looks so often it seemed it was the only look they had for each other any more. I hated the look exchange - their unspoken awareness made me feel guilty and at the same time, conspired against. My sister, brother and I stopped speculating, somehow feeling it was sinful and forbidden, and gradually we began to forget that there ever was Bernadette-Before, and she became simply Bernadette, here and now.

The day that Bernadette bit Aunt Grace and shaved off all of Angela's blonde curls was the first indication of a shift in the direction and intensity of her undesired attentions, previously aimed exclusively at me. The stuff she did to me seemed like favours once she got started on people smaller than her.

Ritualistically, we piled into the car twice a year and were taken to Aunt Grace's house for haircuts, a custom viewed by us as akin to being sold into slavery or sacrificed for witchcraft.

'Why do we have to go to Aunt Grace's?'

'Because that's where you have to go.'

'Gabe doesn't'

'He's older.'

'I'd go to a barber. That'd be cheap too.'

'We don't go because it's cheap.'

'Yeah, dummy, it's not cheap, it's free.'

'Don't speak to your sister like that.'

'Why do we then?'

'Because she's your aunt.'

Aunt Grace lived in an upside down house, where upon entering you were greeted first by a tidal wave of odours then a staircase which led upstairs to a kitchen and downstairs to the plastic coated living area. Growing there in the stairwell entrance was the largest plant I'd every seen. It was an avocado plant and the size of a tree, growing up through two floors, and was the only thing enjoyable about going to Aunt Grace's. The concept of plants growing indoors was something we didn't explore in our house. I liked to sit alone on the stair under the tree and read until it was my turn.

'Your mother used to grow lots of things,' Uncle Tony told me later. 'She had the greenest fingers. Your great grandfather was a botanist, you know. Plants all over the place when she was a girl.'

I didn't know. She never told us that.

'Why didn't she ever do anything with our garden, with us?'

'She was too busy. Too many children, too much to do, not enough support. Don't you remember your beautiful porch garden, before...'

'Before Bernadette was born? That's what you were going to say, wasn't it?'

'Not just Bernadette, Gloria. It was a whole pile up. All those young kids, babies; who's got time for gardens? Especially indoor ones. Other things overtake. Priorities change.'

Once out of babyhood, we had to keep our hair short until we were able to care for it ourselves. Maureen kept hers short to avoid vanity, I grew mine and had it trimmed on the biannual maintenance visit. Bernadette, always the exception, was allowed to grow her hair despite her inability to look after it properly.

Mother and Aunt Grace would start the morning with a cup of tea laced with underlying tension, as they maintained a relationship of mutual tolerance. At age eleven, I considered myself an experienced observer of the human condition and clever enough to detect that they hated each other for some reason never divulged nor spoken of, in keeping with family custom of burying the truth in a shallow grave. Just enough to see there was a body there, not enough to identify whose it was.

After the tea, we'd go under the scissors in order of our ages, starting with the eldest, while Mother supervised the rest of us, inadequately, judging by Aunt Grace's regular interjections, shouted from her cutting room:

'Mary, can't you quieten that baby. Mind my china cats. I hope you're not letting them drink that stuff in the living room,' All the while snipping and smoking, tugging our ears and hair, and shifting us roughly into the required positions. I watched myself in the mirror, sitting in the pumped up chair, while Aunt Grace click clacked to and fro to the ashtray, dragging on her cigarette, clipping some more hair. When she got to concentrating she'd let the cigarette hang out of her mouth, the ash end growing longer and longer. I watched with sideways eyes to see if it would fall on me, but she always caught it just in time.

I was sure both Mother and Aunt Grace found the haircut days as much of an ordeal as any of us and much as I hated to admit it, Aunt Grace was somewhat generous in allowing Mother to unleash her seven scruffy children on her immaculate house to stampede and wrestle, on top of cutting their hair for free.

The first time Angela came to Aunt Grace's for a haircut she was merely a spectator, being a tiny baby and wouldn't need her hair cut for several years at least. She was born with an abundance of hair, silky blond and curling into easy care ringlets that were invitations to touch and smell.

Gabe missed Angela's first visit to Aunt Grace's on haircut day. He was too old now, he said, and wanted to grow his hair long. I thought, rather unfairly, it was his fault that Bernadette created such havoc that day, as the battery powered shaver Aunt Grace would normally use on his short back and sides was left unemployed and available for Bernadette's use, as the baby slept safely, we thought, in her carry cot on the kitchen floor. I was full of anger and the need to blame someone, but, even distressed as she was, Mother wasn't going to punish Bernadette.

'Bernadette, that was very naughty,' She said to her in the car afterwards.

Very naughty? She must be joking. I stared at Mother, disbelieving.

'She was just playing, like with a real live doll. She didn't mean it.'

It happened very quickly, and conveniently, at the end of the line of haircuts when, having finished Mother's cut and curl and tucked her head under a dryer, Aunt Grace returned the teacups to the kitchen where she found Bernadette razing the last of Angela's curls from her soft baby head. Angela was just beginning to cry. Aunt Grace screamed, bringing us all to the room where we saw her lunge angrily, grabbing for the shaver in Bernadette's hand.

'Give me that you horrible child,' she hissed at her.

Bernadette's eyes widened and she stood frozen for a moment, with Aunt Grace's hand around her wrist. Then, with reptilian speed, she bit Aunt Grace, who recoiled as if from a snake, looking at her bitten hand and back at the place where Bernadette had stood, for Bernadette had vanished. I had a fleeting moment of gratification, wondering if Aunt Grace had met her match, but the crime committed by my sister was so terrible that I quashed the thought. Anyway, I had to agree with Aunt Grace. She was a horrible child.

Mother, always calm in a crisis, and though I never did ask her, I later wondered whether I confused her serenity with sheer exhaustion, picked up Angela and stroked her poor bald baby head. When satisfied that no physical damage had been done, she gave her a mother's cuddle and said, 'My poor Angela, my poor baby. Come on, out to the car. Gloria, you and Maureen, take the twins.'

We lugged our belongings and our sisters out to the car where we found Bernadette, and piled in, filling all seats and laps. We waited for Mother, who remained inside with Aunt Grace. She emerged eventually with Angela, to a car filled with silent children, for even the twins, still babies themselves, could sense something momentous had happened.

However, once Bernadette was chided for her naughtiness, leaving me to fume about the injustices of crime and punishment, Maureen broke the unnatural silence.

'Are we still going to Bay State Park this afternoon?' which was where we'd go on haircut days, freshly groomed, with Aunt Gloria and our cousins.

'Of course we are,' she said.

So, that was that. We were going to pretend it never happened. Just like when the candles blew out on my question about names. Another overlooked wrinkle in our lives. Well, they won't be able to keep it up this time, I thought. Angela's bald. How could they ignore that?

'We'll stop at Gloria's for lunch first, and to get Gabe.'

Although also full of copious amounts of children and pets, Aunt Gloria's home was very unlike ours, being much bigger, spacious, tidy and ordered. There were rules, regimes and routines in their house, but it was not an unhappy place. Our orderly Uncle Nick liked things well organised. He was a man that wore a suit, and sat in the same seat on the regular daily train to and from his job in an office. He assigned each one of my cousins a household chore, which changed with a weekly rota that he typed and posted on the kitchen notice board each Sunday night. No such systems existed in our haphazard home, the only official rule being the slightly eccentric requirement to name pets after fish. My cousin's pets had their own houses and beds.

We entered, still subdued, through the front porch, removed our shoes and left them in a neat row by the door. I passed Uncle Nick's armchair, where he sat and read in the evenings. Neatly folded over the arm of the chair was yesterday's newspaper, which he would use to make the fire in the hearth when he got home that evening.

We walked through to the kitchen at the back of the house where we met Gabe, already gathered with my cousins Nick Jr, Christina, and Joseph. At first sight of Angela, Aunt Gloria and mother exchanged a look, clearly speaking twin talk as nothing audible was said. All eyes in the room were of course on Angela, but following the leads of the mothers, not a word was spoken about the dramatic change in Angela's appearance. It was happening, the impossible. They were ignoring it. Their silent message to us was loud and clear, we should do the same.

The table was set with plastic brightly coloured plates and cups. A napkin folded into a triangle was beside each plate. Aunt Gloria busied herself pouring juice and setting out trays full of a variety of sandwiches, also in triangles. There was egg, ham, cream cheese and tuna, a luxurious feast compared to the statutory peanut butter and jelly we were used to. Following the sandwiches were cupcakes, baked, iced and decorated with Christina's help. We were permitted to take them outside while Mother and Aunt Gloria prepared for the visit to Bay State Park.

As soon as we stepped over the threshold and out of earshot there was an eruption of whispering between my cousin Christina, who was my age, and myself.

'Do you believe that?' I said.

'If I'd done what she did I'd be grounded,' said Christina, 'at least.'

Gabe and Nick Jr came to join us.

'What the hell is going on? What's with Angela's hair?' hissed Gabe, accusingly.

'Bernadette shaved it off.' I felt shocked. Saying it out loud made it true, before there had been the prospect of wakening to find it was an awful imagining. I told Gabe what happened, expecting commiseration for weathering the episode without his company.

'Where the fuck were you?' was his unsympathetic reaction. Gabe was aghast.

'You should have been watching her, you're the oldest. What the fuck were you doing? God, poor Angela, she looks – anything could have happened, Gloria, what about that soft part of her head.'

I was offended by both Gabe's new vocabulary and by his placing of the blame on me. 'She looks bald, I know.' I said, crushed, unable to find any other words. Gabe was right, I hadn't thought of the horror of possibilities, of the soft spot on her head. I should have been watching her. Christina defended me.

'She's not the oldest, stupid, you are. It wouldn't have happened if you were there.'

We left for the park in two cars, as the numbers exceeded lap capacity. Bay State Park was a regular destination for family outings, being a short drive away, not involving any bridges or ferries, near enough almost to walk or cycle to. It comprised over 3000 acres of woodland, bordered on the far side by beach and bay, most of it wild, yet well designed, discreet picnic and play areas were evenly spaced nearer the parking area, complete with barbecues and wooden tables. The wildlife was abundant; sea birds, deer, beavers, wild turkeys, rabbits and chipmunks roamed freely, carefully monitored by park rangers. There were signposted paths forged for walking, Wildlife Walk, Rhododendron Road, Marshland Mile, but further into the park were also vast tracks of undeveloped land, beach and marsh left open and accessible as long as one followed the park rules, clearly posted in the window of the ticket kiosk. No litter, No feeding animals, No fires, No horseplay.

When we arrived at the end of the long curving drive approaching the ticket kiosk, we saw several police cars strewn along the central reservation and shoulder of the road. Aunt Gloria, driving in front of us, slowed and spoke to a policeman, who leaned into her window. When he was finished, he straightened up, and turned to wave us, in Mother's car, through the gate.

'I wonder what that's all about,' said Mother. After she'd parked the car, we soon forgot the policeman in the excitement of spilling out of the cars and joining all our cousins, anticipating the afternoon. Considered a safe environment, we were left to our own devices in the park, and allowed to wander unsupervised provided we came back to check in at regular appointed times. This proved no hardship for us, as having already eaten lunch, the hamper was filled with only good things, sugary drinks, cookies, pretzels, sweets and fruit for snacking on during the afternoon.

After helping Mother and Aunt Gloria carry everything to the chosen base, we separated into clutches determined by age and prepared to disappear into the undergrowth. Mother, holding Angela, in a huddle with Aunt Gloria, called to us.

'Gloria, Christina, would you mind taking the twins on the swings first before you go off?' We did mind.

'Can't they go on their own? They're getting big enough.'

'You know they can't. They're too little. I want you girls to stay with them. Just for a while. Maureen can stay here and help me.'

Theresa and Mary were thrust upon us and we led them away to the fenced enclosure. We hoisted them up, side by side into the slatted wooden boxes with leg holes supported by strong chains. I pushed them gently and they happily swayed and dangled together while Christina and I wandered around the periphery of the small area.

What felt like seconds later, I turned around to the sight of Bernadette pushing the swings, too high, too fast. Theresa and Mary, their frightened faces level with the branches on the trees, were screaming. Something prevented me moving. I was rooted to the spot, Christina as well, stood and stared.

'Bernadette, that's too high,' I tried to sound calm, not angry, frightened of Bernadette's response. The swing park was on the other side of one of the ranger stations, in a small wood, out of vision of our table. Mother and Aunt Gloria were unaware of Bernadette's latest crime.

'They like it,' she replied. 'They're laughing.' She took a swing in each hand and crashed them together, and then turning them round and round, twisting the chains to the very top before she let them go, unravelling at an alarming rate, the twins extended arms and legs spinning. I felt sick as I ran, making my way through treacle. I fell and was helped up by Christina. I shouted to Bernadette as I ran, begging her to stop.

'You're hurting them,' I cried, assaulted by the image of kittens swinging, tied by their tails. Bernadette regarded me coldly, looking past me as though I wasn't there, and began to twist the chains again. Theresa's face was bloody now and both girls were crying uncontrollably. It was only moments, lived as if in slow motion. Christina stood still, frightened by the situation. When I reached Bernadette I tried to pull her away but she turned and rushed at me, releasing both the swings, pushed me in the stomach, knocking me down, winded.

Christina untangled the twins and handed them to me one at a time. I sat and held them, tucking one under each arm and the three of us sat on the dusty ground and wept, while she looked on.

'Where did Bernadette go?' I said.

'She ran away into the woods.' She indicated a direction. 'Just let her go, Gloria. Let's take the girls to your mother.'

Christina helped me clean them up. I took my t-shirt off from under my sweater and soaked it in the water fountain in order to wash Theresa's face, bloody from a nosebleed. After a while they'd calmed down, and were standing, cuddled against me, keen to walk back to Mother.

'How could she do that to them? They're just babies,' I said to Christina. Christina shook her head, she didn't answer. It was a question which didn't require an answer.

We brought Theresa and Mary back to the picnic table where Mother was. She embraced them both and asked, 'have you girls been crying?' She directed the question at me.

'They got tangled in the swings and got scared, and Theresa had a nosebleed but its fine now,' I said, adding, 'We're going to go for a walk.'

'Not now girls,' said Aunt Gloria, 'Stay here where we can see you.'

'Oh come on. You said we could. We took them to the swings,' I said.

'Not today. You saw those policemen when we came in,' said Mother.

'They're here, looking for a little boy. He's missing,' said Aunt Gloria.

'He's only two years old,' said Mother.

'He's been missing since last night,' said Aunt Gloria, gravely.

I remembered Bernadette, running off into the woods, but said nothing.

'But we're not gonna get lost,' said Christina.

'We could go and help find him, even.'

'No. Absolutely not. You can pray for him, but you must stay near here.'

Defeated, we went to the bigger swing park where we discovered the rest of our cousins, and while swinging, climbing, balancing and hanging upside down, discussed how one might survive overnight here in the park.

'There's loads of berries this time of year, and grapes grow here too.'

'You'd need to know the poisonous ones, though.'

'I didn't know grapes could be poisonous.'

'Not grapes, stupid. Berries.'

'It's getting cold at night now too. You'd have to build shelter.'

'There's tons of mussels, and clams are easy to get.'

'It could be really fun.'

'It's just a two year old, though.'

'It's not about surviving. Not that way,' said Gabe. 'They think someone might have taken him. That's why the police are here.'

'You mean like kidnapped?'

'Yeah, and maybe murdered.'

That remark killed the conversation. I thought of horrible things happening to the little boy, in the woods, in the dark, and thought how helpless and innocent he would be. I wished that I'd never heard about it, my imagination could only make it worse. We found ourselves gravitating back to the picnic table, closer to Mother and Aunt Gloria, whose grave faces turned to alarm when after a quick scan Mother said, 'where's Bernadette?'

'I think she went for a walk earlier,' I said, 'but I don't know.'

'Oh! She did!' said Christina, glancing at me, 'I saw her go off into the woods.'

Mother gasped, jumped up, blessing herself, upsetting a glass of cola, splashing panic all over. Her colour drained.

'Gabe and Nick, go and look for her. All the rest of you stay here and look nearby.' It was unsettling to see Mother, who rarely showed a negative emotion, put her head in her hands.

'Oh God,' she said, 'let her be safe.' A small shuddery sob escaped from her. I noticed she didn't say please.

Christina and Maureen took the twins and made a show of checking in and behind bins.

'We'll go and check the toilets,' volunteered Christina.

'No!' said Aunt Gloria. 'Nick and Gabe'll do that. Stay in sight.'

I wandered aimlessly, staying in their vision, masking my guilty lack of concern for Bernadette's absence by calling her name.

'Bernadette!' I called, half-heartedly. To my astonishment, she emerged from under a nearby tablecloth, giggling, to be greeted with relief, motherly hugs and some chocolate cake.

'We're just being silly here,' said Mother, 'worrying so much, and so selfish when some poor mother is really missing her son.'

'We'll go home as soon as Gabe and Nick come back,' said Aunt Gloria. I could feel Christina looking at me.

'Can we go for a walk now?' she asked.

'All right. Don't be long.'

Christina and I wandered off, having been given a list of nervous restrictions.

'Why didn't you tell them what she did to the twins? Why did you lie like that?' she said.

I looked at her blankly, not really able to answer. I'd forgotten what I'd said. I was exhausted.

'What did I say?'

'You just said they got tangled and had a nosebleed - you left out everything about Bernadette! It was Bernadette who did it to them!' Christina was full of rage with me and with Bernadette. I felt overwhelmed with defeat.

'I don't know. I don't know why I didn't tell her.'

I did know, though, and it was because I knew it would make no difference. To me, to the twins, or to Bernadette. This was our life now.

'Well you didn't tell her either,' I said, a weak defence.

'She's your sister. Not mine.'

A day later we heard on the radio that the missing boy had been found and returned safely to his home after being checked by doctors. I was immensely relieved both to hear of his safety and to turn off my troublesome thoughts, for I had been worried about the boy. I wondered briefly what I would have felt if the child in question had been Bernadette. Of course I would have been relieved, I thought. Of course I would have.

****

Chapter Ten

Uncle Tony came to stay with us in the late Indian summer, the weeks before my birthday. The nights were cooling and the crickets and cicadas quieting, winter also around the bend. It was the season of anticipation, hopeful and remorseful in equal measures. This year the remorse would tip the scales when the birthday threw up an unwelcome gift.

It was the last time Uncle Tony would play the role of official babysitter, not because any terrible fate befell him, the misfortune was all mine as the position was bequeathed to me, soon to be a year older and considered mature and reliable.

'On your birthday, Gloria, I think you'll be old enough not to need a babysitter anymore, and you can take over looking after the others.'

Although the eldest, Gabe's gender automatically disqualified him as a suitable applicant. He would have been far more able than I, being much bigger, more foul-mouthed and heavy-handed, especially considering Bernadette's predatory temperament, but the idea of suggesting a boy do childminding never dawned, so he came home for meals and to put out the garbage, the only demands made on his free time. I accepted this privilege of authority reluctantly and ungraciously.

'Why can't Gabe baby-sit?' I asked. 'He's the oldest. Not me.'

'Because he's a boy. He wouldn't know how.'

This from Dad, father of seven. Never mentioned was the fact that Uncle Tony, a man, had been doing the job, which had at times included washing, cooking, cleaning and all manner of domestic tasks, more than adequately for the past fifteen years.

'Why can't Uncle Tony still do it?'

'Uncle Tony's too busy, his business is growing. He has more important things to do.'

'I don't want to do it.'

'Well, you're doing it.'

Happy Birthday to me.

On this particular night, Uncle Tony's last to look after us, he came early to cook for us. Hamburgers and hot dogs, cooked outside. The air grew a chill as the sun sank and darkness settled quicker and earlier, but there were no lightening bugs to catch. They'd completed their life cycle, which unfortunately wasn't the case for some of the mosquitoes. There was a salty breeze and already, a few leaves dropping and blowing across the grass.

'I got you some clams, Gloria,' said Uncle Tony.

'Eww. Yuk,' said one of the twins, through tomato ketchup teeth, 'Snotshells.'

'Shut up Theresa,' I said. I especially didn't want Bernadette to hear her, give her ideas. 'Snotshell' was just the sort of thing she'd find inspiring.

'They're for you and Gabe and me. In the fridge. Sauce, too. We'll have 'em for dessert.' Uncle Tony appreciated food. Gabe and I took after him, but rarely got to indulge.

'Mmmm. Thanks,' I said.

We moved inside to watch television, all hemmed in by walls now.

Uncle Tony held Angela on his knee, and a twin sat either side of him on the sofa, making them feel more attended to and important than anything else in his life, even though it was clear to me that the clams were winning by far. Maureen and I sprawled ourselves over armchairs while Bernadette, tense and ticking like a bomb as always, lay on the floor leaning on her elbows staring at the ceaselessly blathering television. Angela was no longer so small and helpless, and Mother and Dad had resumed allowing themselves a limited nightlife.

They'd gone to the Floating Restaurant as dinner guests of Davis, who was Uncle Tony's silent business partner. When Uncle Tony first introduced me to Davis I was surprised that he could speak, and told him so, expecting a silent partner to be mute. He very kindly, and with much self control, resisted laughing, as I was at a vulnerable age when girls can't abide laughter aimed at themselves, a state that for most remains permanent.

'Silent doesn't mean quiet in the business world, Gloria,' Davis had said.

This had occurred at a barbecue, long before there was Angela, the twins, or Bernadette, when it was Gabe and Maureen and I. Bertie, a woman, had come along with Uncle Tony and Davis and I had assumed that she was Uncle Tony's beautiful and exquisitely dressed girlfriend. Bertie had explained in clarified childish detail the workings of the barge business world, leaving the three of us feeling smugly enlightened and hungry for more of her company.

'Are you going to marry Bertie?' I'd asked Uncle Tony, who this time, along with Davis and Bertie, did laugh, embarrassing me into myself and thus closing the subject forever. Uncle Tony wasn't given to the shameful silences in response to awkward questions as my other relatives were, but he found other ways of avoiding answers that could be equally stifling.

Davis owned the Floating Restaurant, which was, as Uncle Tony would describe it in disparaging good humour 'Nothing but a barge with a lid on it.'

It was actually a proper restaurant fixed to the mainland, overlooking the bay, where one could sit and take dinner while stationary and appreciate the aspect over the water, or hire one of the satellite private dining rooms and cruise the bay while dining on three to six courses and drinking in the sight of the bay sparkling at sunset. There were four floating dining rooms and they were, as Uncle Tony inferred, 'barges with lids on', albeit dressed up and nicely furnished. The menu, of course, was mainly fish, and Davis treated Dad and Uncle Joe to a night out with their wives regularly in return for nautical favours that came his way via the Fish Shop. They never went to these dinners as a foursome, though, but always on separate nights.

'Why don't they all go together?' I asked Uncle Tony.

'Who?'

'Uncle Joe and Aunt Grace, and our parents? Why does Davis treat them all, but not on the same night?'

I had always been led to believe that the reason for this was because Uncle Tony was needed to baby-sit and couldn't be in two places at once and had only just realised that this must be parental deceit, because those other cousins hadn't needed a babysitter for years. Uncle Tony regarded me thoughtfully, and I knew instantly that this was one of those bone-shaking questions, I was picking at a skeleton. He looked around the room at my younger sisters, then back at me.

'Davis likes an excuse to go out as much as possible,' he said, winking at me. I knew, by this rite of passage wink, that he was lying. I knew that he would have told me the truth if my sisters hadn't been there, and that the truth was something wicked, scandalous, violent, sexy, blasphemous or forbidden, and that he would tell me someday, I was going to learn that secret. He had communicated this to me with one small wink, and I had looked back at him with what I hoped was an expression of wisdom and understanding, and felt I had an inkling of what it was like to be adult, to have twin language, to have doors open. As far as birthday presents went, this kind of thing was more like it.

My birthday fell on Halloween, making it a day both more special to others yet less of an occasion for me. It was a hectic day for Mother, with costumes, candy and birthday cake to worry about alongside the usual routine of life.

In the birthday tradition, I was also permitted to choose the dish we would all eat for dinner. This could be as extravagant as I liked, being part of the gift. This opportunity to eat well was an oasis in a year round desert of pale food that blended into one pan of cheap white fish, pasta and eggs. In previous years I had taken the egalitarian path and chosen meals that would be enjoyed not just by myself, but also by the rest of my family, chicken cacciatore, lasagne, lobster. This year, however, motivated by nothing but selfishness, I chose calamari, loathed by my sisters. Yuk, they would say. Squid. It would be like eating a monster.

Mother gently tried to dissuade me.

'Are you sure? It's a very grown-up dish, especially cooked that way.'

I had deliberately chosen Calamari Ripieni con Sarde' for its sophisticated ingredients, dry white wine, garlic, fresh parsley, and the inclusion of sardines, which sat on almost as low a rung as squid on the ladder of my siblings food preferences, as well as the appealing instruction in the recipe's first line: 'reserve tentacles'. There would be no deep fried batter to disguise the wriggly-even-when-dead creatures.

'I am sure. I love it that way and I never get to have it. It's my birthday, right?'

'Yes. It's your birthday.'

'You like it, don't you?'

'Well, no, I wouldn't say it was one of my favourites.'

'Do you know how to cook it?'

'Yes, of course I know how to cook it.' Mother said, miffed. 'I've made it for your father.'

'He likes it. And so does Gabe. That's good enough.'

She didn't answer.

'It's my birthday, right?'

'Okay Gloria. It's your birthday.'

I didn't care. I was going to eat what I wanted. It was my birthday, I was thirteen and eager to be difficult, feeling justified under the circumstances, having been given unwanted gifts such as childcare responsibilities, menstruation, swelling breasts and a truly vile, unwanted, unflattering woollen pinafore that I would no doubt be forced to wear and photographed in to forever preserve the indignity.

'I'll cook it myself if you want.'

'No, no, I'll enjoy cooking it,' said Mother, patiently disregarding my provocative offer. 'And I was hoping you'd take the younger girls out trick or treating while we get things ready here.'

'What about Gabe?'

'He'll be out with friends.'

'Oh, great, so I get landed with them.'

'Gloria, cheer up. It's a party. And your birthday.'

I bit my tongue and tried to enter into the spirit of the afternoon, the frenzy of anticipation growing along with the mountains of torn fabric, old clothing and cosmetic aids that were creating outfits. This year the holiday had fallen on a Friday, meaning that it could be a later night for us all and the adults could have their own costume party. Even Bernadette's mood was lighter than usual. The prospect of going out in disguise and being given several pounds of sweets was appealing to every child, though I expect she was also looking forward to the opportunity to throw a few eggs and upturn the odd dustbin. I irritably acted as the wardrobe assistant, unable to remember and yet missing the excitement I once felt on Halloween night. Angela, now aged two and with her blonde curls grown back in, was duly dressed as an angel, with wings and halo, a little white and sparkly being. This was to be her first time out trick or treating. The twins were identical black cats, and I helped them paint whiskers on using an eyebrow pencil. Bernadette dressed herself in sort of generic, non-specific, universal Halloween costume wearing dark oversized clothing, streaking her face with charcoal, stuffing her hair under a hat and transforming herself into something between a ghoul and a tramp. Maureen, like Gabe, was out with friends, leaving me to stew over my single-handed hardship on my birthday until my cousins turned up to lend a hand and some buoyancy to the atmosphere, bearing birthday gifts which proved most effective in lifting my spirits.

'Open the big one first,' said Christina.

She watched me, eagerly.

'It's a book!' I said, turning it over, opening it. 'It's blank.'

'It's a diary,' Christina said. 'You can write in it. All your thoughts and stuff, and secrets.'

'Oooh!' squealed my sisters. 'I bet I can guess where you'll hide it!'

'Thank you,' I said. 'It's pretty. Can I open the little one now?'

'Oh, yeah, that's a pen.'

The diary would remain empty. This wasn't the sort of house to hide written secrets.

The diary, hair clips, a watch. Teenage presents. No more playthings.

The kitchen began to fill with Aunts and Uncles, dressed up, and already fizzing with pink champagne, beer and red wine, they took turns to answer the doorbell which had started to ring and would continue for the next few hours as a steady stream of guisers presented themselves for their sweet reward. Mother and Aunt Gloria were matching black witches, proprietors of Theresa and Mary's little twin black cats. Aunt Grace wore a long black cape, winkle picking high-heeled boots and an eye mask. She smoked her cigarettes out of a long holder and exchanged her usual coral lipstick for blood red. Dad and Uncle Joe made a good effort with a funny wig each, intending to be Moe and Larry of the Three Stooges, thoroughly relishing hitting one another over the head. Only Gabe, who had watched the Three Stooges on a friend's television, fully understood the joke. The rest of us were not permitted to watch it as Mother, ironically, considered it too violent and so the referred humour was lost on us. Uncle Nick was very effective in black clothes onto which he had painted a skeleton, no doubt each bone thoroughly researched and precisely positioned.

Uncle Tony loved Halloween and was always dressed in spectacular fashion, one year a pirate with a real peg leg and parrot, another as a large bear in a fur suit. He arrived tonight as an enormous nun, his voluminous habit perfect in every detail, his strong face framed with stiff white card crowned with black veil, much to the delight and hilarity of everyone present, except of course Aunt Grace, who attacked him for it later, as the empty pink champagne bottles accumulated.

It was colder and darker than any other night so far that year, and I donned a big coat and dutifully walked for what seemed like hours through a patchwork of new neighbourhoods, standing back while my little sisters knocked on doors their empty pillowcases filling with what all parents feared were apples stuffed with razor blades and drug spiked candy corn. Bernadette disappeared ahead of us into the dark, and I let her.

We stopped at neighbour Alice's house, a poison-free zone but dangerous in that she'd finally replaced her worn out old dog with a new, overly exuberant model. It was still a puppy, but a large one, and strong, and she, a frail lady, had difficulty restraining it. The two black cats got away unscathed. I carried the little angel. As we left I could hear Alice, gently trying to teach her puppy how to bark.

When we got home, each child's pillowcase was handed over and picked through and each piece of fruit home grown by little old ladies was discarded along with anything that came out of the bag in the terrifyingly horrific state of being unwrapped. This was common practice in every home, and yet still accounted for about one third of the goods gleaned that evening. Either people had not realised that their apples and unwrapped goods were going to waste, or there really was an epidemic of child murderers and drug pushers.

In the kitchen, Mother had finished fastening the stuffed squid sacks with toothpicks and was decorously arranging a few extra reserved tentacles before my calamari went into the oven, much to the disgust of the majority of my cousins and sisters.

'Eww. That's disgusting.'

'It's shark bait, that's what it is. We're not eating that.'

'It's my birthday and I can eat what I want.'

'Well all we have to eat is cake.'

The evening wore on, the meal was delayed and due to the surplus amount of people, pets and activity, there was barely a square inch of floor space free and even on such a cold night, the house was overheated.

Younger children were dispatched to the back porch where buckets were filled with water and stocked with our own razor free apples for ducking. It turned out we didn't need razors for dangerous apples.

The open door of the porch cooled the kitchen somewhat, where the atmosphere had become sweaty and stifling, which may have had more to do with its well-oiled and heavily clothed inhabitants than ventilation. Aunt Grace was needling Uncle Tony, absurdly accusing him of disrespect and blasphemy for dressing as a nun.

'For God's sake, Grace, it's Halloween. It's just a bit of fun,' said Uncle Tony.

'It's not that and you know it.' She hissed at him, pointing her cigarette holder, cape swirling around her.

Maureen and Gabe had returned home and sat with me in an unobserved corner, captivated by the kitchen theatre. Dressed as she was, Aunt Grace gave a flawless performance.

'Honestly,' Aunt Grace was slurring slightly now, 'I hate to think of the things you people call fun.'

She stressed the phrase '*you people*' in the same disparaging tone that, ironically, my school nun had said '*that man*'. Poor Uncle Tony. Just because he made his living collecting garbage.

Uncle Tony stood up and opened his arms wide, exasperated, filling the room. 'Then don't,' he said. He was clearly unconcerned about her comments, but I detected an undercurrent of unease in the room. I thought someone clearly should have challenged Aunt Grace, or come to Uncle Tony's defence, instead, time took a breath and no one spoke.

There was a brief interval of relief before Theresa's screams broke the silence and she stood, sodden, in the door between the porch and the kitchen, wet black whiskers running down her face, no doubt a victim of an underwater apple.

'What is it, Ter?' Dad scooped her up, wrapping her in tea towels.

There came more cries from the porch.

'Bernadette,' Theresa sobbed.

The next few moments, or perhaps it was longer, as crises have time zones of their own, melded together in a theatrical mixture of surreal images and sounds, of arms and legs and costumed panic. Sloshing water, apples bouncing across the hard floor of the porch, Bernadette's frozen posture and unblinking eyes as Dad yanked her away from the bucket where she held Angela's face forcibly under the water. Angela, already dressed for heaven, had stopped spluttering and lay still in the arms of her Witch Mother, head back, mouth open, slung floppily over a shoulder, arms dangling and disappearing out of the front door and into a waiting car, poised there so readily it was as if it had been rehearsed.

The kitchen was chilled now, and empty. It was very quiet, the only sound being the sizzling of my forgotten birthday meal coming from the oven. Uncle Tony, having shed his wimple, got up, shut the porch door and removed the squid from the oven. Gabe and Maureen remained, still in the same corner. Aunt Gloria and Uncle Nick had taken the twins home with them. Bernadette had disappeared upstairs.

'Who's going to eat, then?' said Uncle Tony.

No one answered him at first.

'It doesn't seem right to eat,' I said.

'Don't be stupid. You have to eat.'

'I feel too worried about Angela to eat.'

'Well don't. Angela will be fine, I had a look at her in the car. I can tell, if there's one thing I know about it's water accidents. But why don't I keep this warm for a bit.' He put the dish back in the oven.

'Let me tell you some things about squid. Come on through to the other room where the fire is.'

He told us about the different ways of fishing for squid, and how my squid was caught by a method called jigging, which sounded a rather tedious pastime of repeatedly raising and lowering a line. This method was used, he said, when really good quality squid was required, such as we were having this evening. So it was nothing like eating bait at all, which was trawled, indiscriminately netted together with any old sea life.

The telephone rang, interrupting his flow.

'Squid are attracted to bright light at night.' Uncle Tony got up to answer it. 'In Sicily, the most delicious squid are caught during the night of the full moon. Hello?'

He held the phone to his ear and listened with one hand and made encouraging gestures to us with the other. When finished, he said, 'Angela's okay. She threw up all over the car and recovered instantly, but they took her in to have her looked at anyway. They'll be back once she's been seen.'

Maureen sniffled. 'I thought she had drowned,' she said. Uncle Tony patted her on the head. 'Well, she didn't, Mo. Now, who's ready to eat Calamari?'

****

Chapter Eleven

Uncle Tony's idea was to take me back to his boat yard with him that night. He felt the day had ended in a manner unsatisfactory, to put it gently. He wanted to make repairs to both my Halloween and my birthday.

'How's your squid, Glor?' he asked.

It had cooked too long, tasted like rubber cardboard, if there could be such a thing.

'It's okay.'

'Not really the right mood for it, is it?'

'Not exactly.' Don't be nice to me, I thought, don't make me cry.

'I think maybe we should go out, Gloria. You and me.'

'But...' I was thinking of Angela.

'No buts. It's your birthday. You oughta feel like it is.'

Angela came home, all washed out. There were dark circles under her two-year-old eyes, telling sad tales. She said hello and goodnight, smiled a bit. Not bad for a kid who nearly drowned and threw up a bucket of water and a pillowcase full of sweets.

I was satisfied then; it would be safe to go out. It was getting late, though, and Mother was concerned. The following day was a Holy Day of Obligation.

'It's nearly bedtime, Tony, can't you take her with you some other time?'

'It's just to watch some TV, eat some popcorn, stay up a bit late. C'mon Mary, it's her birthday.'

And what about Mass?' she said. 'It's All Saint's Day, remember?'

'Don't worry, Mary, we'll get to Mass. Let's leave it up to Gloria.'

He turned to me, hands on hips.

'Gloria, would you like to come?' There was no way he would lose this one. I smiled and nodded. Uncle Tony's boatyard apartment was considerably more interesting than going to bed with my sisters on a ruined Halloween night. More importantly, it would remove me from the lingering cloud of trauma.

'All right then.' She kissed me goodnight. She had too much to do to consider it for more than that.

'See you tomorrow, we'll do the cake then. Happy Birthday Gloria, sorry it wasn't a better one.'

What Uncle Tony hadn't told me or my mother was that on the way there he was calling in at Davis's restaurant where his annual Halloween blast was in full flow.

'We won't stay here long, but I think you deserve a different kind of excitement on your birthday.'

Davis' restaurant was dressed in its own Halloween mask, dimly lit and cavernous, loud music pounding, smoke watering my eyes and nose. It was unrecognisable as the airy and spacious place I knew in daylight. I tried to take in what seemed like thousands of people masquerading in hoods, cloaks, long fingernails and exaggerated eyelashes. Uncle Tony sat me on the outer deck of the dining room where I could look out at yet more parties bursting the seams of the floating restaurant barges off shore, while he went to speak to Davis. At regular intervals extreme and monstrous faces approached me.

'Hi Gloria, Happy Birthday,' they would say and then offer me a drink or a sweet, or an apple, 'without a razor blade' they all said, each thinking themselves to be hilarious, the originator of the joke, that in itself making it funnier every time. They looked like gruesome strangers but their voices told me they were old friends, barge boys, restaurant staff, fishermen, bay men, marina and Fish Shop people I'd been speaking to all my life suddenly swirling around me in disguise. For the first time that night, and far too late, I wished I had dressed up.

I felt confused and fit to burst, as though I was on the cusp of something, aged thirteen and about to embark on a stage of life that could offer me exotic evenings like this. A few hours ago the idea of donning a costume seemed childish, now I longed to be adult enough to do so. Uncle Tony returned with Davis in tow, who, always extravagant, presented me with a gift that confirmed my notion of maturity, beautifully wrapped in gold and black paper, inside filled with a selection of expensive, deliciously scented toiletries bearing exclusive names and logos that I was not yet familiar with.

'Sorry to keep you so late, Gloria,' said Uncle Tony.

'I don't mind,' I said, 'I'm not tired, we can stay.'

'You may not be tired but I'm bushed. We'll go home now.'

We went back to the apartment where I was installed in a sleeping bag on the sofa and I lay there, too excited to sleep.

When Uncle Tony woke me up for Mass, my eyelids felt heavy with tiredness and my eyes sore and bloodshot from lack of sleep and the irritation of smoke.

'Do I have to go to Mass?' I moaned from the depths of my sleeping bag, hoping for yet more privilege.

'Yes, you do. I promised your mother I'd take you. Get up.'

In the car on the way to Mass, perhaps it was exhaustion relaxing my inhibitions or clouding my judgement, or because I'd felt I'd crossed a bridge into another era, I said to Uncle Tony,

'Do you think there's something different about Bernadette?'

Uncle Tony said nothing until he parked the car by the church, and then he switched it off and sat and looked at me.

'What do you mean, different?'

'Different than she used to be.' I was losing my nerve now, his gaze drilling into it, not sure what I wanted to say.

'How so?'

'She's always wanting to hurt things. And people.' Then I told him about the kittens tied to strings, and the twins in the swings, things I had not told my parents or indeed spoken to anyone about. All he knew about was Angela's dramatic haircut and the events of last night.

Disappointingly, Uncle Tony didn't automatically say something to magically repair that part of my life, but merely continued to look at me. He removed the keys from the ignition. Then he looked straight ahead, took a deep breath, then let it out.

'I don't know, Glor. I don't know. C'mon, we'll be late for Mass.'

My birthday cake, double chocolate fudge, was deferred until that night due to the 'unfortunate accident', which was glossed over 'in the family way' as I began to refer to the practice of never mentioning vital points needing addressing, such as letting Bernadette get away with near murder. This time even Angela, the injured party colluded with her.

'She tried to help me,' said Angela.

This would be what Bernadette had told Angela, under threat. Angela was too frightened of Bernadette not to back her up.

'I was trying to help her get the apple she wanted,' said Bernadette, curiously unmoved by Angela's traumatic visit to the hospital but convincing nonetheless. 'I didn't realise she was under the water.' Along with Bernadette's incessant denials and unshakable conviction, memories became confused and conflicting. It was unclear what really happened on the porch that night, the scene having been so chaotic anyway, and the only reliable witnesses being the candlelit pumpkins, their mute and flickering faces watching from the shelves.

Once again, my cousins were gathered to sing to me, once again, the cake was presented complete with orange Halloween face on top of the fudge icing, now history, and once again, life went on without anyone speaking publicly about why we'd postponed the event.

There was no pink fizz due to the overindulgence of the previous evening resulting in the depletion of stocks, but there was a momentous announcement to mark the occasion. Once I'd had my cake and fair share of attention, Mother stood up, an action I thought altogether unnecessary considering what was about to come. She tapped a glass with a spoon, ding ding ding.

'Okay, now I have an announcement to make.'

All eyes upon her, I scanned the crowd. Dad knew what it was, I could tell. She continued.

'We have something else to celebrate tonight.'

Oh shit, I thought. She's pregnant again.

'I've got a job!' she said, giggling like a little girl.

She was going to work for the parish, to act as secretary and reception for both the nuns and the priests. She'd be housed daily, for a few hours after school, in her own small office at the front of the rectory.

She stood there, awarding herself accolades such as undeserving, privileged and unworthy, lamenting the fact that there was no pink champagne available to bless this holy achievement, while her sisters and brothers, nieces and nephews, fussed and congratulated her, seemingly forgetting that we'd originally been gathered here for the purpose of celebrating my birthday. There was obviously nothing older than yesterday's news.

Now I wished she'd said she was pregnant.

Happy Birthday, Gloria.

I heard only selected phrases from her proclamation. 'Every day', 'afternoons', and 'Oh no it'll be fine, Gloria will be here to watch them'. 'It's the beginning of a whole new era for us,' she said.

She wasn't kidding. For me, instead of stepping over the threshold into my dreams of a new and exciting age of meeting boys, wearing dresses, going to parties and gossiping with girlfriends, it was the teenage girl equivalent of doing time. My life was about to be robbed from me. It was my first year in High School, the ultimate destination in my somewhat limited aspirations to date. It was a much bigger school than the small Catholic institution where I'd spent my childhood, and my mother hers. Up until this time I had my cousins as companions and had yet to discover what it was like to have real friends, people my age that I wasn't related to. I wanted to have the time of my life, and look forward to the endless possibilities that would follow. Maybe I would become a vet, using the energy from my fondness of animals to help them, or perhaps I'd take a more artistic route, and go to drama school, become an actress.

Dad said, 'Don't be silly. You couldn't do those things.'

How encouraging of him. But he was right. I wouldn't have time.

She started work the following Monday. I was to come home from school every day and cross paths with her, receive daily instruction concerning the evening meal and any specific tasks or assignments required for that day, take over all household duties and care of my younger sisters. For my efforts I received nothing except a promise.

'It won't last forever, Gloria, I promise. Just until we get back on our feet a bit, then I'll stay home again.'

But Mother didn't set foot in the house ever again in the afternoon unless it was a holiday or a weekend.

Dad became distracted when Mother went to work, although he was often home earlier than she was. He didn't like being there when she wasn't.

'Hi. I'm home.' I came in from school to Mother, who was always running late, frantically preparing for departure, dressing, writing notes, washing a face or wiping a bottom, setting out cat or dog food so that there was at least one meal I didn't have to worry about. She did this every day. The longer time passed the more bemused I was by the fact that she never got any better at it.

'It's all right. I'll do the dog food. I don't mind.'

'Are you sure Gloria? You have so much else to do.'

'Really. It's okay.' At least I liked looking after the dog.

Mother and I no longer had time for each other after that, she was too busy leaving and I was too busy coming home. On weekends we both frantically and futilely tried to catch up on what we missed during the week. That involved her staying in the house and me leaving it.

I put my books, bundled together in a piece of elastic, down in the position they would remain in until the next morning. Maureen, if she came home with me, would absent herself either to do homework or read or pray her rosary.

Over time, I began to believe that Maureen really did have spiritual privileges. She seemed to rise above us, sealed into a sanctimonious aura unable to experience anything that wasn't pure. She was curiously unaffected by those awful afternoons, almost as if she were unaware they happened around her. She was so nice it was irritating. But she was no help to me. I became angry and resentful of her. I took turns cursing her uselessness and feeling guilty about doing so.

Mother left with a squeeze, a kiss, and a verbal menu, often still doing up her buttons as she started the car. I watched out the window and waved as she drove away. Every day at that time I felt like sitting down to cry. I didn't, because I couldn't appear weak. I knew that when I turned and faced the overcrowded living room at my back, the sound of mindless afternoon television now joined by the bubbling fish tank, recently transferred from the Fish Shop under the mistaken notion that I might find it a comfort. The rest of the day would unfold pretty much out of my control.

After Mother had been at work for a few months, Dad came home in the middle of one day, in a borrowed pick up truck loaded with containers. He carried them in, gingerly and lovingly, one by one.

'I miss you down the shop, Gloria,' he said, 'I thought you might like to have these here.'

'But what about you? Won't you miss them?'

'I'm surrounded by fish. Dead and alive. I can look at them here.'

'What about Uncle Joe?'

'So? What about Uncle Joe? They're my fish, not his.'

Moving a tropical fish tank is not a simple operation, and involved considerable preparation, carefully researched and executed meticulously by Dad. Dismantling and reassembling an entire ecosystem, bit by bit, fish by fish, required surgical precision, preserving bacterial balances, temperatures and of course, life. It would have been far easier to simply get some new fish, but that was out of the question. New fish would not be these fish.

It was a large fish tank and most of the water had to be made ready and moved with along with the fish. Dad cleaned the tank and replaced the water in it in gradual amounts in the weeks before the move. He used some of the water to fill plastic bags to put the fish in, divided into small groups according to size and species, to travel, sealed in tight with elastic bands. He'd then put each fish filled plastic bag into another one and blown air into the layer of space between the two to create a cushion effect. He packed all the bagged fish in a box, like bubbles, and covered them, as they would be less active in the dark. In order to keep things as clean as possible the fish weren't fed for a few days prior to transit, which he hoped would take no more than an hour. The remaining twenty-two gallons of water was stored in several containers.

Upon arrival at their new home, the fish would stay in their darkened bags for a little longer while the containers were decanted into the tank, the filter connected and allowed to run for two hours while stones, miniature shipwrecks, and plants, also transported by way of filled plastic bubbles, were put in place. Then it was finally time to release the fish. Old home, new location.

Needless to say, however thoughtfully designed, this would not be a fish's preferred method of travelling if it were able to choose and in spite of all his loving care, a couple of the fish died.

Poor Dad was devastated. He sat, holding the small plastic bags, body bags for fish, and shook his head. 'Oh, Gloria, I'm so sorry,' he said, 'I did everything I was supposed to do, I don't understand what went wrong.'

'That's okay, Dad. Don't worry,' I said. I really meant it. I didn't mind, not about the dead fish. I minded more that he was upset about it. He was trying to do a nice thing for me and he'd got it wrong.

He didn't really understand the situation, or me. He wasn't there enough. It was him that was needed. Not tropical fish. I'd already been coming home every afternoon to the living hell that was looking after Bernadette and my sisters and I didn't want this delivery of the fish tank, locking the door behind me, keeping me in. I wanted the fish tank to still be at the Fish Shop so that I could go there and see it. Like I used to.

I was not a prisoner who wanted a luxurious cell.

****

Chapter Twelve

There were three years of those afternoons. Three years and three types. After a while I gave them names. The Runaway, the Uneventful and the Worst.

They all began the same way, ten minutes to four, looking out of the window, waving goodbye, the feeling of dread and despondency growing with every inch the car gained reversing out of the driveway.

I was head of the house for the next two and a half hours, give or take ten minutes, a period of time which is relatively brief, yet these were the only hours of my day during that three years I can recall. To my sisters and me, these were the only hours in the day.

I would turn from the window and survey the area of my responsibilities, in which there were several constants. The television was on, unless it was broken or there was no power. There was a plate of cookies and a jug of milk on the kitchen table. Bernadette was lying in the centre of the room, propped up on her elbows in front of the television.

I would sit down in an armchair and wait, already overcome by a kind of depressive exhaustion brought on by anticipating what lay ahead in that two and a half hours. Theresa, Mary and Angela would be eating cookies while watching television or playing and bickering in the way that little girls do. Maureen would take her after school sustenance on a separate plate and make her ascension up to the bedroom, up into her top bunk or outside in the garden if it was a fine day, to get on with her worship. Dogs and cats, again weather dependent, would be milling about, begging for food, sleeping on the furniture or outside roaming.

Gabe had all but disappeared from our lives, and certainly from the afternoons. His appearances at home were erratic and brief. He was withdrawn and smelled of tobacco, and if I sought him out he would defer his companionship rather than heartlessly reject me.

'Hey Gloria. Sorry, gotta go. I'll see you later, ok?'

But later never came, and I missed him terribly.

The most frequent type of afternoon was the Runaway. This would be when Bernadette, despite appearances, was not watching television at all, but listening to her sisters around her, simmering away. When she reached her boiling point, she would stand up and head for the nearest vulnerable target – one of my three smaller sisters, usually Angela. Her crimes ranged from swiping cookies, which she would not eat, but destroy by crushing onto the floor; to hair pulling, pushing, and all manner of physical bullying, to stealing a preferred plaything and hiding, destroying or placing it out of reach.

For a long time, my little sisters never saw it coming. Whether they were resilient or naive, I didn't know. They were reborn every day, gullible and innocent. It sometimes made me angry that they could be so stupid, sometimes sad that they were so helplessly trusting. I hated to see her hurt them, hated it every time. There was a lot of hatred milling about within me, gaining momentum.

The next thing, kitchen chairs would tumble onto the floor. Then came the plates, followed by spilled milk and then a screaming, wailing little girl, genuinely shocked and affronted at this undeserved, unwelcome attention.

'Gloria she hit me, she's pulling my hair, she knocked me over, she won't leave me alone. Help me.'

They thought I could protect them.

'Come on, Bernadette, leave her alone, she's not bothering you.'

I started the pointless exchange, reasonably enough, trying to be heard over the chaos. Maybe today will be different, I thought. If I keep my voice calm, level, gentle. I was as innocent and gullible as they were. As though my tone of voice could make a difference.

'Make me,' said Bernadette, launching another attack, this time on the twins, who she liked to pit against each other by knocking their heads together suddenly from behind, or pulling their clothes off, skirts down, shirts up, again by surprise. She would grab Angela again, now only three, and hold her by her hair, disarming her by pinning her hands behind her back, and march her to the top of the cellar stairs, threatening to throw her down, tie her up, lock her in.

I would step in now, forced to become involved against my will, the innocent bystander who witnessed the murder, who would really prefer to step over the body and be on her way.

'Bernadette, please stop it. Leave them alone. Go and watch television. They haven't done anything to you. Stop being such a bully.' That would be the turning point, I knew, for the situation. Call Bernadette a name, accuse her of something and her wrath was instantly directed away from my sisters and onto me.

Once I had Bernadette's full attention, I could usually successfully fend her off in a small scuffle while directing the twins and Angela to our refuge – the basement or the bedroom, whichever was closer. Once they had been despatched I could extricate myself from Bernadette, who by this time, with the removal of her prime victims, would begin to lose interest and gravitate back to the television. I would join the others. We would barricade the door with furniture and spend the remainder of the afternoon in our den, telling stories, tending wounds, playing little games, anything to make us forget that we were too scared to wander freely in our own home.

Bernadette would sit in the living room alone, staring at the television. I don't know if she watched it. If we needed anything from the kitchen, we sent Maureen, if we were in the bedroom. Bernadette didn't worry Maureen.

'We have to pray for Bernadette,' Maureen said. 'We have to forgive her and pray for her.'

'Yeah, sure Maureen. Let's leave praying to you. Put in a good word for me, will you.'

Maureen paid no mind. She sat up high in her bed, closer to God, and said rosary after rosary, Hail Mary, Glory Be, Our Father who art in the top bunk. Maureen would descend the stairs and Bernadette would at best, ignore her, at worst, glare at her unpleasantly.

When she returned, she would knock so we could disassemble the furniture blockade and we would press her with questions.

'What is she doing? What did she say? Is she sorry?'

'She's watching TV. I asked her if she wanted a glass of milk and she said no. She didn't look sorry, but I'm sure she is, deep within. That's about it. Here's your stuff.' She would hand over our supplies, return to her prayer position, and we would carefully replace the chairs and tables that blocked the door.

Perhaps Maureen's prayers were working for her, or perhaps it was because she kept herself so separate, or because she got the lucky draw in the birth order. Who knew. She didn't help us with the barricade, she didn't need it. Bernadette didn't threaten her. She didn't feel as though there were a monster downstairs on the loose.

The second kind of afternoon was the Uneventful. This happened less often. In some ways it carried a heavier tension than the others in that we were compelled to tiptoe around Bernadette, never knowing which one of our actions or words would be the one to ignite her short fuse. It was a nervous waiting game. So we would be very quiet and still, always watchful of Bernadette who was fully in control. We didn't feel the relief of the Uneventful Afternoon until it was over, and then only briefly, as we were already exhausted from worrying about what could have been. We then began to fret about the next day.

There were four occasions in three years when I had an afternoon off. Once I had a dentist appointment to remove a wisdom tooth. The day after I was ill and Aunt Grace came to stay with us. Twice I had to stay after school for detention, although I lied to my family about these two.

The day I had the wisdom tooth removed I left school early, handing in to the school office the note from Mother that I had carefully rewritten in my own handwriting. An investment in the future.

It took the dentist longer than my allocated time to remove the wisdom tooth and seemed to cause him a considerable amount of exertion, at one point bracing himself on the chair while he tugged. When he finished I felt happy, and decided to walk to the rectory to visit Mother at the end of her working day.

I enjoyed my visit to the dentist, his office a sharp contrast to my usual afternoon surroundings, clean, controlled. Blissfully quiet. No sisters. He said it was a tough extraction, it'd be sore later; he'd disturbed the jawbone. I didn't care. I liked sitting in the chair and being attended to, raised up and down, asked to open and spit. So rarely did I get to be the centre of attention.

I arrived too early to visit Mother. The school across the street, my old school, was just finishing for the day and I sat down on the rectory steps and watched them while I waited. I wasn't going to go home if I didn't have to. It had been arranged that Dad was going to be home this afternoon. Children spilled out of the doors, shouted after by black and white nuns in pairs evenly dotted throughout the playground.

'Don't run,' they said. 'Slow down. Be quiet.'

I saw Bernadette come out of school, her uniform dishevelled and her schoolbag hanging open. She walked along with her head down, but shifting from side to side, as though looking out for something. She was alone. Most of the children had friends with them, though she certainly wasn't the only child on their own. I wasn't surprised she didn't have friends. She climbed on to her bus and sat next to a window, near the front, looking out. She didn't see me. I sat down to wait for mother, my numb face and jaw starting to tingle with reawakening.

When she arrived, Mother was surprised to find me waiting on the step.

'Hello!' she said. 'How was the dentist?'

'Good,' I said.

'Let me see.' She looked into my mouth and tried to disguise her sympathetic wince.

'Does it look bad?'

'Come on inside. I think I'll need to call one of your aunts to mind the girls tomorrow afternoon for you.'

She brought me inside and showed me her office, where she answered the telephone and the door. It was very clean and uncluttered. She sat at a big brown desk with a blotting mat and a telephone on it and a neat stack of papers. Her chair was green and spun around on an axis and like a big screw, could go up and down as its height changed.

'Sit down here,' she said, pulling the chair out for me.

'Would you like a cup of tea?'

I sat in the chair, feeling like one of the visitors, watching my mother in her work persona. She acted differently here. It was tidy and efficient.

She was important. One of the priests came in. He was wearing a paper mask that crinkled when he breathed. His breathing was heavy and wheezy. He nodded to me.

'This is Father Gruelo, Gloria. Father this is my daughter.'

'Hello Father,' I said.

He nodded again and muffled a greeting through his mask, then leafed through the stack of papers on the desk, looking for something. Mother reached over and found it, handed it to him.

'Thank you Mary,' he said, and left.

'He's a visiting priest,' said Mother. 'He has asthma, and doesn't speak much English. Would you like to see around the rectory?'

Of course 'around the rectory' was a closed door. Women weren't allowed into the priests' residence, but she showed me the route from her desk along a modern carpeted corridor, turning a corner suddenly into a darker, gothic age and into the sacristy where there were vestments hanging up, and locked glass cupboards containing gold cups, another door and another passage and then like magic, we were backstage at the altar. I spent so many hours kneeling on the other side of it that the reversed point of view made me dizzy.

'I'll get my things, Gloria, and tidy up. You wait here. I'll be about five minutes. We can leave by the front of the church.'

Left alone, I took the opportunity to climb the narrow, semicircular steps up into the pulpit which had a nifty little handrail curling round the inside, out of sight. I looked over the rows of empty dark brown pews, and imagined it full. I picked out places I sat regularly. Then, Mother's stony approaching footsteps echoed from behind, and I scurried down. My jaw was beginning to hurt, and my face swelled.

The next day Aunt Grace came to stay, because we couldn't get anyone better. It was like a Runaway afternoon with Aunt Grace, another undesirable companion, creating an exodus, everybody heading for the safety of the bedroom as soon as they got home. I lay, my throat and face aching, in my sickbed and my sisters appeared, one by one, armed with snacks, books and trinkets to pass the time. I couldn't eat solids, too sore to play. Still, I enjoyed the afternoon. It was time off.

Bernadette stayed in her domain of the living room, lording over the television. Aunt Grace, her neglectful godmother, was uncomfortable around Bernadette. She stayed in the kitchen nervously smoking cigarettes, drinking a can of Schlitz to calm her nerves and flicking through magazines. I strayed into the kitchen once, exhibiting my swollen face, to find something liquefied to eat. Aunt Grace said, 'You look terrible,' her only words to me that day. Bernadette said 'You look like you need to wear a bra on your face.' I didn't mind because although she didn't have much time for Aunt Grace either, Bernadette's active evil side lay dormant in her presence. Aunt Grace, likewise, didn't pick on us anymore; she now preferred to ignore us.

The third type of afternoon was the Worst Type. This was similar to the Runaway afternoon, but instead of taunts and threats it was more violent, often involving the use of household weaponry. The Worst Type of afternoon differed in that it was predictable from the instant I entered the house after school, I could look at Bernadette, only home fifteen minutes before me, and everything from her posture to her clothing shouted angrily, and she had usually set upon one of my sisters or myself either verbally or physically before Mother was fully out of the drive.

Scissors and clipping garden tools were favourites of hers, given her predilection for hair removal. Angela's blonde curls were under threat and she would cower under the kitchen table while Bernadette circled like a cat, brandishing the shears. The twins, more resilient, feeling the double inner strength of each other's support, would try to challenge Bernadette, taunt her. They very irritatingly and also understandably wanted to hurt her back, and this always backfired.

I became notoriously fast in the bathroom.

'Did you wash your hands?' Mother would say, at other times.

'Yes, I did.'

'How could you possibly wash your hands in that time?'

'I did, honest.'

It was practice. But she was faster. In under forty five seconds, the time it took me to have a pee and rinse my hands, Bernadette could deftly tie the twins hair, or legs, or join them by belt at the waist, and push them down the stairs together, I could hear the bumping, rolling tumbling down, and their cries, above the flush.

Sometimes her torture would take more creative forms. Bernadette would astutely intercept Angela's last minute route to the only bathroom in the house and stay there, door locked, silently, until we were forced to go down the street, en masse, because I could leave no one unattended, to our neighbour Alice's house, begging relief. We hurried back, fearful and guilty for leaving Bernadette alone, to find her emerging from the bathroom, newly energised and on the offensive with her fingernails filed into sharp points.

She would go outside and return with hostages, new kittens that she threatened to kill with sharp kitchen knives. She demanded no ransom other than our terror. Bernadette had stopped hurting animals by then, but we didn't know that, we could not be sure.

I would have to stop her, physically, forcefully. Bernadette was surprisingly strong for a girl of nine, and she fought like a cornered wild animal, like a creature fighting to the death for its life. She had no regard for eyes or membranes of any sort, and thought nothing of pinning one down on the floor by their hair, all executed in a maliciously gleeful fashion. I was convinced that Bernadette actually enjoyed hurting us. I had some terrible, terrible fights with her. I thought she might kill me. I tried to fight defensively, and not to hurt Bernadette, not that I didn't want to. There were times when nothing would have given me greater pleasure than snapping her arm the wrong way at the elbow. But I knew even the tiniest scratch would be evidence against me at the end of the day, and in our kitchen court, the jury always ruled in Bernadette's favour. So, I would be dragged by hair or feet up and down stairs, through rooms and around furniture, always taking care not to poke her in the eye, break skin or cause a nosebleed – nothing that would leave marks on her to be punished for. I hid my own bruises; my distorted childhood logic telling me that was the best thing to do.

I lay in bed at night thinking of the things I could have done to hurt her, and then worry that she would attack me in my sleep, set the house on fire, murder my family while I was out. I began to have nightmares.

We would retreat on the Worst afternoons as soon as possible. Once my sisters were calmer, I would return for any pets under threat. The basement was darker and in the winter, colder than our own bedroom. It lacked most creature comforts and Maureen, our gopher, but it was perfectly adequate as an emergency bunker. The basement had Mother and Dad's old clothes to dress up in, and mice, and books. There was soft discarded furniture covered in bedspreads to sit on. There was plenty to do.

'Why does Bernadette hate us so much?' said Theresa. Mary was quiet. Theresa was the one that talked.

'I don't know. C'mon. I'll read you a book,' I said.

'I hate her too. It's her that's the bad one,' said Angela.

'Why is she so bad?' Theresa again.

'I don't know,' I said. 'What should we read?'

'*The Cat in the Hat.*'

'Not again. I'm tired of reading that.'

'But we like it.'

'The sun did not shine. It was too wet to play. So we sat in the house all that cold, cold, wet day.' I sped through the text.

It never occurred to any of us to go directly to our room on arriving home, or down into the basement, to perhaps avoid a conflict. It would mean defeat, giving up all hope that someday we would come home and watch television and have cookies and milk and enjoy them, and play and read and argue with our sisters like other people we knew did. Like normal people did. Normal. It was not a word we would say aloud.

All afternoons ended the same way. Dad came home at six thirty. The sound of Uncle Joe's car crackling the gravel in the driveway. We would be out of our bunker and into our living room positions before he was in the house. Dad and Uncle Joe would come in and say hello to all of us.

'Look at you lazy bums,' Uncle Joe would joke. 'Nothing better to do than sit around watching TV all day.'

I would smile and get up and move into the kitchen to start cooking supper. Life would return to what we could call normal.

In the beginning we sought justice. When Dad came home, we told him about Bernadette. He would sigh, and say; 'Tell your mother.' When Mother came home, we told her. She would bless herself and sigh, and say, 'I know it's hard for you girls, but it won't be for much longer. You must try and be patient with Bernadette, she's very sensitive.'

Later on, Theresa said to me, 'Sensitive, my ass.'

'Theresa! Where did you learn to speak like that?' I said.

Theresa giggled. 'Uncle Joe,' she said.

'Well that's a naughty thing to say,' I told her, unsuccessfully trying to stifle my own laughter. We knew it was hopeless talking to them about it so we gave up, sick of all their sighs. Time marched on; Bernadette got worse. It was just our life. We had to live that way, and that was that.

Everybody would eat my dinner. I learned how to cook with the ingredients and menus and recipes left by Mother, and I put it all together and became a more skilled cook than she was.

Mother came home after the priests had their supper. Dad would jump up off his sleepy sofa and greet her with a kiss and a glass of red wine. He missed her. She would come and find us in the bedroom, me reading a story, the little ones preparing for bed.

'Here Gloria, give me that, I'll take over.' She always kissed me and thanked me for the afternoon. I'd hand her the book and make my way downstairs to find some solitude, listening to her reading as I went.

Should we tell her the things that went on there that day?

Should we tell her about it?

Now, what SHOULD we do?

Well…

What would YOU do

If your mother asked you?'

****

Chapter Thirteen

December was down time for the Fish Shop. The marina, bustling with industry and activity from May to November, was windswept and deserted. Leisure boats had been lifted from the water and towed up to safety on breeze blocks in the garden, covered under thick canvas tea cosies.

The smaller seafood restaurants had closed for the dark winter months, the jingling ice cream trucks were gone and the Italian ice kiosk was boarded up for the winter. Old men came and sat in their cars to see the bay, looking out at the wind creating ripples in the water and blowing grooves in the sand along the beaches and the long grasses turning brown. Seven miles across Piper bay, the view of Beacon Island changed daily, sometimes a misty grey stripe, sometimes so crystal clear you could pick out the houses, clumps of little cubes on a watery shelf. Sometimes it wasn't there at all.

However, if you took some time, paused to look more closely you would detect an undercurrent of activity that would help spawn the next summer season - the diehard bay men, those that fished for a living, checking their lobster pots and crab cages, carpenters maintaining docks and moors, discussing the forecast over a cup of hot clam chowder while Uncle Vinny tried to sell them next year's marine insurance.

Uncle Tony and his barges still operated across the narrow inlet, with his reduced winter population of barge boys as well as those of the ferry captains and crew, water taxi drivers, clam diggers, their faithful water dogs, and seagulls. Davis's restaurant remained open, but only Thursdays through Sundays and without his floating satellite dining rooms, stored away in cosy winter boathouses courtesy of Uncle Tony.

Marina life in winter spent more time indoors, in small huts gathered around braziers or electric heaters, drinking coffee, re-charging, storing up energy for the next busy season. Times were harder, people tried to spread the summer takings sparingly through the winter like thin margarine over cold toast.

Ironically, Uncle Vinny was one of the few who did rather well during the winter, capitalising on the boredom and forced inertia. He opened his clam shack, six days a week, before sunrise to provide fried egg and bacon sandwiches and strong black coffee to the dawn workers. By midday he would have a collection of customers made up of cold and hungry fishermen, ferrymen, et cetera, all with too little to do but needing to pass the hours in a way somehow connected to salt water, fish, and each other.

When Uncle Vinny took control of the chowder bar, he did so with great enthusiasm, as he did with every one of his new schemes. He had experimented unsuccessfully with several business ventures, ice cream van, hot dog truck, and hamburger joint. Aunt Mo, his wife, Mother's big sister, was a Professional Woman with a Career, a rare breed at the time, especially within our extended family of baby-makers. She was a teacher; a position that allowed her both to look after the children and bring in enough income to support the family while Uncle Vinny indulged and exercised his dubious business prowess.

Food was his preferred product and with the chowder bar, he finally succeeded in finding a way of selling it to people for profit.

He moved into the shack with a designer's eye, convinced as always, that this would be the final opportunity, the one that would work. This time he was correct, and it did.

He decorated the shack in the style of his favourite Piper Bay eatery in the town, a tiny Italian cafe inexplicably called Schwartz's. As Uncle Vinny's shack had no tables, he wallpapered its interior with red and white checked paper, hung empty Chianti basket bottles from the ceiling, and framed his serving hatch with coloured lights. He hung a sign on the hatch: 'Vinny's Chowder Bar' and wore a striped apron over his t-shirt with 'Vinny' monogrammed across the front in large letters and tied a bandana around his neck. With his muscular arms sticking out of rolled up t-shirt sleeves, tattooed, 'Mo' on the left, a mermaid on the right, always on display whatever the temperature, he looked exactly right for his venture and perfectly at home. His menu was limited, a factor which was, he said, one of the keys to his success.

Clams any style
  ½ doz $2
  Doz $4

Chowder: Manhattan/New England
  Cup   50c
  bowl   65c

  Egg Sandwich
  any style   75c

Coffee   30c

Various other dishes, however, could be available by prior arrangement. He leased a coke machine which stood outside the Fish Shop and he would provide change if needed.

In the winter the hatch stayed closed and his customers were known locals who would enter through the back via the Fish Shop. There they sat in the festive glow of the coloured lights until the afternoon light faded, and they drifted home.

Even on the coldest days, with his skeletal clientele made up of mainly his friends, Uncle Vinny wore his apron and wrote out a bill, however small, for each of his customers, tallied and collected at the end of their visit. The winter provided him with a tidy sideline in insurance brokerage, an ailing business he'd conducted half heartedly out of his study at home before the advent of the chowder bar. The chowder bar's success had a knock on effect on Uncle Vinny, increasing his business confidence and proving to be the perfect sales venue.

'You never know, with some of those little boats you guys have,' he'd say. 'You never know what can happen.' He'd shake his head sadly, looking out at the heaving December sea.

'No, Vince. Not worth me forking out for insurance. I only take the boat out two, three weekends a year, over to Charlene's beach house. Rest of the time I'm someone else's passenger.'

Uncle Vinny leaned forward on his elbows, the mermaid swimming under his bulging muscles, 'Suit yourself. Nowadays, you don't carry boat insurance you could be open to a lawsuit.'

'Who's gonna sue me?'

'Maybe a seaplane crashes, swimmer in trouble, another boat capsizes in a sudden storm. You're out there, trying to save people, they get hurt getting into your boat. Or run over. People sue for everything nowadays. Like I said, you never know what can happen. You could lose Charlene's house, your house. Bet you wish you'd forked out then.'

Uncle Vinny left some to wonder whether he was issuing a warning or a threat. Whichever, they bought and renewed insurance. Business thrived.

This was a favourite time of mine to go to the Fish Shop and its environs, when it was quiet, cold, and grey, populated only by members of a very privileged and exclusive club to which I belonged: the year-rounders.

Because of my afternoon babysitting obligations these visits to Dad and my Uncles were severely curtailed, but I ached to go, so I did, frequently but surreptitiously, as it was usually during times when I was legally required to be in a classroom. The necessity of self-concealment sapped any enjoyment I might have had, as my pleasure was mainly derived from the eavesdropping as well as chats with my Uncles and Dad, who would have angrily sent me back to school if they'd seen me. The added stress of that possibility soon put a stop to my unauthorised marina trips. Having to hide like a fugitive from my nearest and dearest in a place that I felt I so intrinsically belonged was too painful. I soon found alternative places to escape to.

The Christmas holidays were a welcome respite from the traumatic afternoons as Mother was given two weeks off. She resumed ownership of the household and I was set free. As soon as school finished I would go directly to the marina where Uncle Vinny would present me with a steamy hot chocolate, tearing the bill for it off the pad, winking, and saying, 'I'll take care of this one.'

I could stay there and listen to their banter, or go back deep inside the

Fish Shop to sit with Dad and Uncle Joe, or watch the inferior goldfish in their cloudy bowl. They were acquired after the removal of the irreplaceable tropical fish, nothing precious about them. There was an assortment of stray cats to woo and feed and one shaggy grey dog, forgotten, neglected or abandoned by its owner - no one remembered.

'Didn't he fall off a boat?'

'Nah, that was Cap'n Giffy's spaniel.'

'I think he just got dumped here by some tourist.'

'People get dogs, then they don't want 'em.'

'He was a stray, just started hanging around for Vinny's clamburgers.'

'Now we're stuck with him.'

'I don't make clamburgers.'

'You do for that dog. I saw you.'

'Take him to the pound then.'

'I can't do that. He's a good dog.'

They called him Grouper, and he sprawled out on the floor, easy to step over; got up to fetch a ball, barked when he was supposed to and dog-smiled the rest of the time. I took him with me when I went out into the cold and wandered along the marina, now bleak and barren, but more beautiful than ever. I could smell icy cleanliness in the air, a meditative, rejuvenating quality in the atmosphere and I would bundle up and curl up in amongst some sandy grasses, shut my eyes and feel warm and safe until someone found me at going home time.

'Come on Gloria. You'll freeze to death, how long have you been there? Home time,' said Dad.

'I'm fine. I haven't been here very long. The sun's warm today, and the dog's warm.'

'Gloria, why don't you want to go over to friend's houses? Don't you have any friends, at your age you should be out with friends, not sitting in sand dunes or clam bars with a bunch of old men,' said Dad, in a rare open display of parental concern.

'Yeah,' Uncle Joe chipped in, 'when Francine was your age she was always out, up to all sorts of no good I bet. Or else I couldn't get them out of the house. Crowds of them.'

'Don't you have friends?'

'I have friends,' I said, in my defence, which was not quite a blatant lie, although it was approaching it. I had no particularly close friends. I knew people to say 'Hello' to. My busy housekeeping schedule didn't allow much time for developing relationships.

'Hey, there's an idea, Gloria,' said Dad, enthusiastically,

'Do like Francine. You can always bring friends home after school. I know you have to take care of your sisters but there's no reason you can't do that with a friend.'

Of course there was every reason I couldn't do that with a friend, even if I'd had any close enough to ask. Dad spoke as though he lived in a different house than I did. He did, actually. He lived in an imaginary home where there were seven happy children and two happy and hard working parents. It was what he saw.

'Okay, thanks. Maybe I'll do that,' I said, appeasing him.

'Good, that's that then. You just go ahead, anytime, you don't even need to ask,' said Dad, satisfied. He figured he'd solved a problem, filed it away in the 'forgedaboudit' section of his head.

When I entered Piper High it was with high expectations and firm resolutions. This was it; my life was about to begin. Everything was going to be okay, fall into place. No more backward nuns, straight lines, zipped lips. Church could be a once a week thing, like it was for the rest of the world. I was leaping out of the pond and diving into the vast ocean; full of like-minded girls and good-looking boys, I could fish to my heart's content and throw back anything that wasn't going to taste good.

It wasn't like that. After a few hours I felt more like a swampland creature, clogged up and struggling to reach the clear water where those nicely scrubbed and dressed girls and boys in my dream were.

It was an unfriendly place, big and busy, everybody always in a hurry. The teachers were like greyhounds let out of the gate, raced through their lesson and then disappeared behind doors into their staff room sanctuaries.

I still carried the infection of old playground gossip; the family who smelled of fish. People avoided me, perhaps not recalling exactly what it was I had, but a lingering memory told them to steer clear lest they catch something. It didn't help that I had no fashion sense, having spent my entire life in third-hand jeans and blouses. With life as it was, the washing machine was running about three weeks behind time and the only thing in our house that got ironed anymore was hair. My grubby clothes, scooped off a pile on the floor every morning developed creases so condensed they resembled the inside of a ruptured golf ball.

My brother Gabe didn't exactly ignore me but was caught up with his own affairs and in my exposed state I felt neglected. I could see that he was swimming in the clean water and he seemed much older than me. I could have used the support of a big brother but bad timing dictated that the two year gap in our ages spanned a wider chasm then than it ever had or ever would again.

The truth was, the only people I said hello to were other oddballs like myself, edgy, unkempt kids that seemed tough and streetwise, yet vulnerable in the institutionalised school corridors. Most were older than me. I recognised the kindred spirit and was attracted by it and after a period of saying hello, I learned names. Some had nicknames: Cootie, Ace, Juicy Jeans, or altered versions of their own names: Richboy, Jessieback, Bevels, Jaybone. I was attracted to them, the level of their delinquency was something I could aspire to without fear of failure.

****

Chapter Fourteen

Dad never learned that it was humanly impossible for nine people to come to an agreement over the perfect Christmas tree. So every December, full of good tidings, he piled us, a bag of sandwiches and a flask of hot chocolate, circus clown style, into that year's clapped out vehicle and suffered us the uncomfortable drive across to the North Shore Tree Nursery run by a relation so distant he was Chinese.

'Keep it in the family, I always say,' said Dad.

'That guy can't be related to us. He's Chinese.'

'He's not Chinese.' 'Don't be so rude.'

'He is so Chinese. Look at him.'

'He is not Chinese. A good Bronx boy. He's your third cousin, twice removed, or something like that. Papa Joe will tell you. You have millions of cousins. Now shut up and look at the scenery.'

The scenery, thirty miles of short scrubby pine trees in sandy soil. We took one quick look and then started arguing instead, it passed the time quicker. The outing had a muscle memory reflex all of it's own, that of conflict. Bernadette usually brought along some small instrument of torture, such as a safety pin or nail scissors, just to keep things interesting.

When we arrived on the north shore, the other side of the island, it was like we'd crossed the deck of a large ship. Everything looked the same, just the sun was in the wrong place. The North Shore Tree Nursery was dressed up for the holidays and renamed Christmas Tree Land. We entered a forest of cut conifer through a twinkling arbour of ivy.

'Hey Tony!'

'Hey Eddie!'

The Chinese cousin and Dad hugged, slapped each other on the back.

'How ya doin? Have a look round, take your time, see whatcha like.'

He wandered off, yabbering away to people, part English, part Chinese, part something else, maybe Italian.

'I told you he was Chinese,' Gabe mumbled.

'He's your cousin.'

'Okay, okay.'

'You have millions of cousins.'

'All right, already. He's my cousin.'

'Don't talk back to me. You're not too old for a smack.'

We looked at trees, and more trees. We stood one up and circled round it, accepted by one, two, rejected by three. The decision had to be unanimous. We only agreed on size, the tree should be as big as possible. Except for Mother who'd rather have a small one, suitable for the tiny room, but she didn't say much, she just waited it out. We all knew what would happen. Nobody got tired of arguing about the tree, so the dispute escalated and got noisy. Bernadette, agitated, would start stabbing pine needles or holly leaves into any exposed skin she could find on Angela. There would be tears. Dad would explode, shepherd us back to the car.

'What the hell do you think this is?' he'd shout, 'people are trying to choose Christmas trees, for God's sake.'

'Tony, don't shout.'

'I'm not shouting. It's these kids, putting on a show. What's wrong with you kids today? Okay, everybody back in the car.'

We sat, with Mother, crammed inside the car eating soggy sandwiches, drinking the lukewarm hot chocolate. He came back with Eddie and together they tied a trussed up Christmas tree to the top of the car. Eddie leaned in the window with a big smile.

'Bye guys – see you next year!'

We were driven home in silence, each nursing a private disappointment. The tree was unloaded and carried in. It stood in the living room like an upended arrow until its net corsetry was removed, branches filling the small space with the sharp scent of the foliage. The boughs of the tree bounced back up gently.

'Whatdya think?' Dad said, proudly regarding the tree, 'Good, or what?'

We agreed it was good.

'We'll leave it to settle overnight, decorate it tomorrow.'

Overnight the tree stood in the darkened living room and as it's branches loosened and relaxed, so did we.

Christmas was the time of the year that came close to Dad's imaginary happy home. It wasn't as stressful as Thanksgiving, being much messier and informal. All of the children and both parents had gifts to open, which made them happy, and happy children made happy parents.

Again, our house was the designated venue for the day's celebrations, a choice utterly inappropriate given its size in proportion to the numbers that had to be stuffed in with the humongous tree and fed.

If I'd known at that time that it was actually Mother's decision to have all the huge holiday gatherings in our home, I may have suggested an alternative. However, the generally relaxed and cheerful nature of the holiday usually eased us fairly painlessly through the day.

It began before dawn with the bejewelled tree, buried under presents, glowing peacefully in the fairy lighting, then ambushed by an overzealous stampede down the stairs of children set on the greedy destruction of that brief moment of Christmas Eve magic, transforming what was left of the living room area around the tree, into a sea of torn wrapping paper, empty boxes and bits of plastic. You could almost hear the angels running for cover.

Mother and Dad sat together on the sofa, sleepily looking on, drinking coffee, untangling a ribbon or assembling a robot, contentedly absorbing this culmination of the year's efforts and periodically reminding us that it was Jesus' birthday.

Soon after, food preparation would begin but this was relaxed food, much of it prepared in advance, cold roast chickens and glazed hams, canapés, bright Santa-red crabs and lobsters stuffed and dressed, shrimp cocktails, marinated squid, mixed salad, bean salad, pineapple and marshmallow salad, salad salads, the most arduous work involved was the display and presentation of the Christmas table, which, similar to its predecessor the Christmas tree, was beautifully and carefully designed for the purpose of gluttonous destruction.

Gabe, whose rare attendance at our home was rivalling Papa Joe's, due to a new job as well as the time he spent out socially, helped Mother and I with the food while Dad, Bernadette and Maureen stayed with the younger girls in the paper pit reading instructions, putting things together and enjoying the spoils of the morning. Even Bernadette, though still a mystery to us all, was passive.

Guests began to arrive, cousins beaming, wearing new boots or sweaters and carrying shopping bags bulging with yet more gifts for us, Aunts bearing extra cutlery and crockery and Uncle Joe in a separate car with huge Papa Joe, who sat in his ceremonious big-enough chair and seemed slightly less formidable than normal. Uncle Tony in a Santa hat, bellowing 'ho ho ho', Aunt Grace in a new fur coat, Aunt Gloria and Mother in twin blue suits each more surprised than the other at this coincidental choice.

Sherry, wine and pink champagne flowed and the day passed in a joyful haze until we all stumbled happily out to celebrate Evening Mass and then came home to collapse.

By the time school started again the holidays were a dim and distant memory. The last shreds of gift-wrap had been cleared up and the memory of Christmas morning reduced to bits of plastic toys to step on, sending shooting pains up legs, transistors that had disintegrated, multiplied and migrated to bedrooms, bathrooms and corridors to embed themselves in dusty corners and underwear drawers for eternity.

School hadn't improved in my absence, not that I really expected it to, but there was always a forlorn hope that on returning, either it or I would have altered in some way, making it bearable. I dodged and ducked classes whenever I could, whole days if I could manage, wandering the small section of coastline I called my own.

Uncle Tony found me sitting in a duck blind early one morning in the middle of cold, dark January. I had walked some way along the edge of the bay, along to the end of wooden pilings around a bend to where the beach became natural, far enough away from the inlet and marina to be safe, I thought. I hadn't counted on Uncle Tony being out in one of his barges. He was collecting the Christmas trees.

'Gloria!' he shouted, startling me out of my reverie. 'Are you all right?'

I waved and nodded to him.

'Stay there,' he said, and manoeuvred the barge to a rickety nearby jetty; an abandoned private dock. Testing its solidity first, he walked to the end and along the rough beach to the duck blind where I had been sitting.

'Not a very good hiding place, is it?' he said, laughing. 'Lucky for ducks. Are you dressed warm enough to come aboard?' He led me back down to the end of the jetty and on to the barge, *The Flotsam*, which was carrying a stack of discarded Christmas trees.

'Come on. Come with me while I load up. What time do you need to go back to look after your sisters?' he asked.

'Three-fifteen,' I said, sheepishly, as we had not yet addressed the matter of my truancy.

'Fine, we can make it in that time. Now get inside the cabin and get down until we're out of the way. There's some hot coffee in there.'

Inside the tiny cabin I hid, and poured myself a coffee from the thermos, listening to Uncle Tony's and other voices and the sound of the trees hitting the deck as he loaded up.

Finally I felt the barge leave the dock and make its way slowly up the inlet. It would pass Dad and Uncle Joe's fish shop on the right hand side, any minute. I heard them shout to each other.

'Hey little Tony!'

'Big Tony! Hey, you want some soup to take with you?'

'No time today – see you later.'

They prefixed their names with the adjectives that described them by both size and age, and so did everyone else, in order to distinguish between them. So if Gabe had been a Tony, what would his prefix be, I wondered. Baby Tony, or Tiny Tony I supposed. Better off as a Gabe, then.

I could hear the dog bark. I felt ashamed, stowed away from my Dad, deprived of the opportunity to share this experience more openly. I wished I could stand and wave, go and get some soup, maybe take the dog with us.

A minute later, Uncle Tony said, 'It's your own fault, Gloria,' and then the engine surged as we left the inlet.

'You can come out now.'

I climbed out of the cabin. Uncle Tony's eyes locked ahead of him looking at where he was going.

'You have to go to school, Gloria.' He was angry. 'You have to go to school. It's the only way, Gloria, the only way.' He shook his head as he spoke.

I had never seen Uncle Tony angry before, and it was upsetting that he wouldn't look at me. His knuckles were gripped white. We both stayed silent for a while, listening to the engine and feeling the sharp windy sea spray on our faces.

Every year the town paid Uncle Tony and his small fleet of barges to transport the used Christmas trees over to Beacon Island and distribute them evenly along the sand dunes, the idea being that this would slow down the process of erosion. People came out from the city to visit the Island, spend a day in the summer. It appealed to them, so close to the city yet so far removed from city life. They started building houses on it, raising both its profile and the price of real estate substantially, creating jobs and needs for the locals. It was really just a sand bar, a barrier beach that from the air looked like a thin strip of sand, a tidal afterthought. It could easily be washed away in a strong enough storm. But now, the idea that Beacon Island could turn into a desirable and profitable place, it would be disastrous to allow it to wash away. *The Flotsam* was Uncle Tony's largest barge and could carry considerably more trees than the other smaller boats.

'Why don't you have a barge called *The Jetsam*?' I asked, to break the ice.

'Because jetsam is the stuff that sinks,' he said, shaking his head again. 'Bad luck. A boat called jetsam would never survive what the sea threw at it.'

Even with its considerable size, it would take *The Flotsam* and the other boats several days and many trips to move all the trees. Gar-barges were just about the only sign of marine business life in the dead of January.

A small fishing boat tooted at us across the water, the skipper, in a baseball hat, waved.

'We must be quite a sight,' I said, 'with this mountain of Christmas trees.'

The pile of trees had a tragic beauty about it; these prematurely chopped, once celebrated, decorated cherished centrepieces, now sailing on the ghost boat to driftwood. The sun picked out shiny diamonds of light created by pieces of tinsel left on their hastily undressed branches.

'Gloria, you should go to visit Venice. Everything goes by boat there. People, furniture, building materials, everything. Even Christmas trees, I'm sure.'

'What about garbage?' I asked.

'But of course,' he roared with laughter and picked up a small Christmas tree from the top of the pile to use as a prop and mimed punting the boat with it, 'And we mustn't forget the gondoliers.' He then yodelled a wordless little tune that he called his 'gondolier song.'

Uncle Tony often dreamed of Venice, and Gar-barges was his realisation of that dream. At the end of his song he bowed deeply.

'Gar-barges Madam? Always at your disposal,' causing us both to laugh uproariously.

'Someday I'll take you there, Gloria,' he said, becoming serious again. 'But you have to go to school.'

****

Chapter Fifteen

Unfortunately I didn't follow Uncle Tony's advice. What was there to go to school for? The few friends I had were not close ones. Neither did my mediocre passing grades and minimal contributions to class win me any extra awards or attentions from my teachers.

My most immediate need was for freedom, and I discovered this was an easily attainable goal - simply by not going to school.

Following the dentistry reprieve, the only other two afternoons I was excused from my duties at home was due to a double detention. I said I had to stay after school to retake a test I had missed. The test was in two parts.

The detention was a punishment for truancy. No one at home knew about the truancy because I stole the mail before it could be opened, and intercepted any correspondence from the school. I didn't attend the detention either because I wrote a note from my parents stating that I was needed at home to do the very things I was evading. By this time I was a fairly expert handwriting thief and my skills at becoming invisible were steadily improving.

The sad fact that no one noticed my crimes led me to believe I was someone unnoticeable, full stop, completely and utterly non-memorable. I could only take this very depressing image of myself and try and turn it into something positive. Aren't I clever, I thought, I can skip school for days and no one knows. I am so good at it, they can't see me. Even my brother Gabe, who was in his last year at the same school, in the same building, failed to spot my descent into worthlessness.

After being caught in the duck blind by Uncle Tony, I no longer went to the marina to pass the many idle hours I created. Instead, I wandered the streets, but very carefully. It was a small town full of my many relatives; second cousins I'd met once might recognise me from a photograph.

'Hey, I saw Tony's daughter the other day, you know, Vito's cousin's son. Married Mary Russo. I'm sure it was her, seen her picture. Nice looking kid, what, she drop outta school or something?'

'Really? You sure? Her? She was just a little thing.'

'Positive.'

'I'll call Al, ask him. Haven't seen Tony in ages, maybe I'll go down there soon.'

'Yeah, she was buying gum, downtown in Oscars. Sure it was a school day too.'

Identifying local pedigree in strangers was a family sport, a bit like celebrity spotting on a more intimate scale. The information would snake its way down to the marina, eventually, I was sure.

I found the back corners and soda shops and was gradually assimilated into the small and unsavoury band of misfits made up of the people I said 'Hello' to that I recognised as kindred spirits. We passed the time playing pinball, smoking cigarettes, trying to keep warm, walking, aimlessly along quiet residential streets or sitting in and around an old oak tree in what we cynically referred to as the Hundred Square Foot Wood.

Some light relief came in the form of Skate, one in the hopeless group of bored, unimaginative and damaged people that visited the same places. He was lanky and longhaired and I perceived a twinkle in his eye. He earned his moniker by his legendary smooth, slippery, graceful, gliding coolness, or so he would have me believe. I am sure now that it was Skate himself that invented his nickname and his ultra hip persona. Several years my senior, he had a car, and two jobs, one as a mechanic another as a night barman at Creel's, a spit and sawdust old man's bar. And now he had me. I wasn't that difficult to get.

'Hey, Gloria, you are so gorgeous today, look at your hair. Come on, let's go for a ride.'

He gave me all of his attention, courted me and made me feel special.

He couldn't have had to work on it too hard, considering he was wooing someone whose idea of special attention was having an impacted tooth removed.

It wasn't long before we joined the cars lined up along the marina, safely at night, long after closing time, looking out into Piper Bay but not seeing much of it from the back seat. I finally understood Uncle Joe's joke and discovered what all those people watching submarine races through steamy windows were really up to.

I began to bring Skate home after school with me. I introduced him by his proper name, Philip, not wanting him or my sisters to discover that he shared a name with one of our cats, named for a fish, an entirely different brand of slippery coolness and graceful gliding that he imagined for himself.

Skate was not the type of boy a parent wanted to be spending the afternoons with their fourteen year old daughter, but so elevated was I by his attentions I was completely unaware of this. Skate, although harmless enough, was known, though not to me, as town lowlife, a second-rate pot head come joy rider who worked part time garages and bars and drove a station wagon with curtains on the back windows.

No wonder Mother had a brief expression of dismay when I first brought him home. She didn't interfere, however. When Dad suggested he might be slightly older than the boys I ought to be dating, I turned on him.

'You said I could bring a friend home after school. I'm just doing what you said I should do.'

My parents didn't mention the relationship to me again. I learned later on from the key holder of the great secrets chamber, Uncle Tony, that they did discuss it. In fact, everyone discussed it, but in the family method of two at a time, pass it on, twist it around, get it wrong, and don't ever mention it in front of anyone, especially me. Uncle Tony said they must have decided to ride it out.

It was only Gabe, who berated me for my association with Skate, of which he knew more details than my parents, information tunnelled up to him from the murky underworld of small town layabouts.

He confronted me in a school stairwell, grabbing my arm roughly, angrily. Of course I knew who he was, but saw so little of him that there was a moment that could have convinced me he was a stranger, but then he spoke.

'What are you doing going out with that asshole?' he said.

I was so shocked I didn't answer him. I rarely saw him in school, and we certainly never spoke to each other apart from a cursory nod or to exchange essential domestic information. He shouted at me in a loud whisper, and I was aware of automotive movement around us, throngs of other pupils changing classes, pouring up and down the steps filling the stairwell. The bell rang and he released my arm and left me, still stunned, to slide down to sitting position in the empty stairwell, now deserted. I stared at the shiny enamel surroundings; bumpy walls gloss-painted the colour of schools and sounding of echo.

However, I ignored Gabe's warning. I was delighted with Skate's presence in the afternoons. It was like having a big puppy. He flopped onto the sofa and watched TV with Angela and the twins, joking and playing with them. He made them laugh. If I sat with him, he would put his arm around me and my sisters regarded me with newfound awe and respect. Above all, Bernadette behaved when he was there, either sitting quietly or more often, going to her room, still silent, but a beast lying dormant. The sidelong looks she cast in my direction warned me of a future balance being struck, of her intention of making up for these lost days.

There was a change in Bernadette, however, that I saw happening. Although she often created havoc among my little sisters and me, she stopped torturing the animals. In fact, she began to treat them with the utmost respect and kindness; patiently wooing them back to receive her affections, a slow and tedious task considering she'd scared them out of their wits for many, many cat and dog years. She would sit outside in a shrub with a small offering such as a scrap of cod or squid, and coax the outdoor cats to come to her. She did this with an intense, focused persistence, oblivious to distractions. Looking out the back door, down the sloping back lawn, partially concealed in the shadows, she resembled a frightened animal herself.

'Bernadette,' I would say in my more responsible moments, 'you ought to put a coat on, it's freezing out there.'

Bernadette had three responses to my suggestions, action, silence or swearing. If she acted, she would simply say 'okay' and come in to fetch an umbrella or a coat and return to her post. If she answered me with

152

silence, I would repeat my request once or twice and then leave her, and if she chose to swear she would verbally abuse me. Profanity was another new element to Bernadette's character, and came in levels of coarseness.

'Get the hell out of here'; 'Leave me alone, bitch'; 'Fuck off you cunt.'

I found this reaction particularly upsetting. 'Fuck you too', I'd think, initially, 'sorry I even bothered, go ahead and freeze to death', although I wouldn't dare say it out loud. But then uneasiness about her settled on me like an extra skin, worrying and bothersome. I couldn't shed it. There was something happening to her.

Skate paid little mind to Bernadette, he was cordial and polite and she appeared to like him because she would smile at him.

'Is there something wrong with that funny looking sister of yours?' he once said, in the presence of the twins, who squealed with laughter.

'She isn't funny looking, she's just quiet,' I said, bristling at his question, defensive for Bernadette in spite of everything. His rosy glow greyed slightly. He never mentioned Bernadette again but I looked at her with fresh eyes, trying to determine what it could be that caused him to phrase his question so offensively, and why I couldn't see it.

Maureen was now in the same high school as me and hated it just as much but for different reasons. She was busily making her application to every Catholic Financial Aid and Scholarship Committee she could find in order that she could switch to a Catholic High School next year, and studying all the time in order to achieve the highest marks possible to better her advantage, spending most afternoons in the library after school. I had no doubt she would be successful. I'd already seen many examples of the power of her faith in action.

I declared that Maureen should share some of the afternoon babysitting, an idea presented to me by Skate, who wanted more time with me to himself, no doubt in the back of his car or deep in the carpet of needles in the Hundred Square Foot Wood, but so smitten was I, I didn't care why, just that I was wanted.

Maureen flew into a rage of almost Bernadette proportions at the very notion of giving up her prayerful, studious hours. Her unexpected and uncharacteristic anger dampened my confidence.

'It is not a good idea!' she was shouting. 'Who told you it was a good idea? I bet it was your boyfriend. You should think for yourself.'

'For Christ's sake, Maureen, it's only two afternoons, maybe even just one, if you're that upset...'

'Don't you dare bring Christ into this and try and turn things around.'

'Me? Turn things around?' I said, 'It's not fair, Maureen, I shouldn't have to do it all the time. You're old enough now, for God's sake.'

The second mention of the Lord's name in vain was Maureen's cue to turn on her heel and exit angrily.

'Well, that wasn't very Christ like of her, was it?' quipped Skate, who overheard most of the exchange.

'Oh, shut up,' I said. He was beginning to irritate me, with almost everything he said and did. I was critical of his appearance, his driving, his eating habits and even the way he carried himself, and yet I still sought his company and was possessive and jealous when I wasn't with him. I was so addicted to being desired that I didn't yet realise I loathed him. I hadn't learned that desire could be a choice I made.

We began to take the girls out in the afternoons. It started with a short trip for ice cream.

'Bernadette, we're just going out to get some ice cream, do you want to come?' I could feel the tension in my sisters as they silently hoped she would say no.

'No.' Release of tension.

'Do you want me to bring some back for you?'

'Yes.'

We left Bernadette at home alone. Maureen was at the library. I worried somewhat while we were out, but we returned and all was well and Bernadette ate her ice cream and even thanked me. I sensed it suited Bernadette to be left alone.

Our trips became longer and more frequent, but only on days when Maureen was at the library. Theresa, Mary and Angela loved the outings. For weeks we went for walks and drives and to parks and playgrounds, anywhere that didn't cost anything.

'Bernadette is fine at home, girls, but we mustn't mention that we

154

leave her to Mother or Dad, so they don't worry,' I said. 'Or Maureen. But she is fine there, honest, she likes being home by herself.'

My sisters nodded seriously. They wouldn't betray me, because if they did, the outings would cease. They weren't exactly the afternoons Skate had in mind but he found them preferable to the messy overcrowded living room. We were all so much happier outside of the oppressive home atmosphere, the stuffy smoky room and the threat of Bernadette.

Skate would try and grab me from behind when the girls weren't looking, groping in my jeans or under my sweater. I would push him away playfully, at the same time wishing he would wash more often. His long blonde hair, once so alluring, flopping over his eyes, now held little more for me than a greasy whiff that I avoided with my nose. It was the same hair, though.

'You were wearing that jacket when I first met you.'

'I know. I always wear this jacket.'

'Yeah, that's the point. Don't you have something else?'

'I like this jacket.'

'But do you ever wash it?'

'Come on, Gloria. Gimme a break. Let's go play handball.'

We played handball in the high school parking lot. I was very good at handball, master skill of the serial truant, and had some heated matches with Skate, who was my equal on the wall. I taught Theresa and Mary, hoping they would never have as much idle time to get as accomplished as I was. Angela was content to chase stray balls and watch.

On the way home Skate looked into his rear view mirror guiltily at the sound of a police siren, then he laughed.

'I always think they're coming for me when I hear that sound, even if I haven't done anything wrong,' he said, as the vehicle, which was an ambulance, overtook him. 'It's only an ambulance.'

'Whenever my mother hears a siren,' I said, ignorant of my prophecy, 'she always drives back and passes our house, no matter where she is in town, in case it's on fire.'

When we arrived back, the house wasn't on fire. But there was a police car outside our house along with Aunt Grace, her face drained of colour. Her lipstick mouth was a pale thin line and her arms were folded. Her body language was crying out for a bomb disposal unit. I got out of the car nervously, shielding Angela and the twins behind me.

'What's wrong Aunt Grace?'

She looked not at me, but at Skate, and very controlled, said, 'Thank you for bringing the girls home. The police would like to speak to you.' Her words were wasted because he'd already been bundled into the police car.

'Now, all of you go inside,' she said.

I went inside and Uncle Joe was there with Uncle Tony. I was so happy to see them and I smiled but their faces were nearly as grim as Aunt Grace's. I started to cry.

'What did he do? What happened? Where's Bernadette?'

'Exactly, Gloria.' Aunt Grace finally blew.

'That's exactly it. Where is Bernadette? Do you know? Who's supposed to know? Who's looking after her?' She was shouting now. 'No one, that's who, because you left her alone while you take your little sisters out joyriding with a criminal.'

Aunt Grace, my sisters and I were now unable to halt our rising levels of hysteria. Uncle Joe took charge of his wife and Uncle Tony took the children.

'Go into the kitchen, sit down and calm down, Gloria,' said Uncle Tony sternly. 'I'll get to you in a minute.' He then reassured the snivelling twins and Angela and sat them in front of the television where they would shortly become oblivious to everything around them, and joined me in the kitchen.

'What...'I began, already becoming tearful again.

Uncle Tony silenced me. He raised his hand in a silencing gesture.

'Quiet, Gloria. I talk, you listen.'

The ambulance had gone by the time Skate and the girls and I had arrived home. Bernadette had fallen out of a tree and broken her collarbone and her elbow, hobbled inside and very sensibly phoned Aunt Grace who phoned an ambulance and ran round the block to discover what she feared, that Bernadette was home unsupervised, and called the police to report Skate as a possible child abductor.

'But that's ridiculous!' I said. 'He's my boyfriend, what does she think she's doing getting the police to come and arrest him?'

Uncle Tony, although he agreed with me that she overreacted, sympathised with Aunt Grace, given the reputation of my 'grimy companion' as he referred to him.

'I told you to be quiet. And they're not arresting him, they know who he is. They'll just tell him off and send him on his way. You're underage, he shouldn't be carting you and your sisters all over town in a car with curtains in the windows. The people who will really suffer the most from this will be your parents. Okay, I'm done, what have you got to say?'

I had nothing to say.

'And if I were you I'd get rid of that grease monkey,' he said.

'I will,' I said.

Skate beat me to the dumping ground, though, by coming to the door shortly after Uncle Tony's lecture and his release from the police car. Uncle Tony refused him entry to the house so he informed me bluntly shouting from the doorstep to the kitchen that I was history.

That was the end of Skate, or the Grease Monkey as I too would end up referring to him, but I was utterly devastated and heartbroken at the loss of my first love. Any negative thoughts creeping into my mind about him instantly swapped places with the positive. Suddenly he smelled masculine.

I thought him so hip and manly and wise, although our conversations were limited, and generally led to his favourite topic, his swollen member, and we'd practice the correct procedures in order to maximise his pleasure, him telling me what to do every step of the way. Inexperienced as I was and idolising him as I did, I took the view that these lessons were valuable instruction in lovemaking. He was my mentor, I was his eager pupil. It wasn't until much later when I acknowledged what a jerk I'd hooked up with that it occurred to me that making a man's penis feel nice wasn't exactly rocket science.

Mother and Dad came home and didn't speak to me for a few hours, working up to it by throwing cold looks my way while engaged in other parenting duties. They dismissed my offers of help. When they had finished and could direct all their attention my way, I endured more castigation until the liberation of being sent to my room. I found Bernadette there, lying quietly with her eyes open. Her arm was in plaster. I felt I should say something to her.

'Does it hurt much?'

'We were trying to catch a bird,' she said.

'Who's we? Was someone with you?' I said, confused.

'The cats. The other cats, of course,' she said, and then meowed at me.

She turned over, cat like, making cat sounds, making paw-like gestures with her unplastered arm.

'We're sleepy now,' she said.

I turned in my bed and faced the wall, ending the conversation. I was really scared of Bernadette. I was frightened of her physically, and frightened of the lack of connection between her words and her actions. She had no reason to be violent towards my sisters and yet she was. Who was to say she wouldn't commit bigger crimes, murder, or arson? The scariest thing about her was that I had no idea what went on in her mind. Of course, I wasn't alone in feeling this fear, but I didn't know that, I didn't know that it terrified Mother and Dad especially, but for different reasons, and it also worried my aunts and uncles, older cousins and Bernadette's teachers. I didn't know because it was a subject that couldn't be talked about. Bernadette's mind was the biggest secret of all.

****

Chapter Sixteen

Although we still referred to it as 'Gabe's new job', he had been working in Davis's restaurant kitchen for some months. He started out clearing tables, trailing the waiters but found himself more captivated by the preparation of food in the kitchen so Davis moved him in there, first washing dishes but within a week he moved to prepping vegetables. Now Gabe was learning how to cook, and embraced his newly discovered passion with vocational commitment.

I suspected my brother had a hidden side to his life, a somewhat shady side on the streets with questionable companions and delinquent pastimes and my suspicions were confirmed when I took up with Skate and briefly trod in his shadowy steps. Gabe, though, had graduated from lowlife before I arrived there. Now, his life was consumed by food. He was in the restaurant kitchen all week, even in his off hours, and when he wasn't in Davis's kitchen he was in Mother's. Previously, Gabe's female companions had been nothing more than a collection of voices on the end of the phone that were usually told he was out. Now he had one steady girlfriend with a name, Beth, a face, and a seat at our table. Beth was a waitress he'd met at the restaurant. He brought her home to share when he cooked Sunday dinners.

It was lovely to rediscover my brother. After the incident in the school corridor when he'd berated me for the company I was keeping, I briefly turned against him, feeling he'd been too harsh. We never spoke about the incident although by the time I saw Gabe again at home I had been over it a thousand times in my head and prepared my indignant speech, as after all, Skate was also one of Gabe's former associates.

However the next time I saw Gabe he apologised.

'Sorry about the other day at school Gloria,' he said. 'I was wrong.'

There was no more complete apology than that, and it was enough for me, as feeling anger for Gabe was like carbonated hot chocolate. Unsustainable.

He was very happy with his saucepans and his girlfriend and it lifted the spirits of the house when he was in it. Beth was a slight, sociable, brown haired girl that laughed when Gabe was funny and nodded solemnly when he was serious and talked to us and Mother and Dad, always animated, gesticulating feverishly, a language we all understood and it warmed her to us. She and Gabe clearly enjoyed the long hours and hard work that was restaurant life.

'Did you see that woman in the suit walk out on her husband?'

'The pineapple?'

'No, not her, it was one of the melons. She started it.'

'We had a domestic in the dining room today – had to call the cops.'

'What's a melon?'

'The other guy, we think must have been the boyfriend...'

'Her boyfriend? But he knocked her into the bay...'

'A melon's a type, they always order the melon.'

'She had to be hauled up onto a passing clam boat...'

Gabe could cook fish. In Dad's eyes, this fact transformed an occupation he considered sissy into what it was, a skilled and creative profession. Gabe, although he wasn't partial to them, learned to make all the standard tourist fish fare, Lobster Newberg, Clams Casino, Stuffed Flounder; frying, battering and breading the creatures to death and he would serve them if necessary. Gabe believed fish should taste like fish, however, and he preferred a more refined, simple menu, lightly grilled swordfish, sautéed scallops, delicate risottos, seasoned baked sea bass, squid, its skin scored, crosshatched with a sharp knife and broiled with chilli and cilantro. He could fillet, shell or shuck anything that swam or skittered across the ocean floor. This earned him hero status in the family, so much so that they would even praise his more feminine efforts such as pastry. He drew the line at cakes, though, that being Mother's domain.

I welcomed the Sundays that Gabe cooked, when we returned home from Mass the house would slowly fill with lovely aromas and extra guests. Mother, so unaccustomed to sitting in the living room enjoying an aperitif, wouldn't readily know which seat to choose, and would then be talking, laughing and listening to us. It was so rare that I felt this; that I was part of a family in spite of having such a sizable one around me. I drank in my parents' presence and attentions on those short afternoons, capped with one of Gabe's tasty masterpieces at the crowded kitchen table.

'So she's dragged up on the clam boat, and the clam guy's looking around, wondering where she came from…'

'She stands up, screaming at the husband across the water…'

'Or whoever he is…'

'And the clam guy's dog knocks her back in!'

'Does a pineapple always order pineapple?'

'No. That was just her hairdo.'

Accidents and illnesses were the landmarks and turning points in our lives, and Gabe's illness was no exception. Gabe kept working when he was ill, his passion to learn more powerful than his need to lay in his bed. He ignored feeling unwell, assuming it would go away, swallowed aspirin and plenty of fluids, which were, because he was living the restaurant life, the wrong sort of fluids late at night in the bar. These were exactly the things he needed to do in order to get worse.

One day, he emerged from his room even later than usual, for his late hours necessitated a mid morning rise even on a good day, and he felt worse than ever. He sat at the table and Mother placed a plate of toast and a cereal bowl in front of him. He stared down at the items.

'I don't think I feel like eating,' he said. His hair and his dressing gown were rumpled and grubby, and he was pale. 'Maybe I'll take a day off.' He then went and threw up and urinated blood.

Mother and Dad had remained loyal to Dr Shapiro even in the years after his misdiagnosis of Bernadette's stomach virus. 'Any doctor would have made the same mistake,' they said. This wasn't true, but it was what he told them and he'd been the doctor since they were babies themselves, older, wiser, educated and respected. So they believed him.

Dr Shapiro no longer made house calls, so Gabe had to limp out to the driveway and be driven to his house, now shabbier than ever, for Dr Shapiro was an old man and was unable to maintain a home. His garden had gone wild, and the property he declined to sell to developers, once surrounded by a matching landscape of woods and meadows, was a dark and haunted oasis in a desert of new style suburban houses and treeless lawns.

Unfortunately for Gabe, Dr Shapiro was also too old to practice medicine, something already appreciated by Aunts Grace, Mo, and Gloria who had defected with their families to younger doctors housed in the new yellow brick clinics and health centres that we eyed enviously out of the car windows when we passed. But Mother and Dad believed in tradition, and that age and experience could not be bettered and they refused to be swayed.

Gabe was not accompanied into the Doctor's office by a parent; he was old enough to go alone. Much later, when he was well, and lucky to be alive and able to laugh, he told me that Dr Shapiro's nose hairs had grown even longer, his stethoscope icier, and his prodding fingers even more insistent, even at age eighteen Gabe had cried out when his failing kidneys were assaulted by Shapiro's rigid digits. He was given a prescription, which came as a foul tasting liquid in a brown bottle, to be taken three times a day for seven days, which he did dutifully, until he became too ill to lift the spoon to his mouth.

It was Aunt Grace who saved Gabe's life. He became a bit paler every day, his skin taking on an eerie blue tinge, veins clearly visible beneath. By the fourth day I was sure I would soon be able to see through him.

It was a tempestuous day; dark and threatening with an ear-nipping, raw easterly wind blowing the last of the leathery leaves off the trees. The bay churned and chopped, clearing itself of all boats; even the seagulls couldn't fly, an omen, perhaps.

'Nothing good ever blows out of the east.' Uncle Tony always said.

Aunt Grace, who loved to visit the sick and cast her experienced eye over, spat back at the weather on the morning of day four, jumped in her car and drove the short distance to check up on Gabe. The night before she had come over and seen the state of him, talked about it later in the kitchen.

'You took him to Shapiro?' said Grace, 'What did he say?'

'He's given him some medicine. It'll just take time.'

Aunt Grace huffed a bit, and left it at that.

But she blew back in again with the east wind that afternoon.

She took one look at Gabe and said

'Mary, this boy needs to see another doctor.'

Mother, of course, had already realised this. It had been a bad night for Gabe. She had already made another appointment with Dr Shapiro, after school, when she would have to give up an afternoon at the rectory. But Dr Shapiro wasn't another doctor, he was the same one. When Aunt Grace pointed this out, in an uncharacteristically gentle manner to Mother, I suspected something was up.

'Well, okay then let me take him over to see Shapiro, Mary,' said Grace. 'You go to work, and I'll take him over and call you the instant we get back.'

Mother looked hesitant. There were only minutes before she had to leave for work. Gabe, now nearly unconscious, was in no position to have an opinion either way. I, not long home from school, stood, unnoticed throughout. I waited for someone to make a decision.

'Well, all right. You will call me right away?'

'Of course I will. I promise,' said Grace.

As I waved goodbye to Mother, Aunt Grace, instead of driving Gabe to see Dr Shapiro, lifted the telephone and called an ambulance after which she called me into the kitchen. She placed her hands on my shoulders and looked at me.

'Gloria, I am going to lie to your sisters now, and I want you to go along with me, because it's the best thing to do for Gabe. Please trust me.'

I did trust her, oddly enough. There was no doubt that she knew what she was doing, and that it was the right thing. She was the only person I'd seen in the last two days that possessed anything resembling control.

The ambulance arrived within minutes, and Gabe was transported into it on a stretcher, frightening me, because he was even more ghost like. I was afraid he would turn into a mist, and disperse into the air, floating away before the stretcher reached the entrance to the ambulance. I wanted to run and shield him from the wind, but could only stand and stare. Maureen, Bernadette, the twins and Angela watched. Maureen clutching a rosary, also stood motionless, taking in the scene. It was so

163

dramatic, the ambulance crew in our house dressed in uniforms, this big flashing vehicle outside, it seemed so large, so much bigger in reality than it was on our fourteen inch screen, the only place we'd ever seen a person loaded into an ambulance. It felt terrifyingly important. Bernadette, usually so quiet, was the first to speak. She, after all, had seen the inside of an ambulance when her elbow broke.

'Why are they taking him?' she asked.

'Dr Shapiro couldn't see him this afternoon, he was taken ill himself. He's going to the hospital because he needs to see a doctor and the quickest way to do it is in an ambulance.'

That was Aunt Grace's lie. It wasn't far from the truth. She put her coat on. 'I'll call later.'

And then she left. I thanked heaven for Aunt Grace's intervention, felt guilty about hating her. This shift of feeling was just another unsettling element to the day.

We resumed our afternoon as we would on any other day. Being left home alone while everyone else rushed to the hospital was becoming almost routine now. I was experienced in that field. I knew there was nothing I could do but wait until the next thing happened. We'd be forgotten now for an unspecified length of time. Maybe a piece of news would be telephoned in. Someone would remember us eventually, and Uncle Tony or Aunt Mo would turn up with a scrap of news and a pizza.

Bernadette, sat in the armchair, looking at the television, she was quiet. I guess she'd had enough excitement for one day. The twins and Angela followed me about, clinging, worried. The east wind rattled the windows, reminding us that we weren't talking about Gabe. Instead, we did homework. We played scrabble. I made no concessions for age, and still lost.

'It isn't fair. You can make big words. Your score is higher.'

'We need long words to open up the board.'

'But all I can make is fox,' said Theresa.

'Fox is lots of points.'

Bernadette passed with a kick at the end, upsetting the board and tiles, her only act of aggression. We'd counted the scores by then. We watched more television. The howling wind buffeted some distant transmitter, causing the picture to flicker and jump, but it held out for us. We needed it as our occupation.

It was Uncle Tony who finally arrived, long after we'd eaten and I had put Angela and the twins to bed. He didn't bring any pizza. He was subdued and troubled and entered the house quietly.

'Are you girls all right?' he asked, and went up to the bedroom to check on my little sisters. Then he sat down and leaned forward, and I was sure he was going to say Gabe had died.

'How did Gabe get to the hospital?' he asked.

'Is he still alive? Have you seen him?' I said.

'Yes, yes, of course he's alive. I'm sorry, I should have said that first,' he said, waving his hand past the side of his face as if brushing away the obstacle of the thought.

'He'll be okay. Gabe is going to be fine, don't worry. Your parents will be home later. Gloria, come into the kitchen with me while I find something to eat.'

I followed him, leaving Maureen and Bernadette. I sat down at the table while he stood leaning against the sink.

'Do you know who took Gabe to the hospital?'

Confused, I couldn't understand why Uncle Tony was asking me this odd question.

'The ambulance.' I said. He looked at me, also confused. 'Aunt Grace called an ambulance.'

Uncle Tony sat down across from me and shut his eyes to mull over this new information, covered his face with his hands, and pulled them down again, stretching his face so that I could see the pink inside of his eyelids. Then he leaned forward, and together we completed a sequence of terrible events, finishing each other's story of what happened in the afternoon.

After leaving our driveway, Aunt Grace had followed the ambulance to the hospital in her car but a collision occurred on her way there, believed but not confirmed to be caused by Gabe's ambulance. Aunt Grace, whose adrenaline must have surely been well above peaking point, stopped to help the passengers in the crashed cars. Aunt Grace, feeling invincible, must have been thinking, today is the day that I am meant to save lives. It wasn't a fatal accident, but there was an explosion, and a fire, and Aunt Grace was right there on the scene. She was now in intensive care with very serious burns. She arrived hot on Gabe's heels at the hospital, also in an ambulance.

Up until now Gabe had been taking medicine that he was allergic to and as he became more and more ill Dr Shapiro prescribed more and more of the brown medicine. Gabe, like Aunt Grace, was in the intensive care unit getting the treatment he needed. It was certain that he would recover although not certain how much damage the bad medicine might have caused.

When Gabe had been brought into the hospital Mother and Dad were called, and immediately made their way there, arriving at the same time as Aunt Grace's ambulance, causing macabre confusion of farcical proportions, considering only an hour earlier Mother had left Aunt Grace in her house phoning the doctor.

'She saw Grace brought in, all burnt,' said Uncle Tony, 'and she knew your brother was already there. She imagined a whole bunch of awful things before she found out where Gabe was.'

Uncle Tony didn't tell me what awful things Mother imagined, so I tried imagining them myself. The house had burnt down? All her children were dead? Aunt Grace had crashed the car with Gabe in it? A fire at Dr Shapiro's? Mother was terribly afraid of fires, she would think the worst, of screams and melting flesh.

Actually, those fears would be quite accurate, if misdirected when applied to her children. The screams and melting flesh belonged to Aunt Grace.

'But you're sure Gabe will be okay?' I asked.

'Gabe will. He's already getting better,' said Uncle Tony, 'but I don't know if Aunt Grace will survive.'

Silenced by this statement, I felt myself hoping that Uncle Tony was being over-dramatic and was surprised at how concerned I felt for Aunt Grace, realising for the first time that perhaps I did love her. She was always there, always the same, bossy, bitchy, capable of cutting hair while dispensing biting insults with a smile, snip snipping. She could always be relied upon to interfere and by doing so she saved Gabe's life.

Uncle Tony put his arm around my shoulders when I started to cry.

'She can't die, it wouldn't be fair,' I said.

'No,' he said, patting me, 'it definitely wouldn't be fair.'

****

Chapter Seventeen

It was the beginning of a new era - the dawning of the ordinary guy's realisation that doctors make mistakes. No one could correct those mistakes but the right lawyer, for the right price, could find a way to dress the wound. So Dad set out to get Dr Shapiro.

He approached his task with gusto, evident at the mealtimes he attended, alternately discussing tactics and railing against the great Shapiro crime, repeatedly making comments like, 'I'd really like to get a more conventional revenge on this guy.' At which Mother would blanch and hiss at him disapprovingly.

'Tony! Don't talk that way at the table.' She didn't have much control over where else he talked that way.

I went to visit Aunt Grace in the hospital with Dad and Uncle Tony on one of her first days there, feeling a sense of duty and also of gratitude both for her role in Gabe's rescue and her own survival.

'Are you sure you want to come?' said Dad.

'She doesn't look too good.'

'I'm sure.'

We went in the morning, after breakfast, and I walked along the shiny hospital corridor peering into each room and its sickly inhabitants, hoping by the time I reached my aunt to have become desensitised to the horrors of hospital patients. As we turned into her room, I said, cheerily, 'I can still smell the breakfast toast.' Dad nudged me in the back, Uncle Tony kicked me in the leg and I took one look at Aunt Grace and the realisation that it wasn't toast I was whiffing, chased my taste buds instantly to the back of my throat, nearly retching up the shock. I wasn't at all prepared for the scorched sight that was unrecognisable as my Aunt Grace; her heavy make-up replaced with charred and puffy white lumps and dressings, no home for a lipstick. The rancid atmosphere of her pain in the room stung, and brought tears to my eyes. I swallowed my sickness and didn't stay long.

Gabe, once properly diagnosed, made a rapid recovery and was home within a few days. Mother took time off work, washed his bedding, plumped his pillows and prepared a limited selection of comfort food. Beth came to visit daily, with chocolate and puddings and even flowers.

'Here you go girls, dig in,' she said, always remembering to bring something for my sisters and me, be it restaurant leftovers or a pack of M&Ms.

'That girl sure knows how to work a crowd,' said Dad, approvingly.

A week or so into his confinement, I delivered a bowl of soup to his room. He'd been up and about, but Mother was still intent on pandering to him, maybe making up for lost times past.

'Hey Gloria.'

'Hey Gabe. How do you feel?'

'I feel good. I was just getting out of bed.' He gave the soup a negative look. 'I don't think I can eat that.'

Mother appeared behind me.

'What's wrong, Gabe,' she said, concerned.

'Nothing, I'm just full. I been eating all that sweet stuff that Beth brought over. I'm sorry.'

'That's fine, don't worry. Gloria can eat it.'

I made a face at Gabe, behind her back.

'I think I'll be able to go back to work soon,' said Gabe.

'Well, don't rush things,' said Mother.

'No, don't worry. You know, there's a place above the restaurant to rent, a small apartment. I may think about that,' said Gabe.

'About what?' She stopped, startled.

'About renting that. The apartment.'

'Well, don't rush things,' she said, leaving the room.

'Come on Gloria, come eat this soup.'

'What do you mean?' I jumped in. 'Are you moving out?'

'Don't worry about it. Go and eat the soup, Gloria.'

'I hate tomato soup.'

'Listen. I've eaten about a hundred bowls of it. You can eat one.'

Aunt Grace finally came home from the hospital to her house, now empty. Her two sons, Joseph and Anthony no longer lived at home and

Joseph had a new young family. Francine, the once difficult daughter was no longer difficult but also no longer home. She was living in the city, learning how to be a beautician, near enough for frequent visits but too far for full time nursing, which is what was required. Aunt Grace was an invalid.

Uncle Joe spent a week racing back and forth from the marina to their home only to find that he was exhausted and never quite got his timing right, constantly finding himself where he was needed least, his eyes and spirit looking more sunken each day.

Mother and Dad discussed his situation over a Sunday meal.

'Maybe if we all chipped in a bit we could get her a home nursing service or something,' said Dad.

'She needs care for too long, for that,' said Mother, 'much too expensive. What she really needs is to go and stay with someone, or someone to move in with her. It's a pity her children have left. If we had room here she could come and stay.'

I did not believe Mother could have expressed this sentiment honestly. I watched her closely.

Gabe was serving up some of his own Braciole recipe, thin strips of fine steak spread with garlic and mushroom pate, carefully rolled up and secured with dainty toothpicks, fried in olive oil and then bathed and steeped in his tomato sauce.

'I hope you don't expect me to pay for this meat,' Dad griped.

'Tony, just eat it and be grateful. And don't talk with your mouth full.'

'Don't worry Dad, I got the meat,' said Gabe jovially.

'Listen, here's an idea. I'm looking into renting the apartment above the restaurant soon, so if you wanted, you could use my room.'

Six pairs of eyes turned hungrily in the direction of Mother and Dad, the bad relations, mulling over the inheritance before the body was cold. If Gabe moved out the girls could have more space and any permutation would be an improvement on our present arrangement. I could have my own room. We could be split into two halves, the three younger and the three older. Or Bernadette could have the room to herself.

Mother ignored us, sat up rigidly and set down her fork.

'So you really are moving out?' she said to Gabe.

'It's just down the road,' he said, 'I spend most of the time there anyway.'

I watched as Mother lifted her glass and sadly sipped, looking at Gabe, her wistful expression travelling back in time. Her firstborn was moving out. Then she shifted in her both her seat, and her attitude, leaning forward.

'Well,' she said, 'I guess things will have to change around here then.'

We held our breath, my sisters and I, waiting for the division of the spoils to be decided and announced. Mother turned to Gabe.

'When do you think you'll be going?' she asked.

'About two weeks?' He said it with a question mark. Mother's unexpected readiness for his departure threw him as well as us.

'Fine,' said Mother, 'we'll tell Aunt Grace then, and Uncle Joe can stay here too. If they want, they can move their own bed in, though I can't believe they'll be getting up to any shenanigans with her in that state. You can of course leave things of yours here if you want, Gabe.'

We could only sit stunned, mouths hanging open in various stages of mastication. Theresa found her voice, and pleading for us all in one, said,

'What about us? We could have more room instead of being all crammed in like sardines, I mean, it's our house, not theirs, we should come first.'

Mother smiled, she had her holy look on.

'It won't be forever, girls. Aunt Grace's needs are greater than yours.'

I watched her, squinting as though the narrowing of my eyes might give me better insight into her motives. Surely this woman couldn't be my mother, volunteering to have Aunt Grace, her distaste for whom had always been obvious to me, come and live with her? Even Maureen, otherwise delighted by this show of exemplary Christ like kindness, found it hard to cover her surprise. And shenanigans? She mentioned shenanigans - at the table.

Preparations were made, Gabe's room was cleaned and painted and two beds put in. Aunt Grace and Uncle Joe couldn't use their own double bed as predicted by Mother because her damaged skin was too tender to be sharing a bed. There was a bookshelf, radio and television. In a matter of days, Gabe was erased from his room.

Dad engaged an attorney, the brother or in-law of one of Uncle Vinny's clan of clam shack marine insurance pals and they set up their first meeting at the Fish Shop one Saturday morning, at which I was present, although not as a participant, more of a hidden spectator, lurking behind the goldfish bowl. It was such an unlikely time and place for a litigation meeting, and the lawyer in question, known only as Tommy, was so fierce looking that I feared the possibility of Dad's desired 'more conventional' revenge and began to feel concern for Dr Shapiro. Months were devoted to planning the strategy of the lawsuit, without anything actually happening, and many more meetings took place both at the Fish Shop and out on Tommy's boat, for as time passed he and Dad were becoming good pals, while I imagined Dr Shapiro tipping overboard accompanied by a concrete brick.

I needn't have worried, though for Dr Shapiro had already died, quite naturally, in his shambling house. Sadly, as he had no family and no patients, he wasn't found for quite some time and as Aunt Grace was too burnt out to spread local scandal, we didn't hear of it until Dad read it in the town newspaper one morning at breakfast.

'Drat!' he shouted, over his toast and coffee. 'The bastard's dead!'

'Tony, not at the table.'

That was the end of Dr Shapiro at our table and in our lives, and the beginning of many others doctors.

Although Aunt Grace wasn't fit to cut hair or spread gossip, we still had her with us, living in our house. She arrived, walking slowly and gingerly, with the aid of sticks, Dad and Uncle Joe on either side of her acting as human shields, Mother behind her carrying an assortment of prescription bottles and packages of hospital gauzes, salves and gels. We gathered for her entrance, Angela hanging back silently, frightened by the monster that was being escorted into our home. This reaction was understandable, as the image of Aunt Grace was reminiscent of those partially unwrapped mummy creatures of horror films.

'It's all right Angela, it's only me, your Aunt.' This came out somewhat slurred, as Aunt Grace's face was badly burnt and still partially bandaged.

Angela was still confused, not able to recognise Aunt Grace because of her distorted appearance and the fact that she was being nice.

'Aunt who?' she said.

'It's Aunt Grace, honey,' said Dad. 'She's had a bad accident and we're going to look after her here for a while. Now why don't you go play.'

The twins had reached the limit of their attentiveness and the drama of Aunt Grace's entrance had unfolded enough to satisfy their curiosity and they left to do as Dad suggested, taking Angela with them. Maureen and I exchanged polite greetings and excused ourselves, while only Bernadette remained, clearly mesmerised, and followed the macabre procession up the steps to the bedroom to complete the installation.

'Bernadette.' I called her from the kitchen. She turned, pierced me with her beady eyes. 'Come down here for a sec.' I said, and she glumly descended the stairway, looking over her shoulder until Gabe's, now Aunt Grace's, bedroom door shut out her gaze.

'What?' Bernadette said.

'It's just not polite to stare like that.'

'Like what? I wasn't,' she said. 'Who is that?'

'Who's who?' I said.

'Who was that lady with Dad?'

'Bernadette,' I said, 'that's Aunt Grace. You know that. She's coming to stay here until she gets better.'

Bernadette didn't answer, just looked at me for a moment, her expression distant and wild, not seeing me, and then left for outside through the kitchen door.

'Leave the girls alone.' I shouted after her, feeling my stomach churn, knowing she wouldn't.

The brief respite brought on by Bernadette's injury passed quickly, she recovered the use of her arm and was up to full power in no time. We still spent most afternoons locked away in our bedroom or basement. We'd given up our desire to live like 'normal' children in favour of remaining whole ones, and now had taken to removing ourselves to one of those locations immediately on arriving home after school, rather than waiting for trouble to start. Giving up the luxury of watching afternoon television seemed a small price to pay for the peace it brought to us.

Bernadette continued to behave violently towards my little sisters, but the incidents were less frequent because we were cunning in our avoidance techniques. When she did strike, her attacks were more intense than ever, and usually the result of some provocation, however small. For me, she took to theft and destruction of property, ruining favourite pieces of clothing or stealing birthday money, so I began to lock things up in a wooden box and wear the key around my neck.

It had been necessary to exclude Bernadette much of the time in order to protect ourselves, but that was less necessary as she withdrew into herself more and more. She built a cubicle in her bottom bunk by hanging blankets around the bed and sat there for hours, talking to herself. We got used to her verbal stream of consciousness that made no sense to us. Bernadette had written a language all of her own punctuated with cat sounds, which was eerie at first. Eventually, though, we stopped listening.

'Siffy bin bin, keep to the track, that's all she had to do to wear the rain. Nerby! Get that fur off into radar or the cross to bear will march to tonga! That's good, calm, calm down, paws never need wiping.'

We had long ago ceased to complain about Bernadette, as our gripes reaped no results, no matter how many cuts, bruises or broken possessions were produced. Likewise, as she grew insular and strange, we saw no point in mentioning it.

Dad appeared in the bedroom. 'Bernadette, come on downstairs and talk to me instead of sitting there all alone,' he said.

'She's not all alone. I'm here, and so is Maureen and Theresa.'

He ignored me and Bernadette ignored him.

'Yeah and she's got that imaginary friend she's talking to,' wisecracked Theresa, unwisely. Bernadette took note of her comment.

'I heard you Theresa,' she said.

Dad tried again. 'Come on honey,' he said to Bernadette, 'come down and talk to your mother and I. Tell us about school.'

'She's not talking about school!' Theresa shouted at him. 'She doesn't make sense.'

After he left, Bernadette was on top of Theresa, twisting her arm, pulling her hair, biting, scratching while muffling her screams with her own pillow until I could forcibly pull her off and she withdrew and went back to her cubicle.

We didn't call for Mother or Dad to help. Sometimes the fighting made me vomit, and sometimes it made me tired. Sometimes it made me want to murder someone, and sometimes it made me want to kill myself. Sometimes it made me laugh, but that wasn't happening much anymore.

'Theresa, why can't you keep your mouth shut?' I said. 'She was perfectly happy, leave her be.' I was aware that I was talking about her as though she couldn't understand me, as though she were a difficult pet. Theresa left the room. Mary stayed quiet, as always. Angela cowered and Maureen, if there, would ask from her distance if I were all right, and ask if Bernadette were all right, and pray for us all.

Due to the reduction of our complaints, I assume it was assumed we were all fine and hunky dory. We were largely left to get on with life ourselves, with little or no supervision, and now I had Aunt Grace grudgingly added to my list of afternoon responsibilities.

In some ways this was less of a hardship than I imagined it would be, or planned on, even. Since the inception of Aunt Grace's convalescence in our house I'd expected to be drinking top shelf martyrdom, with stark visions of pus filled bandages, impatient, biting comments in the bleak smelly room that once belonged to my adored and mournfully pined for older brother. But it wasn't like that at all. In actual fact the room was newly curtained, painted, bright and fresh smelling. The bandages were dealt with by crisp visiting nurses or other aunts, and most unexpected of all, there were no sharp comments or cross words. It was as though Aunt Grace, the wicked witch had melted and been remoulded into someone better, with perhaps not such a striking surface. She was so badly injured it was difficult not to pity her, to want to help her feel well, when it was clear every move she made caused her pain. She never complained, which I would have, but doggedly struggled to perform the ordinary daily actions that most of us do without thought, like eating and getting from lying down to sitting up. I helped design a simple frame that could straddle the bed and hold a book, so she could read, keeping the weight of the book off her body, and Uncle Joe built it. Every day we made an elaborate, extended straw so that she could drink without having to reach and lift her glass. I even spent time in her room to speak to her, her molten face twisting into a grotesque smile, appreciating the company.

The extra strain came when evening approached and dinner had to be made and with two additional adults, one requiring only certain foods, this was a much more difficult task for me, as Mother, anxious to please and impress, left more detailed and complicated menus. Sometimes Maureen would offer assistance.

'Gloria, what can I do to help?'

'Oh, thanks. You can peel and chop that squash so it's ready to cook.'

I didn't think it was necessary to tell her to take the seeds and pulp out of the middle of it, but God didn't smile quite as brightly on Maureen when it came to culinary skill, and she invariably created more work than she saved.

Uncle Joe now returned with Dad, meaning the house was always too crowded with hungry people filling space and creating garbage, that no brother was there to remove.

Doctor Madalan, the new doctor, came to visit twice a week, so the house had to be tidied, which I did by simply redistributing the mountains of newspaper and clothing, and throwing the litter of shoes down the basement steps.

This was the glamorous young doctor we always yearned for, his office located in the yellow brick medical centre, with a waiting room with armchairs, current magazines and a tropical fish tank. It was the fish tank that swung Dad's decision in Dr Madalan's direction when reviewing the health centres, as well as its name and location, at the foot of Dog Pond road, exactly halfway between home and the marina. It was called the Marina Bay Medical Centre.

Instructions were left for me to make the doctor a cup of tea after he saw Aunt Grace, which was something we ourselves never drank, nor did he, apart from one or two polite sips. I found this tea making ceremony an excruciating and embarrassing old-fashioned idea of Mother's, who couldn't even be there to partake. I had to make embarrassing inadequate small talk while Dr Madalan took the minimum required amount of tea sips before he could bolt, smiling patronisingly all the while.

Home was like living in a hospital wing, with so many nurses and the doctor coming and going. One day, while Dr Madalan and I sat itching for the tea break time to be over, he smiled and said,

'Your younger sister certainly has an affinity with animals, doesn't she?'

I had five younger sisters but knew he meant Bernadette and knew it was somehow a loaded question. He wanted to have a conversation with me about Bernadette, but I didn't have time for that, there was too much dinner to cook and I had homework, not that I ever did any homework.

'Yeah, she does,' I said, flatly.

Theresa turned casually from her television armchair.

'She loves them now, but she used to torture them. Now she thinks she's one of them.'

'Theresa!' I said, involuntarily, shit, I didn't want this doctor to know our secrets, ashamed that I had a sister that tortured kittens and babies and now thought she was a cat sometimes. It was one of those moments when I could feel myself being my mother but I ignored that. Anyway, we never told the last doctor anything, why should we tell this one. It seemed like it would be entering dangerous territory, or opening a can of worms, as they say, although I never understood that expression. Maybe I hadn't opened any cans of worms but I had opened countless bags of them. It was just worms inside.

'Well she does!' said Theresa. 'And now she tortures us.'

'Don't be silly,' I said, throwing a shut-up look her way.

I looked at Dr Madalan.

'She doesn't even know what torture means.'

He took his last sip of tea and left.

****

Chapter Eighteen

Maureen got her scholarship. I knew she would. Not just for one place, she ended up with a selection to choose from, so many of the crème de la catholic high schools were falling over each other trying to entice the wannabe nun into their school. Maureen, to her credit, had single-handedly and painstakingly researched and written to every Christian funding body in the northeast and beyond, filled in their lengthy applications, wrote their reams of required essays and answered all their queries quietly, while sitting cross-legged, crouched in the space between her top bunk and the sloped ceiling. Then she attended their interviews and set to making her difficult decision.

'Why not just go for the one with the fish tank,' I said.

'Honestly Gloria. Don't be stupid. I couldn't do that.'

'It was a joke, Maureen. You're the one that's stupid.'

In the end Maureen, no fool, picked the one who offered the most money, Holy Family High, whose foundation were even prepared to pay for her books and transport. This news arrived in late spring, in a rather grand envelope addressed to Dad. Maureen was thrilled to think that come September her dream of catholic high school was becoming a reality. Dad read the offer, and although proud and happy for Maureen, couldn't help but be somewhat miffed by the offer, insinuating his inability to provide.

'Well, get a load of them, on their high holy family horse, will ya?'

'But Dad, this is great,' said Maureen. 'I couldn't have possibly gone there without this.'

'Well I could have paid for your books at least.'

'Take it easy on Dad, Mo,' I said to her later. 'It makes him feel bad that he can't send you to those places himself.'

'Well, that's just silly. He should be happy for me.'

'There you go, being stupid again.'

This was the beginning of Dad's blue period, his slow descent, his total loss of enthusiasm and optimism, his dampening spirit, and although he never quite arrived there, he began to live as though the rest of his life was just a series of stops on the way to rock bottom. He changed into a different man. It wasn't a drastic or dramatic change as if he had become a violent drunk and starting abusing his family, which would have been more straightforward to deal with. It was more subtle than that, and gradual, a piece of him went missing. We didn't really notice it.

Mother had a job, a bit of her own money and was even more tired than ever, if that were possible, yet her job fed the very core of her soul and no one would dare suggest giving it up. His only son was gone and now here was Maureen, just about paying her own tuition. His eldest daughter was a lying truant and looked after the rest of the children, completely inadequately, including at least one who was highly dysfunctional, although technically he didn't know about the lying truant bit and thought the childcare situation was well in hand.

He wanted to be needed, and he was of course. But he didn't see that, because it was an unwelcome, unfulfilling need, and not the kind that would supply him with the instant gratification he craved. He wanted to be needed to fill our worlds with the things he wasn't able to give us anyway, so he was on a one way trip to depression.

He was needed to do some of the housework, and to leave Uncle Joe at the shop sometimes while he came home and spent an afternoon with us being a father, on weekends, fixing things, taking us places, talking to us.

But he didn't, the Fish Shop was under threat; the marina was changing. It was growing and developing; strangers were coming. He had to be there, to fret with Uncles Joe and Vinny. It was Uncle Joe who would come home, with just a distracted head pat and a nod to us before he disappeared behind his and Aunt Grace's door.

Then Maureen got a job.

'How can you have a job?' I said. 'You have to be sixteen to have a job. It isn't legal. You can't do something illegal. It's a sin.'

'It's on a very informal, off the books level,' she said. 'And it's only a few hours. I need the money for school. Of course it isn't a sin.'

'But Maureen, how could you work there? Why can't you go and get a paper round or something. What will Dad say when he finds out?'

'Oh, he'll understand. I mean, of course I'd go and work for Dad if he could afford to pay me, but he can't.' Maureen's emotions were all used up on her love for God. She went to work at the Surf Emporium; a sparkling glass fronted freshly built shop with flags, surfboards and inflatable toys outside on its surrounding deck, all colour colour colour.

The view from the Fish Shop across the inlet was a peaceful swatch of reeds swaying in the breeze, a small deserted beach bordering a point of headland that jutted out about five hundred yards further into the bay than the patch that was ours. Just visible was a ruined barn, a previous life rotting away. It was private land, owned by the Crosier family, difficult to reach, for the road to it dead-ended abruptly at thick scrubby high hedges. You wouldn't even know it was there, unless viewed from our side, the marina side, of the inlet. All those years that I sat on the ground outside the cupboard that became the clam shack, looking across the lazy inlet and watching that point of land where nothing much happened, the odd barge or clam boat passing, I never imagined it would ever be any different. The Crosier's, though, were Piper Bay's foremost realtors, with a keen eye for developing opportunities and as the town grew, so did their empire.

The little piece of headland was their high school graduation gift to their son, Glen, a former barge boy, who saw a gap in the market, ploughed through the hedges, razed the land, built a dock, a parking lot and the Surf Emporium, its shiny aisles filled with wetsuits, surfboards, swimwear, picnic sets, paper goods, sweets and giant lollipops, beach umbrellas and things for boats and fishermen.

'They don't sell bait,' said Uncle Joe. 'They couldn't do better bait than we do. And lollipops! How stupid can you get. Who wants lollipops with all this sand?'

Mother tut tutted. 'All those poor birds! And the view!' Building anything was a crime in her eyes.

Dad hated the place. He couldn't even talk about it, and when he did it was an eyesore, an atrocity, a monstrosity, a hideous creation of the devil. My parents didn't look favourably upon progress, and in this case I couldn't blame them, as it was stamping out life as they knew it.

Ironically, the Fish Shop didn't suffer because of the Surf Emporium, only the spirits of the people who owned it. They didn't go out of business, as feared. They actually benefited, as the Surf Emporium attracted visitors who could see the Fish Shop across the inlet, now busy with Boston Whalers and speedboats piloted by sun-kissed young people.

From their side of the inlet, the Fish Shop looked like what it was, a series of ramshackle wooden shacks, nailed together haphazardly. It became an odd attraction, this pile of driftwood in the midst of all the colourful modernity. It was nostalgic for the older people and novel for the younger ones, because the older ones talked about it and misremembered, inventing a romantic and magical past for it, making the younger ones think that they were witnessing the original American dream. It became renowned for its special bait, and various legends of the shark chum circulated, thankfully none containing kittens.

Their steady and loyal clientele stayed with them and glared at the strangers, adding to the charm, as did Dad and Uncle Joe themselves, swarthy men clad in white undershirts. The rented boat space was slightly increased, and the new visitors, although mainly there to gawp rather than spend, were not short of money and usually bought something, even if it were just a bowl of chowder.

Dad worried anyway, needlessly and incessantly. He didn't see the change as a positive thing, as progressive. He wanted things to be the way they were, with Mother at home and Aunt Grace not a cripple and tropical fish in the Fish Shop and maybe only a couple of normal kids, and to be ten years or more younger. It was all too much for him. He began to exist in his world rather than live in it, adding sloshes of red jug wine to his cream soda, taking up the signature cocktail of his own father. He didn't get drunk, just mildly anaesthetised, still capable of functioning inside of his envelope of numbness, but no longer as the chief participant in his life. He became a jovial but passive observer, somewhat removed, watching the world in the same way he gazed at the gold fish, complaining of their inferiority to the tropical variety, seemingly forgetting it was he who removed the latter.

Life back home, meanwhile, continued to fester and multiply. Uncle Joe still had to maintain his own home but in order to reduce the amount of to and fro travel, moved their cat and dog in with us as well. The cat, Kilroy, or Killer as we called it, constantly tried to increase the house's population by presenting us with the other creatures it hunted out. His technique was to get the animal in the house, whole and unharmed, then release it for a period of recreation before the final fatal bite. Aunt Grace, who couldn't bear to see an animal harmed, gave orders that whenever Kilroy entered the house with a victim, we were to abandon everything else and concentrate on launching a rescue operation. We had no objections to this plan; it provided instant light relief from either mundane chores, dull television, or difficult homework. It was one of the few things we all could have fun doing together, even Bernadette. Bernadette was excellent at it as well, especially catching the birds, which seemed drawn to her, presumably unaware of her feline aspirations. It was during one of these rescue missions that the new wave of sudden silences began.

We were chasing a chipmunk, such easy prey for Kilroy that it was more like a trip to the Kitty Cat Food Court than hunting. These chipmunks were doubly condemned as they made their home under the woodpile at the back of the house and were regularly fed by my sisters and I and even Aunt Grace, which made them tame and less wary than ordinary chipmunks, who even at the best of times were not very challenging game.

This confused chipmunk would have emerged from the woodpile expecting a walnut or grape and instead found itself removed indoors and dropped on to a strange linoleum landscape where a crowd of children joined the cat in the chase. We chased the chipmunk cartoon style, overturning furniture and making sudden U-turns, with Kilroy hot on our heels. The chipmunk was in grave danger, a cause for great concern yet we couldn't help being amused by its plight, howling with laughter all the while for one cannot live in such a violent household without a bit of cruelty creeping under their skin and into their soul.

Aunt Grace's door was slightly ajar, about a chipmunk's width, and after a heroic leap up the stairs it disappeared through the crack. We followed instantly, tumbling into the room to find Aunt Grace deep in conference with Mother, Dad and Uncle Joe. Their expressions when we appeared halted us and they stopped talking instantly. Not in an ordinary way, but in a sudden, guilty, head-turningly suspiciously secretive way. That guilty manner turned it into a significant moment. Everyone in the room felt as though they were doing something wrong.

'Get out of here,' said Dad, quietly, to us.

'But there's a chipmunk...'

'It's all right, we'll find it ourselves,' he said, 'Just get that cat and close the door.'

We found ourselves rejected on the landing with the door shut in our faces and surplus levels of unused adrenaline, a problem addressed immediately by Bernadette, who pushed Angela and Mary down the stairs. Theresa started screaming and went after Bernadette, having discovered, as I had, that fighting back with Bernadette was an exhausting yet effective device for shortening the length of the conflict. Mary lay on the bottom step silently sobbing, while Angela screamed. Theresa, grabbing a handful of hair, thumped Bernadette against the wall. Not very hard, because she was so small, but it was impressive nonetheless. Bernadette withdrew and it wasn't until we resumed what we called normality that anyone came out of Aunt Grace's room, in spite of the noise we made.

'Is everything all right?' Mother asked, wearily. Always distracted now, as well as tired, Mother often appeared to live a pre-programmed robotic life, she said things, but didn't think them, or hear herself.

'Yeah, we're fine, now.'

'What was all the fuss?'

'Angela fell. And Mary.'

'Bernadette pushed us down the stairs,' said Angela.

'Shhh,' Mary shushed. 'I'm trying to watch TV.'

Mother sighed. 'Are you all right, girls?'

There was no answer.

'No broken bones?' She smiled, this being an attempt at light heartedness. No fractures, no blood, that's fine then, forget about the push.

Maureen appeared, apparition like, suddenly. 'They haven't got bones yet, they're mainly just cartilage. Complete ossification doesn't occur until early adulthood.'

'Hey that's really helpful Maureen,' I said. 'Now why don't you go do something useful like pick up a duster.' Maureen just smiled her detached smile and drifted away. Behind her, Dad and Uncle Joe emerged from the bedroom, heads bowed, hands in pockets, following Mother into the kitchen where they would again be silent until sure not to be overheard.

'We got the chipmunk and let it out the window,' said Uncle Joe, as he passed.

'Thanks Uncle Joe.' Nice of him to tell us.

We of course were no strangers to sudden silences but I felt resentful, considering myself graduated into the age of participant and should no longer be excluded from such discussions. What could they be talking about that I couldn't hear, perhaps it was me? Even If that were so, than I was old enough to be included in the circle.

This was lonely speculation now that Gabe was gone and Maureen had managed to remove herself from the house in every way except bodily as well as becoming someone I didn't want to talk to anymore anyway. I had no one to gossip with. I was beginning to feel like a Victorian servant, required only to perform necessary services and then to stay out of sight the rest of the time. I had little else in life and few friends and no prospects. I suppose I should count myself lucky that they sent me to school, I thought bitterly.

I made my way upstairs, only to be intercepted by Aunt Grace.

'Gloria, can you come here for a moment,' she called from her bed. Oh god, what does she want now. I stopped, and went in.

'What do you need?' I asked, flatly.

'I just wanted to tell you...' she started, but stopped suddenly when Mother appeared in the doorway behind me.

'Grace, would you care for a drink?'

Another statement suddenly arrested, another amputated conversation, and she had that same old shifty look, too. It was the last straw. That was it, I'd had enough.

'I'm going out.' I announced. It was Saturday; I could do what I liked. I had to escape this claustrophobic mess. I went to the bedroom and put on my shoes, angrily pulling at each lace, distraught and angry, although I didn't really know what I was at the time, I just felt rising rage.

'Where?' Maureen asked.

'Just out.'

'With who?'

'Just out. With friends.'

'Well for how long, then? It's getting late now, you'll miss dinner…'

'Shut up Maureen and mind your own business. I'm going out to get laid, okay? Now fuck off.'

'Gloria!' Maureen was shocked, which pleased me. Bernadette's eyes widened from inside her blanket curtained space. Even Bernadette could be shocked. I loved the moment of shocking them by being coarse. Especially Maureen. It was the only time I ever felt I made an impact, but in the long run the experiment actually made me feel worse.

I was already feeling suffocated in this overcrowded house, and so lonely and neglected. Now I'd added self-loathing. I was a bad foul-mouthed person.

I passed Dad on the way out, sitting on the sofa passively sipping his brain Novocain with Uncle Joe.

'I'll see you later,' I said, exiting quickly. 'I'll probably be late.' I was vaguely aware of parting well wishing comments following me through the closed door.

Of course I had nowhere to go, I just needed to be out, so I wandered the streets for a while, heading downtown, away from the bay, where I peered into bars and avoided drunks. I was surprised at how many drunks there were, but then I wasn't familiar with downtown life. I knew this was where people at school would go on weekend nights. I passed Rick's Pizza, where two boys I knew were sitting outside the shop front, on the ground, eating pizza. Raymond, one of them, nodded hello. I slowed but they didn't engage me in conversation so I went inside and ordered a slice of pizza. I sat at a table and ate it, feeling awkward eating alone in public. I watched Rick throw the pizza dough. Several more customers came in while I was there, each time I looked down and concentrated on the tin ashtray until they sat down. Rick, the pizza guy, came away from his ovens and around the counter with two more slices of pizza for the boys outside.

'On the house,' I heard him say. 'People see you guys sitting here eating, they come in.' He came back in smiling, wiping his floury hands on his apron. 'Those guys are free advertising,' he said.

I finished my pizza and left, seeing that two girls had joined the boys. None of them spoke to me.

I walked some more, this time ending up at the marina, concealing myself while watching the diners in the floating restaurant and on the dining boats, the distant flashing of the Beacon Island lighthouse, listening to the clanking of the halyards against the masts until I felt calmer. A long time later, hours, I went home, my legs aching from the tension and walking miles. I'd had a miserable time. Aunt Grace had come out of her room and been set up in an easy chair and sat with my parents and Uncle Joe in the living room. Aunt Gloria and Uncle Nick had joined the party. Once again there was a sudden halt to their discussion.

'Hi Gloria,' someone said.

'Hi. Goodnight. I'm going to bed.'

I wondered where Uncle Tony was. If he had been there he may have come looking for me, I thought. Perhaps I could have talked to him, perhaps not.

My sisters were all asleep and I found Kilroy in my bed feasting on the remains of a chipmunk, which he gathered up warily and carted off as soon as I arrived, leaving its face behind. He never ate their faces.

Oh, great, I thought. An offer I couldn't refuse. Surely this couldn't be a good omen, especially if it were the same chipmunk. I wrapped it up in toilet paper and threw it out, washed my hands, and collapsed.

****

Chapter Nineteen

It was difficult for Aunt Grace to get around so Uncle Joe made her a wheelchair, or to be more precise, an armchair that could roll, on wheels that he retrieved from a discarded go-kart that Gabe had made as a boy. This chair was the embodiment of the phrase 'it's the thought that counts' as it was in fact, almost useless for the purpose it was created, which was to make life easier for her. It had no enabling features. There was no mechanism for her to push it herself, nor could anyone else move it without a good deal of resistance. It was heavy, navigated awkwardly through doors and the wheels, originally stripped from a retired supermarket trolley, were permanently jammed into the opposite of her chosen direction. It rolled freely only when Aunt Grace was in it alone, trying to reach something, on a dangerous incline. But she employed it regularly because it was, after all, so thoughtful and caring of Uncle Joe to build it. And for all its failings, it was quite comfortable. I found her slouched in it on a twilit evening in the back garden, sniffling into a box of photographs. It was an unusually warm evening for early June.

'Are you stuck there, Aunt Grace? Do you want some help?'

She shook her head. 'Maybe a tissue,' she said. If she'd wanted me to go away, she'd have waved me off. Asking for a tissue was the signal to stick around. The unfamiliar territory of having to comfort an older relative made me uneasy, but I felt I had to say something, however feeble. The light was fading and in the darker shrubs around the edge of the garden I saw the first blink of lightening bugs this season, feeling the same sense of excitement, unchanged since my first ever sighting of them.

'Look. Lightening bugs! Over there! They're the first I've seen this year.'

'Where?' She peered into the fading light, feeling excited as well even in the midst of her crisis.

'There. In the hydrangeas. Must be because it's so warm.' I came closer to her and had a look in the box on her lap. She was looking at her wedding photographs, among others. I picked one up. It was stained, coloured sepia, and had raggedy scalloped edges.

'Can I please look?'

Aunt Grace, looked down, wiped her nose on her sleeve, and nodded.

The black and white picture was of a young couple smiling out at the camera, taken in our parish church garden. It was posed like all wedding pictures I'd ever seen, long white dress arranged in a swirl around the base of the bride, clutching her bouquet, the taller groom leaning in with one arm disappeared around her waist, the other gently touching her arm, both beaming into the lens. Except that these people were younger versions of Uncle Joe and Aunt Grace, all dressed up in cake-top clothes. Aunt Grace looked nice, not quite as overly made up as in later years, more natural and pretty. The garden was covered in snow.

'You must have been freezing,' I said.

Aunt Grace smiled, having recovered from her short episode of grief.

'My feet were. I had little white satin wedding shoes on. Sandals. They got soaked through standing there.'

'The church's trees have grown a lot haven't they?' I said.

She fished another photo out of the box, this one colour, of a later, painted version of herself, in front of the new split ranch house, pointing up at the window that was her hair salon.

'Turn on the porch light, will you Gloria?' She squinted at the picture while I did as asked.

'Good god, would you look at all that make up,' she said, shaking her head. 'If only I had seen what I looked like. I looked like a witch then.' She stared at the photograph, shaking her head.

'And now I look like a monster.' She sighed, in a resigned, matter of fact way. The tears were finished for now.

I said nothing, following Thumper's mother's rule, the rabbit from the Bambi movie. If you can't say anything nice then don't say anything at all. I was so sorry for Aunt Grace, yet my first thought was that we, as children had thought she looked like a witch too. She did, and she acted like one sometimes. I looked at her now. She certainly didn't look like any of the Aunt Grace's in the photos. It wasn't just her face, but the skin on her hands and her arms, all over her, sinewy, melted and shiny.

Underneath, though, she was better. The wicked witch was dead and the newborn monster was tame, and friendly.

The shrub suddenly effervesced with an outburst of lightning bugs.

'Oh, would you just look at them!' she sighed.

There was nothing like the magic of lightning bugs to cast a positive glow on almost any situation. They were always a good omen. Summertime was here. Living was easy. School would finish. The weather would be nice. Business would be good. Fish are jumping. The profits are high.

I began to push, or manhandle the awkward chair in order to get her inside but she stopped me.

'Wait a minute Gloria,' she said. 'I tried to talk to you the other day, but your mother came into the room.'

'Oh?' I wondered what this could be about. My radar detected a secret coming on.

'You know Doctor Madalan? The doctor who comes here to see me all the time?'

'Yes. I have to make him tea.'

'Yes, I know,' she smiled. 'He's told me. Well, he's recommended that your parents go see another doctor in the Medical Centre.'

I didn't quite understand what she was trying to tell me, my imagination at first thinking she was going to confess to a love affair between herself and her doctor, secondly that my parents were dangerously ill.

'Is there something wrong with them?'

'No, it's not about them. It's about Bernadette. A different kind of doctor.'

Aunt Grace was whispering now, so uncomfortable was she talking about That Different Kind of Doctor. Her patronising delivery of this piece of news irritated me.

'You mean a shrink?' I said.

'Gloria, there's no need to use such language,' said Aunt Grace.

'Shrink isn't language.'

She ignored my comment.

'What I mean is a doctor who is more specifically trained to deal with the sort of problem Bernadette might have,' she said, pronouncing each word precisely, evenly spaced.

The use of the words 'Bernadette' and 'problem' in one sentence and relating to each other was momentous. I thought I'd better keep quiet and listen.

'I just thought you'd like to know that', she said, and clammed up on the subject. 'Do you think you could help me inside?' The temperature had dropped suddenly; it was cold. The fireflies were gone.

I carefully manoeuvred her inside the house and abandoned the chair at the bottom of the stairs. I then gingerly helped her lift herself out of the chair and supported her as she made her way to bed, slowly, one step at a time. She still tired easily, and I sometimes forgot just how much of an invalid she was, even as she sat there in front of me all twisted and melted and wincing. Her pain had transformed her and her life, and I was irritable at the inconvenience it caused me. I realised that the rate of my sympathy wearing thin wasn't in tandem with the progress of her skin grafts, and felt a pang of guilt, especially as she had almost become my friend, and was now sharing information that I would certainly get from nowhere else.

'Sorry to be snappy, Aunt Grace,' I said. 'Thanks for telling me that about the doctor. When are they going?'

'I'm a bit tired, Gloria. Maybe later,' she said.

Telling me was one thing, discussing it was another. I was left to ponder in my own head what might be getting examined inside Bernadette's.

I resolved to try and be more patient with Aunt Grace, both physically and emotionally. I was still getting used to liking her.

To celebrate the arrival of a weekend, June, and the fireflies I decided to visit Uncle Tony so I took the cheap ferry over to the Beacon Island and then walked along the ocean to his house. The cheap ferry was a recycled yacht that had belonged to an old esteemed New England family, the Hillingtons, who had long since upgraded. It was adapted for passenger use by adding serviceable benches and a coat of glossy white paint and its stencilled new moniker Maiden of the Waves. It wasn't much of a maiden though, more of a doddery old crone, but I was fond of it. It cost 50 cents and took twice as long as any other ferry that crossed the bay. It deposited you basically in the middle of nowhere, at Breakwater Point, the only public beach on the island, a forsaken sweep of sand, a range of dunes with a small wooden shack built around a toilet and sink to denote its unrestricted status. There was a wooden sign listing the rules, no alcohol, no littering, no horseplay, no swimming beyond the red flag. It was early in the season, there was still crispness in the air and no haze to filter the sunshine, and the ferry was nearly empty. I climbed up to the top deck to sunbathe for the duration of the voyage.

A girl, familiar from school was already up there, the only other person on the deck. Rangy, long-legged and dirty blonde, she was wearing a baseball cap backwards, cut off jeans, a sweatshirt and no shoes, stretched lengthwise along a bench. A slash of white zinc cream, sun war paint, protected her raw nose in the middle of her otherwise angular, suntanned face. I stretched out on the bench across from her.

'Howdy Gloria,' she said, completing the carefree picture. Just looking at her made me feel good, my only problem being that I couldn't recall her name. She leaned forward and reached out to shake hands. I shook her hand. It was a masculine gesture.

'Robin,' she said, 'from Chemistry, Mr Grimsdale, Mondays 2.15. Wanna beer?' She reached down into an army green canvas bag and produced two cans of Schaeffer, and handed me one.

'Gotta drink 'em while they're cold.'

It was only eleven in the morning, and I wasn't really a beer drinker, or a drinker of any sort apart from the odd sip of birthday pink champagne but the sun was heating up the day, and there seemed to be little space in her offer for refusal, so I accepted.

'Thanks,' I said. 'Sorry, I'm not so good with names.'

'That's okay. You don't go to chemistry much, anyway, do you?'

'No, I'm sort of a habitual truant.' This news seemed to please Robin, who after a brief summary of the work I'd missed and a much lengthier assessment of Mr Grimsdale's sexuality, clearly questionable in her opinion, handed me my second can of beer and an opener, with which I now, with no hesitation, punctured the can. The warmth of the sun, the drone of the engine, the paragliding seagull escorts, the cool ease of my companion, the salty sea mist combined with the spray from the beer all contributed to my growing feeling of confident well-being, the promise of summer, and beachy glamour. Hey, I thought, I'm a free spirit beach bum, with a great life.

By the time I was halfway through my third can we'd arrived on Beacon Island and all thoughts of visiting Uncle Tony had retreated to the expanding pickled walnut section of my brain. The priority now was to get to the nearest shop to buy more beer, and we could do this in Pirate Harbour, a place a mile or so west along the shore where Robin's older sister could be found, a means to legally purchase alcohol.

The ocean was rough and Robin wanted to go swimming, but was dissuaded when she was knocked down by a breaker before even removing her clothing. We then engaged the sea in a dangerous game of chicken, making heavy losses including a sweatshirt and her purse, saturating our clothing through to our skins, and any belongings we managed to retain. Remarkably, this didn't concern us even as the changing weather darkened the sky and chilled the wind.

'You'll have to pay for the beer,' she said, arriving finally at Pirate Harbour, walking along the boardwalk to the bay front where there were shops. Pirate Harbour was the biggest community on the island, with a supermarket, a liquor store, a drug store and two hotels. It was also home to the island's suppliers of power, telephone service and post office, police station, courthouse and volunteer fire department and was self governed, unique among Beacon Island communities, with an elected board of trustees, and a mayor, renewable every four years.

All this for a few hundred homes, most only occupied for the summer months, and by short-term rentals, and like everywhere else, only reachable by boat. Some of the older houses were more substantial than elsewhere, with a few equipped for winter though they still stood high above the ground on stilts, a perpetual reminder of their tenuous ever-shifting substratum. Pirate Harbour was built on a part of the island, or strip of sand, that probably hadn't existed above water a mere hundred years earlier. This fact didn't seem to worry the residents, though, most of whom were transient holidaymakers, and although it worried the year round people somewhat more often, they treated it in the same manner they would if their house was situated under the flight path, or in a bad climate, or in a habitat that nurtured fatally venomous spiders. They complained about it once in a while but mainly ignored the issue and got on with life.

Every couple of years a shudder swept the little town when a hurricane wiped out a few houses, sending them hurtling into the ocean, but no one guessed it would never happen to them. Occasionally the Great Hurricane, back in the thirties, before hurricanes were properly christened, was discussed. It destroyed just about everything. Whole communities, whooshed out to sea, gone, existing only in faded snapshots and perhaps at the bottom of the ocean if you were a romantic fantasist. They talked about the Great Hurricane like they talked about Hitler or the Titanic.

'Something like that could never happen again.'

As if nature learned her lesson.

But of course it could happen again, as could tyranny and ships that sink, except that hurricanes came every year and were therefore far more likely.

'Not in our lifetime, anyway.'

To hell with their grandchildren.

As well as and no doubt because of its elected self-government, Pirate Harbour was also known for its predilection for rules and regulations, long lists of NOs posted on tasteful painted wooden boards throughout the community, (for it was a rule that all signs had to be tasteful and wooden) the most absurd being No ice cream to be eaten in the street. They were plainly determined to put their courthouse to good use. We called it The Land of No.

In such a community it was necessary for the purchase of beer for consumption by a minor to be a covert operation.

'You wait here,' said Robin, indicating a bench outside the

supermarket. She returned momentarily. 'I need some money. I might take a while, get yourself a sandwich or something.'

I hesitated. 'I haven't got very much,' I said.

'We don't need much. Let's see whatcha got.'

Reluctantly I fished in my pocket, producing a small fund for her to count.

'That's great, plenty.' She helped herself, assuming I suppose, that I had more. 'I'll pay you back later, I'll get it off my sister.'

I'd handed over what was to be my lunch money, as well as my return ferry fare on the assumption that Uncle Tony would bail me out and feed me, when I eventually got there. She disappeared again, leaving me with seven cents and my empty stomach, wishing I were able to pay for and eat ice cream in the street. I'd been too insecure to admit to her that it was all the money I had.

A short time later I saw an older, sexier version of Robin enter the liquor store, flicking her hair in the face of the man at her side. They came out with a brown paper bag and vanished around a corner. I waited a while longer, and finally Robin joined me on the bench.

'Okay,' she said. 'Let's go pick up.'

We walked a zigzag of boardwalks, Robin looking round furtively all the while, unnecessarily so I thought, until we were close to where we started, where she reached into a specified shrub, reached beneath it and produced her canvas army bag, fully replenished.

'C'mon' she said, 'let's hit the dunes.'

Any guilt I felt by walking across the dunes, contributing to their erosion, was soon obliterated by the next injection of Schaeffer. Robin's sister joined us with her boyfriend and an assortment of other weekend Pirate Harbour Hostages, as they called themselves. They brought more refreshments, most in liquid form, including vodka, orange juice and tequila and one boy had a bag of pretzels and some oatmeal cookies. The group split into two halves, Robin's sister and her crowd, several years older, and the rest of us, idling away the hours until sunset with drinking and chat.

The pretzel boy moved to sit next to me.

'Ralph, this is Gloria, from chemistry, but she never goes. Ralph has Grimsdale too,' said Robin, with an evil giggle. 'He loves Ralph.' There was than much lurid discussion of the dastardly Mr Grimsdale, suspected perverted queer, a threat to all boys in school, but in particular to Ralph who he definitely had his eye on and was just waiting for the right moment to move in and strike.

'What will you do then?' I asked.

'Hit him right where it hurts,' replied Ralph, to a captive audience. I didn't understand what he meant. I decided to switch to vodka and orange juice, and knowing nothing about alcohol, did this on the basis that it would be more nutritious, and ate as many of the pretzels as I could get to come my way, which was quite a few since Ralph had taken up residence by my side.

Later, we staggered back up the boardwalk in the twilight and into a doorway, up a narrow stairway that led to two small rooms. Our numbers had diminished, with only Robin, her sister and boyfriend and Ralph left. Robin led me by the arm, jovial and laughing, shushing me. Once again, stealth was required. I experienced this walk through an erratic, whirling haze. We were upstairs above the hotel, where Robin's sister worked, and one of these rooms was where she lived. The other room was closed. There was a single unkempt set of bunk beds, a familiar sight, a chest of drawers and a clothing rail. There were clothes, shoes, papers, books, empty bottles and other rubbish filling almost all of the limited space, also familiar. Robin's sister and her boyfriend, whose names I never learned, or if so, have forgotten, flopped into the bottom bunk giggling and canoodling. I watched the boyfriend reach down into Robin's sister's trousers, and looked away, amazed they could be so oblivious to the rest of us. Robin ignored her sister and flopped herself lengthily on the floor, without removing any obstacles, as utterly relaxed as when I first saw her, and seemingly unchanged by alcohol.

'So, guys,' she drawled, 'let's rest up a bit for the evening session, shall we? If we wait until after nine, we can slip into the bar through the back downstairs and my sister will serve us.'

Somewhere between her descriptions of Tonsils, the manager to look out for, the unrivalled excellence of the Pirate Harbour Hotel bar, and the removal of the sister's undergarments, I remembered Uncle Tony, where I had planned to be many hours and several miles ago. I had no desire to sample the near supernatural effects of legendary barman Billy the Squid's grapefruit tequila slammers.

'I have to go.' I said, standing up. I immediately sat down again. I was unprepared for balance. 'I have to go to my Uncle's house.'

When, after meeting and defeating their protests, it emerged that my Uncle lived a mile the other side of Breakwater Point, Ralph elected himself to escort me, which could have been a great asset to my safety, or not, as I remember little about the journey. He reckoned I would have died without him; I have my doubts. Whichever, his decision to escort me altered the future considerably, and was the event that set the tone of our ensuing relationship – my dependency on him. He would claim countless more times that I would die without him until, helpless, I eventually believed him.

We had three miles to walk along the ocean in the dark. The weather was turning bad and I was, for the first time in my life, very drunk, fortunately anaesthetising me against how frightening such a walk could be.

I remember only four things about our pilgrimage, before we arrived at Uncle Tony's house. 1. I lost my shoes. 2. I was wretchedly sick in the toilet shack at Breakwater Point Beach, and being so naive about the effects of alcohol, didn't understand why. 3. Ralph gave me chewing gum. 4. We consummated our relationship in the dunes and the only thing I remember feeling about that was guilty because it eroded the dunes.

'Gloria! Are you all right? It's so late! I was getting worried. Gloria?' Uncle Tony told me later he had been beside himself with fears about my safety, but I was too distracted to notice. 'How did you get here? The weather...' he looked past me.

'Oh, this is Ralph.' I said, pleading, before he could say anything else, 'Uncle Tony, could I have something to eat, I'm so hungry.'

'Sure, come on in, hi Ralph, come in, take these' he hugged me, gave us towels, put the kettle on, and made toast.

'You smell like a distillery,' he left the room.

'I'm sorry.' I called after him, meekly. 'It was an accident.'

He came back with two blankets and a pillow.

'Bedtime. Gloria, take the spare room on the left. Ralph, you're here on the couch.' He handed over the bedding, waited till I was in the spare room and then switched all the lights out.

Davis was there in the morning, his gleaming motorboat docked next to Uncle Tony's barge at the end of the rickety pier. They were having breakfast on the porch where it was already warm, although the sun was still low and hadn't yet reached the bay side of the house. I emerged from my room sheepishly, wrapped in a blanket. I glanced at the empty sofa with a pang. 'What happened to Ralph?' I asked.

'He got up early and left. Good morning Gloria,' said Uncle Tony.

'Oh, I'm sorry, good morning. Morning, Davis. Did he say where he was going?'

'Come have some coffee,' said Uncle Tony.

'Back to Pirate Harbour, I think. How do you feel?'

'I feel fine,' I said. He poured me a coffee out of a thermal flask on the table.

'No hangover?'

I shook my head.

'The miracle of youth,' said Davis.

'This is good coffee,' I said.

'Davis brought it over. Have a croissant.'

'Thanks. I'm starving,' I said, wincing at the returning memory of the Breakwater Point shack.

Not much else was said during our lazy breakfast, other boat people on the bay paused to exchange greetings with us; the water taxi guy, a fisherman on his way back from checking his cages, an early season renter exploring the island who wandered down the boardwalk only to shy away, finding himself practically in Uncle Tony's kitchen when he reached the end. This community had grown as well, although only to sixty odd houses and Uncle Tony's had the distinction of being slightly removed from the rest, and its own private boardwalk was easily mistaken for a public one, as it joined a sandy pathway leading off to the beach. I nestled into my towel.

Davis left, and Uncle Tony began to pack up.

'Are we going?' I asked, surprised, because it was still early on a Sunday.

'Yep. Now take a shower and get back into your pukey clothes, I have a meeting on the mainland this afternoon.'

'They're not pukey. Just wet,' I said, suddenly tearful. 'I'm sorry.'

Uncle Tony laughed and gave me a bear hug.

'Go get them from out back, they're hanging out on the deck. Hurry, now, cast off in fifteen minutes.' I did as I was told as he loaded our things onto his barge. I soon joined him, and felt better as we crossed the bay. We were fantastically alone, as no one had ventured out after last night's storm, but the conditions couldn't have been more perfect, the warm sun, and the bay was glimmering and flat enough to walk on, so still that fish were visible beneath the surface. When we reached the middle of the bay, Uncle Tony killed the engine so we could enjoy the quiet, and we sat there, soaking it all up for a time without speaking.

At the end of our interlude, normal relations resumed and the transition from island head to mainland mind engaged, and we chugged along amiably.

I was sad to see the marina looming, because I hated to leave the warmth and tranquillity of the bay, but was looking forward to the prospect of clean clothes and perhaps a bit more sleep. It wasn't often that I regarded my hand-me-down down wardrobe and cramped bunk bed as luxury items.

We had to bypass the marina to get to the Gar-barges boathouse. I automatically stood to wave to the Fish Shop and after squinting for any sign of recognition for some time, stated the obvious.

'Uncle Tony, there's no one there.'

A few minutes later, the grim faces of Uncle Tony's employees met us on the dock, and the Gar-barges standard was at half-mast. Reggie, the oldest barge boy, was weeping softly.

****

Chapter Twenty

Even though he was my own grandfather, I hadn't quite realised how just much Papa Joe had meant to the little marina community of Piper Bay.

This was a man I hardly knew, whose prime had occurred long before I was born. He and I had little interest in, and no affection for each other.

Deposited there on the dock in my pukey clothes and then forgotten, I milled about for a while, unnoticed among the various big men weeping, staring into space, hitting the bottle or getting on the phone, busy contacting the people needed to bring the death machine to life, relatives, priests, undertakers. Grief rubs off on people, and even though I didn't feel particularly sad, I was sent into a reverie of my own. I walked home thinking of everything I knew about Papa Joseph while the tide of grief swelled around me.

Of course, I knew the famous stories about him, how he removed his family from a miserable existence in a deprived outlying urban neighbourhood and came out here to Piper Bay Village. How he bought the dilapidated shack, made it serviceable, selling trays of worms through a little window, digging the bait himself. The pittance he and his family lived on at first, and his unflagging hope and determination in a landscape and climate that was described to me as akin to the Wild West.

Then there were the tales of his befriending all the fishermen, boat owners and other bay people, mistrustful at first, building up his bait business and becoming a self proclaimed figurehead, a sort of marina godfather who paved the way for Dad, Uncle Joe and Gabe, who started their working lives helping out on fishing excursions, digging clams and painting boats. And of course the story of the tragedy of my grandmother's early death and his sorrow and yet how he struggled to carry on and single-handedly raise the family, Papa Joseph featuring as the chief sufferer in that story as I can't even remember the cause of my poor grandmother's demise. He was literally a legend in his own time, and judging by the reaction of all the big strong, rough men around me on the dock, crying themselves to pieces, some of it must have been true.

These stories multiplied considerably over the next few days and the facts of some of these accounts were so wildly varied that you'd be forgiven for thinking several people died instead of just one.

They were all, however a far cry from the Papa Joseph that I knew, who visited our house twice a year, was to be feared and not crossed, sat in the only chair in the house that would accommodate his great mass and knocked back gallons of cream soda and red wine. I had, I felt, almost no connection to the only grandparent I'd ever met – in fact, didn't even like him very much. Neither did Gabe. By the time we came along, he was finished with children. He adopted an 'ignore them and they'll go away' attitude toward us and if we didn't, he'd throw us a coin and growl threateningly and then we kept well clear. We made a point of getting the coin first, though. When we were smaller youngsters, Gabe and I referred to him as 'the big fat guy', a habit we were to revert to after his death. I therefore participated in the mournful days to come in very much spectator fashion.

Multitudes of visitors attended the wake, and much eating, drinking and repeating of words and phrases 'end of an era', 'great man', 'the debt we owe him', 'bedrock', 'if it hadn't been for him' and more heroic tales. He could tear a phone book in two, he could crack a walnut with one bare hand. This latter feat was annually demonstrated at Thanksgiving but performed more as an act of violence than a conjuring trick.

Once again, we did the open house. In amongst the piles of newspapers, empty grocery bags, piles of dirty laundry, piles of clean laundry, dogs, cats and dirty dishes we had to fit in and entertain the extended family, many of whom we didn't even recognise.

There was even pink champagne.

'But this isn't a celebration,' said Theresa, confused. 'Papa Jo's dead. Isn't that sad?'

'All life is worth celebrating,' said Uncle Joe, in his wise man 'there-will-always-be-fish' voice, 'Have some cake.'

Gabe and I wandered around the house largely unnoticed, like urchins at a fun fair, spotting relatives who were now strangers.

'Who's that guy, over there?' said Gabe.

'Where?'

'Grey beard, dunking cake in his vodka.'

'That's Uncle Gabe, you dope. You're named after him.'

'No. Really? That's not Uncle Gabe?'

'It is. He's old now. And grew a beard, it's all grey.'

'Wow. That's amazing. Have you seen Francine yet?'

'Yeah, I saw her yesterday. She got pretty.'

'And nice.'

'Hey, look. There's the Chinese Christmas tree guy.'

For three days I slept at Uncle Tony's in order to make sleeping space available. Maureen took the twins and Angela and stayed in Grace and Joe's empty house, along with a whole slew of other grown up, now adult sized cousins.

Mother took a week off work to do the catering, and the funeral, which was so crowded that those who came to pay their respects spilled out of the front of the church and onto the lawns, was paid for courtesy of the town of Piper Bay, including the unexpected (but not unsurprising) expense of a rapidly custom built extra large coffin. Apparently there wasn't a standard, off the shelf coffin made wide enough to accommodate the man's enormous bulk. The church was stuffed to the vestibules with flowers. Papa Joe travelled the short distance to the cemetery in a white limousine, courtesy of O'Connor's Cabs and Cars and was laid to rest next to my tragic forgotten grandmother, about whom I knew even less.

Having no tears to shed, I instead concentrated on Ralph, who soon won my heart with his waggy doggy tailed looks and lopsided smile, and came hanging round my door in true hound dog style, panting to please me. True to what I thought was my type, like Skate, he was lanky, with wispy fair hair and a happy-go-lucky countenance. He was the opposite of myself, with my dark thick hair, olive skin and uneasy, anxious outlook. We'd been inseparable since the episode on Beacon Island, and I now for the first time had someone to walk the school corridors with, when I was there. He was a free spirit with no fixed group of friends, and took up randomly with whoever suited his mood. It could be Robin and her sister one day, or the boys in the football team the next. I found his unrestricted lifestyle incredibly attractive, and now he had taken up with me.

Uncle Tony knew from the start that Ralph was wolf dressed as Labrador but again I was a victim of my own need for attention, and just as with Skate, the Grease Monkey, I would have been better off with a real puppy. Ralph, however, was a different breed. I had known that Skate was a roller coaster ride, liable to crash and inevitably coming to an end, whereas with Ralph I thought I was on the road to heaven, from here to hereafter.

Years later, I asked him about it.

'Why didn't you tell me?' I said to Uncle Tony, who laughed ruefully.

'Would you have listened, Gloria?' he said.

'No, I guess I wouldn't have,' I said.

'No, of course you wouldn't. And you would have hated me for it too. I couldn't have borne that,' he said.

'So you suffered in silence.'

'I think you suffered more than I did.'

Ralph, who was a year above me at school, came from a decent Piper Bay family. He was an only child of hard working parents, lived in a freshly painted annually split ranch with a two-car garage in Grace and Joe's old neighbourhood. He was polite and clean and well dressed, had a part-time job in a paint and wallpaper shop and went to Mass on Sundays. He mowed lawns in the summer, shovelled snow in the winter, raked leaves in the fall, dug over gardens in the spring.

He took me for long walks in parks and along the beach on weekends, with our dog Trout, Fluke's successor, who he would furnish with a bowl of water to wait while he treated me to coffee or an ice cream in the snack bar. We collected bags and bags of shells and beach glass and would make pictures out of them in the afternoons with my sisters. If he stayed for dinner he would occupy the twins and Angela while I cooked, drawing with them, reading to them, or building houses and villages out of playing cards that Bernadette would invariably ambush and destroy just as they reached their crowning towers of glory.

'He seems like a nice boy,' said Aunt Grace, and getting to the crux of the matter, 'What does his father do?'

'He's a policeman.'

'Oh!' she said. 'How interesting.'

'And his mother's a nurse,' I volunteered. 'He is nice, isn't he?' I was pleased that Aunt Grace approved, I felt I'd brought something home I could be proud of, like a cat, presenting the outcome of its hunt.

'That's quite common, you know, police and nurses marrying, a bit like the Irish and Italians,' she said. 'Gloria, could you be a doll and get me a glass of water?'

There were no complaints about Ralph, or worries or disapproval of the amount of time I spent with him, or probing questions about him. Apart from his looks, he was the antithesis of Skate, a boy every daughter's parent would be happy to have in the house. In saying that, both of my parents were so otherwise preoccupied and had been for so long that I doubt they would have commented if I'd brought home Dracula or the Dalai Llama, provided I turned up for all my duties.

It was only Uncle Tony who showed some reticence, which undoubtedly was due to his protective nature and I assumed it would dissipate as time passed, as I was anticipating much time with Ralph.

Uncle Tony invited me to stay in his island house for the three weeks in the summer that I would be free, during Mother's vacation, and had offered to give me a key to come and go as I pleased on weekends. We sat together, legs dangling over the dock at the boatyard as we discussed it.

'I just feel you could use a place to go, Gloria, a bit of a refuge,' he said, 'with Gabe now moved out and Maureen working and heading off to Holy Family in the fall, and now with Bernadette's illness, it just seems like your turn for a bit of a change. I know it's not much, but…'

'What do you mean "illness"?' I said.

This wasn't the first time I had heard Bernadette referred to in such reverential tones lately. Aunt Grace had intimated a similar state of alteration to Bernadette's status after the visit to That Kind of Doctor, and the sound of Bernadette's whispered name was fresh as there had been an influx of hushed conversations in corridors, driveways and over breakfast. My parents, who were already more than occupied with the struggle to run their overcrowded household, as well as the Fish Shop and the rectory, stretched income, grief, overgrown lawns and broken down cars, now had another worry to absorb them, this one usurping all the others. I spotted two jellyfish just beneath the surface and watched as each jelly lung expanded and contracted, trailing tentacles. I thought they looked like two waterlogged and bloated gouged out eyes.

'You know what I mean,' he said. The trouble was, I didn't really know, but I had a suspicion, a dangerous area for the imagination.

'No I don't know. What illness does she have? Can you tell me, or are you not allowed. I suppose it would be breaking the rules for me to know anything useful about my sister?'

He looked as though he were being tortured. He took a breath. 'Well, I think it's going to be a while before they really know, but...'

'So is she crazy then? Is that all? What else is there to know?'

'Gloria. C'mon. Give me a break' said Uncle Tony, shoulders slumped, looking awkward in his large frame. He took a deep breath and sighed it out. 'I don't know. They want to give her medicine but they...'

'Oh, they have to find out how crazy, or what kind of crazy, crazy enough to kill kittens? Or just enough to drown little babies? Have they got pills for that? How about talking to cats – how about the cat answering you?'

I threw a stone at the jellyfish and they disappeared in the ripple. I felt anger and guilt, and no compassion. If anything I hated Bernadette even more, just the sound of her name made me angry. Now the riddle of what was in Bernadette's mind was perhaps solvable, her difficulties were to be celebrated, her vileness excused, her evil spirit would now become her troubled soul, she needed looking after, medicating, sympathy and counselling. She would be indulged. I would have to indulge her. The thought made me feel sick.

The jellyfish reappeared and this time Uncle Tony threw a stone at them.

'They look like plucked out eyes,' I said, when they resurfaced.

'Gloria.' Uncle Tony shook his head. 'They don't, that's gruesome.'

'Perhaps I should go see That Doctor then? What's my excuse?'

He shook his head again, it seemed to be the only thing he could do and be sure about. 'I'm sorry Gloria. Let's just leave it for now, but tough as it might be, you could spare a thought for how Bernadette might feel.'

We sat in silence for a few moments, watching the jellyfish remove themselves from sight under the dock beneath us.

'Can Ralph come over to your house with me?' I said. I now felt if he was going to offer me a place of refuge I may as well have some company.

Uncle Tony sat up. 'Would your parents allow that?'

'I didn't think I'd mention it.'

He shook his head again, and sighed again.

'Let me think about it,' he said. 'Come on, let's go over to Davis's and get some ice cream.'

Ice cream, our panacea, lightened the mood. It was a Saturday morning and the Floating Restaurant was closed, though busy with staff vacuuming and polishing, setting tables, chopping and filleting, replenishing bar supplies and marrying ketchups. We entered via the kitchen and Uncle Tony fetched us two scoops each of mint chocolate chip from the giant tubs in the walk-in freezer. I sat down on a keg of beer and waited nervously as the thick door of the freezer drifted open, releasing a frosty cloud to swallow up my uncle. Never had I entered the freezer and since time began, had feared for my life every time the door opened, lest I was somehow drawn in and imprisoned. I knew it had a handle on the inside, it was impossible to be locked in, but I knew the door would jam if I was in there, and the walls would begin to slowly slide inwards, and the floor and ceiling. There would be no air, as the room got smaller the cold cloud would become more and more dense. Apprehensively, I watched until Uncle Tony was safely sitting on the keg opposite me. Gabe was there, de-veining a vat of shrimp. He was surrounded by crates of food, some containing live lobsters and crabs, shifting noisily. He put the shrimp down and leaned over his work surface to talk. Uncle Tony went off outside to talk to Davis as he oversaw the servicing of his satellite dining rooms which were being prepared for the summer season.

'So did you hear about Bernadette yet?' I asked Gabe.

'Yeah, I did,' he said. 'So it's official.'

We laughed, in that bleak sort of sharing a leaky lifeboat way.

'Who told you?' I said.

'I managed to wrangle it out of Uncle Vinny, funnily enough. I could tell something was up by the way Dad clammed up anytime I went into the shop. I asked Uncle Vinny what was the matter with him, and he just told me the whole thing. Who told you?'

'Uncle Tony, but there isn't a lot of detail.'

'No, well. You're a girl, remember. You can't know stuff.'

'Yeah, I know. I'm only the one that takes care of her,' I said.

Gabe shrugged. 'There's not much to know. She's been to a doctor, she has to go back. Probably forever. She'll take medicine. Probably forever too.'

'Was it a shrink, like a real one?' I said.

'Yup. Like I said, it's official.'

'So that's that then?'

'Looks like it.'

'What if I go crazy now? Do you think I'll get to see a doctor? What if Theresa goes nuts, or Mary, or Angela? We just get to be screwed up, that's it, and consider ourselves lucky I suppose.'

'You'll be able to move out soon, Gloria. You can finish school, go to college, whatever. It seems like a long time now, but it goes quick.'

'It's all right for you. You were a boy. You never had to do anything there, you could just go out all the time, and now it's all john hunky dory and you're a fucking hero because you can cook fish.'

'I know. I'm sorry. I really am. I know it sucked for you.'

He picked up a wriggling crab out of a nearby crate, its claws pegged and banded, and tossed it to me.

'Quit yer crabbin',' he said. I threw it back, missing him, laughing.

'See?' he said. 'You even throw like a girl.'

Uncle Tony arriving back, picked the crab up off the floor absentmindedly, and stood with it in his hand, deep in thought.

'Gloria,' he said, suddenly, 'Davis just gave me the most fantastic idea. Why do you think I don't have barge girls?'

'I don't know.'

I looked at Gabe, for help, he shrugged again and went back to his shrimp.

'Is this a riddle?' I said.

'No. Just answer the question. Why? Tell me what you think?'

'I don't know. Because girls aren't strong enough?' I guessed.

'No!' he shouted. 'Wrong! No! There's NO reason.' He was gesturing wildly.

'They never come and ask for jobs, that's why. And I never thought of it, till now.'

He was booming now, the subjugation of earlier that morning vanished.

'How about it, Gloria, do you want to be the first barge girl?'

This idea should have felt like a dream come true, but because it was never in the catalogue of things to dream about, a concept that was so impossible it didn't even exist, I simply sat there dumbly.

'Could you put that crab down. I can't think.'

Gabe threw aside his shrimp and whooped. 'What a brilliant idea!' and the three of us commenced to make plans and were so excited you'd think we'd just invented the internal combustion engine.

I told Ralph as soon as possible, walking the three miles to wait outside the paint store he worked in.

His reaction was the first breeze in the tornado of negativity that would batter me until the end of the day.

'You can't do that,' he said. 'It's a guy's job.'

'No, it's not. Uncle Tony said there's no reason for it to be. It's just that he's never hired a girl, until now. I'll be the first,' I said, proudly.

His face clouded. 'They won't like it, the other guys that do it. They won't like you, either, because you're his niece, and a girl. They'll give you hard time. Anyway, you'll probably screw it up. Girls aren't supposed to run boats.'

I had expected him to share in my good fortune. I thought he'd be excited for me but instead he spat doubt in my face. At first, of course I knew he was wrong, and tried to convince him otherwise, and we argued, ending with me standing in the street, alone, crying, full of misgivings, regret and their sidekick, guilt.

'I thought we were going out tonight?' I cried, running after him. He swatted me away, a pesky, desperate, bloodsucking insect.

'I'll call you later.'

I went home and waited in agony, thinking of only how to repair the damage and get back into his good favour, terrified that he would abandon me. Of course by that time I had totally forgotten that I had done nothing wrong.

There was more adverse reaction to my new career that evening.

'You?' said Uncle Joe incredulously. 'A barge boy?'

'No,' I said, 'a barge GIRL.'

'I've never heard of anything so ridiculous,' he said, further crushing my self-esteem. 'I'll need to talk to Tony about this.'

'It won't interfere with any of the work you do here, will it?' said Mother. 'I'll speak to Tony, too.'

It wouldn't occur to them to speak to me, I thought, sneering inwardly at her use of the word 'work'. The subject was then closed, and I retreated to Aunt Grace's room. She listened with empathy, recalling the rejection of her snack bar idea some years back.

'I tell you, Gloria, my snack bar would have had class. Not like that clam dive they've got now.'

I didn't actually agree with her about the clam shack, but appreciated her kind words.

Ralph didn't speak to me until the next day after school when my act of contrition, some fast and furtive sex in the duck blind, coupled with the news that we could stay alone at Uncle Tony's beach house in the summer softened his mood.

'I'm sorry about yesterday,' said Ralph. 'I'm just so edgy, these days you know. That bastard touched my hand today.'

'What?' I said.

'Grimsdale, the queer,' he said. 'He looks at me. You know what he wants me to do?' He then spoke to me of unspeakable acts being forced on him, violently and painfully by the clearly deranged chemistry teacher. Ralph became extremely aroused when he spoke to me about Mr Grimsdale's perceived debauchery.

'That's awful, does he really say that stuff to you?' I asked, which Ralph answered with a breathless, 'Come here, I need you,' and proceeded to engage in behaviour similar to what he had just described only this time with me. His handling of me was rough, and hurt. It sometimes resulted in bruises, which I hid, or lied about if necessary. But it made him feel better, so I obliged, and didn't complain. Making him feel good made me feel good, like I was useful. Instead of used.

'I thought Mr Grimsdale seemed pretty normal,' I said.

'Yeah, well he's not, he just can act that way, it's a double life. Don't let him fool you,' he said, vehemently, 'You're just a stupid, naive girl. They're all pervs, they just cover it up. They all lie about it.'

Ralph was right about one thing, and that was I was a naive girl, and probably quite stupid too. I thought, though, that he was the fount of all knowledge. I believed anything he said; he was my everything. He fed me what I needed, the need to be needed, and if I didn't oblige his every want, he got very angry, dangerously angry, angry enough to threaten me, and that, I mistakenly thought, gave me power, and it was the most exciting thing in my world.

****

211

Chapter Twenty-one

'You shouldn't listen to all that crap, Gloria,' said Uncle Tony. 'See? You can run a barge just as well as anyone. They'll get used to it in no time, you'll see. Next week it'll be old news.'

Uncle Tony was reclining on a long sofa that was wrapped entirely in silver foil and adorned with a large white bow at either end. This, and a case of champagne, were the only items on the barge, which looked primitive and grimy in contrast to its glittering cargo.

Summer had finally arrived along with the hangover veil of haze that capped the bay in the early mornings to be later distilled by the sun's heat. School was out and I was the newest member of the Gar-barges team.

Piloting the barge was, contrary to my expectations, and contrary to what almost the entire male population in my acquaintance tried to persuade me to think, quite straightforward. It was about the simplest kind of motor powered boat there was. The motor started with a key, similar to a car, and this one had a wheel to steer with. When you turned the wheel to the right, the barge would turn right, but slowly. You had to be patient, and have a light touch. Some of the barges had rudders instead of steering wheels in which case you sat in the back and if you wanted the barge to go right, you pushed left, and it reacted a bit quicker than the steering wheel type. That was it. Docking could be a bit tricky but again it was just a matter of some rope and a couple of poles. It was not a feat requiring scientific precision, an engineering degree or Olympian strength.

Although I thought better than to mention it, Ralph was wrong about the other barge operators, as Uncle Tony now referred to us. They were very friendly and welcoming, even helpful, perhaps treating me as something of a curiosity. Maybe they zipped up before coming out of the toilet now, instead of after. But there was no indication of jealousy or outrage about my appointment.

'Why, then, is everyone so against it?' I said, 'especially Dad and Uncle Joe.'

'I don't know,' said Uncle Tony. 'People don't like changes

sometimes. It scares them. Papa Joe dies, a week later you take a boat out on your own. They can't handle two big things in one week, their minds set up a connection between the two. Don't think I haven't had my share of grief about it.'

'Oh. I'm sorry.'

Uncle Tony laughed, rocking the barge. 'Hey. It doesn't worry me, it shouldn't worry you. Stop apologising all the time, Gloria, you apologise too much.'

'Sorry,' I said, before I could stop myself.

This was my first voyage of delivery, to Sandy Hills, one of the towns on the Island I'd never been to.

'Why is that sofa all wrapped up like that?'

'Because it's a present, the guy said.'

'That's a pretty big present.'

'That's nothing, Gloria, compared to some of the stuff that we take over. You'll see.' He pointed, and got up. 'That way, over there,' he said, coming to sit beside me for the final part of the journey.

We drifted slowly offshore of the island into the Sandy Hills harbour, nothing like any place on the island, or indeed anywhere I'd ever seen. The houses to the east and west that I could see looked like small space age palaces, with acres of glass through which one could catch a glimpse, in the brief moment we glided past, of more acres of glass inside, and polished wood, a small swimming pool, an orchid, a pair of terriers, a Jackson Pollock, and then the vision would be swallowed up by the thick trees or high stone wall surrounding the garden, putting an end to my voyeurism.

The small dazzling harbour was my next surprise. Beacon Island communities didn't generally have harbours, just jetties, and if there was any harbour it was very basic and functional. This harbour was full of gleaming cabin cruisers and the kind of sailboats I'd only seen on the occasions that my Dad had pointed, awed, and said 'Oh my God look at that sailboat!' On land, just beyond the dock was a clean kempt boardwalk, telephone kiosks, landscaped flowerbeds, whitewashed benches, a few select boutiques, two restaurants, a florist, and a pet grooming shop. The only familiar Beacon Island amenity I could locate was the grocery and general store, and even that looked chic. The barge rammed into the side of the dock before I realised we had arrived, so engaged was I in my first sight of Sandy Hills.

'Oh!' I said. 'I'm sorry Uncle Tony! I'll just grab...' but he had already secured the barge. He was grinning at me.

'I said stop apologising. You'll come here quite a lot, you'll get used to it. There's a lot of wealthy people here, but if you take a walk it's not all like that. And this is friendly place, regardless. Money doesn't have to be nasty and offensive. It'll seem quite everyday, after a while, you'll see.'

'Are those palm trees?' I was incredulous.

'Something like that. They move 'em inside in the winter.'

'But this looks like some exclusive European resort,' I said. 'Or at least, what I imagine that would be like.'

'This is better, though,' he said.

'Why?'

'Because there aren't any roads, for one thing. It's quiet. And, of course, they've got to get rid of their garbage,' he said, chuckling.

'Better than Venice?' I asked.

'Well, no, I wasn't counting that. No comparison, it's different.'

Sandy Hills was the furthest east on the island that I'd been, I was really only familiar with the stretch between Uncle Tony's and Pirate Harbour. I had no idea any place like this existed. I'd been gazing across the bay at this barrier island all my life, thinking of it as my own. It was only just dawning on me that I didn't know much about it. I felt like I'd jumped under a microscope.

'Are there other places like this? I mean here?' I asked.

'Nothing quite this exclusive that we service, but they're all different. You'll get to know them,' he said. 'There's only one private place I don't go to, Beacon Bay Haven, it operates like a club. You can't buy a house there unless you're voted in, and renting isn't allowed. It's much richer than this. Gar-barges isn't good enough for their garbage, they have their own arrangements.'

I sat for a while, taking it in. There were few people about, it was still pre-season, but it was hot. There was a woman standing outside the pet place, idly reading the sign. She wore a strapless black dress and stupendous high-heeled sandals. Shiny jet-black hair toppled out of her hat onto her angular brown shoulders. She was wearing sunglasses and carrying a minuscule dog of no breed I recognised. I was mesmerised by the scene, this remote, sparsely populated place inhabited by otherworldly goddesses like her, with the ability to sustain two restaurants and a pet beauty parlour.

I sat on the gift-wrapped sofa. 'What happens to this sofa now? Do we have to move it?'

'We'll help. Someone should be here to meet us. I expect they'll be along in a minute.'

'It looks like its going to a big giant Barbie house,' I said.

'Doesn't it just!' said a voice, belonging to a man that seemed to bounce out of nowhere. 'Sorry I'm late, Tone, I'll just go get the big wagon. And who is this?' he said, indicating me.

'Gloria, this is my friend Peter, also one of our best customers. Gloria's my niece, and newest captain, at least part-time.'

'Oh how exciting!' squealed Peter, a bit dramatically, I thought, but I did appreciate not being called a girl for once.

'Oh, come, you must see the house, have you got time? Two secs,' he said, and without waiting for an answer, trotted off to get the big wagon, a long flat-bed pull-along trailer. We lifted the sofa onto and wheeled it along a network of boardwalk streets to its destination, giving me a further opportunity to observe the Sandy Hills community.

Uncle Tony was right, some of it was quite ordinary, but it was newer and better kept than any other place on Beacon Island I knew of, and very different. It had an unusual flavour, a sort of ultra hip, heart of downtown feel, but was more driftwood paradise than city slick, and, in common with Pirate Harbour and Deer Path Cove, was peaceful and quiet, with the perpetual sound of ocean.

We walked along Bay Walk, which was the main street, a 'street' being just a raised wooden path, where we passed two more shops, an art gallery come jewellers, and an ice cream parlour, the last one the only business other than the grocers I'd seen so far that made sense to me. The houses had names instead of numbers, as was island custom, as well as being painted bright colours. There were many, many houses here and as we walked endlessly along Bay Walk I read the names. *Seaview, Bay Walk Cottage, Blink'n Beautiful*, next door to *Blink'n You'll Miss It, Seaview East*.

The gardens were lush. I'd seen the odd bedding plant or non-native ornamental grass plant on other parts of the island, but my picture of a beach house exterior was of sand, shells, grass and maybe a pine cone here and there, all provided by nature. The gardens of Sandy Hills defied the sand, it seemed the residents could get anything to grow in it, the more colourful the better. The colour was ultra vivid against the pale beach grass and white sandy landscape, flowers were everywhere, roses framed doorways and vermilion geraniums spilled out of window boxes and down walls. Imported tropical plants had thrived. One house even had a small lawn; clearly farmed turf shipped over from the mainland, perhaps on one of Uncle Tony's barges, and rolled out like a carpet. Thin vertical jets of water from a sprinkler swayed gracefully back and forth over it, a few drops landed on me as we passed. Others had themes, a jungle garden, a Japanese garden, a blue-and-white-hues only garden, a sculpture garden, a fresh water fountain garden. Somehow, all of this colour and innovation blended in with the landscape, seeming almost natural. There was nothing garish or tawdry about it.

I guessed Peter to be in his twenties. He was an appealing man with curly blonde hair and a big all-the-time smile, even when he wasn't smiling. His face held his muscles permanently in that smiley position. He was suntanned and very physically fit; a fact easily observed because he wore only a pair of flip-flops and tennis shorts.

He and Uncle Tony 'chatted amiably as we walked, including me in their conversation, which centred mainly around the sofa, a joint gift from Peter and his friend Jerry to Jerry's sister, until we came to a corner where Bay Walk sagged and was overblown with sand.

'Not far now, said Peter.

The three of us had to push, shove and manoeuvre the wagon over the obstacle and around the corner towards the ocean, on to Sandpiper Lane, a narrower stretch of boardwalk of a higher elevation, making it more precarious, and the conversation halted while we concentrated on the move. About halfway between the bay and the ocean we stopped.

'Here we are! Welcome to the big, giant Barbie house!' said Peter.

Peter's house was a two-storey old style house, painted pink with white shutters. It was called The Pink House.

'Jerry!' he shouted into the house, 'The sofa-mobile has arrived!'

He turned to us. 'You are coming in?' I looked at Uncle Tony, who looked at me, and then his watch. 'Ok, Pete, but just for a few minutes.'

Jerry came out on to the porch, another man cut from the same mould as Peter, this one the dark version. They fussed over the wrapped sofa for a few minutes and decided to leave it outside for now. Introductions were made and we went in. As I expected, the house was a treat, with open plan design, open fires, open windows. A widow's watch at the top of the house had both bay and ocean views. There was art, natural wood, and lemonade and wine, chocolate and potato chips. We sat on a deck facing south, high above the boardwalk with a view of spindly, stilted houses sprawling out and ending at a vast expanse of ocean beach. A dog, an albino spaniel, whose name was Pink begged for scraps.

'Now behave, Pinky. Not a very original name, I'm afraid,' said Jerry, 'It wasn't me, though, she came with the house. I bought it three years ago and she was a condition of sale.' He scooped up the dog and cuddled it. 'We love her, though.'

Peter and Jerry entertained us as lavishly as the fifteen minutes we had to spare would allow, sending me home with a camellia from the roof garden in my hair.

'Maybe see you Tuesday, if you're here,' said Uncle Tony, when we parted. Tuesday was a garbage collection day in Sandy Hills.

'What nice people,' I said, to Uncle Tony, still slightly in awe.

'Yeah, too bad they're not all like that.'

I loved being a barge girl. I became popular in the Gar-barges boathouse, and soon developed a rapport with the other barge boys. There were six, four of them year-rounders and two extra for the summer season, plus me, the part-timer. There was one large and three smaller gar-barges and an assortment of small motor boats acquired by Uncle Tony over the years, some conglomerates, several old boats meshed into one, and there was always a boat being put together, taken apart or repainted, and a dismembered engine in the kitchen. Uncle Tony was unable to say 'that boat's no good anymore'. I always took the barge with the steering wheel on my excursions, probably because it was easier, not just for a girl, but for the youngest and most inexperienced member of the team, and it became known to them affectionately as 'Gloria's barge', 'Glorious barge', or 'Gloria's glorious barge'.

Unfortunately I couldn't share any of my new working life with Ralph, who seethed and became surly at any mention of Gar-barges, however unrelated, to the point where I concealed my enthusiasm for the job. My desire to please him ensured that I never spoke of it, and would even turn down opportunities to make an island delivery in favour of a few hours spent with him. Ralph, combined with my other commitments, didn't afford me much time out on the bay. If Uncle Tony had been an ordinary employer, I would have been fired. He loved me too much to fire me, and at this stage, the purpose of my appointment was to give me something to look forward to and a sense of worth for myself. It was good, but it wasn't enough. No matter how much he gave, there was too much bad garbage coming at me from other directions, including inside myself.

Back home, we still lived around Bernadette, who was beginning to undergo changes since her visits to That Kind of Doctor started. She spent more time with the animals, particularly cats and birds, conversing openly with them and reporting their conversations regularly, usually at dinner or similar public gatherings. I looked forward to these declarations, amused by the theatre of the adult discomfort pitted against Bernadette's lunacy.

She wore a hat now, all the time, even to school and in bed, for protection against the cats inserting thoughts into her head, or her own thoughts escaping. It was not a baseball hat or anything that might pass unnoticed, but a felt hat with a rim, like a man's. It looked out of place on a young girl, particularly on hot midsummer afternoons when she would sweat sideburns. Bernadette was much more comfortable with her madness, it seemed, and took pains to explain to us the meaning behind her hat, and the cats' remarks. Mother and Dad, on the other hand, and aunts and uncles, kept true to form by ignoring her behaviour, nodding pleasantly at her bizarre commentary.

'That's nice Bernadette, Maureen could you pass the ketchup please?' they would say, tight lipped and white knuckled, until they could retire for a feverish discussion out of earshot.

Bernadette took medicine now but the various substances and dosages were still in the experimental stage and it would be sometime before the drug situation was a stable one, information I got via combined intelligence from Aunt Gloria, Uncle Tony and eavesdropping. They still never talked to us about it, "they" being our parents and "us" being Bernadette's sisters. It was as though it was none of our business, we weren't involved.

Bernadette's attacks on the twins and Angela were less frequent and tended toward short, sharp and verbal rather than violently physical, I supposed because of the soporific effects of her medication. It could almost be classed as ordinary sibling rivalry, although having lived in Bernadette's defensive battleground for so long we had little concept of what ordinary was. Sadly, their fear of her was not so easily quelled. I discovered Mary at three am, teetering on a chair at the cupboard removing what appeared to be Bernadette's prescriptions. Annoyed at first to have my childcare duties extend into the early hours, I challenged her.

'Mary.' I whispered. 'It's the middle of the night. Back to bed. What are you doing?'

Mary had always been the quiet twin, and as she grew older, she grew quieter, the shadow of her noisy sisters. She never spoke out of turn, or unnecessarily, and this time was no exception.

'Nothing.' She said, screwing the top back on a bottle. My annoyance turned to worry.

'You haven't swallowed any of that, have you?'

She shook her head.

'Are you sure?' I asked.

'Of course she's sure.' The voice came from the corner behind a box of old newspapers, cardboard, and a bucket of kindling. It was Theresa, her spokesperson.

'She's counting them,' Theresa sat in her corner cross-legged, arms folded, 'to see how long they're going to last.'

'It won't ever run out, it doesn't work like that,' I said. 'It keeps getting renewed. Now go back to bed and get some sleep.'

I followed them upstairs and listened as they relayed this whispered information to Angela, the lookout, who lay wide-eyed, waiting for their return. I felt sick as it sunk in just how frightened they were, aged only six and seven, counting the remaining tablets like days on death row. What's the remedy for that?

Maureen was the only one who slept soundly. Bernadette, tossed and fidgeted in her sleep, her blond curls spilling out from under her silly hat onto her pillow. I watched her sleeping and wondered what she dreamt, and whatever happened to the beautiful baby bouncing Bernadette, the one we loved once. Was she still in there somewhere? Why did this happen to her? Why not me? Maybe I would catch it later in life.

I discovered the best solution to coping with these unwelcome feelings and general difficult areas of life was by not coping, i.e. pretend it's not happening, a condition which has now been given the official, and much more convenient label of 'denial'. I thought the best thing would be to escape whenever possible, and I did that entire summer, out on the bay and to Uncle Tony's beach house, where he begrudgingly turned a blind eye to the presence of Ralph, who he disliked and disapproved of, but refrained from saying so out of the kindness of his very big heart.

Every Tuesday morning I rose early for garbage collection at Sandy Hills, on the largest barge, accompanied by Uncle Tony and one of the other barge boys. After dropping off whatever deliveries we had we'd separate and head to our designated boardwalks, each with a flat wagon. When we were finished, we'd decant our wagons onto the barge and go back for a second load. Then we had coffee and Danish pastries at the Pink House with Peter and Jerry, or Marta and Pat's, or at Robin's Rest with Rob and Raymond. Afterwards, we'd head back home as the barge was full, to empty it before Uncle Tony returned for the rest, without me as it would be time for me to be at home.

I made many friends in Sandy Hills, but especially Peter and Jerry. Sometimes I'd see them on the mainland, catching or leaving a ferry, and we'd share an ice cream or a coffee at Davis's restaurant. They were amused by my naivety. I was about halfway through the summer before I finally realised, and then not until a word in my ear from Peter, that there was something special about the community of Sandy Hills, and it wasn't just the amount of wealth.

'Honestly Gloria,' said Peter, 'I don't think I've ever met someone like you. You're as innocent as you are street wise. It just doesn't figure.'

I didn't think, talk about or even recognise the existence of Sandy Hills or my barge career while I was with Ralph, who would have blown a gasket if he'd known how much I enjoyed these things, considering his opinions. This again was widespread behaviour that earned itself a label in the modern times we lived in. So rather than referring to it as 'keeping secrets' or 'hiding the truth' or just plain 'being fucked up', it was 'compartmentalising'; much snazzier. It meant I kept the different parts of my life separate and never mixed them up; in my case, for fear of an explosive cocktail.

I still worshiped Ralph in spite of his moodiness, jealousy, possessiveness and increasing violence. I saw him, mistakenly, as my ticket out of my trap, my ultimate escape. I bent over backwards, sometimes literally, to keep him happy and he would promise me lifelong devotion, a little yellow house with a white picket fence life. He liked to talk about 'our future' together. I spent two weeks at Uncle Tony's house with him, and didn't go home once. It was blissful. Ralph had to go to work a few times, once, luckily for me, on a Sandy Hills Tuesday, when Uncle Tony ferried us both back to Piper Bay, the two of them, not speaking a word; silently despising one another. The other Tuesday I missed the Sandy Hills collection in favour of a day with Ralph. Uncle Tony stayed on the mainland in his Gar-barges apartment, whenever Ralph was with me, a fact that I found both a relief and a disappointment.

When I couldn't be on the bay or at Uncle Tony's house, I was at home where I whiled away the hot afternoons reading trashy romances or staring into the tropical fish tank, leaving my sisters and Aunt Grace to fend for themselves for everything bar absolute essentials.

I never visited Dad at the Fish Shop or Mother at the rectory; spoke to my parents only when absolutely necessary, and spent as much time away from their house as possible. It was an almost perfect summer, until the last week when it all fell apart.

****

Chapter Twenty-two

The nice boy who gave me chewing gum gradually disappeared and metamorphosed into someone else, somehow without me realising it. This happens to women all the time, but I didn't know that. The easy way to take the 'almost' out of the perfect summer equation would have been to extract Ralph from it, though.

This was another example of the thing that was renamed 'denial', although, I still prefer to describe it the original, more accurate, way - pretending it wasn't happening. In order to deny something you have to acknowledge it to begin with. I was new to the experience so I didn't see it coming. It would be a very long time before I did, long after the episode came and went, which is something that also happens to women all the time. Perhaps if I'd had more practised girlfriends, they would have warned me, and I would have a string of people lining up to say 'I told you so'. In the end it was only Uncle Tony who noticed, and he was wise enough to realise that saying anything against my relationship with Ralph would only damage my relationship with himself.

I learned quite a bit about Ralph during the summer. He began to confide in me, long, heartfelt, tortured tirades that I accepted like gifts. It turned out that Ralph's family wasn't the ideal suburban model after all. His father was a tough city cop; he'd seen it all, as he continually reminded Ralph. He rose at the crack of dawn and commuted into work every day to 'wipe up the scum' as he put it, before it spread out to us. His mother, a nurse, worked mainly nights. She did the best job she could looking after Ralph during the day considering she was asleep most of the time.

'Wake me up if you need anything; if anything happens; if you want me, if it's urgent.'

There were a lot of things Ralph needed, but mainly he needed his mother to be awake. He didn't find that reason sufficiently urgent, so he let her keep sleeping.

His parents fought when they were together, loud, long, plate-throwing arguments. It was his father who threw; she was the crash wall.

There was one weekend Ralph brought me to his home. His father sat in a reclining armchair in front of the game on TV, in his undershirt, like many other fathers, drinking a beer and smoking. The cigarette smoke drifted out of his mouth, was whipped away by the electric fan and blown out into the hot summer haze.

'Dad, this is Gloria.' Ralph grunted at him. We were just passing through the room. 'Hi Mr Gilmour,' I said, smiling, trying to impress. He turned and critically appraised me for a moment or two before he nodded dismissively and returned to his game. I was insulted and therefore most sympathetic when Ralph confessed to his hatred of his father. In the kitchen, his mother was up to her elbows in the sink, playing the perfect wife. I thought I might be greeted with gleaming teeth, cookies and milk, but no, crash walls don't smile. She was pretty, though, but with downcast eyes and a soft voice barely audible, like she was trying to blend in to her surroundings, go unnoticed.

Ralph was an only child, who liked to surf, listened to music, grew his hair, and definitely didn't want to be a cop. He didn't know what he wanted to be, but what he was turning out to be was a man full of rage and anger with a tendency towards violence, all covered with a thin coat of surfer boy curls and a crooked grin. Only the smile and the curls were inherited from his mother, everything else came from the dad he abhorred. Unfortunately I only acknowledged the veneer.

I was determined to have the perfect end to what I had considered to be a perfect summer, and on Labour Day weekend, with a slight amount of manipulation and a lot of luck, I was able to divide my pleasures into the remaining days without any conflicting crossing paths. At least that was how it was planned. The luck packed up and did something else that weekend.

The plan was, Friday night would be spent at Uncle Tony's with Ralph, whose departure for work on Saturday afternoon would be perfectly timed with the arrival of Uncle Tony and friends on the Glorious barge to collect me, and we'd all go over to Sandy Hills to the annual all-night-end-of-the-summer party, after which we would collapse and fall asleep on the beach for a few hours. Sunday would be spent leisurely swimming through coffee and making our way back to Uncle Tony's for anytime breakfast and more coffee and then, finally, back on the barge to the mainland. Perfect.

Friday evening came and I sat in the ferry terminal at sunset, reminiscing over the summer, if one can reminisce over such a short time, drinking a can of that old family favourite, cream soda. I was joined by Peter and Jerry who were heading over to Sandy Hills. After hugs and kisses of greeting they settled down on the bench with me. Jerry opened a bottle of some sort of French drink I didn't recognise, with a twist cap, the latest innovation in refreshments. Ring pulls weren't far behind. I still punctured the tops of my cans the old way, in the coke machine.

'What are you drinking?' I asked.

'He's drinking water,' said Peter, 'which he paid over a dollar for. Soon we'll have to mortgage the house for the summer supply of the stuff.'

'It's not just water, it's carbonated spring water,' said Jerry, 'much better for you. Here, have a sip.' He offered me the bottle. 'It's full of minerals.'

'You're full of minerals,' said Peter.

Quite a lot of people didn't like to drink the brackish water on the island, they thought it would make them sick and so brought over barrels of the nicer tasting Piper Bay tap water, and when they ran out, had more sent over by Gar-barge or with friends on ferries. I drank the native Beacon Island water. Although it didn't taste very nice, it never made me ill. Jerry's fancy water bit my throat and I marvelled at how rich people found new things to spend money on, and then claimed those things were better.

They chatted excitedly about the Sandy Hills party, describing to me how the beach would look, how they were to join in the construction of the stage, the elaborate clam bake preparations and how the entire event was flawlessly timed around low tide.

'Where's Tony? What are you two doing tonight?' said Peter.

'Uncle Tony's not coming till tomorrow. I'm having a friend over,' I said.

'Oooh. A friend !' Jerry teased. 'Anyone interesting?'

'Oh, no, nothing, just a girlfriend,' I lied to them.

We sat together on the *Cap'n Kidd*, a runty, squat, utility boat that had been used as a rum-runner during prohibition, and didn't appear to have changed much since then. The Beacon Island ferries were all second-hand, all had previous hard-working lives and were now living out a gentle retirement sailing to and fro across Piper Bay, like old horses giving pony rides. I didn't normally travel by ferry, but Uncle Tony wasn't coming and he would not allow me to take a barge over on my own after dark.

The little ferry was full to capacity, and would stop at tiny Deer Path Cove, on to Sandy Hills and Sandpiperton, a small family community whose residents consisted mainly of blue-collar workers from the town of Breadmill, directly across from it on the mainland. There were more hugs and kisses for farewells at Deer Path Cove, where only myself and another woman disembarked, and I sat down on Uncle Tony's dock and waved the boat off, heading west, overstuffed with parents, kids, dogs, good looking young men and groceries.

I immediately walked up to the ocean and took a long walk in the fading light, returning to Uncle Tony's just as the natives – the mosquitoes – were getting restless. I hoped to find Ralph there, as he was due anytime but there was no sign of him so I went indoors and made myself a cup of tea and some toast, and sat on the screened in porch to watch the sunset's afterglow and anticipate his arrival. The one remaining ferry came and went, and as the night grew older the bay traffic quietened. Half a loaf of bread and two pints of tea later there was still no Ralph. It was nearly midnight and too late to phone, but I still waited, faithfully inventing his excuses for him, sure all sounds, distant motors or nearby rustling shrubs were announcing his approach, and was crushed by each passing water taxi or browsing deer. I fell asleep in the chair, woken by the cold morning, swollen bladder and a stiff neck, not having spoken to a single soul since I left the happy bustling ferry so long ago the previous evening. I waited again, for most of the day, beside myself with worry, grief and teenage lovesickness, a terminal illness, in my case.

He finally arrived, inconveniently, half an hour before Uncle Tony was due. By that time I had phoned his house, where there was no answer, several times, and mourned his death by every car and boat disaster imaginable, had him murdered and robbed and left for dead, suffering a heart attack and falling down his cellar stairs where he still lay, unconscious. It never occurred to me that I may have been cruelly stood up, I never considered being angry with him. Instead, I threw myself at him gratefully when he stepped onto the deck, and sobbed uncontrollably with relief. He seemed irritated by my exaggerated show of emotion, pushing me away.

'It's no big deal. I just didn't feel like coming. It was never that definite, anyway.'

'Oh I know, I'm sorry, I'm just such a stupid worrier.'

'Yeah,' he said. 'You are pretty stupid.' His tone was matter of fact.

Of course it had been a definite arrangement, but he had an uncanny power over me, if he had told me I had blonde hair I would have gone to the mirror to check.

We decided to leave the house when he discovered Uncle Tony's arrival was imminent, the scorn between them was mutual.

'I better leave him a note,' I said, 'he'll be expecting me.'

'Why? Had you got other plans?' he said this aggressively.

'No! But he's my uncle, he'll worry.' I scrawled a quick note. 'Maybe catch up to you later. Gone out with Ralph, love Gloria.'

We walked down to the ocean and along the shore to Breakwater Point where we got a coke and some french fries, then walked back to Deer Path Cove where we sat on the beach. It was dark by then. Uncle Tony would have left for Sandy Hills and the party without me. Ralph was quiet and preoccupied and rejected any attempts I made at conversation.

'Would you just shut up, Gloria.'

'I'm sorry,' I said. I stroked his arm. He pushed me away.

'I'm going for a walk,' he said, and left me there for a very long time, where I was mosquito bitten and then cold, and again, full of worrisome thoughts concerning his safety. I considered going back to house to get a sweatshirt, but even though the trip would have taken all of four minutes or so, I stayed, afraid to miss his return, or his body washing up on the beach, or other such tragic imagined reunions. I stood up when he finally came back, avoiding any embraces or actions that would be likely to upset him.

'We can go back to house now, if you like. Uncle Tony will be out.'

'Oh yeah? Where'd he go?' he said. His tone was frightening. 'To Sandy Hills maybe? To the party?' He smelled of alcohol.

'I – don't know.'

'Oh yes you do, Gloria. I saw you with those queers at the ferry terminal. Dirty queers like that uncle of yours.'

He then drew his arm back and punched me in the mouth. Dumbstruck, I'd been attempting to open it and defend myself, and my uncle by – what else – denial.

I suppose it was at this point the perfect summer idea took a nosedive.

Unsteady, shocked and already reeling, I stood, open mouthed and bloody, staring at him, and, before I could recover enough to speak, he beat me senseless. Senseless in the way that I then lost whatever sense I may have possessed, not in that I lost consciousness. He was too smart for that. He punched me and kicked me and threw me on to the sand and hit me a bit more, enough to hurt me but not do serious damage, then he pulled me to him and we had some rather violent intercourse, which anyone else might have described as rape. This was my act of contrition and his reconciliation and it was the beginning of an evil cycle and my crash wall career.

Then, he left.

'Look, Gloria, I'm too upset to stay, I've got to go. I'm sorry.' He kissed me passionately, stood up, arranged his clothing.

'Please stay,' I begged. 'Where will you go?'

'I got friends down the way. I'll see you tomorrow.'

I watched as he disappeared into the night, then sat and cried for a time, and when I'd finally convinced myself that he didn't mean it, he was just troubled and moody, and besides, I'd upset him, I took my aching bruised and bitten body back to the house and fell into bed, exhausted. I avoided dwelling on his observations regarding Sandy Hills or my uncle, dismissing them as remarks made in rage. People say things they don't mean.

I awoke in the early hours aware of a light inside the house, and got up to investigate, finding it came from Uncle Tony's room. He must have fallen asleep with it on, I thought and when I sneaked in to turn it out was left with my mouth hanging open for the second time that night. There was Uncle Tony and Davis in bed, sound asleep, curled up in each other's arms like two kittens. I hastily exited, hearing one of them stir in the bed as I closed the door behind me.

****

Chapter Twenty-three

The deeper I thought I was in love with Ralph, the more he abused me, a situation I won't dwell on, because one, he's not worth the paper, and two, it's all a bit depressing, and three, I feel a bit foolish about staying with him for as long as I did. It's amazing what a human being can get used to.

He was as clever a bully as I was passive victim. He never overstepped the mark, never injured me enough to need medical treatment, or hit me on my face or hands, anywhere that might be visible. He was genuinely distressed and angry as he recounted the tales of his own and his mother's beatings, yet it seemed he made no connection. I, in turn, saw him as the victim. He was the injured party, not me. The poor guy couldn't help it; he was the innocent bystander of his father's creation.

I was able to minimise his 'upsets' as I came to call them, by becoming astute in avoiding the circumstances, subject matter and behaviour that would provoke him. I lived my life in the tense area of two steps ahead. I chewed gum nervously and my stomach hurt. Ralph had been my escape from my lousy life, my ticket to somewhere, to being something better. I had been so wrong. Out of the frying pan, into the fire, I jumped without a parachute, and now I was squashed and burning.

'I'm so sorry, Gloria, you know I would never really hurt you,' he said, 'I don't mean it, anyway it's like it isn't me, it's like it's someone else.'

He would hold me, look into my eyes, tears free-running down his face.

He was crying, I was bleeding.

'That's it, the last time, I'll never do it again,' he said.

I believed him. I couldn't resist those tears.

Ralph was finished High School and working full time now in the paint store, making enough money to get drunk on a regular basis. He spent a good deal of his time off work intoxicated, when he also passed the time getting angry, fighting and driving, the things that eventually killed him, but that was later on, when people started to die. We dreamt of going away and living happily ever after, having baby boys that he could play baseball and go surfing with. Baby girls were not included in the formula for the perfect life.

'We gotta get outta here Gloria. Go west. Get off this fucking island.'

'I'd love to do that.'

'Let's do it, let's plan it. We'll take our savings, you got some money, right?'

'A little bit, enough to start out. I could borrow more if I needed to...'

'From who? That faggot uncle of yours?'

If I was lucky these conversations would end in Ralph passing out.

I was in the middle of my last year of High School and failing badly, mainly because I wasn't there much. When I did attend, I was usually thinking about how to get out again. School is much more interesting when participated in full time. I was there so infrequently that I lagged far behind, and didn't know what the teachers were talking about. I knew I wouldn't be able to graduate if I didn't make an effort, but I just pushed that thought aside and chewed more gum, while saliva worked hard on an ulcer.

Uncle Tony and I didn't discuss what happened on Labour Day weekend, and were living in a fraught state of he thinks that I think that she thinks that he thinks that I think he thinks that she thinks, etc. We smiled, and were polite to each other, but there was a nervous edge that wouldn't let us over into honesty, yet. In spite of my desperation to talk to him, I didn't make the time, preoccupied with Ralph, whose scorn for Uncle Tony caused me more inner turmoil. I was full to the brim of guilt and shame and self-loathing. It was easier to avoid Uncle Tony, as well as anything else I felt bad about. Now, six months had passed since Labour Day, and already the daffodils were coming up in our garden and boats in driveways were being uncovered and painted, preparing for another summer.

I stopped spending time at the marina. My Gar-barge hours were further reduced due to winter and to allow me to devote my energies to school, where everyone thought I was. I had lost interest in the Fish Shop, which was not a place for a young woman to spend her idle hours. I'd heard everything there was to know about shark bait by now anyway.

When I didn't go to school I hung around the new shopping mall, where I could grab a coffee with Ralph sometimes, or else I walked on the beach alone.

My duties in the afternoons remained unchanged, except that the girls were older now and more self-sufficient, and would dress themselves, play and do their homework largely without any input from me. My only job now was to be there, and to feed them. The Bernadette wars were over. We still avoided her, but only because she was so weird.

Mother had told me, a long time ago, that it would get easier, here it was. The easier time was here. She also told me it wouldn't be forever, and now I could see an end in sight.

Aunt Grace, who would never fully recover her former form, was well enough to move home in the autumn. This was cause for a celebration, although as it was pointed out tactfully, and repeatedly, not because of the actual leave-taking of Aunt Grace, but because she was healthy enough to be able to return to her own home. There was pink champagne and chocolate chip sponge with vanilla icing. There was a symbolic bonfire in the back yard which smouldered into the evening, her ceremonial burning of the invalid chair.

Aunt Grace was feeling strong and positive, and felt sure that everything was going to fall into place when she moved back into her home.

'The first thing I need to do is clean from top to bottom,' she said, pushing the sleeves of her blouse above her elbow as she spoke about it.

'Don't overdo it, Grace,' warned Aunt Gloria. Grace ignored her and continued to hold court, mapping out her plans as she made them. The usual crowd had gathered, including Gabe and Beth. Uncle Tony was there, and so was Davis, giving us another opportunity not to speak properly to each other. Davis was as amusing and gracious as ever. I didn't invite Ralph.

'Where's your boyfriend honey?' asked Aunt Gloria. All ears tuned in as they feigned interest elsewhere.

'Working,' I lied, and turned to Grace. 'When is Francine coming home?'

Francine had achieved her beautician-ship and was going to partner her mother in a new salon. Aunt Grace would still cut hair but Francine's new skills would be able to provide new procedures and fragrances applicable to all sorts of body parts, including feet.

'Feet? What the hell do you want to be messing with feet for?'

'They're so important! You can find your whole body in your feet. You should take care of them.'

The men laughed at her.

'Yeah, sure Grace. Your whole body.'

Aunt Grace ignored them too.

'We'll do pedicures as well. And once we're up and running I'll install a sun bed,' said Aunt Grace.

'A what?'

'You're joking.'

'Who needs a sun bed living here?'

'It's the sand. People don't like sand, and all the wind and flies and things that go with the beach. You get a nice even tan, no burn.'

'But the whole point of going to the beach…'

'Yeah, why cover yourself in oil and crispy fry on a gritty beach when you can do it in the comfort of your own kitchen in a pair of blackout goggles.'

'I've heard everything now.'

'You wouldn't understand. You're a man.'

'Papa Joseph will be spinning in his grave.'

'Well, if he'd have paid more attention to taking care of his body he might even still be here to voice an opinion, or at the very least, be able to spin faster.'

Blasphemy! I could detect a bit of the old Aunt Grace returning as well, but we were friends now so I found her funny and wouldn't hear a word against her. That was just who she was. I would, in many ways, be sorry to see her go.

'You'll come and visit me Gloria, won't you?' she said, 'even if it's just to cut that hair. I can straighten it for you, or make it curl more. There's all kinds of new stuff to do that with. Safe stuff, that won't damage it.'

Her departure however, would once again throw open the arena of an empty bedroom to compete for. Already, we were preparing to plead our individual cases.

Naturally, we all thought ourselves to be the most deserving candidate, because I'm the oldest, the youngest, the pair, the most hard working, tired, studious, responsible, well-behaved, or the sort that needed extra privacy.

However, the decision was made before we'd even begun to compile our lists and the allocation of this coveted piece of real estate was announced at the party, casually dropped into the conversation in-between cake crumbs.

'Are you going to paint it before they move in?' I asked.

'Heck, no, it's nearly new. I mean, it's not like Grace draws on the walls or anything,' Dad said.

'Who? Before who moves in?' said Teresa.

I looked around, and Maureen's face gave me the answer. I looked at Maureen, throwing her a silent question. You? She nodded.

'Maureen is going to move in, honey,' said Mother.

As muscles tensed and the springs of the outcry tightened, Mother spoke again.

'And Bernadette will go with her. Just the two of them. You four will stay where you are.'

Outcry arrested. There would be no more discussion on the subject and the party resumed its celebration of Aunt Grace.

If one considered the numbers involved the arrangement was vaguely unfair but we couldn't resist being satisfied and grew to view Mother's decision as an inspired solution.

Maureen was chosen because she, as the academically minded member of the crowded bedroom community, needed the peace to study. She also wouldn't mind having Bernadette as a roommate, and Bernadette had always tolerated Maureen. I doubted if I had made the shortlist on either count.

The twins, Angela, and I were excited. Two people would be leaving the bedroom, which equalled one entire set of beds, meaning that the remaining sets could each rest against a wall, removing the dormitory, or hospital effect. It would look like a bedroom; there would be space between the beds that would accommodate more than a pair of knees. Ironically, I would never get to enjoy it, my life lived at home was about to end.

As usual, anything concerning Bernadette sat on scales, if I was happy about Bernadette going to The Doctor, I was sad that it was due to That Kind of Illness. The long ago little girl with the blonde curls always dragged herself out of the past to weigh down the negative plate.

I was happy about Maureen moving out of my bedroom and could say that to her, gloat even. I wanted to be happy about it. With Bernadette it was indefinably different. It was tricky to hate someone that you love and give that feeling an identity.

'I hate her! I wish she would die!' I had shouted once, in the heat of the moment.

'Gloria!' Mother had shouted back, the exceptional raising of her voice leaving an indelible impression. 'Don't say such things! You can't hate your sister. It's impossible. Now go to your room and say a rosary.'

I never said that rosary.

Bernadette was deemed fit enough for ordinary school, That Doctor said. As long as she took her medicine she would be able to learn as well as anyone. Anyone normal, they meant, but no one would say that lest it imply she wasn't normal, which of course she wasn't.

She was twelve now, in Junior High School, a building integral to the one I was in, albeit rarely, and for this one year we'd shared the same corridor space.

Bernadette was different from the other girls in her year, in other ways, apart from The Illness. She was older, having repeated a year in primary school, a circumstance that branded her dim and slow. She was smaller than her classmates, by a long shot, putting her at a physical disadvantage as well. The living room terrorist we had been so frightened of seemed meek and fragile in these surroundings.

Bernadette had another problem, a paradoxical, unfair problem, and that was that if she took her medicine, she felt better, and when she felt better, she stopped taking it, believing herself to be fully recovered. This belief was a delusion. We could tell when this happened because she said her thoughts were escaping, and she would revert to wearing the hat. She had added a long woollen coat to the costume; its collar high, and refused to remove these items, partially concealing her face and hair, and persistent, if a bit washed out, beauty. It would take a number of small crises and a couple of weeks to put her back on the acceptable track. It happened a lot. She had to be watched carefully to avoid this, but it was difficult for Mother and Dad, who were still trying to hide the truth. At first Theresa had questioned the regular dispensing of drugs.

'If Bernadette is so sick, why does she have to go to school?'

'It's nothing dear, it's not sickness. Bernadette has to take those, they're like special vitamins. You go and play.'

Special Vitamins? Theresa knew, even at her young age, that this was boloney and that was the signal to use alternative methods of procuring information about this particular topic.

Thus, we couldn't be enlisted to ensure the regular intake of the Special Vitamins in any way, because we weren't supposed to know about it.

When I went to school I avoided Bernadette wherever possible; when we did meet or cross paths I found it painful. When I did see her, she would look past me, as though she found the encounter equally unwelcome. I had heard rumours of bullying.

'How are you finding school, Bernadette?' I asked.

'Fine.' She kept her head down, no eye contact.

'Is everyone nice to you?'

'Fine.'

'Are you sure? Someone told me you were being picked on the other day.'

'Everything is fine Gloria.'

My last day of school was short, and in March, and I don't recall everything about the day, it stays in my memory in fragments that constantly rearrange themselves.

I walked to school in the snow, bleakly worrying that the daffodils pushing up through it would be frozen. Once there, the corridors were as usual, teeming with pupils in transit, shaking off snow, picking up books.

I heard a commotion coming from the stairwell, the same one where three years previously my brother had confronted me about my dodgy associations with The Grease Monkey.

I walked toward the stairwell. There was a cluster of pupils in the small tiled area looking up at the three sets of staircases zigzagging upwards. Some were open mouthed and silent, some shouting. There were more people on the stairs, all looking up at a small group at the very top, swinging a large parcel over the banister, at the top, and letting it dangle over the chasm. The parcel was Bernadette. A hat fell, made its way from above, seemingly in slow motion, floated past me and landed.

I looked from the ground floor, horrified, opened my mouth, but nothing came out. As I strained, along with everyone else, to see what would happen, two angry teachers descended upon the group at the top. The spectators were shooed away. I stayed, unable to move, straining my neck watching, as the parcel, in a long woollen coat, was led away by the two teachers.

Another teacher arrived at the bottom of the stairwell, where I was, dispersing the crowd. I knelt down and picked up the hat, my mother's voice echoing in my head, 'You can't hate your sister. It's impossible,' and thinking of the thousands of times I'd envisaged committing similar acts of cruelty as way of revenge.

'Leave that. Show's over,' he said.

'But that's my sister,' I said.

The teacher took the hat from me.

'Go. Forget it. We'll take care of her. Get to class.'

Bastard. Here was a person who could have been kind to me, and missed the opportunity. Had he been kind to me, the rest of the day may have been different, or maybe not. It was one of those moments that could have changed things. He could have taken me upstairs, to go with Bernadette to the school nurse, to see her after she was all right, not that I felt I deserved it. He could have asked me if I was all right, surely it must have been obvious that I wasn't. Instead, he said WE will take care of

240

HER. There was no room for Gloria in that sentence.

It was the last straw for me. I fell into a black hole of disgrace and self-hatred. Now it was my turn to go crazy, albeit temporarily.

I looked up. The stairwell was empty. I left by the front door and walked home, this time disregarding the daffodils I stepped on.

There was no one home. I paced the floor, and my heart was beating, I could hear it. My movements were jerky, robot-like. Under the sink I found a bottle of household ammonia and poured half of it into a bowl, and lowered my face to the bowl. The fumes pushed me back, though, so I added some water to it. I was thinking it would still work with water. This time I was able to get my face down into it. I wanted to be blind. I didn't want to see any more, or have to watch other people, or look after them. Maybe if I were blind someone would look after me.

I wasn't blinded, I think I may have been crying too much, or added too much water, although my eyes and face were very sore after it. It didn't work, I couldn't even do that right. Disgusted with myself, I cleaned up, making sure there was no evidence of the act, of my failure.

Then I went and phoned Ralph, hoping to catch him before he went to work.

'Hello?'

'Ralph?'

'Yeah, Gloria?'

'I'm going away. Somewhere far. I have to go now.'

'I'll come with you.'

****

Chapter Twenty-four

I was adrift almost three years before returning. Luckily, Mother died or I may never have got back on course. Of course I didn't feel that losing my mother prematurely was good fortune in itself, but I chose to believe that she did it, partially anyway, for my benefit.

I spoke to her a few days before it happened, when she was fine, but I wasn't, and pretended I was, as was so often the case in my telephone calls home. The only difference this time was that she knew.

'Gloria, are you sure you're all right?' she said.

'I'm fine, honest,' I said. 'Maybe just a little tired.'

'No, you're not. I can tell.'

For her to make such a comment, or indeed take any extra interest in me, was unusual, as our standard conversations were short and formulaic, her distracted receipt of my weekly check-in. We would exchange pleasantries, the list of how is he's and she's, give my regards to all, bye for now. This time, though, she was reluctant to get off the phone.

'Are you sure you don't want to come home for a bit? Even just a weekend? It's been so long.'

'No, I'm too busy just now. I'll try for Thanksgiving.' I always said that.

Or Christmas, or my birthday, or Easter, or Labour Day, whatever was closest. I never went, even after I started to want to. Something always came up at the last minute. Nothing could get me to come home. Up until then.

'Well. Take care of yourself then. Don't work too hard. I love you.'

That's what she said, my last conversation with my mother. She had never said that before. Luckily I had the presence of mind to say, 'I love you too,' before I hung up.

Initially that first spring, although no search parties were sent out or cavalries called, they beseeched me to come home. Why did you go? Why. I couldn't explain that to them, not being altogether certain myself.

We'll make things better for you, they promised. Come home, please. All was forgiven for a short while, and then it wasn't, as it became clear that I wasn't coming back and was living, unmarried, with a man. By the time the daffodils had gone, they stopped asking and got used to my absence. Communications became less frequent and more strained, but of course, try as one might, it's impossible to completely drop out of a life where there are people you love, and that love you back, so messages were siphoned through Gabe or Aunt Grace, who was still able to speak to me, although she disagreed with my sudden exit and 'drastic version of happily-ever-after', as she referred to it. Through them, I picked up bits of news.

Bernadette didn't go to school anymore; instead a special teacher came to the house until she turned sixteen, after which she attended classes in a Place for That Kind of Person, but she didn't always go, because after taking her medicine and feeling better she didn't think she was That Kind of Person anymore. Her cycle of sickness carried on as normal. Normal for crazy, that is.

Aunt Grace sent photos of my family to me, and from them I could see that the twins and Angela had grown from innocents into pre-teens, and my absence from that transition stung. Mother and Dad were getting older. This was easier to see on the hard still surfaces of photos than it ever had been in person. I looked at their faces smiling out of the snapshot; I even touched it, but felt only the shiny polaroid paper. Their images tugged, but didn't bring the same searing pain as those of my little sisters, whose lives I felt I was missing. The distance between my parents and I had come gradually, long before I made it geographic. The Fish Shop, the marina, the bay, the island, were all the same but these were the particular areas my homesickness focused on every day I breathed the stale air and looked at my pallid skin tones. All of the photos had been intercepted and destroyed by Ralph in one of his many spiteful moments.

He found me late one night, asleep on the sofa, the pictures lying beside me, watching. I had so far kept them concealed from him.

'What the fuck are you looking at?' He said, snatching them up. He rapidly flicked through them, disgusted. He was, as usual, drunk.

'Waste of time, Gloria,' he said, then flaring up again, as the thought arrived in his slow-witted mind, 'Where did you get these?'

He tore them up, staggered to the window and flung out the pieces like confetti.

'With the rest of the trash, where they belong,' he said before staggering back toward the sofa. Luckily he fell, used up, before he could trash me. I let him stay there, sleeping on the floor, while I crawled off to bed. The apologies were no longer forthcoming upon waking. As time passed, Gabe rang less often.

'Hey. How's everything?'

'Good, great.'

'How was Christmas? Sorry I didn't call that day.'

'That's okay. It was nice. Quiet. Just the two of us, but okay. Yeah. How 'bout you?'

'Yeah, the usual, you know. Christina, remember her? She has another baby now, so there were kids around. I didn't get much time off work. Lots of fruitcake, you know. Usual stuff.'

'Well, okay.'

'Okay.'

'See ya.'

'Okay. Bye.'

I lied to Gabe and Aunt Grace, was evasive and vague and said I was fine; everything was okey dokey, hunky dory. I didn't know how to go home once they'd stopped asking me to.

Because the terrible whim that initiated our flight was entirely mine, and not Ralph's, I was culpable whenever things went wrong, which of course they did, horribly, from the very beginning. We had some money saved, although Ralph had more and was therefore more powerful. Any savings I had went first. We made our way inland, hitchhiking away from the coast; away from all the things I loved. His direction. Instead of the romantic, adventurous life on the road we had dreamt about, we had arguments, got cold and hungry and in the early stages of the exodus, even had a night sleeping rough, outside in the cold, on leftover dirty snow in the thin brush lining the highway, more out of Ralph's desire to prove a point than real necessity.

We had got as far as the other side of Baltimore. Not exactly the Wild

West he was looking for. We eventually lodged above a dry cleaner in a pokey apartment that smelled permanently of the premises below in a nondescript stretch of satellite suburb, a desert of road construction and strip malls, beyond which was a succession of scientific rat-like neighbourhoods. There was no bay, no ocean, no Fish Shop. Ralph got a job in another paint store, and I worked in fast food restaurants until he got me a job downstairs in the dry cleaner, where, as he often liked to say, he could keep an eye on me, a perverse remark considering this was the only use he had for me now, as a prisoner.

It was partly true, what I told Gabe. Christmas was quiet, but it wasn't just the two of us. Twice I spent it sitting alone, watching out the window wondering if he'd come home. He didn't. No presents. No pink champagne. No cake.

I came to hate Ralph and existed in a sort of frantic state of immobilisation, if that's possible. Mired in a routine, however dreadful, time passes. Monday finishes, Friday comes, and then it happens again. More than two years passed and I was still trying to adjust to our arrival.

He was just as violent, still hit me, but now I fought back, which, I discovered I was quite good at. Who would have thought all that practice at home with Bernadette would come in handy. But Ralph was stronger than I was, and the amount of satisfaction I derived out of fighting back was outweighed by my injuries.

After he broke my arm, I decided to escape as soon as it healed. I didn't know where I would go and I was under constant surveillance, obstacles that were challenging but not insurmountable. I was determined to go, and schemed and planned. Then I discovered I was pregnant.

Pregnancy dampened his sexual interest in me, 'for the duration' as he said, and thankfully, curtailed his physical assaults. This lack of physical attention was a great relief, and for a while I reclaimed my body as my own and shared it with my baby.

Apart from the dry cleaning chemical atmosphere I breathed, I took good care of myself, resting, eating well. It never occurred to me to see a doctor. I knew I was pregnant and felt fine; my experiences of doctors were not promotional. Actually having the baby seemed so far into the future that I didn't consider it, even as time passed and I grew bigger.

Ralph found girlfriends elsewhere, yet he still exercised his might and control over me, as he felt was his right as the father of the baby I was carrying. Aunt Grace had been so wrong; this was no happily-ever-after.

This was the tetrachloroethylene squalor that I was trapped in when, on a hot Indian summer day I was called away from a sweltering mangle to take the urgent phone call that ironically, probably saved my life.

'Gloria.' It was Gabe. 'I'm sorry. I've got terrible news.'

A flood of relief is not the typical first reaction to the sudden decease of a parent but I was in such a desperate state that the good feeling in the cocktail of emotions produced by the news of Mother's death floated to the top. I hastened to quash my inappropriate happiness of relief in some suitably thankful prayers, thanks for letting it be quick, thanks for letting me speak to her the other day, thanks for getting me out of that heat, thanks for everything, because this time I had to go home. I packed a small bag, enough for a few days. I didn't have much, anyway.

'I'll be back after the funeral,' I said, knowing I wouldn't be.

Ralph grunted. 'Just don't spend any unnecessary money.' For once he didn't argue so I silently promised only to spend necessary money and waddled alone down to the bus station with all my worldly possessions.

Unfortunately, I hadn't told anyone that I was expecting a baby, in another feat of life mismanagement. I'd been postponing the announcement until I had the strength to field the reaction, and telling Gabe on phone at that moment didn't strike me as good timing.

I decided there was only one way to go home. I was quite large now, and no matter how much I tried to understate that; any entrance I made in the midst of my shocked and grief-stricken family couldn't fail to be dramatic. It wouldn't be good for anybody. Pregnancy can cloud the mind, not to mention the daily inhalation of dry cleaning fluids, but I was fairly certain of my judgment in this instance. I would go to Uncle Tony over on Beacon Island. He would know what to do.

Uncle Tony had the distinction of being the first person on Beacon Island with a telephone answering machine, a relatively new innovation that within a few years would catch on and become as essential as the phone itself. At that time, though, they were a novelty, considered by some as pretentious, unnecessary and frivolous, views sometimes shared by Uncle Tony, as, he said, most people just hung up on it anyway.

I was grateful for the machine when I phoned him from a rest area on my journey. 'Hi Uncle Tony. It's me. I'm on my way home, but I'll come to your house first' – I halted, thinking of what else, what to say next. Click. The machine cut me off, seemingly it thought I'd finished. Well. That would have to do. I would try again later. I bought myself a pack of Lifesavers and sat on the bus, with a polarised heart, numbly staring out of the window at the scenery. So happy was I to be going home, and so sad. The photos Ralph had destroyed included some of the last taken of Mother. I hadn't seen her. I stood apart and hid under a sun hat while I waited for the ferry, not that anyone would have recognised me. I wore a man's white shirt over my old shorts, unzipped and fastened by shoelaces that I'd tied together and slipped through the belt loops. I'd taken this shirt, and a few others, from an unclaimed supply at the dry cleaner to serve as my maternity wardrobe. There were men who owned so many shirts that they could forget about some of them. Ralph, true to form, wouldn't lend me any of his shirts. 'They won't fit you. I'm not that fat,' were his exact words.

There were only two other passengers on the ferry other than myself, Labour Day had come and gone and even though it was a Friday, for most visitors, that was the signal to close the summer lid and think about raking leaves. The sky was dark and overcast, and deteriorating every minute, which was another contributing factor to the reduced population. I spoke to no one.

I could see Uncle Tony standing on the end of his dock as the ferry approached. It had started to rain. The dock had been strengthened, much of the wood had been renewed and more added. It was still narrow but no longer rickety. There was a heron standing on the shore a few yards along, like a handy umbrella, motionless but for its feathers ruffling in the rising breeze. I began to feel nervous.

I hadn't spoken to Uncle Tony since I left, and we'd never resolved that previous Labour Day weekend incident. Now I was about to step off the boat, almost three years later, nine months pregnant, surprise, and ask him what to do about confronting my family. Oh, yes, and my mother, his baby sister, was dead.

He blinked, and that was all. There was no staggering back, mouth dropping open, hand to chest or crying out. He blinked, and then he hugged me. The heron flew off, the boat left, I cried.

'Well Gloria,' he said. 'I think you'd better come in and sit down. You must be hungry.'

'I'm always hungry.'

Uncle Tony lit his hurricane lamps and we talked over French toast and tea and wine into the evening, starting with my apology for missing the party at Sandy Hills three years previously. It took us about three minutes to realise there was no point in discussing it. We had no problems, or baggage, or issues, words that are now used to all mean the same thing. We invented our own word for it.

'We could call it flotsam,' I said. 'Right? If jetsam is the stuff that sinks, then flotsam is the stuff that hangs around, you can't get rid of. That can be what we call our baggage.'

'Could be,' said Uncle Tony. 'But at least you can deal with flotsam, clean it up. Jetsam sinks. You can't see it but it's still there – maybe it rots, maybe lies in wait, drags a line, creates an obstacle. Is that more appropriate?'

'Oh, yeah. I didn't think of that. I don't know.'

Uncle Tony laughed. 'Perhaps we could have categories of fucked-upness,' he said, 'flotsam, jetsam, seaweed, baggage, luggage, overnight cases…'

I started to laugh too, then I started to cry again, and then stopped. It was exhausting, all this emotion.

'How is Davis?' I asked.

'He's fine, great, he'll be thrilled to see you. He'll be here in the morning to pick us up. I haven't got a boat here.'

He looked at me, concerned.

'Christ Gloria, you are huge. When is this baby due?'

'I'm not sure. I think soon, but I didn't know exactly when it happened.'

I started to cry again, and told Uncle Tony how happy I was to see him, and about the smell of the tetrachloroethylene and that I hoped it hadn't damaged the baby. I told him about how Ralph bullied me both emotionally and physically, and how it took five different machines to press and fold a shirt, and how I'd brought home a wild baby rabbit that I'd found and Ralph had killed it, and all about why fast food is sometimes slow. I told him how Ralph made me stay in when he went out and sometimes locked me there and took the keys from me and I would worry there would be a fire and I would burn to death. I told him about Gabe's phone calls and Aunt Grace's photos, my lonesome Christmas's, and cakeless birthdays and how I'd hang up the phone and almost die of homesickness.

I laughed at that point.

'Now, I'm supposed to be feeling real grief and I'm just so happy.'

'Don't worry, you'll get there,' he said. 'You're in shock.'

I took a deep breath and carried on, told him about the journey, and the hitchhiking and how Ralph made me hitchhike while he hid behind shrubs so that we'd get lifts faster, and sleeping in the bushes under a billboard in the late spring dirty snow, and about putting my face in the bowl of ammonia and what happened to Bernadette on my last day of school.

Then, when I'd reached the beginning, I stopped.

'And I never finished school like I promised you and now I'm going to be a mother and I don't have one of my own. The baby won't have a grandmother. My mother will never see my baby.' And then I wailed, and cried for a long time, getting up only once, to throw up in Uncle Tony's bathroom, returning to the sofa to cry some more.

Uncle Tony didn't say anything; he made tea, hugged me, patted me and gave me tissues and a towel until I'd stopped, then he went to the freezer and got us both some ice cream.

'Here,' he said, handing me a bowl. 'Raspberry Ripple. Your favourite.'

His kindness produced another bucket of tears, but I finally was able to eat my ice cream, in between sobs, after which he put me to bed and tucked me in.

'You'll feel better after a good sleep,' he said.

'Yeah, I think I will.'

The wind woke me some hours later and I found Uncle Tony standing in his front porch, lamps lit, looking out to the darkness of the bay. He was listening to a transistor radio.

'Oh no,' I said. Uncle Tony didn't smile.

'I'm afraid so,' he said. 'There's a boat coming from Sandy Hills at first light to take people back to the mainland.'

'What about Davis?'

'He'll sit tight now, everything's changed.'

'I had no idea, I haven't heard a weather report in months.' I was afraid to ask the next question.

'Is it coming this way?'

He didn't answer me at first.

'Can't tell. You know how these things are. You ought to try and sleep a little while you can.'

I went back to my room, listening to Uncle Tony making phone calls, overhearing scraps of his sentences. '...no, not that boat...dawn, any minute now...the Langston house?... See if you can talk him out of it...nothing so far...it wouldn't stand up...Doodle, Jack and who else...' I was too frightened by the escalating sounds of the wind and the water to stay there, and there was certainly no question of sleep, so I returned to the porch. Time slowed down for the next few hours, and then suddenly sped up.

I had lived through many hurricanes since my first, and worst, Hurricane Grace, the one that brought Bernadette. My memories, mutating from excitement to fear to desolation, were not happy ones, but the four walls in them were fairly sturdy. Uncle Tony's house on the island felt like a paper tent in a rodeo arena in comparison.

I could make out shapes in the bay that revealed themselves to be bits of debris as the day dawned. I was disturbed to see a piece of freshly painted windowpane floating amongst it.

'That's the phone dead.' Uncle Tony put it down, and came over to me, and put his arm around me. Water was sloshing over the boardwalk next to his house, the water now ankle deep in his front yard.

'Time to go. Don't worry Gloria. We'll be all right, whatever happens.'

'What's that?' I pointed.

'That's it, *The Beacon Island Belle*.' It was coming from the west.

Ten minutes later the chugging of the engine was audible and the ferry had nearly reached us. The bay surged, pelting and tossing the *Belle*, but robust and tugboat like, it withstood the forces of nature and sidled into the dock, rocking and sloshing through the increasing wreckage.

Uncle Tony's garden was underwater now, the stilts his house sat on were no longer visible, and the water was rising. The ocean was sweeping the island.

Captain Mack came out on the deck, shouting and beckoning to us to come aboard. His shouts were lost in the wind. Uncle Tony grabbed me, and we braced ourselves against the wind, which was so strong it was all our effort not to be blown off the dock.

There were about twenty people on the boat.

'We're not going anywhere now,' said Captain Mack.

The boat was taking a beating from the rubble rising against it, and was now wedged into a corner against the dock with the help of part of someone's roof. It just as well the dock had been strengthened. I could see the water rising into Uncle Tony's windows, but the house was still standing. We put our life jackets on, and stood in silence, hoping the boat would stand up to the abuse. Even the few dogs present were still and silent.

'Uncle Tony,' I whispered, 'something awful is happening.'

He pulled me closer to him. 'I know Gloria, we'll get through this, this is a good boat.'

'No, no, that's not ...' I doubled over, unable to suppress my groans any longer.

It was at that point time accelerated.

****

Chapter Twenty-five

Uncle Tony, to his great credit, said, 'Gloria, this isn't something awful, it's wonderful,' although he did wait until the wind had subsided somewhat before making his comment.

I wasn't so sure. The other passengers feared for their lives for the several hours that we stayed on the boat, while it rocked and rolled. I saw them, holding onto one another for support, staggering to and fro with the erratic jerking and pitching of the boat and searching each other's fearful eyes.

They didn't know what fear was, I thought; they ought to try lying down on the floor and passing a basketball from their business end in this weather. I forgot about life, being so totally immersed in it. I had been whisked into the tiny cabin for the sake of a modicum of privacy, albeit superficial, as there was only a swinging wooden panel, loosely called a door separating me from the rest of the people. My screams could be heard along with the howling wind, no doubt contributing to the general terrified atmosphere, but I couldn't help it. I gave a short sharp birth to a baby girl, with the help of Doodle, a friend of Uncle Tony's from Sandy Hills. It was Doodle who encouraged me to scream - not that much encouragement was needed.

'Doodle,' Uncle Tony had shouted over the wind. 'Get in here with my niece.' He didn't say my name.

'Who is he?' I said, affronted, as the strange young man handled me.

'This is Doodle. He's a nurse.'

Doodle took control, relieved to have a distraction and the opportunity to be one of the few people on the boat who felt useful and competent.

'Let it go, Gloria,' he shouted, 'scream as much as you want.'

Uncle Tony left me literally in Doodle's hands and left the cabin then, to rejoin the small and diligent group of people on the dock fending off the growing detritus, trying to make sure the boat we were on stayed intact.

Just as it had on the day of Bernadette's birth, the meteorological roulette wheel had gone full circle and landed on the letter G and this storm was also born a girl, her name Hurricane Gloria. Uncle Tony had remarked the previous night as we ate our ice cream, 'You may not be the only Gloria to surprise me today.' The significance of his comment flew past me, as I was otherwise preoccupied at the time.

Hurricane Gloria had spent a week travelling hundreds of miles across the Atlantic, born as a tropical depression, evolving into a tropical storm and hit Beacon Island as a full-blown Cat 3 hurricane, with sustained winds of 112mph and gusts to 130mph. Gloria had the lowest recorded barometric pressure since Hurricane Grace, sixteen years earlier, possibly assisting Doodle in the rapid delivery of my daughter.

By the time she arrived the winds had dropped and the water subsided, all that remained was a heavy, steady rain. Uncle Tony returned to the boat, his smile was huge, his arms extended.

I handed him the baby.

'I guess this makes me a Great Uncle.'

'You were always a great uncle,' I said, lying back, exhausted and overwhelmed with relief.

The other castaways, myself and my baby had taken refuge in Uncle Tony's house while we waited for the *Beacon Island Belle* to be freed from its wreckage trap in the bay. Uncle Tony had been engaged in that process and in the inspection of the rest of Deer Path Cove, happily reporting back that there were no major losses, only two roofs blown off unoccupied properties, thankfully. There were always the one or two pertinacious types that refused to budge from their homes. A party had been despatched to salvage what they could from empty houses; food, blankets, coffee and alcohol were brought back and employed or consumed. I enjoyed the fuss made over my new baby and myself; there was nothing like brand new life to inject some passion into an already intense situation.

A water taxi had been radioed to transport me to Bayview Hospital, courtesy of O'Connor's Sea Cabs, the new faction of the up until recently landlocked livery service, now expanding into marine territory. This was their first and only boat, the *Sea Cat*. My fare had been waived due to the extraordinary circumstances.

The speed of weather change after a hurricane can leave the mind running to keep up. By the time I was skimming across the bay in a water taxi the sun was setting red in a clear purple sky.

'It's not every day people have a baby in a hurricane,' said the pilot of the taxi.

'Well, maybe not every day,' Uncle Tony had replied, 'but it seems to happen to us a lot,' reminding me with a jolt of the ominous circumstance of my child's birth.

'Look at that sky,' I said to Uncle Tony. 'How can that be, so soon?'

He shook his head.

'Have you talked to anyone yet?' I asked him. 'Does anyone know?'

He shook his head again.

'We missed the funeral,' I said, sadly.

'No, we didn't,' he said, 'it's been postponed until tomorrow. You might miss it, though, Gloria, depending on what the doctor says.'

I thought how much easier it would be to miss my mother's funeral, and then I thought how much harder it would be.

'I didn't know funerals could be postponed,' I said.

Death was so unstoppable, it seemed only right that funerals should follow suit. Fortunately for Piper Bay, Beacon Island and especially the *Beacon Island Belle*, however, Hurricane Gloria hit at low tide, lessening its storm surges and therefore probably postponing a few more funerals. We rode the rest of the way in silence.

The funeral was held off for two days; the same length as my stay in the hospital, before my little girl and I had been signed out, deemed fit and healthy despite the tumultuous ordeal of her birth.

Only Gabe and Davis visited me there. Davis came first, bearing flowers and chocolate, fussing over the baby and me. His visit was brief, and the next scheduled visiting hours came and went with no guests. Finally, in the evening Gabe turned up.

'Look at you!'

'Look at you!'

'You've got a beard!'

'You've got a baby!'

'I guess I win.'

He stayed longer than rules dictated, but the nurses turned a blind eye, considering my circumstances. Gabe held the baby and we both watched her sleep as we talked.

'Why has no one else come? Have they all disowned me? I guess I'm pretty much the family scandal, right? Shame and disgrace.'

'Nah. Nothing like that. They're all too busy,' Gabe said, 'they keep saying "must go see Gloria", but then the days just run out.'

'How is it?'

Gabe thought for a minute. 'Sad, and happy – there's a lot of laughing – and then crying. And weirdness.'

We both laughed. Gabe could have been describing any day out of our lives, and not just Mother's wake.

'Pretty much normal, then,' I said.

'It's busy, though,' he continued, 'so many people come to see her, and then to the house. And there's tons of food and flowers, and kids, and it all has to be managed, by us, this family, and no one is completely on the ball, but we're OK. It's happening.'

'How is Dad?'

'He's a mess. Him, Uncle Joe, and Aunt Gloria. Oh, and Maureen. They're the worst. Everyone else rallies.'

'What about Bernadette?'

'I can't tell. She stays in her room most of the time, is very quiet, but that's how she is. I don't think it changes things for her, much.'

'How about you?'

'I'm sad too, I mean, she was our mother.' Gabe removed one hand from around the baby and wiped his eyes and blew his nose. 'But you know, I wouldn't tell anybody else this, but I've missed her for much longer, her dying, of course I always liked to see her and everything, but...'

'I know what you mean,' I said. 'It's like she's been gone since...'

'Yeah,' he said, 'since. But Angela doesn't feel like that, or the twins. It's just you and I. You know, I went around everyone and asked them who they thought her favourite was.'

'That wasn't very tactful.'

'No, no, listen, it was a while ago, before she died. And everyone said themselves, everyone said, I'm her favourite, even the twins, separated themselves.'

'You didn't ask me,' I said.

'No. You weren't here. Okay, who do you think her favourite was?'

'Maureen.'

'Definitely. Me too.'

'Maybe not when we were really small, though, before the others came along. Maybe then it would have been me.'

'No, because it was me then.' We both laughed.

'I can't believe she's not here,' I said, suddenly overcome. 'It was so sudden. I wish I'd been here.'

'Here,' said Gabe. 'Someone else is about to cry.'

He handed me my waking daughter.

'Everybody is excited about this baby, you know, who also seems sudden, as no one knew about her,' he said.

'Yeah, I know,' I said. 'New life and all, lots of tragedy of death, miracle of life type talk going on, I bet. I feel awful that she'll never meet her. I could really use a mother right now.' I buried my face in the baby, both of us crying now.

Gabe put his arm around me. 'It's getting noisy in here,' he said. 'They're wondering what you're going to name her.'

'Oh shit.'

'Yeah, just thought I'd warn you.'

'I've already named her. Anna. But I haven't told anyone, except you.'

'Yeah, well, you know they'll all be pushing for a Mary.'

'It's too late.'

'That's a nice name.'

'Thank you.'

'Why Anna?'

'I like it because it can't be changed by turning it around. Because it's spelled the same way frontward as it is backwards. And because I don't know anyone, and no one in our family, is called Anna. And because I like it'

Later, when Anna was seven, she asked me the same question, and I gave her the same answer, which she was quite pleased with.

'Except me, of course,' she had said.

'You know me. I'm in your family.'

Mother had died suddenly, of a heart attack, at work, where she appeared to be short of breath, and then collapsed, in the presence of two priests, Father Sinclair and Father Best, who called an ambulance and accompanied her to the hospital, where they administered the Last Rites. It happened within a short space of hours, and nothing could have been done to save her. It came as a terrible shock to a family who never expected her to die at all, and certainly not so prematurely, without giving any warning or reasonable notice, or leaving a list of instructions and a lifetime supply of prepared food.

Dad was a wreck, as Gabe said, but he was still standing. He didn't say much, I don't think he could, and most of our communication happened through touch. He hugged me, repeatedly, and held Anna, stroking her head, and looking into her eyes.

'She looks like your mother,' he said.

Her funeral was very well attended, as had been the four-day extended wake. The pews were crowded with grieving, overcome mourners in black, there were forests of flowers, and the air was thick with incense. She was buried in the cemetery next to her own parents, and a gravestone's throw from Papa Joseph. It was a beautiful clear day, with a few thick branches still strewn untidily over the ground to remind us of the hurricane that had delayed her departure.

There was a lunch afterwards, laid on by Davis at the Floating Restaurant. She was Gabe's mother, and Uncle Tony's little sister. He said it was the least he could do. Much of the food had been prepared by Gabe the previous day.

Bernadette stayed away from both the funeral and the lunch, actions that were only questioned by distant acquaintances who didn't know about The Kind of Illness she had. Bernadette didn't like large gatherings anyway, and was never publicly emotional. Bernadette's emotions were a mystery to me at the best of times, at this, which must surely be the worst of times for her; I couldn't begin to imagine how she would cope. Maureen, it seemed, was now her primary contact and the person best able to communicate, or interact with her in any way. She kept tabs on Bernadette, monitored her medication and checked her regularly. It was ironic, I thought, after all those years of refusing to baby-sit, or even contribute to the afternoon childminding shift. Perhaps things would have been different if she had. Perhaps Maureen would have quelled Bernadette's hostility. There was no point in dwelling on it now, though.

The post-funeral festivities complemented the lengthy process of Mother's internment by stretching far beyond lunch. Davis didn't mind, it was Monday; the restaurant was closed anyway, and the pink champagne was drunk late into the evening. Gabe and I had discussed the propriety of the pink drink earlier.

'I think she would have wanted us to have pink champagne, don't you?'

'Of course. It's a celebration of her life, right?'

'And you have a new baby, too.'

'Maybe we ought to check with Dad.'

We did; he thought pink champagne was most appropriate, as well as cake, as long as he could drink his cream soda concoction. We weren't sure what to do about the cake, as it had always been Mother who made the cakes. Aunt Gloria volunteered, wanting to do something, she said, to feel her. Mother always had different cakes on her own birthday, which she made for herself. No one knew what her favourite cake was. No one, that is, except, Aunt Gloria. A huge void must be left by the loss of one's twin. However, she was enormously comforted by the creation of the lemon cake, topped with a fluffy white substance that was a cross between meringue and vanilla icing, and by Uncle Tony and Aunt Mo, her remaining siblings as they reminisced.

No one made any audible comments to me about not naming my baby Mary, but this obvious oversight on my part was conveyed nonetheless, through innocent remarks and exaggerated body language.

'Anna?' an eyebrow raised. 'I wasn't aware that was a family name.'

However, Anna was too much of a new baby to be resisted and a great fuss was made of her, in her short bursts of wakefulness.

People can be unpredictable when grieving, as well as when drinking too much alcohol. Dad and Aunt Gloria, who had been paralysed by their sadness up until now, rose to the occasion and played most gracious hosts to the guests, Aunt Gloria had gone to great extents, including cutting and colouring her hair, in order to minimise her resemblance to Mother, a symbolic gesture that, along with making the cake, helped ease her own pain as well.

Maureen, also incapacitated by grief, decided uncharacteristically to allow booze to take over in the evening. This made her unable to control her tears and she carried a large box of tissues with her for the evening, as every sentence she uttered, however trifling, was followed by a moist emotional outburst.

'I'm so sorry you had to come home under such sad circumstances, Gloria,' she said, diving into the tissue box.

'It's been so long since we spoke. And you have a baby!' she wailed.

'Well, I'm glad I'm here.'

'I'm not going to be a nun,' she confessed, suddenly.

'Oh!' I was surprised. 'I didn't know that, sorry, I guess I've always assumed, since, well, forever.'

'I've just decided.' Maureen looked heavenwards after this comment, still with the tissue over nose. I took this upward glance as an indication the decision wasn't hers alone.

'So God has other plans for you then?'

'I'm going to stay here,' she said.

'Here? What, here here? In Piper Bay? Maureen, what's here for you?'

I couldn't remember Maureen ever not working towards leaving, getting away, going somewhere more spiritual, less populated. She wanted to be alone, isolated.

'I've never really appreciated what's here for me,' she said, 'and now I know.' With that, she excused herself to leave me wondering until Aunt

Grace interrupted my musings. She, also, was propping herself up with long-stemmed glasses of pink champagne. Aunt Grace was now fully recovered, and looked better than ever. Plastic surgery and skilful application of cosmetics made the scarring on her face almost undetectable, and any on her arms and legs she concealed with her immaculate clothing. Francine had returned from the city with an eye for sophisticated style, remodelled Aunt Grace and her salon, moved it out of the house and into the town centre, aiming to attract a more upmarket clientele. She called it 'Creative Trichology' thus excluding all but the most gullible, pretentious and richest customers, and became one hundred percent more successful than she had been as 'Grace's Beauty Parlour' at home, whilst doing exactly the same thing.

'So. A baby,' she said, teetering slightly. 'And where is its father?' Grace was the first person apart from Tony and Gabe, when I told my story, to mention Ralph.

'He's not here, Aunt Grace. I left him,' I said.

'Good,' she said. 'I never liked him.' I didn't think this was true, but she was slurring her words, which I had learned from Ralph, was a condition in which it was unwise to challenge a person. I tried to smile enigmatically.

'So. She's finally gone. Your mother. You must be sad.'

I nodded.

Aunt Grace shook her head. She was very drunk, I realised. She had a look in her eyes that never quite reached me but boomeranged back into herself.

'Your mother was only eighteen when she did the same damn thing. That baby didn't weather any storms.' She looked around. 'Just as well.'

She sat down at a nearby table and slumped over, head in her folded arms, clearly having come to the end of her night.

I didn't know what Aunt Grace was talking about, and assumed it was drunken ramblings. Uncle Joe came up behind her, threw a quick small smile at me, and took her gently by the shoulders.

'Come on Grace, we better head home,' he said.

She reeled around, stood up and pointed her finger at his chest displaying energy that a minute ago I wouldn't have thought physically possible.

'And you, you bastard,' she shouted.

'Been hiding, having a good cry, have you?'

Uncle Joe, with the help of Uncle Tony, who she hurled yet more abuse at, led Aunt Grace away.

'Time to go, Grace' Joe repeated, and Grace, suddenly docile, complied.

I watched the scene, detached, suddenly feeling the bequest of death, childbirth and two days in the hospital. I turned to go and found Uncle Tony was next to me.

'Did you see all that?' I asked him, and he nodded, and shook his head. 'Where am I staying?' I asked.

'You can stay with us at the apartment if you like,' he said, 'or you can go back to your house.'

After checking with my sisters and Dad it was agreed Anna and I were better off having our own room at Uncle Tony's, where I gratefully retired, but not, unfortunately to sleep just yet. Just as I put my head down, the parcel beside me began to squeak.

'Oh no,' I said, and joined Uncle Tony, having a nightcap in the living room. 'Have a glass of wine, Gloria,' he said.

'Do you think I should? Feeding the baby?'

'One glass won't hurt. Might make her sleep.'

He raised his glass.

'Here's to your mother.'

'What was Aunt Grace talking about Uncle Tony?'

'She was just drunk.'

'No, I thought that at first. But I could tell by Uncle Joe, it was more than that. Do you know? You do know. I know you know.'

'It's just life, Gloria. Have another glass of wine. Two won't hurt. I'll tell you a secret.'

He then told me the reason why Gabe was called Gabe, and not Tony, after Dad, the question I had asked all those years ago that caused such a stricken silence at the birthday party.

Once upon a time, Aunt Gloria had met Uncle Joe at school and dated him a few times. On one occasion as a prank Mother had stood in for Gloria to see if Joe would know the difference. Of course Joe did and although Gloria's dalliance with him wasn't serious and was short-lived, it was the beginning of a liaison between Mother and Uncle Joe.

'So, aged 18, your mother, like a good catholic girl, soon found herself pregnant …'

'Whoa, hold on a minute.'

'I'm sorry Gloria. Is this too much for you?' said Uncle Tony.

'It's not a problem for me, but maybe for you…'

'No. No, it's not too bad,' I said. 'I'm not that shocked, really, just, it's like hearing about someone I didn't know. Anyway, could you refer to her as Mary, though, for the purposes of this story, and not "your mother"?'

Uncle Tony obliged and finished the story, which was quite sad, and lasted well into our already late night.

Mother and Joe ended their relationship before she discovered her pregnancy, and by that time Joe had fallen for Grace, who he met, ironically, while accompanying mother on a visit to Grace's beauty salon.

Mother never told Joe about the pregnancy, but instead confided in Dad, who had, like Joe, been a close friend throughout childhood. Dad, having been in love with Mother for years anyway, asked her to marry him, keeping the secret of his own brother's baby from him, adopting it as his own. And so they married.

'Gabe? Is Gabe that baby?' I said.

'No, no. It was a long time before Gabe.'

Grace and Joe got married the same year and Grace also became pregnant, so they were both pregnant at the same time, but Mother and Dad lost that baby, Joe's baby. It was a boy, born prematurely, and died after only a few days. They were devastated. They named him Tony, and he had a funeral, a sad baby funeral.

'Grace had Francine that same year. She's always known something fishy went on between Joe and Mary, though.'

'How do you know all this?' I said.

'We were all friends here together, Gloria. It's a small place, and it was smaller then. We fished together, your Dad and I. And he helped me out when I first started the business, with just one barge. Before he and Joe had the shop. He always told me how much he liked your mother. He thought she was special. Up until then he was too shy to do anything about it. Maybe because I was her brother, maybe that's why he talked to me. Remember, I'm a guy, too,' he grinned. 'We get to know stuff.'

'Did Mother know he told you?'

'No. Your father was so upset at the time, he told me, but I swore never to tell Joe or Mary, and he never told her either. So it's just me, supposedly. I'm the one with the big secret.'

'That's typical. But now you've told me.'

'I never promised not to tell you – we didn't think that far ahead,' said Uncle Tony. 'And anyway, Gloria, you've been through so much, and now there's Anna, and after Grace's remarks tonight I thought...'

'It's okay. I won't say anything.'

'So, five years later another boy was born and that was Gabe.'

'And the reason he's not named Tony is because there had already been a Tony, the baby that died.'

'Right.'

'What about Aunt Grace? She seems to know something.'

'Well, yes and no. What she knows, she's surmised by eavesdropping and theorising.'

'That's how I find out things,' I said.

'Exactly,' said Uncle Tony. 'That's what makes them family secrets. That's what everyone did. Probably everybody knew. Romance, pregnancies, babies. People talk about those things. Sometimes, though, things are best kept in whispers, behind closed doors. Your mother wanted it that way.'

'All those years and she never told us a baby died,' I said.

'She was too religious, too guilty. She thought God made Bernadette sick as a kind of penance. She lived her life like one big long act of contrition. She thought anything bad that happened was punishment.'

'For having a baby?'

Uncle Tony shrugged again.

'She believed it was wrong not to be married. That was a big sin for her.'

Uncle Tony and I talked for another hour, until we ran out of ways to cover the same territory. There was nothing left to do but digest this information.

I looked down at my baby, Anna, finally sleeping.

'I have to go to bed. Is there anything else I should know first?'

'Probably, but I can't think offhand.'

'You'll tell me if you do? No more secrets?'

'Promise.'

'Can I tell Gabe?'

****

Chapter Twenty-six

Eleven years later Uncle Tony and I sat in the same two chairs, on a Friday night in late June. He and Davis had converted the loft above the apartment, adding height and panoramic windows that looked out to sea, and we sat up high, taking in the sunset and watching Anna cavorting along the marina with her dog, dipping in and out of the Fish Shop, bothering the fishermen and tournament officials, who were busy making their sinister preparations. She was demob happy, having finished school for the summer that afternoon. A lot of things happen over the course of eleven years, but somehow, at the same time, nothing also happens. Anna wasn't a baby anymore but she was still my daughter. People die, but they have a way of sticking around in spite of that. Same sun, same bay, same fish.

Uncle Tony poured me a glass of red wine.

'Do you think it's all right – you know, with the baby?' I said.

'A little bit won't hurt you. Just a glass.'

I was six months pregnant and asked Uncle Tony the same question every Friday night when we took time out for a drink to discuss business, gossip or just sit, relax, and look at the bay, at our world.

Comforted by his ritual reassurance, I sipped my glass of wine, guilt free.

'Well it didn't do Anna any harm,' I said, and lifted my glass. 'Here's to my week off.'

Uncle Tony and I now shared the Gar-barge business, which we had split into two factions. Original Gar-barges included the workhorse garbage and delivery boats, and the smaller Glorious Gar-barges created a new part of the business. A Glorious Gar-barge could be rented by the hour, day or evening, with a pilot for short sightseeing, sunrise or sunset sails, individually tailored to the customer's whims, whether it be a birthday celebration, a romantic liaison or an extravagant means of transport. We had three Glorious Gar-barges so far, each one designed by a local artist to be unique and comfortable. The Sandy Hills Special, our largest, was painted purple and gold and equipped with two plush velvet sofas and fixed mahogany benches with brass details. The other two, diminishing in size respectively, were less gothic in theme by equally as bright, and we planned to add another if this season proved successful, and it was already looking promising. Clients were welcome to bring along their own refreshments; we supplied only the atmosphere, not wanting to cross purposes with Davis's floating restaurants. We could provide high calibre live entertainment from stand up comedy to strings, or simple background music, china, crystal, flowers, extra chairs and cushions, facilities for pets, you name it. So far we hadn't had a request we couldn't meet. Beacon Island was proving to be the ideal marketplace for such frivolity.

The Original Gar-barges expanded and prospered, as more houses were built on the island. Because of its unique nature and prime location many of its visitors were fabulously wealthy people who squandered and wasted, wined and dined, so that we, the humble Piper Bay people who swept up after them, could capitalise on their excesses.

'Rich people don't have better garbage,' said Uncle Tony, 'they just have more of it.' His distinctive laugh would follow. They were our livelihood. We loved them, and their garbage.

Beacon Island attracted its share of celebrities, who came to get away from it all, to hide away from the people who wanted a piece of them. Piper Bay natives obeyed their supposed wishes and refused to recognise famous faces, to us, people were just people. Most of the celebrities complained then. There was nothing there on Beacon Island, not enough people, nothing to do. Left alone, unrecognised, they got bored. So fortunately for us most of them left again, proving Beacon Island to be a most efficient personality filter. The few that stayed were ones that fitted, and they could rest assured that their garbage, like all the other residents, would not be picked over and sorted through.

The expansion of the business didn't make us as rich as the people we served, but we were quite comfortable, and I was able to provide Anna with the sort of things I had to go without as a child, such as more than one pair of shoes per season, rides on the coin operated horses outside the shopping malls and ice cream, twice a day, more than once a year. Uncle Tony finally got his trip to Venice, and he and Davis were planning another visit for Carnivale in February.

Dad had died, sadly and suddenly, in a car accident, six years after Mother. His last years were too quiet for him; he looked and acted older than he was, just going through the motions of life. Driving home one night from the marina, a deer leapt out of the pines into the road. Dad slowed down, we all agreed afterward, that's what he would've done. Slowed down to watch the deer, wait for it. The oncoming car, however, swerved to avoid the animal, applied his brakes a little on the exuberant side, and lost control of his vehicle, causing a fatal collision for everyone involved, including the deer.

Dad's death was followed directly by a hurricane in a bizarre mimesis of his wife's passing. His funeral was not postponed, however, as Hurricane Bob's severity was diverted elsewhere and only whipped us a bit with a tail wind. It had the distinction of being the first male hurricane to hit the island, although it was the third, albeit last, Hurricane Bob. While we remained relatively unscathed, Bob wrecked enough lives for the World Meteorological Organisation to strike him from the name list. Bob was replaced with Bill.

Dad's death was sad, but his funeral was a low key event compared to Mother's, as he had been a mere shell since she died, passive and depressed, and we had expected him to sleep away quietly with his broken heart before the tragic accident took him.

Maureen was planning a family reunion, on the next anniversary of his death in order to memorialise him properly. She never felt he had an adequate send-off, for some reason. Probably because nobody made a cake and there was no fizz being drunk.

Whether anyone would attend this reunion was unpredictable. Maureen was the only one who thought this was a good idea. I couldn't imagine a more depressing occasion and would certainly try and time the birth of my baby to avoid it if at all possible.

Gabe and Beth were married. Beth worked at Davis's restaurant right up until she gave birth to twin boys, Anthony and Joseph. I was their

Godmother.

'I thought you didn't ever want to use those names for your kids?'

'I know, well, I thought I didn't. They were going to be Thomas and Andrew, right up until the last minute.'

'What happened?'

'I don't know. I just couldn't go through with it. It seemed, I don't know. It was like a pull or something.'

'What's Beth think?'

'She likes those names. She's got Tony's and Joe's in her family too.'

'Yeah. Well, they're nice names.'

'Yeah, I know. That's why I'm giving them to the boys.'

Gabe was head chef at the Floating Restaurant until Uncle Joe bowed out of the Fish Shop, having lost his enthusiasm, and was happy to retire and let Gabe, who had inherited Dad's half, take charge. Gabe left the shop more or less unchanged, except to tidy it up a little bit. He bought Uncle Vinny out of the clam shack and extended it, adding yet another tacked on little wooden room in keeping with the original tumbledown style of the building. He kept it simple, but upgraded the appliances and installed an espresso machine, making it necessary to add a lockable window to the open hutch. Now an accomplished cook, he made the Fish Shop's reputation for food as legendary as its chum.

Fortunately - or not - Dad did not take his secret chum recipe to heaven. Gabe still cooked it up annually, and was doing so at this moment, as I watched the boats I could see him ladling out buckets of the stinking gruel. He alone knew the recipe, and kept a note of it stored in a safe deposit box at the bank with instructions for its transfer in the event of his relinquishing the chum crown at short notice, an arrangement I thought as stupid as the shark tournament.

'Just please tell me one thing,' I had asked him.

'That there aren't any kittens in it.'

'Nope. No mammal ingredients whatsoever,' he laughed. By now we had shared all of our ghastly childhood secrets concerning Bernadette, as well as the Big Secret About That Baby, which, I had been annoyed to discover, Gabe already knew.

'You know? How could you know?' I had said, incredulous.

'Dad told me. I can't remember when. A long time ago, we were out clamming.'

'Why didn't you ever tell me? How could you not tell me?'

'I don't know,' he said. 'He asked me not to. And it didn't seem like a big deal. And you were a girl. You would have made it a big deal.'

'That's not fair.'

In retrospect I wasn't surprised that Gabe hadn't told me, and he was right, it wasn't such a big deal. The biggest deal about it was that it was a secret.

It was the eve of the shark tournament, the annual slaughter that had now stretched from a twenty-four hour contest into a week long gore-fest, with the addition of side shows, stalls and marina-side amusements for all the family. You could buy cuddly sharks, wind-up sharks, inflatable sharks, water pistol sharks, shark-shaped chocolate, shark steaks and shark recipes as well as ice cream and cotton candy and have the pleasure of wading ankle deep through shark blood while you did it, if you so desired. It took two days to set up, a week to run its course and another day and a half to strike. It was why I timed my yearly summer vacation when I did, and took flight across the bay to Uncle Tony's house in Deer Path Cove until the last drop of blood had been hosed off the boardwalk. It wasn't that I was particularly fond of sharks; on the contrary, I was scared of them. The fact that they died wasn't what disturbed me; it was the macabre glee with which they were spread all over my world like jam on toast.

Anna came in with her dog, Trout. The naming of pets for fish tradition lived on, in spite of the limitations imposed by the suitability of species names. This was the third Trout that I could remember, succeeding another dog and a gerbil.

'Please, can't we stay, just for the weekend, to watch?' she asked.

Anna had never seen a shark tournament before as I always made sure to be well away before the carnage commenced.

'You would hate it,' I said, as I watched the gallows being erected down below me. Out of storage came the purpose built structures that

271

could hang as many as six of the toothy beasts alongside each other at a time for facilitating the beer-swilling hunters with close-up comparisons and gruesome photo opportunities. The evolution of the shark tournament meant that there were now high entry fees and strict rules and regulations, although most of them were designed to prevent cheating and protect the fishermen's interests. They didn't have much to do with the fish themselves.

'You can stay till Sunday if Uncle Tony doesn't mind, and puts you on a ferry that morning,' I said.

'I don't mind at all,' said Uncle Tony, and Anna, thrilled, returned to the marina.

Ralph was dead now, too. He had been killed shortly after Mother's funeral in a drunk-driving accident of his own making. He'd finally had that one too many and hit the correct crash wall. I went to his funeral, which was, because of his father, overflowing with uniformed policemen paying their respects. I had to refrain from showing my relief at having my biggest problem sorted, although maybe I wouldn't have wished it be resolved in such drastic fashion. But then again, I didn't shed any tears and I dare say I could have put away a fair portion of cake and a bucketful of pink champagne had there been any available. He never saw his daughter, nor did he express any interest in seeing her. His parents visited, irregularly, for the first eighteen months of her life, but had since moved to the west coast and dropped all contact, including Christmas and birthdays.

I tried hard to break my own family's tradition of covertness. I was sometimes brutally honest with Anna and never answered her questions with awkward stony silences and shifty smiles. There were a few areas where I tended towards vagueness. One was her father. I somehow couldn't bear to come completely clean with her about the sort of character he was and the deterioration of our shaky relationship. I couldn't really say 'your father was probably the biggest mistake I ever made', so I tended to concentrate on what I thought might have been his good side, which I had long forgotten, and the rest of the time I was vague. She guessed, though.

'He wasn't nice, was he? My father,' she said.

'Well. Not to me, anyway. He had problems. I'll tell you about it someday, but not now.'

She guessed most things that I was cagey about. I told her about That Illness, but we never discussed why she had never been inside the home I grew up in, in spite of its close proximity, and never pressed me to go there. I wouldn't allow Bernadette to babysit for her, although she was always available and offered regularly. I didn't ever put Anna in a position where playing with Bernadette might result. Bernadette begged to play with her.

'Why can't you leave her here to play with me? Little girls love to play.'

Bernadette was a grown woman now, in her mid-twenties. She was still very beautiful and quite strange. Her medicine made her docile and she slept more than average. She could have, had I allowed it, been an excellent playmate for Anna as she was able to see the world through a child's eyes, and didn't tire of the games. But there were some things that couldn't be fixed. Some stuff sank, and some stayed afloat. There was no way she was getting near my daughter. She never questioned my decisions about playing with Bernadette.

Bernadette wasn't ever going to get well, but the drugs she took kept the tortuous demons in her mind at bay. The demons that tortured Bernadette, that is. We didn't know what became of the ones that tortured us. In the latter afternoon era, when our retreats to the basement were as routine as military drills, Theresa used to joke, 'Bernadette is exercising her demons.' It was one of our favourite Bernadette jokes. We had a lot of those jokes.

Bernadette went to see That Kind of Doctor once a month; Maureen ensured she kept the appointment, and her prescriptions magically seemed to renew themselves. We weren't allowed to know what That Doctor and Bernadette talked about, no one was, so we never found out about why Bernadette didn't think little girls loved to play when we were little girls, or if she even remembered; or perhaps she just had the games muddled.

When I went back to work after Anna was born, she came to work with me, and became the celebrated Barge Baby.

Maureen remained in the house after Mother and Dad had died, and the rest of my sisters left, one by one, each taking with them their legacy, the defects left with them as a result of Bernadette's Illness. Theresa moved to California and phones once a month, sends us a Christmas card every year of her own design; she is employed as a graphic artist. She spends her Christmas each year with her twin Mary, whose escape took her even further afield, Yellowknife, a town in the Northern Territories of Canada where she went on a canoeing vacation with a friend and never came back, cutting herself free completely from the rest of her family. She's twice divorced and now lives with a mining surveyor. She swears this time it's the real thing, and we believe her. All news of Mary is channelled through Theresa, who assures us that Mary often says she would welcome any of us to visit her in Yellowknife, bar Bernadette, at any time, with open arms, she'd love to have us, but not to expect her to ever come back to Piper Bay Village.

Angela took most of the brunt of That Terrible Time Before They Knew About the Illness, which was, in essence, the whole of her childhood, depriving her of any useful nurturing. She was the one I would have expected to move furthest away, to another planet if possible, but she didn't. She stayed in the Piper Bay area, remarkably balanced and devoid of bitterness.

'That's life,' she shrugged it off.

'It could have been worse. I'm okay now, better than she is.'

Along with Gabe and me, she loves the bay and its environs and is studying marine biology at City University with a view to coming home and working in the Piper Bay Aquarium, another new development resulting from the attractive locale, which I feared would slowly disappear under buildings. The Aquarium was a way of immortalising our sands, grasses, fish etc, for the more delicate visitor to experience without having to put up with the rain, wind and sand in their eyes. They also got the bonus of performing dolphins for the price of their ticket, which were imported from somewhere else, as Piper Bay was too far north for dolphins. Angela had a summer job there presenting the dolphin show but once she acquired her degree would hold a more senior, less frivolous position.

'I'll still play with the dolphins, though,' she said. 'They're my friends.'

Maureen looked after Bernadette, that was her vocation, she said. She replaced Mother at the rectory, and threw herself into the job, working full-time and taking a hands-on role in the parish's administration, a situation that satisfied her need to serve God. At home, she saw that Bernadette was fed and clothed and medicated. Bernadette, who had been assessed and deemed someone who was unable to survive on her own, received money from the State to assist in her care, but of course Bernadette didn't believe she couldn't survive on her own. So Maureen lived with her in a manner that led Bernadette to think she was completely independent.

None of us had stepped inside our family home since Dad died. It was bequeathed to all of us, but as far as we were concerned, Maureen could have it. We sent her cheques every month to help her maintain it and Bernadette. It helped to assuage our guilt for not doing anything else.

'Thank God Maureen stays there,' said Gabe, to Angela and I, one evening sitting at the bar in the Floating Restaurant. 'No one else would do it', he laughed. 'What would we ever do if she died suddenly?'

This was meant to be a humorous rhetorical question, but when we exchanged looks, the sobering reality of the inescapable answer flattened the joke somewhat. If Maureen were to die suddenly, we would give her a funeral and do nothing about Bernadette, we would become 'in denial', i.e. pretend it wasn't happening, or worse, and Bernadette would probably be 'homeless' another new no-fault word for the late twentieth century which actually meant 'abandoned', and we would be terribly guilty. We didn't want to think about this, about Maureen's sudden accidental death. We didn't want to think about Maureen's death at all, especially if it was before ours.

Aunt Gloria, Mother's twin sister, visited Maureen and Bernadette regularly, as did Aunt Mo. Maureen herself was near deranged in her happiness, feeling so sure, as she did, that she had discovered God's mission for her, and wore the fixed-smile expression that can often be observed on very religious people, or as Aunt Grace would say, 'She looks like she's had an alien visitation.'

Aunt Grace, incidentally, had telephoned me the day after her outburst at Mother's funeral to apologise.

'I'm very sorry, Gloria, I have no excuse except to say that I got drunk and emotional. I don't remember what I said to you, and I'd rather not be reminded. You have a beautiful baby.'

We agreed to forget the whole thing, thankfully, now that I knew the truth I had no desire to hash over the subject with Aunt Grace. She still voiced her opinions on other matters as loudly as ever, though, and believed, along with her theory of Maureen and the aliens, that we all, and not just Bernadette, had a madness of our own, and hinted at this perhaps being an inherited trait.

'Look at Mary, up there in Siberia, for goodness sake, refusing to talk to anyone but those Eskimos.'

'It's Canada, and they're Inuits, Aunt Grace, not Eskimos.'

'Well, whatever they are. And you, without a husband. Gallivanting around, having babies. Driving boats. You'd think you would have learned by now,' she indicated my pregnancy.

'Learned what?' but with this, Aunt Grace just rolled her eyes.

'Don't be ridiculous, Aunt Grace. It's hardly gallivanting. We've been together years now. Richard's a good guy,' I said.

'That's what you said about Ralph,' she said, blessing herself, superstitiously, I thought.

'It's what you said about him, too, remember?'

'Well, you ought to be married,' she said, and clicked away in her red stilettos to harangue someone else.

'Let me know if you need anything,' she shouted over her shoulder.

My pregnancy was the result of a four-year relationship with Richard Crosier; another school dropout who survived. Richard came from the real-estate family who owned the Surf Emporium, opposite the inlet from the Fish Shop, that Dad had seen as both a threat and an eyesore, where Maureen had worked so long ago to help pay her way through Catholic High School. Richard had been on the edge of the crowd that I had met when seeing Skate, the Grease Monkey. Richard and I had probably smoked cigarettes together on the same spit of land that his father bulldozed to construct the Surf Emporium.

Richard got further than Baltimore. His rebellion extended to him quitting school and absconding to South America to take drugs and hitchhike, among other things. His teenage belief that his rich parents didn't care for him was, of course, mistaken, and they invested vast amounts of time and money trying to find him, and when he turned up in a hospital in the Florida Keys they were overjoyed to fly him home, and all was forgiven. He'd fallen off a motorcycle and fractured his skull, an injury that no doubt helped hasten his absolution.

He went to work for his brother Glen, in the Surf Emporium, which he inherited when business began to pall, around the same time I returned and had Anna. Glen moved into to the booming real estate industry, where the real big money was.

Richard scaled down The Surf Emporium considerably, taking away the glass and the glitz and renamed it The Beach Shop. He took great pains to break and remove much of the concrete around the building and re-plant the indigenous beach grasses that had grown there, which he claims was all part of a long-term plan to woo me. He consulted with Dad and Uncle Joe, who still had the Fish Shop, to contribute their ideas in order that the two shops could independently profit and yet benefit the marina collectively. He rented dock space to surplus boats that Dad and Uncle Joe had no room for. He opened an account with Uncle Tony at Gar-barges to handle all his deliveries to the island, and lavished attention as well as free gifts on Anna from the time she was six weeks old.

I finally gave in when she was seven, and now we were like an old married couple, without the documentation. We lived in a large apartment above the Beach Shop, and could always hear the sounds of the bay.

Richard had gone ahead of me to Deer Path Cove to get the house, which hadn't been used since the autumn, ready. Uncle Tony and Davis had bought a second house on the island in Pirate Creek, another secluded community, a bit further east, however it was larger, with a daily ferry service as well as a shop and a hotel. The new house was insulated for winter so the Deer Path Cove house was now closed up at the end of the summer season.

Below me on the marina, I'd been watching market stall traders start to arrive and set up.

'They're early,' I commented to Uncle Tony.

'Well, there's an informal tournament opening party tonight,' he explained, 'a beach bar, a bit of music, a few clams, that sort of thing.'

Anna was suddenly back, draped in what looked like strings of teeth.

'Like my shark's tooth necklaces?' she said.

'Uncle Gabe got them for me.'

'Time for me to go,' I said.

****

Chapter Twenty-seven

As the time approached, Maureen's idea of a small family reunion gained as much momentum as the hurricane that spat out Bernadette all those years ago. I gave birth to a baby boy, in a hospital, on a clear balmy night. There was only one possible name for him, and he became another Tony. Unfortunately my timing was off, as his arrival contributed to the event's burgeoning stature. The phone rang incessantly.

'Nothing like a new life in the face of death,' said Maureen.

'Maureen, Dad died six years ago. Death is not exactly in our faces.'

'Yes, but it's a memorial, and we'll be thinking of him. And you've even named your baby after him.'

'There's also Uncle Tony, remember. Anyway, I'm busy Maureen, I have to go, I've got a new baby, remember – what was it you wanted?'

'I just heard his baptism is that same morning,' she said.

'Yeah, so?'

'Well, I'll be a bit busy, getting things set up, that's all. It might be difficult for me to get there,' she said, presumptuously.

'Sorry Maureen, I thought you knew.' I lied, 'It's very small. Only the godparents and Richard and I are going to be there. And Anna.'

'Oh. Who are the godparents?'

'Uncle Tony and Davis are,' I said.

'Oh!' she said. 'I was going to ask Uncle Tony to help out with...'

'Don't worry. We won't be late for your party.'

Uncle Tony had never been asked to be a godparent. He was thrilled.

The last time there had been a significant gathering was at Dad's funeral. It was a miserable, sad day, as expected but it was difficult to shake the image of him in his last year; grim, uncommunicative and depressed, his sudden death not only killed him, but any hopes that we might have had for him. It was the realisation that he had been dead for so long, already.

Because of this chronic pain, and the abrupt nature of his funeral, as well as its accompaniment by a hurricane, not everyone made it - at least not every second and third cousin and their spouses.

Now, five years on Maureen thought it fitting to mark the anniversary in a festive yet sanctimonious way. A memorial party that would double as a family reunion and she was inviting people I'd never heard of, yet assured me they were all bona fide family. Gabe and I were dreading it. We had new lives now, different families. At first we tried to dissuade her.

'Maureen, what if the weather is bad?' I said. 'You remember the hurricane. Mary has a long way to come, and Theresa's all the way out in California. It'll cost her a fortune, she'll have to fly.' I felt myself inventing excuses for the twins, as I didn't think they would come.

'Nonsense,' she said, in her no nonsense voice.

'I've checked fares, it's a cheap time to travel.'

Theresa phoned from California. 'Have you heard about this Maureen thing? Like a memorial reunion or delayed wake or whatever it is?'

'I have heard,' I said. 'You're not coming, right?'

'No, I'll come,' she said. 'I'd like to see Mary and people and I'll be able to pick up some of my old stuff. Maureen says she got boxes of it stored away.'

'You don't have to come, you know,' I said.

'Yeah, I know I don't. But I will. Mary said she'd go if I went, you know how it is with us. But can I stay at your place after it? And probably Mary, too. I don't want to be in that house any longer than I have to.'

That House. None of us wanted to go to that house. It had been eleven years since I'd been in That House, and fourteen since I'd lived there. Anna had never been there. I worried about it, and had nightmares about it, nightmares about the nightmares I'd had there, about being frightened, about drowning, and falling, about it burning down with me inside, trapped. It was a house with too many secrets.

I asked Gabe how he felt.

'I hated that house,' he said. 'It was so damn crowded.'

'But you had your own room.'

'That made it worse, somehow, like being the only one in camp with a dry tent. That's why I never came home. I was so happy when I moved out.'

'What do you think it's like now?'

'I don't know. Less crowded, I guess,' he said.

'It scares me. It's like visiting some haunted mausoleum or something, full of skulls and cobwebs.'

Gabe laughed at me. 'Well, actually, no Gloria, it's not like that. It'll be fine. I'll be there. And Anna will, and Uncle Tony, and everyone. It's just a house.'

On the appointed day, we drove to the airport to collect Theresa and Mary. Anna sat in the back seat with the baby Tony, dividing her attention between him and me.

'Is it going to be a big party?' she asked. 'With all your cousins and their kids and everything?'

'Yeah, pretty big, I guess,' I said.

'I didn't think you liked things like that,' she said.

'I don't,' I said.

'I think it will be fun, seeing them all. All your cousins. And mine too,' she said.

'I'm sure you'll have a great time and I'm sure I'll have a nice time too, once I'm there,' I said, not quite so sure.

'Is it like an official family reunion?' asked Anna, beginning her probe.

'Sort of. At least that seems to be Maureen's plan. It's probably the only time we'll ever do something like this.'

I tried to present the idea as something positive.

'What is it that you don't like about family parties?' asked Anna.

'All the people there,' I said. 'And all the people missing.'

I was not looking forward to attending an event that was being billed as the biggest cake occasion of the century, without Mother and Dad. Surely I would be able to hear their voices coming from the group in the next room.

'Is Bernadette going to be there?' asked Anna, knowing she would.

'Yes,' I said.

'Does that bother you too?' asked Anna, knowing it would.

I laughed then. 'Why are you asking me all these questions when you know the answers?'

Anna just smiled and watched the side of the road pass, humming to the conveyor belt rhythm of the cracks in the road as the car rolled over them. Badump, badump, badump.

After a while, she said, 'I guess it isn't possible to ever have a family reunion without people missing.'

The rest of the journey was silent. We stopped home dropping the twins off to get showered and changed, and exchanged them for Richard.

'Scoot over, I'll drive,' he said.

'Thanks.'

He took my hand in his.

'Are you ready?'

'I guess I am,' I said.

The church was now kept locked. Gone were the days when holy or troubled souls could wander in off the street any time to offer praise, ask forgiveness, a question, or even shelter from the rain while considering the eternal flame. Nowadays the visitors too often wanted God's home for the whole night and then to make off with the tabernacle to boot so it was necessary for all appointments to be pre-arranged.

We were met at the door by a smiling nun, dressed in the merest hint of habit, a modest scarf type affair holding back her hair. With a hefty set of keys she escorted us, stopping to unlock and relock each clanking metal door we passed through.

The interior, however, had not changed, especially so in the west vestibule, to which we were shown. The wrought iron rails and circular stone steps looked as though they hadn't been dusted since my own baptism. As we waited for Father Viola, I listened to the distant dripping sounds I remembered hearing and fearing as a child.

Anna pointed to the baptismal font. 'What is that? It looks like a birdbath,' she whispered.

'That's what I thought when I was a girl,' I said. 'Actually, it still looks like a birdbath, doesn't it?'

'Why are you getting him baptised, anyway? You never got me baptised,' complained Anna.

'There's nothing stopping you doing it now.' I told her.

'God already knows your name, you used to tell me. Well, then how come God doesn't already know his name?' she said.

'I don't know. Things change, I guess. We talked about this.'

Richard, Uncle Tony and Davis smiled at this. Anna smiled at me.

'I'm just trying to make you laugh,' she said.

It was a quick, small and quiet ceremony. No sooner had he said, 'I baptise thee in the name of the Father, the Son and the Holy Spirit. Amen,' than we were key-clunking briskly through the building and locked outside again.

The rest of the family were assembled back at the house for the party.

'Well, time to go,' said Uncle Tony. 'Are you ready Gloria?'

'People keep asking me that,' I said.

'Well, are you?' he said.

'Yes. Absolutely.'

Overgrown shrubs and wild uncut grass did not obscure the house as I imagined in bleaker moments, nor was the paint peeling and wooden roof rotten and full of holes. The front lawn had been mowed, and the rest of the garden looked well maintained, the hedges were cut and the flowerbeds free of weeds. Cats meandered over the lawn and in shrubs. The stump of the felled tree that had been our childhood plaything had been carved into a birdbath and nut feeders hung from the lesser trees around it. The sight of it, tidier than it used to be, eased my tomb-raiding dread somewhat.

Maureen was there, inside, and managed to breathe her own warm life into it in spite of the cold draughty spaces, perhaps coming from under the floorboards, that I imagined still chilled me.

Our entrance caused mayhem.

'What's his name?' shouted Uncle Nick, glass raised.

'His name is Tony,' I said.

They cheered. 'After your father, uncle or a hurricane?' someone shouted. This was a joke and there was an eruption of laughter.

'All three of them,' I rallied. More laughter, and then we raised our glasses and drank to my new baby.

The house whirled around me. I looked around at the furniture, some of which had been reupholstered. Gone were the stacks of newspapers, old overflowing toy boxes and piles of laundry.

'I'm just going to change the baby.' I said, and went upstairs and looked in my old bedroom. Two single beds were neatly made up on either side of the window, which was letting in the sun. It was warm, clean and smelled of beech wood. Jesus and Mary looked on from the walls. I looked in Bernadette's room. A bed, a desk, a bookshelf. There was a cat sleeping on the bed. Gabe was right. It was just a house. I returned to the throngs of relatives below.

Bernadette stepped forward out of the crowd and reached out. She was wearing a baseball hat. I stared at her. She looked fragile and pale as though she spent all her time indoors.

'We've updated her style somewhat,' said Maureen, indicating the hat. She spoke about Bernadette as though Bernadette couldn't hear her. This surprised me, but I was even more surprised that Maureen would have any knowledge of baseball hats as a statement of style.

Bubbling In a corner I could see the old fish tank, the only area of neglect I could discern. A plant had become dislodged from the gravel bed and floated on the surface, but could be salvaged if given some attention. I could see only one fish, and the tank was cloudy. I made a mental note to ask for it.

'May I hold him?' Bernadette said.

'Sure. Go ahead,' I said, and handed her the baby to hold. Bernadette took the baby and cradled him gently, leaving me with both hands free to enjoy my cake and pink champagne.

The End